Faith

ROADIES SERIES

ERIKA VANZIN

Faith

ISBN: 978-1736645277

Staci Frenes, Line Editor
Shelby Goodwin, Proofreader

Cover Design by Elizabeth Mackey

Want to get more FREE from Erika?

Sign up for the author's New Releases mailing list and get a free copy of the short story "Eliot." You will periodically receive free short stories and unique chapters.

Click here to get started:
https://www.erikavanzin.com/newsletter.html

To the Groupies who are keeping this dream alive.

The Jailbirds Are Back with Great News!

Hi, Roadies!

There's big news on the heels of the split from their old record company announced five months ago. As already anticipated by the title of this post, the Jailbirds are back, but not with the news that everyone expected. They did not, in fact, find a new label but decided to form Jail Records, a new entity in the music scene that will deliver to fans their future albums and also music from other talented artists looking for a home.

The record company has not yet announced the guidelines to submit demos, but we're sure a press release will soon clarify the details of this latest ambitious project.

After coming out in the open and admitting their status as ex-inmates—during the hottest Christmas season in music history—the Jailbirds gave birth to their most incredible adventure.

Are you excited about this unexpected project?

Be kind and Rock'n'Roll,

Iris

38182 Likes 27782 Tweets 23698 Shares 7482 Comments

CHAPTER 1

Michael

"Oh, yes, baby. Keep it up. Do that thing with your hips again. It drives me crazy." My voice is raspy. The blondie straddling my lap seems to appreciate my hands on her buttocks pulling her toward my pelvis, allowing me to sink even deeper into her.

"When is it my turn?" The complaint coming from the couch next to me reminds me I was taking care of Tiffany's generous breasts, or was it Brittany? Carolina, maybe? Anyway, the twin of the blonde who is striving to make me have the most overwhelming orgasm in history.

"Come here, honey. Sorry. Your sister makes me forget your name when she keeps moving like this."

The girl giggles and approaches me again, slamming her huge fake breasts in my face. I've never been one who discriminates against a woman just because they're not entirely natural. After all, if she prefers that, who am I to judge? Plus, let's be clear, these two are to-die-for sexy, both dressed and naked. When I met them at the club last night, I had no doubt how the night would end.

Jennifer, or maybe Amanda, seems happy with the attention I'm paying to her upper body—so much so that when I slip a hand between her legs, I find her wet and ready to welcome me.

"Honey, I've neglected you. Do you want to come and take over for your sister who looks tired?"

In fact, the girl straddling me seems less than enthusiastic; perhaps because, like me, she can no longer orgasm easily after a night of sex. It almost seems like I've lost sensitivity down there, and the effort I've been making to chase that pleasure for at least half an hour is exhausting.

I am reminded of the words of my friends who tell me that, sooner or later, my penis will fall off from of all this sex. Maybe they're right. I have to remember to Google it. Is there something like impotence from too much sex? The mere thought terrifies me. I almost don't notice the two girls have exchanged places. If they didn't have necklaces with different letters hanging from their neck, I couldn't tell them apart. I already struggle to remember the face of the girls I take to bed, let alone distinguish between two identical twins. "G" and "P," I'm almost sure these two letters should ring a bell. Maybe they're the initials of their names?

I don't have time to overthink it because a slight knock on the door draws my attention.

"Who the hell could it be this early?"

I grab my phone from the coffee table and peek at the time. It's eleven o'clock in the morning. Damn, I was supposed to be at the recording studio two hours ago! I have about twenty calls and messages from my bandmates that begin with asking me where I am and end with openly insulting me.

"Excuse me, I have to go and check who it is. I think it's my friends." I move Melanie from my legs and pause for a second to think. I'm not sure it is them because they would have

entered with the keys or broken through the door. The slight knock from the corridor for the second time convinces me that it cannot be Damian, given his heavy hand.

"Do you mean the others will be joining our party?" Liberty's eyes light up.

"Why, honey, am I not enough for you?" I ask her, annoyed while looking for my clothes.

They both giggle, and I lose patience when I hear a knock for the third time. To hell with it. If they're in such a hurry to see me, they'll have to deal with the nude version of me. I approach the door and, seized by a momentary flash of clarity and decency, I grab the first thing I see and cover my private parts, still hard and wrapped in a condom. I welcome the hotel manager and the two security guards one step behind him, with a see-through vase full of fresh flowers to cover my erection. From the expression on his face, I gather they have bad news and that I've made it worse by exposing myself. I must admit, though, the manager is really good at maintaining a poker face. If it weren't for a slight movement in his jaw muscle, you wouldn't know he's pissed off.

"Mr. Wright, I'm sorry to divert you from your…morning activities." I follow his gaze behind me to see that Amber and Beverly are watching us with interest, without feeling the need to cover up.

"Is there a problem?" The vase in my hand is getting heavier and heavier. Few times in my life have I felt inadequate, and this is one of them, at least from the clothing point of view. I've never been one of those guys who boast at the bar about his sexual exploits. Of course, I tell my friends the juicy details, but my current lack of modesty makes me uncomfortable.

The man clears his voice and returns to study me. "Mr. Wright, we are forced to ask you to leave the hotel. Here's the formal request, which also contains the invoice for the balance of the duration of your stay." He hands me an envelope printed with the hotel logo but, stunned as I am at the news, I don't reach out to take it, so the man slips it between the flowers.

"Why the hell are you kicking me out? I always pay on time, and I've never been a problem! Is it because of the unregistered guests I bring to the room?" I nod my head towards Elizabeth and Lola.

The two security guys dressed in black close around the director in an almost imperceptible way, but I notice it. I spend my life with people like them who look over my shoulder at every step, and when I raised my voice, I triggered the "protection mode" required in their job. I don't want to make a scene and make myself look ridiculous any more than I already am, so I inhale deeply and try to get the smile back on my face.

"Really, if it's about the guests, I'll try to run them by registration from now on," I promise more calmly with almost a plea in my voice.

The manager seems to relax and his expression softens, but the words out of his lips do not change the situation. "I'm sorry, Mr. Wright, it's not your fault. Indeed, you are a very discreet guest of our hotel. Never a complaint from the neighboring rooms. The problem concerns the journalists and paparazzi who have been pestering our guests over the last five months. This is a hotel that offers reliability and privacy, and we can no longer guarantee it since the news of your…past accommodations…reached the newspapers," he explains to me calmly.

I can't blame him. Since we decided to make our prison

record public, freeing us from the weight of lies, the press has not given us a break. At first, we let them target us, hoping that the news would wane with time. After a month, we began to worry; after two months, we were sure that only a government crisis could bump us from the list of journalists' priorities. I can see how five months is exhausting even for those forced to live with our fame. I'm sure the high-profile businessmen who spend the night here with escorts, to have some distraction from their wives, do not want to risk finding their face plastered on the front pages of the newspapers.

"I can try to do something. I'll call my manager and the police if needed. I can issue a restraining order for the paparazzi," I try to convince him, but the compassionate smile that appears on his face makes it clear that the decision has already been made.

"A restraining order for every single paparazzo in this city? Mr. Wright, we have called the police several times and, apart from a few hours of respite, the situation has remained virtually unchanged. The police district threatened to shut us down if we made one more phone call. I tried in every way to help your stay, but unfortunately, this is the only solution that allows us to run our business smoothly."

I doubt that the police can shut down a hotel, but I understand his point.

"And where the hell will I go?" I say more to myself than to the person in front of me.

The manager smiles. "Manhattan's real estate market is always attractive. I'm sure you'll have no problem finding new accommodations that make you feel at *home*."

Buy myself a house? Has he gone mad? "How much time

do I have?" I ask, resigned at his firmness.

"Normally, checkout time is noon, but we understand it is difficult to organize your exit in an hour. You have until six this evening to leave the room."

His generosity leaves me seven hours to pack my stuff and disappear from his sight. I give him a forced smile and nod then take a step backward, not sure how to close this damn door without the manager seeing me completely naked, but he insists on staying, as if to make sure I'm packing. I decide to throw away what little dignity I have left. I place the vase on the side table then spread my arms to grab the door handle and smile at him.

"Have a nice day," I say, before returning to hide my naked body behind the layer of wood.

When I turn around, Samantha and Barbara look at me, pouting. "So the party's over?"

I look down on my private parts, noticing that my erection is only a distant memory. "I would say yes."

"So, now where do we go?"

I realize they didn't understand that we'll all have to leave this room, but not together. "You to your home, I assume. Me…I don't know."

I grab my phone and lock myself in the bedroom, but not before picking up the girls' clothes—who, finally, understand and are getting dressed to get out.

"Where the hell are you? I've been trying to call you since this morning." Our manager's voice is serious but not furious.

I decide to avoid the explanation that includes the two blondes putting their clothes back on, and I immediately get to the heart of the matter. "They evicted me from the hotel."

The silence on the other side of the line lasts a few seconds too long. "What the hell did you do this time?" Evan's voice is a mixture of resigned and desperate. Sometimes I feel bad for the poor guy.

"Nothing, I swear. The paparazzi are always stationed in front of the door, and the hotel guests have begun to complain. When you cheat on your wife with a prostitute, you'd prefer not to have a lot of witnesses, especially if you're a prominent member of the rich, puritanical New York."

I hear him inhale deeply and exhale slowly. I think he started using the gift certificate for the meditation center that we gave him for Christmas. He was so stressed we were afraid he'd blow a gasket. "Let me make a few phone calls, and I'll call you back. I'll also send you someone to help you pack your bags."

"Thank you for the calls, but as for the suitcases, I don't need any help. I can do it myself."

"Really?"

"Don't be so surprised, I'm used to packing for tours…and it's not like I have much else to do."

Evan remains silent for a few seconds. "You should be in the studio with the others, idiot!" he rants. His meditative moment lasted precisely forty seconds.

"So they can berate me for not showing up this morning?"

"You know they're right, don't you?"

"I know, but I've just been evicted. I can only handle one crisis at a time. I don't want to be scolded because I didn't show up at the studio." I realize I'm whining like a kid who doesn't want to do his homework.

"It's a hotel room, Michael. It's not your home. You can

find dozens identical to that one," sighs Evan in despair.

"See? Even you say I don't have a home."

"Go pack your bags, Michael, before I come and kick your ass."

"Evan, can I ask you something without you getting angry or making fun of me?"

I feel his hesitation, but then he urges me to continue.

"Can you become impotent from too much sex?"

He says nothing for an endless time, and I look at the screen to see if he hung up.

"Evan?"

"If only, Michael. If your dick does fall off because you use it too much, at least you'd be on time for your appointments for once in your life, not between the legs of a woman."

He hangs up, leaving me no time to reply.

***

It is almost evening when Max, our driver, lets me out in front of the red brick building that has become so familiar over the years.

"Surprise!" I singsong when Simon opens the door of his house on the Upper East Side.

His face is puzzled, then looks worried when he notices four huge suitcases behind me and several garbage bags on the sidewalk next to Max. Apparently, over the years, I've accumulated a lot more stuff than I thought.

"Are you going somewhere?"

"I was evicted from my hotel room."

He studies me for a few seconds to see if there is a follow-up to my explanation. "Can't you find another one?" His voice becomes more suspicious.

I shake my head and flash one of my most beautiful smiles. "Evan tried, but as soon as he gives my name, suddenly all the hotels in Manhattan don't have free rooms. Apparently, the paparazzi scare guests and the word has spread," I say, motioning across the street where the photographers are having fun with our outdoor conversation.

Simon looks up, annoyed, and beckons Max and me to come in. I pick up the suitcases as fast as I can, along with the bags that our driver cannot carry, and I run the five steps that separate me from the landing of my friend's house.

"So you're looking for a home? Why did you come here?"

Out of all of us, Simon is the one who needs calm and stability. He loves silence like I love women. I understand the annoyance of my sudden appearance, but I'm desperate. I'm basically homeless. Max takes his leave and walks out in a hurry, no doubt afraid that Simon will turn me down, and I'll end up sleeping on his couch with his family.

"Where else do you want me to go?"

"I don't know. There are four of us in the band. Am I really your last resort?"

He invites me into the living room of his townhome, which extends over seven floors. It looks like a jungle in here. There are more plants than in Central Park, and I suspect there is far too much oxygen; I read somewhere that too much oxygen can be toxic and that you can go into narcosis. I think it was an article about scuba diving, but you can never be too cautious about certain things.

"Damian and Lilly fuck like rabbits on every surface of that house. Thomas and Iris walk around naked taking artistic photographs at their navels. Do you think I can go and live with them?”

A smile raises a corner of his mouth, and I know I’ve won him over.

“I see your point. They scare me since finding their women. I was used to their outings. Seeing them move in together within a few months is disorienting.” He chuckles as we leave the formal living room to move into the kitchen that overlooks the back patio.

We sit at the table near the floor-to-ceiling window overlooking the small garden, which opens up to a lot of natural light on the warm-colored furniture in here. Simon hands me a beer from the fridge and I take a generous sip of it.

“So, what do you plan to do?” he asks me after a while.

Him and his need to plan for the future. He could just live day to day like other rock stars, but instead, he’d like to start a family and settle down before the age of thirty. He’s even investing in funds for his future children and their upbringing. He doesn’t even have a woman and he’s already thinking about kids. In my opinion, he’ll never find someone to start a family with—only a psychopath invests in kids who are technically still sperm.

“We could live like we did when we shared the room at Joe’s before we became famous!”

The bottle of beer he is about to sip from stops in midair. His wide-open mouth and eyes make me almost burst out laughing. He’s terrified at the idea of having to live with me for more than a few days. I love him, but I think I would go crazy with the multitude of plants here. But I want to keep him on the spot a little longer.

“You’re kidding, right?”

"No, why not? It will be fun. Like the old days: beer and chips for dinner, action movies on the laptop in bed, and porn when we want to warm up a bit!"

"You were the one who ate beer and chips. I was trying to make decent meals. You were the one obsessed with *Die Hard*, I wanted to watch something else. And most of all, you were the one getting off on the loud porn when I was trying to sleep!" he blurts out, outraged.

I laugh and drink my beer. "It's too easy to get under your skin. You're too funny."

I hear him muttering something incomprehensible as he goes to the sink, rinses the bottle he just finished, and slips it into the recyclable bin under the sink. Doesn't he have a cleaning lady, this guy? I hope he doesn't force me to make up my bed every morning because I swear, I'm going to sleep on the street with the pigeons.

"So? Do you have a cook for dinner? A catering service that provides meals?" I ask when I feel my belly grumbling. Considering I no longer have room service, I am a bit disoriented.

Simon turns around and looks at me like I've gone crazy.

"I'm a grown man. I usually feed myself!" he replies in disbelief when he realizes I'm serious.

"Why should you worry about it? You have the money to pay someone to do it for you." I'm genuinely interested.

At least when Damian and Thomas were single, they ordered takeout or went out to dinner. Simon looks like the perfect couch potato, middle-aged, divorced, who eats meals alone in a kitchen without a TV, who rinses his dishes before putting them in the dishwasher, and who prefers to read a book instead of sitting in front of the computer and killing himself

with porn.

He shakes his head and turns to grab the laptop lying on the island's marble counter. "You know what? This is far too much news for today. I don't feel like cooking. We'll order out." He gives up, or maybe he simply lets me win so as not to argue.

The sense of disorientation I felt while leaving what has been my home for three years loosens in my stomach, and I finally manage to relax. As much as I try not to take myself too seriously, I was distraught that Simon might tell me to find other accommodations.

***

Immediately after getting up well-rested and having breakfast, we walk to the new record company building, which is also the house where Thomas and Iris live, in about twenty minutes on foot. Outside Simon's townhome there are still paparazzi, but it's a beautiful day in May, the sun is shining, and, according to Simon, it's a waste to use the car. I honestly would have preferred to finish my coffee comfortably seated in Max's SUV rather than spill it while walking, but I'm a guest at his house, and he dictates the rules.

"Do you know why Evan was in such a hurry this morning to have us in the studio?" I ask Simon, who doesn't seem worried by our manager's call.

"I don't know, but he didn't seem strange to me."

"Really? He seemed agitated. I almost had the impression that it was a matter of life and death."

Simon giggles, amused, and it makes me suspicious. "Maybe because he wanted to be sure to get *you* to come to the studio since you didn't show up yesterday."

Yes, this could be Evan's strategy.

We arrive at the big gate that opens to the back of the house and garden, and ring the bell. Thomas and Iris decided to keep the entrance of the record company at the back to separate it from the rest of the house where they live. The garden is not huge, but it is remarkable when you consider we're in the center of one of the largest cities in the world. It is surrounded entirely by a red brick wall that prevents it from being seen from the outside. At the end of the small stone path that leads to the stairs leading to the patio of their kitchen, a door opens to the reception area of Jail Records. Next to the white counter is the door to the conference room, and behind that, a small corridor leads to the two recording rooms.

Ingrid, the receptionist Evan hired, smiles at us and lights up as soon as we enter. She gets up to greet us by resting a hand on my arm and fluttering her eyelashes instead of answering the ringing phone. She rushes to have coffee with us more than she stays behind that desk.

"I think work is calling you." Simon points his finger at the phone with a bit of annoyance.

"Oh, yes, so silly of me," she giggles and returns to sit at her desk.

Evan, meanwhile, leaves the conference room where I already see Damian, Thomas, Iris, and Emily.

"You're here. We were waiting for you to begin." He seems to almost glow as he says it, which gets my attention.

What the hell does he have to say that's so important that he has to bring our asses here at nine o'clock on a Wednesday morning? We enter and sit in the comfortable sofas of the conference room. Not having much space on this floor, we decided not to set up the room with the classic table and chairs around which important things are discussed. Instead, we put colorful sofas and armchairs with a bar counter on the far wall so we can both discuss work and sometimes relax. I must say that I like this less formal environment much more than the one in the old record company.

"What do we owe all this haste to?" I ask, intrigued while sipping my coffee.

Evan closes the door behind him and sits in the chair next to Emily. Those two together have become a real war machine. I didn't think Evan could find a person who's so in tune with him and who can keep up with him. I've always seen him give the orders to his assistants, but she's more of a right-hand man, the one who helps him come up with ideas, not just execute his orders.

"Last night, we were locked in here until midnight thinking of strategies to give an injection of life to your career after leaving the old label," Evan begins.

Injection of life is a very optimistic expression. Our career has to be totally relaunched, but I don't say anything. I don't want to be a Debbie Downer this early in the morning.

"We thought we'd do the exact opposite of what the old record company demanded of you, which was to hide your past," continues Iris.

"What do you mean? Do you want to flaunt the court documents with our convictions?" asks Simon, amused. It was his idea to come out into the open and clean up our image, but I don't think he had this in mind. We all laugh at his proposal. Emily throws him a balled-up piece of paper.

"No, idiot," Evan says. "Emily has a pretty good idea: to use your past to change your image. You're the perfect exam-

ple of making mistakes, atoning for your sins, and living an honest life. You're the emblem of hope for thousands of kids who find themselves in the same condition but who are treated like scum inside juvenile prisons. That's why we thought you should bring your voice right into these prisons. Turn to the kids, not to those outside. Our idea is to do a charity concert inside the facility where you met. Before I call them, I want to know what you think."

Evan's speech comes at me like a bucket of freezing water. I feel a cold vise starting from my stomach and expanding to my chest, freezing my heart. I look at Damian, who seems, on the one hand, surprised, on the other worried. Thomas has an indecipherable expression, almost calm. Perhaps because Iris has already told him about this idea and he's had the opportunity to digest it. Simon stares at his coffee and seems to think about it.

"It's not a bad idea," Damian says. "We can do a gig for the kids. Document the thing and put it on the blog. This could show people that the guys locked in there aren't monsters. I wish I could talk to them, tell them they can get out of that shit." His words grow more and more distant, and the lump in my throat is the only thing keeping me from vomiting in the middle of the room.

"No! Absolutely not! I will not go back to that place. I'd rather die than go back in there," I blurt out as I get up from the couch under everyone's surprised gaze and walk to the door, opening it wide and marching quickly out into the garden.

I walk to the bench on one side of the green corner, sheltered from the trees. I sit down and take deep breaths to try to calm my heart that's exploding in my chest. I don't notice

Simon's presence until I see his feet in front of me.

"Are you alright?"

"No, I'm not. I'm not even close to being okay. How the hell does Evan think he can ask us such a thing?" I say all in one breath as I put my hands through my hair.

Simon inhales profoundly and stares at something in the distance. Some time passes before I hear his calm voice again. "Michael, you're not that helpless kid anymore. You're a grown man who has left behind all that crap and built a life for himself. Don't be afraid. You won't be treated like a criminal…and that night you'll go home and sleep in your own bed, not inside a cell with people you don't trust."

I feel the lump in my throat closing again at the mere thought of the nights inside that cursed place. "Do you have any idea how long it took me not to have nightmares after we came out? Years." My voice is almost a whisper.

"I shared the room with you. I know how hard it was to get over it. But remember my room is just down the hall. You're strong, Michael. You're the strongest of all of us because you managed to get up every time. I'm sure you'll be able to walk into that place with your head held high and teach those kids not to be afraid."

Simon's words warm my chest. He's not one to give empty compliments; what comes out of his mouth always comes straight from his heart. I appreciate his trust in me, but I'm not sure I can do it this time. Because, for the first time in years, I'm scared again.

CHAPTER 2
Faith

"Mother?" I stick my head inside the Mother Superior's office after knocking and waiting for permission. The boarding school headmistress beckons me to enter and waves me toward the chair in front of her desk while she finishes filling in the attendance on the register.

I approach with a light step to avoid making noise on the stone floor in the austere room. The walls are thick and also stone, the windows small, the furniture sparse and made of solid, dark wood. A desk, a filing cabinet, the wooden chair of the headmistress, and two chairs on the other side of her desk make up the furniture, together with the low table and a stool in a corner where there is a landline telephone.

The building was a former cloistered convent, converted into a boarding school; the communal rooms are large, and our steps rumble inside the rooms with little furniture. I think they do it on purpose, so it's easier to hear when we sneak from room to room after ten in the evening, the mandatory bedtime curfew.

"Are you here for your weekly phone call?" Her stern gaze rests on me and makes me straighten my spine. The Mother Superior is a very rigid person. She doesn't like to see the girls of her school slumping or paying little attention to posture.

Her all-black attire, including the veil, makes the pale, hollowed-out skin of her face even edgier, giving her an intimidating, stern look.

"Yes, Mother." I try to keep my voice clear and strong like she prefers. She is not a person who likes soft-spoken girls with little backbone. The exact opposite of my father, who always scolds me if my voice is louder than my brothers'.

"Take a seat, but this time remember to keep your conversation appropriate to this environment."

"Yes, Mother." I am tempted to look down in shame, but I know I would be scolded for it.

Last week, I asked my father to hug my mother for me since I couldn't go home for her birthday, and Mother Superior scolded me because these shows of affection are not suitable for the ears of those outside the family. We do not have privacy when we make calls—this is the only phone in the school accessible to call outside—and we are not allowed to use cell phones. Not that I need one, since I found out about their existence only a year ago, at twenty-three, when I started working around people who didn't grow up in a closed community like mine.

The Mother Superior returns to lower her gaze on her books, yet I know that she will listen to every single word. Not that I have anything to hide, but it always makes me nervous because I'm afraid I'll say something wrong and make her angry.

I sit on the stool, dial the number, and my father's voice thunders on the other side at the first ring. I imagine him, like every Sunday morning at eleven o'clock, waiting for my call sitting in the armchair next to the phone in the living room.

"Faith."

"Good morning, Dad."

I glance toward Mother Superior and see her hand stop and rise from the sheet. I should have called him "father," with the respect that befits a parent.

"Have you been to church praying this morning?"

"Yes."

One of the conditions under which my father let me leave the Community of the Sacred Heart of Jesus, where I grew up, to work as a nurse in another state, was that I stay in a boarding school run by nuns where prayers and discipline are respected. It took me months to convince him, but he finally gave in and found this place for me. Every morning at five o'clock we gather to pray in the small chapel inside the school. I am exempt from this task only when I have the night shift at the prison, and I do not return before eight in the morning.

"Did you go to work this week?"

"Yes, I had the day shift." It is the shift that my father prefers. He doesn't like it when I am locked up inside a prison during the night, even if there are only kids in there.

"Have you talked to any of the inmates?" His stern tone reminds me whenever he disapproves of my choice to leave our community of just over six hundred inhabitants to work in the infirmary of a juvenile prison.

According to the teachings of our community, the woman must stay at home to look after the children and take care of her husband and the house. It was a scandal when the locals learned that he had allowed me to move out. On the other hand, my father permitted me to study to become a nurse, making me want to explore the world. I am the rebellious daughter he didn't expect to have. Amid eleven other children—the emblem of obedience—I am the one who at twenty-four is not yet married and has no children running around the house. My sister Hannah is twenty-one and is already pregnant with her third child.

"I have not had any conversations outside of those I need to understand the condition of the patient who is taken to the infirmary. There was no improper conversation."

"They are prisoners, Faith, not patients. They are in there because they committed crimes. Did you forget about that? It seems to me that you are taking those criminals too much to heart. Maybe it's time to come home and set your head straight."

The shiver that runs down my spine just to hear about the life that awaits me in my community makes my jaw tighten as I inhale deeply. The image of Jacob waiting for me on the doorstep, his boots dirty with manure, expecting me to clean them, and the smell of pigs he can never get off his skin almost makes me vomit. The guilt and shame at my disgust for my future spouse make me blush.

"No, Father. You're right. I got the word wrong."

I hear him inhale deeply. I know he would like to continue the conversation, but on the phone, it is difficult. He doesn't like technology. We were the last family to have a computer at home, but it was the only way to make us all study and keep social services out of our house. We had one in the kitchen to use under the careful supervision of my parents or one of my older siblings.

"I'll hear from you next week."

"Okay."

My dad hangs up. I would like to breathe a sigh of relief,

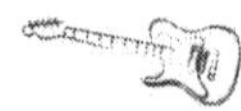

but I hold it back because the Mother Superior would not forgive my act of insubordination towards a parent. I wouldn't risk her denying my permission to go out with my co-workers this afternoon.

"Thank you for letting me use the phone." I turn to the Mother, who raises her head from her records again.

"Go. And remember that you have to come back by eight o'clock this evening."

"Yes, Mother."

I never thought about skipping the curfew. As much as my family considers me a rebel, I follow the rules. Even if I have access to sinful foods, forbidden movies, or books outside my community, I have never purposely gone against my father's teachings.

***

"You've finally escaped the convent!" exclaims Linda as soon as I sit in the back seat of her car and close the door behind me.

"It's a boarding school, not a convent." I smile at the joke she makes every time they come to pick me up to go out on a Sunday afternoon.

Linda and Cindy are the other two nurses who work with me at the prison, and sitting in front of me on the passenger side is Penelope, the psychologist. They are all older, married, and with children, but once in a while, they allow themselves a few hours of "girl time" to go to the beach without having to look after their children. I think of my mother and sisters, and I can't imagine them doing such a thing. For them, there is no free time to "take a breath without the family," as my colleagues say. The whole idea was taboo until I started hanging

out with them.

"From how you dress, you couldn't tell." She winks at me from the rearview mirror and smiles.

I know she's just teasing me, not making fun of me, but that doesn't stop me from noticing how different my attire is from theirs. I'm wearing a long skirt, long-sleeved shirt, and boots, while these three are in shorts, sleeveless shirts, and flip-flops. I know I stick out like a sore thumb, but I'm too embarrassed to expose all that skin to strangers.

"Stop embarrassing her, Linda." Penelope comes to my rescue. "If she likes to dress like that, what do you care?"

She is the oldest, around sixty-five, and has been working in prison for at least thirty years. She's the one who took me under her wing when I arrived here a year ago, disoriented and intimidated by the world, and taught me the basics of modern life, like the existence of cell phones and coffee shops that sell everything but ordinary black coffee.

"You know I don't mean any harm, right?" Linda smiles at me from the mirror.

I nod and smile at her. I know that it was entirely counterintuitive that the four of us eventually became friends. We couldn't be more different, with completely opposite families and personalities that would never get along on paper. Yet here we are, ready to get out of the car to spend a few hours on the beach breathing the salty air together.

"Have you heard the news?" asks Cindy as soon as we sit on the sand not far from other people. The three of them have already undressed down to a bikini while I took off my boots and socks and sank my feet in the sand. I love the feeling of sand between my toes.

I shake my head and wait for one of the three to enlighten me. It seems to be something vital because they've been in turmoil since we left.

"The Jailbirds are doing a concert at the prison."

I had heard that someone was going to come and play—they built a stage in the dining hall—but I never stopped to ask for details. When the women see that I don't react to their excitement, their eyes widen.

"You have no idea who they are, do you?" asks Linda in disbelief.

The only one who doesn't seem surprised that much by my ignorance is Penelope, in whom I confide the most, someone who knows that the outside world, for me, was a mystery until a year ago.

"Should I?" An embarrassed half-smile appears on my lips.

"They're only the biggest rock band in the world. Why on earth would you have heard their music? Unbelievable!" Linda laughs as she pushes me slightly.

Her way of touching people always leaves me a little disoriented. At first, it bothered me. I'm not used to strangers hugging me. Even at home, we're not used to displays of affection. We hug for special occasions, such as holidays or birthdays. You certainly don't touch the people you're talking with. It's Linda who pulled me out of my shell and showed me you can do it without being ashamed or embarrassed.

"I don't listen to rock music." My confession comes out like a whisper, but the three of them heard me because they stare at me with curiosity. I don't want to tell them that my father would punish me if I even thought about listening to the devil's music. I've found it's hard for other people to under-

stand the specific dynamics of my community. I soon realized that the rest of the world does not live like us, and though it excites me to discover new things, it also scares me because my father would never approve of my conduct since moving here.

"It doesn't matter. We'll give you a crash course before they arrive next week when your poor heart gives in under the wave of testosterone." Cindy smiles at me.

"Testosterone? I would like Damian to slam me against the wall," Linda sighs, pulling a laugh from the others.

I smile, but I feel my cheeks flare up. I'll never get used to their open references to sex. At first, I didn't understand them, but since they've explained it all, I want to plug my ears to avoid the constant embarrassment.

"Linda, you're a married woman, and Damian is a monogamous man!" rebukes Penelope.

"No one touches your babies, don't worry. You can lower your claws, Mama Bear. Do you know it was Penelope who formed the band? They were her special project in prison, back when there were still the funds to do something decent for the boys."

"Really? Are they former inmates? And they allowed them to be a band?" I can't hide the outraged nuance in my voice.

Penelope smiles and studies me with the usual patience she uses when it comes to my closed-mindedness. Little by little, she is teaching me to see the world with different eyes from my father's, and I'm afraid this is one of those times when I'm judging without thinking with my own head.

"Not everyone who arrives at the juvie is a hopeless case. In fact, most are scared kids who made a mistake. They were good people, we managed to save them by giving them a

chance not to become criminals, and they grabbed the opportunity with both hands. You would never know they've been in prison," she explains patiently, and I nod, without fully understanding how it is possible.

I grew up being sure that only criminals, those who have a soul stained by sins, end up in prison. When they lock you in there, no one can save you. Your soul will end up in hell with that of other sinners.

"So this band is famous?" I try to make conversation out of curiosity for these former inmates.

"Every person on the face of the earth, apart from you, has dreamed of meeting them at least once in their life." Cindy enlightens me about their fame.

Linda scrolls on her phone and shows me a video. It looks like a concert in a stadium. The singer with long hair and a magnetic look is singing obscene words that make me blush to the tips of my ears. He moves entirely uninhibitedly in front of the microphone, pushing his pelvis forward in a gesture I shouldn't even think about, let alone see.

"It seemed right to baptize you with 'Sex on the Beach,'" she giggles, amused at my wide eyes and shocked face.

You should never talk about the sexual act, not even in private, let alone in public, in a song about sex on the beach. If my father knew I was watching this video, he'd wash my eyes with soap, like that time my friend Marianne showed me *Dirty Dancing*. I'll never forget the embarrassment I felt at seeing the actors rub that way in front of the cameras. How do actors go home to their spouses after sharing such intimacy with a stranger?

"Oh, Jesus, forgive me," I whisper in a low voice, closing

my eyes and covering my face with my hands.

Someone, however, forces me to regain contact with reality, removing my hand from my face.

"Faith, there's nothing wrong with this video, nothing sinful. Stop thinking about your family thousands of miles away. This is your life. When you finish this video, you can choose whether to watch others, but it should be *your* decision." Penelope encourages me to bring my gaze back to the phone, holding my hand.

This time a different guy is framed, the one with the guitar. He has light brown hair with golden tips and eyes of such a particular color that they appear gray. He is so handsome he takes my breath away. He's like one of those actors from western movies that are so intense they seem to come off the screen. But what completely confuses me is his gaze. That mischievous smile of a trouble-maker who knows he'll get away with anything because he manages to convey an innocent sweetness on command. Only there's nothing innocent about this guy. The way he moves, winks at the camera, how he slips his tongue over his lips and then gives us an evil grin.

My stomach explodes in a sensation that almost makes me catch my breath. It's as if someone has tightened a vise in my bowels, down to the bottom, where a tingling makes me blush. My cheeks burn, and when my brain understands these sensations, my father's voice thunders overbearingly in my head: "What you feel in your stomach when you look at a boy is the devil trying to catch your soul and drag it to hell with the rest of the lustful ones."

I squeeze Penelope's hand hard and find myself fighting between the feeling that invades my stomach and my head that

tells me to look away. I can't do it. I'm magnetized by those eyes, those lips that do not allow me to look elsewhere. When the video ends, my stomach is far from normal again. My heart beats in my chest so furiously I wonder if everyone else can hear it.

"After so much heat, Cindy and I are going to take a dip. Are you coming?" asks Linda, putting her cell phone in the bag.

Penelope and I shake our heads, and the two women move away, chuckling towards the shore.

"Oh dear Jesus, help me," I exhale the air I was holding in my lungs until they were out of range.

Penelope looks at me and smiles. "So, was it that bad to look at?"

I clamp my lips and bite them. I'm blushing when I shake my head and admit that the video wasn't so bad. Sinful, but not ugly.

"I saw you blush. You liked one of them, didn't you?"

I bring my hands in front of my face and take a trembling breath. "I shouldn't feel my stomach twisting when I see men who will never become my husband. It goes against all the teachings I have received in my life."

Penelope inhales deeply and rests her gaze on the ocean. For a moment, I have the feeling that I have offended her in some way.

"They kept you locked in a box with no cracks for so long that the world is a discovery for you. The squeeze in your stomach is pure and simple excitement, attraction to a man you like physically. There's nothing wrong with that, even if you feel it for more than one person. It is in the nature of every human being to be attracted to someone, or else our species would have become extinct thousands of years ago. I know it's hard for you to accept because all your life you've been taught it's a sin, but you have to try not to feel guilty."

Her tone is calm, the one she always uses when explaining things to me.

As soon as I left the community and started to live in the outside world, the people I spoke to treated me like I had mental problems because I didn't know what a cell phone or a bar was. Penelope never treated me as if I were dumb just because I haven't ever tried certain things. She understood my condition and was teaching me to live differently.

"I don't know how to reconcile what I feel with what I've been taught. I've never felt a squeeze in my stomach so violent looking at the guys I've known my entire life. Why now? My father says that the devil is out here. And maybe that's it. The evil that is tempting me. How else can I explain why, until I left the community, I never felt the squeeze in my stomach like when watching that video."

Penelope looks at me and smiles at me lovingly, as my grandmother did when I was a child. "Or maybe your community is too small. How many are you, just over six hundred? Sometimes it happens that you are not attracted to the people with whom you have grown up and lived all your life. You can feel brotherly love for them, but not that impulse to procreate and give life to a new family."

I lift my shoulders because I'm short of words.

"Who did you like the most in the video? Apart from Thomas, who you can't see behind that drum. Was it Damian? The singer with long hair? He is usually the one who shakes up

women's hormones." She smiles as she asks me.

My cheeks go on fire again, and I shake my head. "The guy with the lightest hair. The one with the guitar who approached the singer and who has the face of sin."

Penelope laughs, amused in that calm way she has. She's not as loud as Linda or Cindy. I like talking to her more because she's never over the top. "Oh, yes, honey. Michael has just the face of sin. He looks like a young Clint Eastwood, those eyes could pierce the screen and make women fall in love."

"That's right, those eyes... Do you know him well?"

"Enough to understand him. He's a cheerful, brazen one. He responds to what life throws at him with humor."

"Is he superficial?"

"No, on the contrary. It's all appearance. He's built so many layers of indifference to protect his most fragile part that I don't think he can reach his heart anymore. They broke him in so many ways when he was young that when Damian, Thomas, and Simon managed to put the pieces back together, there was nothing left of the insecure and frightened boy who entered the prison. He has become Michael, the one who never misses a joke at anything."

"You talk about him as if he were your child." She talks about her children and grandchildren with the same passion with which she described the guy who was only her patient.

Penelope looks at me, smiles, then looks at the ocean. "Michael was the one I was most worried about in all my years inside that prison. I was afraid he would come out of it in a black bag, with no one coming to claim his body. He's a rare gem that few have been able to recognize, unfortunately."

My heart keeps pumping in my chest as hard as it did when I watched that video. My head spins full of information, unable to make them coexist. The idea of the criminal who has been locked up in prison and the boy who Penelope has just described to me—two people enclosed in the same body that I cannot unite in a single name: Michael.

CHAPTER 3

Michael

A minivan. Evan rented a minivan with tinted windows to get to the juvie. I understand that between Manhattan and New Jersey the private jet is a bit too pretentious, but a minivan? There are eight of us locked up in here attempting small talk since we left. As we get closer to the prison, however, the jokes have become more and more infrequent.

My bandmates are nervous, even if they don't show it. Our chatty mood has subsided since we left town and the houses have given way to fields of grass and some sporadic trees. This view of nothing but land reminds us of the complete loss of hope we felt when we would go out to the courtyard in the afternoons and there were only fields as far as the eye could see. The only road in sight ended at the front gates topped by barbed wire, where no one ever passed through but the prison employees.

Having only this view for more than a year can undermine your sanity. At some point, you start to think there is no future for you beyond those fields, and that even if you tried to escape, you wouldn't find anything or anyone waiting for you. In a facility with more than six hundred boys between fourteen and seventeen years old, you feel alone, as if no one in the world cares about you.

For the four of us, that was our reality. Apart from Thomas, who lost his family while in prison, none of us had anyone wondering about our wellbeing in that concrete building. If we had died in there, we would have ended up in an anonymous grave, without a funeral, buried at the expense of the state without much fanfare. When I got out, I was only seventeen years old, yet no one came to pick me up, no one worried that a car would take me home. I walked to the nearest town, got on a bus with the fifty dollars Penelope had given me before crossing the threshold, and went to Manhattan. I walked off of that bus with a different last name and Joe's address that Simon and Damian had given me while waiting for Thomas and me to get out after serving our sentence.

"Listen, Evan, when you rented the minivan for the trip, did you also think about some snacks? I'm hungry!" I break the silence by leaning toward the front seat where Max and our manager are sitting.

Damian bursts into a thunderous laugh. Simon shakes his head in despair while Iris giggles, amused. Evan turns around and looks at me with a scolding gaze.

"Is it possible that you can't go more than two and a half hours without a meal? We've already made two stops since we left because you have a peanut-sized bladder. And now you're hungry?"

"Listen, it's not my fault that I have to drink often to keep myself hydrated." I pretend to be offended. "Do you know how many liquids are consumed by having sex?"

Simon laughs. "You've been living with me for a couple of weeks, and you give me hell every night because I won't let you bring women home. When the hell did you have sweaty

sex?"

"Do you know how many times I have to jerk off because of you? Do you have any idea how much sperm I spill?" My roommate makes a disgusted face while the others snicker.

"What the hell do you have between your legs, a hydrant? How much fluid can you lose during ejaculation?" asks Emily, amused.

I turn to her and throw her my best mischievous smile. "You'd like to find out, wouldn't you? You would like to try my *hydrant*. Let's just say it's enough to make me dehydrated." I raise my eyebrows invitingly. I would never sleep with her, not because she isn't attractive but because it would be embarrassing to work with her.

Emily makes a disgusted face. "Michael, not all women want to live in a porn movie. Not all of them dream of being flooded with the sperm of the alpha male who possesses them."

"You only say that because you've never been flooded by me." I wink jokingly. I'm sure this conversation counts as harassment in some court, but luckily, she seems more amused than offended.

"Can we stop talking about your sperm?" Thomas intervenes, disgusted. "Pretty sure not even a brain transplant could erase the image of your seminal fluid flooding women all over the country." The others laugh, amused.

Silence falls again when the metal fence topped by barbed wire emerges after the turn, and the correctional facility appears in front of us like a concrete block with red doors. Although this is not a prison, it is a correctional facility for underage boys who have violent tendencies and are not eligible to serve a less restrictive sentence. The problem is that seventy percent of the kids in there aren't violent when they enter, but they become violent to survive the abuse they are subjected to on a daily basis.

***

Leaving the old record company and its tyranny has its positive side. You can make the decisions that are better for your career and not for their bank accounts. You can be honest with the people around you without feeling like a slimy liar trying to hide your past. You can enjoy the girls competing to end up between the sheets of the bad guy: a *real* bad boy with a prison record. I thought a rock star's life was fantastic, with women dropping their panties at the mere sight of your beautiful face, but I was wrong. Former inmates have a line of women ready to do whatever you ask them.

The worst part of leaving your record label, though, is that you no longer have an organization that does everything for you. You don't have interns who follow you to remind you of your appointments. You don't have assistants who call to make sure that people hired for a job are doing it for real, and above all, you don't have an organizational machine that provides you with the best help for your life to run as smooth as oil. With less than fifteen days to organize this concert, the juvie's bureaucracy that drove us crazy, and the budget of the new record company still to be defined, we didn't find a sound technician or any professionals who could set up the stage.

So now, I find myself kneeling behind my amp, trying to connect the power outlet to the battered power strip that the prison provided us, trying not to be electrocuted. While Damian is in another room answering the kids' questions and doing the actual charity, the three of us are setting up the instruments

for the concert on a makeshift stage the prison put together. If it were up to us, we would have played on the concrete floor. Here, the boys will be crammed into benches around the dining hall tables. You can't even move those seats because they're bolted to the ground. Not a great setting for a concert by a longshot.

"Do you need help?" Simon approaches and peeks behind the stack of amps.

"I hope this place doesn't catch on fire. These sockets have been here for at least twenty years and the wires are exposed." I get up and start turning on some instrumentation, hoping it doesn't explode in my face.

"We don't need a stampede *and* frying the instruments in the process," Simon grumbles subtly.

We are all a bit low on morale, even if my bandmates don't admit it as openly as I do. To come back in here means to relive memories that none of us want to dig up. The pain and fear we felt within these walls are still too vivid. Only Damian seems invigorated by this situation because he has embraced the mission of helping these boys, giving them the hope they need to overcome the sentence and get out of here with the desire to live a better life. He's like that. He's always donated generous amounts to charities that help women victims of violence or children at risk.

I'm not that kind of person. I feel nothing but resentment for this place because I would have died here if it wasn't for Penelope, Simon, Damian, and Thomas. Crushed by something bigger than me for a crime I was forced to commit. I didn't go into that house to steal because I wanted to, but because the alternative was to be beaten by my father. My mother, instead

of stopping him, prayed that I would not die.

When Damian returns from his meeting with the boys, we have already finished assembling everything. He looks exhausted, but he's smiling and his eyes are shining with satisfaction. I bet he managed to get rid of some of his own demons. I don't think he pulled any punches—it's not like Damian to polish the truth—but I also believe he gave hope to these guys along with the brutal truth. Because, after all, we managed to get out of here. Even I, who had lost all hope, came out of it and changed my life. This is the only thought that makes me stay on this stage and repress the instinct to bolt out of here without looking back.

Damian doesn't tell us anything about how it went. I know this will be a conversation for later, when we're all inside the van and away from this place. When we can finally breathe a sigh of relief again.

"The director told me not to play 'Sex on the Beach' because it's too explicit for minors," he chuckles quietly while putting the guitar around his neck, and the room fills with the murmur of the boys taking their seats.

We all laugh, and when they finally tell us to start, the first chords of "Sex on the Beach" resonate in the large room. We glance at the director, who shakes his head squeezed inside a starched white shirt with a tie that was fashionable a few years ago and a well-ironed but dated suit. If he hadn't forbidden us to do so, we wouldn't have even played it because it wasn't on our set list. But who are we to deny a bit of rebellion to the boys locked inside these walls? We've never been good at following the rules.

The roar that rises isn't like from the stadiums we're used

to hearing—there are far fewer kids in here—but the enthusiasm on their faces is priceless. These are not the faces of rich boys who can afford to pay seven hundred dollars for a front-row seat. These are kids who have nothing and who have been given the rare opportunity of a private concert. And you can see on their faces they don't take it for granted.

They don't care that the acoustics suck in here, that the echo eats half of our words and the rumble of the drums is deafening. They don't give a damn. The only thing that matters is that the most famous band in the world is playing only for *them*. Someone today noticed that they exist, and the smiles on their faces are enough to make us forget where we are.

I turn to my bandmates and see they're as ecstatic as I am. Song after song, we don't care about being perfect, about performing a technically superb show that has no soul. It's our first concert after leaving the record company and for the first time in years, we're back to playing like we did when we were just starting out, when only our love of making music mattered. For the first time in years, I feel reborn, savoring the freedom that first made me passionate about music.

When we get to the last song, the boys all stand up, screaming and jumping, and not even the guards care about getting them being seated anymore.

Damian thanks them, and the boys begin to flow out of the room to return to their cells. I turn to Simon, who's smiling from ear to ear.

"That was crazy." Thomas breaks the silence as he gets up and takes a towel from Evan, who is handing us wipes and water to get us back on track.

"Michael, you're bleeding like a slaughtered pig." Emily

looks at me, puzzled.

I lower my gaze to my hand and realize that in all the excitement I've torn up my fingertips. It's not the first time, it happens when I play with my all, and my fingers move as if possessed. The worst part is that the blood stains my guitar and clothes.

"Does anyone have a Band-Aid?"

Evan, Iris, and Emily look around bewildered. They didn't think about this detail. If we had a record label backing us, an assistant would be ready with the first-aid kit and disinfectant in their pants' pocket.

"I'll show you to the infirmary where you can clean yourself up." The prison director who has approached us in the meantime, offers to guide me as if I didn't know how to navigate this place. I ended up so many times in that aseptic room, with its disinfectant smell, I could walk there with my eyes closed.

I notice Simon casting a worried look at me, but I gesture that I'm okay. I have no problem going in there.

Retracing the halls, with its nine-by-six rooms with the two bunk beds on each side, reminds me how this place is not a prison but has all the appearances of one. The boys are out in the yard, the cell doors are open, and the silence is almost surreal. Both the director and I want no small talk. Like an old couple, we didn't split in the best way. According to him, I was a problematic and violent boy. In my opinion, I had been beaten by my cellmates and the guards who came to 'quell the brawl.' Irreconcilable differences, they would have called it in a divorce. I call it turning a blind eye to abuses that should never have happened.

A muffled sound makes my head snap in the direction of a room a little further on. I recognize that grunt. It's the sound air makes coming out of your lungs when they beat you. Those beatings are so intense you can't even shout. I bolt toward the room where the sound comes from and I find a guard kneeling on the back of a little boy so scrawny he almost disappears under the hulk of the man. The blood covering his face frames an expression of pain and fear that I have experienced too many times. Without thinking, I violently push the guard and grab the little boy by the arm, drawing him behind me.

"Michael, what the hell are you doing?" the director shouts, following me into the room.

The guard, who was ready to jump on me, hangs back at the sight of his superior.

"What does it look like? I'm saving a little boy from a beating," I hiss with a fury that for a moment catches him by surprise.

"It's not a beating. He needs to be put back in line." The guard tries to defend himself, but I nail him with my eyes.

"And to do that, you need to beat a little boy bloody who is a third of your size?"

"Michael, if we think kids need a little firmer method for breaking the rules, you can't intervene in our corrective strategies." The director's voice is firm, but his gaze still holds all the anger and hatred that have not lessened for me over the years. It always bothered him that we became a band, and when we got famous, we had to pay him handsomely to make him shut up about our true identity. He always considered us scraps of society and never accepted the fact that we lived in luxury.

I pull up the little boy in front of me; his eyes are wide and his face is covered with blood from a cut on his eyebrow.

"Look him right in the face. It seems to me that he clearly understood what his *mistakes* were. How about getting him to the infirmary?" The director does not even move to breathe. "You know, it doesn't take any effort to Tweet to the whole world what your 'corrective methods' are. I don't know if you realize how many eyes are on us now. A single Tweet is enough for me to unleash public opinion and put the breath of your superiors on your neck once the media smells this story."

His jaw contracts and his gaze becomes sharp. He hates me, but at the same time, he's weighing my threats. He knows it would take very little to make his life hell.

"Stand up and come with me."

The guard seems to want to protest, but the firm gaze of his boss is enough to make him desist. A dry nod makes him back away from the room. I grab the little boy by the arm and support him to get him to the infirmary. He is light as a feather and shaking so much I can feel his scrawny arm trembling between my fingers. The blond hair, the blue eyes, the face with delicate features make him look helpless. He's at that age when you recognize how good-looking he's going to be, but without the facial hair to make him look masculine; he's easy prey in a place like this.

We enter the infirmary with its white walls, two stretchers in one corner of the room, and a doctor's desk on the opposite side, and a shiver chills the sweat on my back. I hate this place. I hate how when you cross this threshold, the humiliation of what they just did to you begins to settle in your heart until you feel like a nobody.

I dreamed endless times of knocking out the nurse, opening the cabinets along the wall, and swallowing as many pills as I could find to put an end to my agony. I never did it because I didn't want to beat the nurse or the doctor on duty—they were harmless. I didn't want to become the violent and problematic person that everyone in here claimed I was.

The room seems empty, but from behind a screen in the corner of the room, the blonde hair of the girl on duty this afternoon appears. When she raises her head from what she is doing and realizes who has entered, she opens her blue eyes wide and stops, petrified.

The air leaves my lungs and doesn't go back, my mouth is suddenly dried out, and the grip on the boy's arm loosens. I have never seen a more beautiful face in my life. The eyes that look so innocent, the thin nose turning slightly upwards, the fleshy lips that seem sulky, and the squared jaw, framed by the bob of blonde waves, is a combination that makes my erection snap to attention in my pants.

Then my gaze slips to her blue blouse buttoned up to her neck, the ironed collar, the long brown skirt, the same color of the boots, and the small wooden cross hanging from her neck with a rope thread. Where the hell did she come from? A convent?

"Good morning, Faith. I have two guys here who had a small accident. Can you take care of it? Normally, I'd send you a guard for the boy, but Michael here can give you a hand with him if you have any problems."

The director's words bring me back to reality like a cold shower. *Does she need to be protected from this little boy, with his face dripping with blood?* I would like to shout at him, but my gaze is still fixed on her angelic face, and my lips seem sealed. Before I can get a grip, the director exits the room and leaves us alone.

"Are you a nun?" I blurt out of the blue while helping the little boy up on one of the stretchers and hearing him giggling. I don't know why I asked, maybe because I feel guilty for having an erection thinking of a nun.

Her cheeks heat up when she looks up at me, her skin so pale that her embarrassment turns her face a delicate pink. I see from her gaze that she is extremely uncomfortable, and I don't know if it's because she recognized me or because the question is entirely inappropriate.

"You don't need to take vows to be devoted to God."

Worse. She has nothing that binds her to chastity but doesn't give it up to anyone. I've never liked girls who chastise themselves for fear that God will punish them. I decide to drop the question and focus on the guy who seems a little more relaxed than before.

"What's your name?" I ask him, and I notice the girl stiffen. Doesn't she ever ask the names of her patients?

"Levi." His voice trembles and it makes me a little angry. He will never survive here if he does not stand up for himself.

"Well, Levi. How about putting some stitches on that eyebrow? You're bleeding like a pig. Girls like guys with scars, but not all the blood that comes out of them." I smile, and he giggles too. The cut looks deep. He must have slammed it on the cot. Those pieces of iron are deadly when you crash into them. I still have scars on my shins.

Faith approaches him with a wet cloth and begins to cleanse his face, using gauze with disinfectant to clean the wound. I

see him tightening his jaw, but he says nothing. He's learned not to complain, to make as little noise as possible, to disappear between these walls so as not to be noticed, not to be targeted. The tightness that grips my chest almost stops me from breathing. I know what it's like to want to disappear and never feeling transparent enough at the sight of others.

The girl walks to the lockers and returns with a suture kit and a vial with a syringe. Levi shudders and tries to jump off the stretcher when she picks up the sterile needle, but I hold him by the shoulders. He is terrified. Faith stops with wide eyes and for some reason, shivers. The silence lasts for several seconds until she breaks it.

"It's just an anesthetic to put the stitches on you. The cut is deep. It will hurt you if I don't numb the section of skin." Her voice comes out almost in a whisper, and I can't help but stare at those fleshy lips that I would like to see wrapped around my erection while those sweet eyes look at me as she crouches on her knees between my legs. The image is so vivid that I can almost feel the warmth of her tongue on the skin stretched inside my boxers. It's hard to shift my gaze to Levi, who is wiggling out of my grasp.

"No, I don't want to. No anesthetic, nothing. I want to be awake, no matter if it hurts." His words form a lump in my throat. I feel anger and sorrow for him.

Faith furrows her brows, perplexed. "It's a local anesthetic, and it won't make you fall asleep," she says in a hesitant voice.

"No. I said no anesthetic."

"Why? It will hurt if I suture your face without anesthesia." Her voice becomes more firm, and her back straightens as if she is annoyed because she can't do her job.

I answer for him. "Because when you close your eyes in a place like this, even for just a second, you find yourself with one hand pressed to your mouth, others that drop your pants, and the weight of someone above you who makes you his whore. He said no anesthesia. Do what he says." The words come out so low and commanding that I see her move away as if afraid of my reaction. Out of the corner of my eye, I notice Levi staring at me with the awareness in his eyes that I would not like to see in a little boy of his age, but I feel him relax.

Faith widens her eyes and a grimace of disgust, which she cannot hide entirely, arches her lips. Even if she says nothing, there is a reproach, contempt, and perhaps even a little fear in her gaze. I don't know why she's terrified of the people locked in here, but if she didn't want to have contact with the prisoners, she should have to choose another place to bring her faith in God and her good morals.

I stare at her for a few seconds to see if she believes a single word of what I said. But she doesn't speak. She puts down the syringe, takes the needle and the suture thread, and begins to sew up Levi's eyebrow. The boy's eyes become watery, and his hand grabs mine, squeezing it until it hurts. It must be agony for him, but he does not breathe, does not say anything, does not complain. He remains silent, praying that the pain will end soon. God, how many times have I prayed like him that the pain would disappear.

Faith is fast, precise, efficient and Levi's torture goes faster than I expected. When she finishes disinfecting him and putting the Band-Aid on him, the guard comes in, and terror reappears on the boy's face. I can't do anything for him anymore except watch as he is taken by the arm and dragged out with-

out a word. When the door closes behind us, the air seems to get almost dense.

"If Levi comes back in here, you need to tell me." It's the only thing I can think of to say and I watch as she stops cleaning up the blood-stained gauze.

"What?" For the first time, she looks me in the eye with fear or disgust, I can't tell which, and my world stops at the innocence that shines through it.

"If Levi returns to the infirmary with other wounds, call me. I'll leave you my personal number. If anything happens to the kid, *call me.*" I don't know what I'll do if they beat him up again, but I feel the need to keep in touch with him when I get out of here.

"How do I do that? I can't…I don't know," she stutters as if I had just asked her to take part in a robbery.

I get up, go to the desk with her following me, worried, grab a notepad, and write my cellphone number. I usually wouldn't give my personal number to complete strangers, but she doesn't seem like a die-hard fan who would put my number online for everyone's use. She doesn't even give me the impression that she knows who I am.

"This is my number. Promise me that you will call me if something happens to him." I look her in the eye until she grabs the paper and slips it into her pocket, nodding.

"Do you want patches for those wounds? They don't seem to need to be sutured, but they certainly need to be disinfected." Her calm voice makes me look at my fingers. I had completely forgotten about them.

It's my turn to nod and sit on the stretcher while she changes the latex gloves and takes the disinfectant and gauze. I watch

her sit in front of me, take a hand into hers, remove the blood now clotted, and disinfect the wounds. Her hair drops slightly down her jaw, setting apart those lips that seem even more pronounced. In my head, she is naked, kneeling in front of me with her long fingers enveloping my erection and her lips tasting it. My hand behind her neck presses her closer and closer toward my pelvis, her blue and innocent eyes looking at me from below, shiny with the effort as I push against her throat to finish even deeper. I'm about to come in my pants and she has no idea what's going on behind my boxers.

Holy Christ, I must be desperate for sex if I'm about to ejaculate while a nun disinfects my fingers. I close my eyes and try to get back to a semblance of normalcy before my bandmates notice and tease me mercilessly. It's not easy because the scent of her fills my nostrils until my head spins. Unlike most women I go out with, she simply smells of soap, clean, and it's driving me crazy with fantasies of how innocent and pure she is. Her hands envelop mine. I can feel the heat radiating through her latex gloves and imagine how it would feel on other parts of my body. Not even a freezing shower could tame the erection her closeness is causing me, and only a miracle is gonna save me from the jokes of my friends.

PRESS *Review*

The Jailbirds Are Back Behind Bars!

Hi, Roadies!

As you can see from the photos in this post, the Jailbirds are back in jail. Don't worry, they didn't commit any crime. The band held a concert at the very facility where they were held as inmates when they were younger.

As you know from the interview I posted on the blog, the band was formed right inside the walls of juvie, and Damian, Thomas, Michael, and Simon wanted to return to meet the guys who are in there now. They wanted to bring a message of hope to those who have gone astray, showing them that it's possible to change and have a better life.

But above all, they wanted to bring a message to you. Due to the continuous cuts in funds to these facilities, it is increasingly difficult to find resources to finance programs for the recovery of children at risk, such as the one they have benefited from. Without these programs, the boys once out are left on their own, increasing the risk that they will return to the streets and have a bleak future waiting for them. For this reason, the Jail Foundation was created, a non-profit foundation that rais-

es funds to carry out programs for the teenagers in these kinds of detention centers.

I asked the band about this recent concert.

How important was it for you to get back in there?

Damian: For me, it was like being reborn. Seeing the expression of hope in the boys' eyes goes beyond any words.

Thomas: Intense. It was helpful to come back and remember what it really means to be afraid for your future. For me, it was an incentive to keep doing something for these guys. Forgetting our past has never been the solution to a very real problem that exists in the world and cannot be ignored.

Michael: I confess it wasn't easy to get back in there. I don't have good memories of that place and being there made it physically hard to breathe. But seeing those guys with smiles planted on their faces was priceless. They're the reason I'd go back a thousand more times.

Simon: It was liberating. Finally, being able to talk openly about our past was a way to tell those guys to not be like us and hide. They can't change what they've done, but they can certainly change their future, and showing them such a blatant example of change is the best way to open their eyes to hope they otherwise wouldn't have.

If you feel generous and want to embrace this cause, I leave you the link below to donate.

Be Kind and Rock'n'Roll,

Iris.

73872 Likes 69522 Tweets 46582 Shares 8784 Comments

CHAPTER 4
Faith

I spent the whole night with my eyes wide open, staring at the ceiling. The encounter with Michael upset me so profoundly it prevented me from falling asleep. The intensity of his gaze made my legs tremble. Those gray eyes that dig deep into me, laying my soul bare, affected me a thousand times more than seeing them in the video. He's so handsome it took my breath away, with that blondish-brown hair, a hint of a beard, and large, strong *manly* hands. I never understood being attracted to a man until meeting Michael in person.

But what struck me about him were his words. Assuming that those boys are victims, not executioners, the subtle anger that boils inside his chest that he tries to control. I felt like I was watching a volcano ready to explode, and it scared me.

Penelope's words come back to my mind, confusing my head and my chest: Is Michael good or bad? According to my father, the people who have been locked up in prison are bad, they will go to hell, end of story. According to Penelope, Michael is good. He is a guy who made a mistake and repented. According to my heart? I don't know. The contrast between the teachings and what I saw with my own eyes clashes too much to lead me to a conclusion.

The way he defended that boy, how he held his hand to give

him courage, the intensity with which he looked at him as if he were a bear ready to attack to defend his cub. And Levi isn't even his son—he's a criminal like Michael who ended up just like him.

I'm used to dividing people into groups of either good and evil. For me, the world is black or white. In this case, however, the shades of gray are so blended I'm losing my mind. Add in the turmoil of my stomach at the intoxicating sensation of touching his skin and I can hardly think straight.

I look up at the empty infirmary before me and realize that I'm almost at the end of the shift, and I have not finished updating the medical records of this week's patients. I retraced every single inch of Michael's face in my thoughts: his lips, his eyes, his eyebrows that rose almost to challenge me when I told him I'm not a nun. I've been asked this often since I left my community, but I've never been ashamed of it. I'm proud of my clothing, and embarrassed at the way other women walk around half-naked. But Michael made me feel inadequate, like I had to justify my decision to fully live God's teachings.

A firm knock on the door startles me. I'm so lost in my thoughts I didn't even realize I was staring into the void.

"Come in." My voice comes out hoarse—I haven't spoken with a living soul since this morning.

The guard drags a boy inside, tugging him by the arm and making him sit on the bed forcefully.

"He closed his fingers in a door. The director wants to know if they're broken and if he needs a cast."

The details of these accidents come to us directly from the guards who accompany the boys. We don't talk to them much except to ask if they feel pain during the diagnosis. In our reports, we write exactly what we're told without questioning whether or not it's true. After the conversation with Michael yesterday, though, a feeling of discomfort fills my stomach.

The boy is slender, fifteen years old, and it's not the first time I've treated him. I've patched him up other times for accidents that were always very clumsy.

"You should be more careful." I look into his eyes as he looks down with a mixture of anger and shame but says nothing, just nodding. I don't even know what his name is. The guard sneers at my statement, and I wouldn't have noticed it if I hadn't had that conversation with Michael.

I come here to treat patients and then go back to the boarding school without asking questions because I have never doubted that what I am told is true. Black and white. But what if this time it was gray? What if there was another story behind these purple and swollen fingers?

"Excuse me, can I ask you for a favor?" I ask the guard with a smile and my heart pounding in my chest.

The man looks at me with tiny black eyes that scare me. The smile on his face is not jovial, it's that of a predator and makes me uncomfortable.

"Tell me everything, *honey*." The way he emphasizes the word makes the hair on the back of my neck rise.

"I didn't sleep much tonight, and I really need a coffee. I can't leave you here with all the medicine cabinets open, or the director will have a fit. Could you please go and get me a cup?"

The man's smile dies on his lips. He knows he can't leave me alone with one of the guys.

"Please, I really need caffeine to keep my eyes open." I

struggle telling the lie—this is *not* who I am, I don't even say the little white ones. My father always tells me that white lies are the ones the devil prefers to drag us to hell. There are no good lies, only lies that stain our soul.

I feel my stomach twist in the grip of embarrassment and fear.

The man stares at me for an interminable time, then nods. "If you try to do something stupid, you know what the punishment is, got it?" He threatens the boy in a tone that makes me shudder.

The boy nods and lowers his head. When he finally leaves the room, I breathe a sigh of relief.

"What's your name?"

His gaze shoots to mine with furrowed brows. I never ask his name. It's not my job to take these patients to heart, and he seems surprised by my question.

"Liam."

"Liam." His name sounds strange on my tongue. "You have to be careful when you close the doors. These fingers don't look broken, but they will hurt for quite a while. I'll have to make you a stiff bandage to keep them in place."

He looks at me and frowns. "Do you really think that at fifteen I'm so stupid I don't know that slamming my fingers in the door hurts?" He seems almost offended by my observation.

"You mean you didn't get hurt like that?"

"Of course, I got hurt like that. What that asshole didn't tell you is that he held my hand on the door jamb while he closed it so hard he almost busted my fingers off."

"The guard did this to you?"

I can't disguise the outrage on my face. I know the boys

often beat each other up. They're criminals, after all. Of course they don't have the slightest respect for others, but guards can't do this kind of thing. They're in here to maintain order, not beat up the boys.

Liam looks at me with a sad smile as he shakes his head. He doesn't tell me anything because the guard comes back with my steaming coffee in his hand and puts it next to the boy.

"Did he give you any problems?" he asks me, casting an accusatory glance at the boy who is getting smaller and smaller under his stern gaze.

I don't know why, but I'm sure if I tell the guard about the conversation I had with Liam I'll get the boy in trouble, and the thought clinches my stomach. Maybe what he said was a lie to make me feel sorry for him, but something in the resignation on his face makes me waver.

"No, he was an angel. No problem." I force a smile as I apply some ice to ease the pain before bandaging him.

Since Michael walked through that door, my whole life has been in turmoil. I've never told a single lie, and since he came into my life, with his magical smile and angry eyes, I've lied twice in a matter of minutes.

When the two finally leave the room, I collapse in the armchair and inhale deeply. No punishment I inflict on myself can ever redeem me from lies. A weight rests on my chest, along with a piercing doubt making its way into my brain: how come these kids come to the infirmary with injuries that couldn't happen if they're locked up in a nine-by-six-foot cell?

I reach for my small bag of personal belongings in the desk drawer, place it on the desk in front of me and stare at it for a while. I haven't used this punishment for a long time because

I've never done anything this serious recently. These last two lies are a clear sign that the devil is tempting my soul.

I fish for the razor blade that I keep in a small hidden pocket. Then I raise my skirt and sink the cold metal into the skin of my thigh. At first, I don't feel anything, then the burning makes its way along my leg with the tiny drop of blood. I repeat the gesture and then dab the area with gauze to stop the blood. Two small wounds to remind me that lying hurts God.

***

My shift is over but I know Penelope stays late, so I knock lightly on the door, asking permission to enter her office. When she sees me she smiles and gives me a knowing look—like she knew it would be me to cross her threshold.

"How did you know it was me?" I'm always curious about how much this woman manages to anticipate my every move.

She leans against the back of her armchair and smiles. "You're the only one who has such a light touch on the door."

I sit in the armchair in front of her desk and nod, fascinated by her grasp of the smallest details. That's why I'm upset by what she tells me about Michael and his band: maybe she's seen things others have overlooked.

"Why the worried face?" she asks when I don't speak. I came here to ask her for advice, yet the truth is that I don't know what I want to know.

I raise my shoulders and inhale deeply. I try to collect my thoughts, but it's complicated to find the thread of the speech.

"Is it Michael? I know that yesterday he came to the infirmary with Levi, and you had to treat them both." Her gaze is as sweet as that of a mother trying to help a daughter.

"Yes, let's say it's about Michael, but I don't know where

to start."

"Start by telling me what troubles you about him."

I blush violently and look down. The idea of being so transparent makes me burn with shame at the turmoil that man causes in my stomach every time I think about him.

"Everything. The way he looks at me and makes me feel inadequate. The way he makes me quiver when he flaunts his beauty in my face. The way he bared his claws and his teeth to defend a young boy he just met... The things he says, the anger that boils inside him."

"What did he tell you? Anything in particular?"

"Not exactly, but the way he assumes that bad things happen to kids in here…I don't know. Do you know that today Liam came to the infirmary and said that the guard almost broke three of his fingers? How is this possible? The job of the guards is to keep people safe, not to hurt the boys. As criminal as they are, corporal punishment is prohibited inside a prison. Was Liam lying?" My words come out confused, my thoughts are a tangle I can't untangle.

Penelope studies me for a while with an unreadable look, then inhales deeply and raises her face to the ceiling, crossing her fingers on her stomach. She has a relaxed demeanor, very different from the one she holds with her patients.

"You came here with the ideas that have been instilled in you since you were a child. You have a specific, well-defined vision of the world, but it's limited by the community in which you lived. A religious community with precise rules that you've followed to the letter your whole life. But they are rules that apply within that piece of the world, not necessarily to the rest of it. The boys they put in here often come from

problematic families, but this doesn't mean they're criminals. They're kids who have made mistakes they're paying for, but they're not necessarily dangerous or planning to engage in criminal activity as a way of life."

"I understand what you're saying. You've already told me this several times. But, if they really aren't criminals, why do the guards have to use such a heavy hand to maintain order? They're the good guys; that's what confuses me. Michael treats this place as if the guards were the bad guys and the boys the good guys. He turns my world upside down, and it throws me into turmoil."

"Faith, there are no completely good people and completely evil people. There are people who, when put in certain situations, act differently and unpredictably."

"So the guards are bad?"

"The guards take orders from above and act accordingly. The directives here are to keep the fear high among the boys to prevent brawls. Often, however, those who impose order use the heavy hand, too heavy for boys who have no fault."

"But it's wrong."

"Life is not fair. The good guys don't always win, and the bad guys, at times, are among those who should defend the law and do justice."

"Why do you work in here, if that's really the situation? It goes against your moral principles."

"Because sometimes you have to live in the enemy's house if you want to help those who really need you. I love these kids, and I couldn't help them otherwise. When they go out, it's too late to save them. Life in here makes them cynical and desperate, and when they cross the threshold to return to society, they're so jaded they can't see anything good in their future. I can give them the hope it takes to keep some of their dreams alive, but to do so, I have to be in here, in the belly of the beast, and fight every day."

Her words settle in my chest, clarifying some of my feelings, and, to my surprise, they're not what I expected. When Michael came in with Levi, my instinct told me to trust him. When Liam told me his story, my belly told me to believe him, as it told me not to trust the guard. His way of speaking, of looking at me, of threatening the boy—there was something deeply wrong I couldn't quite understand, and that my eyes didn't want to see. Penelope's words silenced my doubts and confirmed that my instincts were right.

"Back to Michael. You like him, don't you?" she asks me with a smile, lightening the atmosphere around us again.

I open my eyes wide and observe her smile. She's not judging me, but admitting out loud what I think about Michael embarrasses me. I nod and look down in shame.

"What do you like about him?"

"Physically?" My cheeks are on fire even just thinking about it.

"Yes, even physically. I don't think you got to talk to him for so long that you discovered much about him from a personality point of view."

"His eyes. They make my stomach tighten when he looks at me. And then his hands. They're strong, and they have those veins poking out that make you think he could knock out a bear with his bare hands if he had to. And his smile. His lips are…are…I stared at them for a long time, and it was rude of me. You don't stare at people!"

Penelope smiles at me and nods.

"And then how he held Levi's hand while I put the stitches on him without anesthesia. I liked that. He seemed to be a person who takes care of those he loves, and it seemed strange because he doesn't even know that boy."

"It struck you, then."

"Let's just say he's not a person who goes unnoticed."

Penelope laughs. "Say what you will about Michael, he's definitely not a wallflower."

***

When I leave Penelope's office, I decide to do something I would never have dared before: go to the guards' breakroom and look for the one who brought Liam to the infirmary. I feel compelled to warn him of the damage he could cause that boy. Maybe I'm not the right person to give advice to the kids here, but I'm a nurse and I know how to treat wounds. It's what I studied and I know how to do my job. That boy was lucky today; those fingers could have shattered and caused permanent damage.

I immediately identify the person I want to talk to sitting in a corner, a coffee in his hand while chatting with a colleague. Luckily there are only two of them.

"So, are you still sleepy even after your coffee?" he asks with a smile when he sees me.

For a moment I draw a blank, then I remember my excuse to get him out of the room. I didn't even sip that coffee. "I'm wide awake." It's not a lie. "Can I talk to you for a moment?" My voice trembles. I'm no longer sure this is a good idea.

"Of course," he says without getting up.

I look at the other guard who is studying me with curiosity. This must be the longest conversation I've ever had with someone working here. "In private."

"Don't worry, Matt and I tell each other everything. It's not a problem."

His answer makes me uneasy, but I'm here and I decided to have this conversation. I'd look stupid if I turned around and left. "It's Liam, the kid you brought this afternoon... His wounds were…quite serious. I know you didn't want to hurt him, but you might have risked severely damaging him."

The guard looks at me, stunned, while his friend looks equally surprised. "Oh, listen to her. You think you have the right to come here and tell me how to do my job? Those guys are criminals, they need someone to straighten them out or they'll end up in jail as soon as they get out of here. What right do you have telling *me* how to behave?" he snaps indignantly while his friend sneers.

Suddenly, I'm not just uncomfortable with this confrontation, I'm afraid for my safety. His attitude is aggressive. I'd always thought guards were here to protect us from criminals, but I'm no longer sure this is true.

"I didn't mean to imply that you don't know how to do your job, just that the injuries Liam suffered could have been much more serious," I try to explain, but the anger in his eyes, as his friend laughs, is scaring me.

"And how should I behave?" he says, raising his voice to a yell. "Go ahead, teach me."

"Faith, please come with me."

The voice of the director behind me gets my attention. I turn around to find his stern eyes greeting me, and though he's always made me nervous, I'm relieved this time to follow him

out of the room.

His office is not far but the walk seems eternal. When we enter, he does not ask me to sit like he normally does. He leans on the desk and studies me for a long moment. "I heard the conversation you had with Charles. I feel compelled to tell you that an aggressive attitude towards colleagues is not appreciated here."

"He raised his voice, but he didn't threaten me," I point out.

"I'm not talking about what *he* said. He felt attacked by your accusations and simply reacted accordingly."

I don't understand what he's saying. Is this *my* fault? "I didn't mean to accuse him of anything; I just expressed my doubts about a situation that could have been much worse." My words come out weaker and weaker as his expression darkens.

"The hard line we take in this facility is for the good of the young people who are sent to us. If we do not intervene with a steady hand, they hurt each other, and you would be dealing with something more serious than a simple wound. That is why we need staff to stay united and comply with the rules. Even the health personnel."

My mouth is sealed shut. I can't say anything in response to this reproach.

"If you are not able to comply with these rules while maintaining certain confidentiality, perhaps this is not the place for you. If you do not believe in this approach, I am willing to accept your resignation and leave you free to find another facility that better suits your needs."

Is he firing me? The idea of leaving this place and going home to my family terrifies me as much as the guard who ranted in my face, but I can stay away from Charles. If I go home, I won't be able to stay away from the man who's waiting to marry me.

"No, sir. I understand. It will not happen again."

He motions with his head for me to go, and as I turn to the door, anger and fear boil inside of me at the thought of losing the freedom I never thought I needed.

CHAPTER 5

Michael

"Shhhhh! Please, if we wake up Simon, he'll kill me. I can't bring girls into my room."

Holy Christ, I feel like a teenager who lives with his parents, sneaking girls in through the window to avoid being scolded. The blonde lowers the volume of her moans but not too much.

"If you want, we'll invite him too. The three of us could have fun for sure," she suggests as she moves sinuously over me.

I can't hold back my laughter. "Simon? He's all home and family. A three-way is as far from his reality as another planet."

"Really? You're rock stars! Shouldn't it be all booze, sex, and drugs?" She throws her head back and opens her mouth slightly, lost in the waves of pleasure.

The vision of her long and inviting neck, her voluptuous breasts bouncing with each lunge, make me lose my mind. I feel the orgasm mounting—until the phone rings and makes me lose my concentration and rhythm. I ignore it and continue to devote my attention to the goddess of sex who is all over me and does not seem to be troubled by the ringtone. The second call starts without waiting for the first one to end, and my impending orgasm has become a distant memory. I look at the screen and realize that it is not a number I have on my phone.

Who the hell calls me in the middle of the night from a number I don't know? I'm beyond annoyed, and when it rings for the third time, I snort with exasperation.

"Shouldn't you answer? They're so insistent, maybe it's important." Clearly, the girl has also lost her momentum.

I grab the phone and bring it to my ear. "What do you want?" I answer, annoyed.

On the other side of the line, the silence makes me wonder if I was a little too abrupt.

"Are you going to talk, or did you interrupt the greatest fuck in history to breathe like a maniac?"

"Michael? It's Faith." A girl's shaky voice gives me pause. I don't usually remember the names of the women I sleep with, but if I gave her my private number it must have been a great fuck.

"Okay, Faith. You'll have to give me a few more clues, honey, because if you count on my memory, we're not going to get anywhere."

"I'm the prison nurse, the one who treated your fingers."

Blowj… mouth. Yes, I remember her perfectly. Fawn eyes, fleshy mouth, dressed like a nun. The chill that spreads in my stomach, however, takes my breath. If she's calling, it's about Levi. If she had any intention of fucking me, she wouldn't have waited three weeks.

I prop up on one elbow, completely forgetting the girl who's still sitting on my pelvis and looking at me curiously. "Is Levi okay?" I ask with a shaky voice, as if saying the words out loud will make my fears real.

"We're at the hospital. It's not life-threatening, but I had to

call the ambulance when they brought him to me."

Words bounce between my heart and brain. I didn't even realize I'd sat up, disregarding the naked girl on top of me. "Send me a text with the name of the hospital and the address. I'll come as soon as possible." I end the conversation without even saying goodbye and throw the phone on the bed.

The girl is now picking up her clothes scattered around the room and giving me my pants. "Michael, is everything okay? Is someone you know in the hospital?"

How do I answer that? I'm concerned about a kid I met three weeks ago for the first time and haven't spoken to since? "He's a guy I know. I asked the nurse to call me if anything happened." She won't understand, I know, but it's the best I can offer her now.

In a rush to grab my shirt near the door, I trip over a chair and it falls noisily to the ground. By now, Simon will be awake since all my efforts to be quiet have gone to hell.

A few seconds later, he knocks on my door. "Michael, is everything okay?"

I open the door wide and find him with messy hair, a crumpled-up shirt, and in his boxers. I must have really pulled him out of bed. When he looks at the now-dressed girl, he throws me a look that could kill.

"I don't have time for preaching about bringing girls into my room. I have to go to the hospital."

My statement brings him to attention, as if I'd thrown a bucket of cold water at him. "Is someone sick? Did Damian pull some bullshit move? Or Thomas? Did Evan have a heart attack? Do you want me to come with you?"

"No, ye…no, you don't need to come with me. It's Levi.

They beat him, I think, and he ended up in the hospital."

"Who the hell is Levi?"

Good question. I never told anyone about what happened in the infirmary because I didn't want them to worry about me. They know how much I suffered in there, and that I didn't ever want to go back. Telling them how I intervened to defend that kid would have set off too many alarm bells.

"I'll explain later. I have to call a taxi…no…I don't know." I grab the phone and see that Faith has texted me the address of a hospital in New Jersey, near the prison. I'll never find a taxi at two in the morning from Manhattan, even if I pay an arm and a leg.

"Do you need me to call Evan? Or Max?" asks Simon, more and more worried, as I approach the door and let out the girl who realizes she's not the only one in the dark about what's happening. Luckily, she doesn't protest when I slam the front door in her face without a goodbye.

"Max has his phone off," I tell him as I stare at my phone and try to figure out how to get to that damn place.

"Evan says he can send a car within ten minutes. I'll come with you. You're not going alone looking like that." And he runs up the stairs to get dressed.

Apparently, I can't stop him and maybe it's a good thing, because I've never been so anxious in my life.

***

The journey by car is endless. Simon and I don't talk much, and the driver Evan sent is one of the companies we occasionally use when Max and Dave are not on duty.

Simon, seated next to me, throws worried glances my way as his phone periodically lights up with texts. I know the oth-

ers are in touch and asking what the hell is going on. Still, I hope our trip to Underwood Memorial Hospital is enough explanation until I can figure out what I'm doing myself.

When we enter through the emergency room door, the reception counter is empty, but the waiting room is quite full of patients who apparently aren't in as serious condition as those already admitted.

"A young boy was brought here straight from the juvenile prison. His name is Levi," I say to the woman who has returned behind the counter. She looks at me as if I were another thorn in her side of this night shift. And I am, because how the hell do I explain being here?

"Are you a relative or the person legally responsible for him?"

I shake my head, knowing we're not getting anywhere.

"He's a cousin," Simon says at my side.

I look at him to thank him but he's making eyes at the woman, clearly to get what he wants—a technique I didn't know Simon had in his bag of tricks, as he's always been the honest one.

"If he's not a close relative or a name that appears on the emergency list, I can't help you."

I'm about to jump at her throat when someone approaches me and, in a small voice, says my name. I turn around and find myself facing the prison nurse. God, I don't remember her being so beautiful.

"Levi is in the operating room; when he arrived at the infirmary, he had broken ribs and one punctured lung that collapsed."

Her words make my legs tremble so unsteadily she has to

walk to a chair and make me sit down before I collapse. "You told me it wasn't life-threatening," I say accusingly, and she blushes with embarrassment but I don't care—she lied to me.

"It sounds much worse than it actually is. They managed to keep him stable in the ambulance, and he was conscious when we arrived here. Unfortunately, I can't go in, but I can ask the nurse if it's possible to get some information. I was on duty, so technically, he was under my responsibility."

I nod, but I don't say anything. Next to me, Simon puts his hand on my shoulder and then gets up to go and answer his phone. I'm guessing Evan wants to know if we've arrived and what the hell is going on.

Hours pass as we remain seated in silence while medical personnel pass back and forth without giving us so much as a look. It's wearing me out. At seven in the morning, I glance out the window behind me to see the sun has been up for a while now, and most of the patients have been taken care of. Almost as though when the night shift goes to sleep, emergencies drop in intensity.

Next to me, Faith keeps still and silent, her fingers intertwined as if she were praying and her head slightly down to avoid anyone's look. How the hell does she stay so calm for hours? I've turned around thousands of times by now in this uncomfortable chair.

Simon has been out making phone calls dozens of times. Evan is undoubtedly a bundle of nerves—not having the situation under control is driving him crazy, I'm sure. This time I'll kill our manager. I can feel it.

I get up and almost end up on the ground; being seated for so long I lost sensitivity in my legs. I pass the desk where the

night shift nurse has been replaced by the day shift and see in the corner of the hallway divided by metal doors a vending machine with snacks. I pull a five-dollar bill out of my wallet and stick it in the slot. There isn't much left, but I select three chocolate bars that will get us by without fainting from hunger. After throwing one at Simon still outside the door, glued to his phone, I return to my seat.

I hand Faith one of the candy bars. It takes a moment before she realizes what I'm giving her, and when she looks up at me, I almost bend down to kiss those inviting and slightly parted lips.

"I'm good, thank you," she replies kindly.

I frown and study her for a few moments and she blushes under my gaze. "Are you allergic?" I hadn't even thought about that possibility.

She shakes her head and lowers her eyes. Why is she always so silent? It's like she's trying to disappear, take up less space and breathe as little air as possible.

"Then eat. Otherwise, you might faint. How long have you been on duty? When did you last eat?"

Hesitantly, she reaches out her hand and grabs the bar. I watch her think about it for a few seconds and then open it as if it will change the course of her life. Before putting the piece of chocolate in her mouth, she pulls up her sleeves enough to reveal a bit of the white skin of her wrist, but no more. Discreet and composed, from the first time we met. I watch as she wraps her lips around the bar, and my erection awakens in my pants. For a moment, she opens her eyes wide, then narrows them, and if she were a little more free she'd probably let out a moan of pleasure. I see her surrender to the sweet taste that caresses her tongue—a gesture as innocent as it is erotic and exciting. She doesn't rush to devour the chocolate but savors it slowly, like it's a mystical experience she doesn't want to end.

I watch her hand return to her knees to join the other, and notice her start to press her nail forcefully into the white skin of her wrist. I want to stop her and say this will hurt when I see the other small wounds, almost imperceptible. I look back at her face, watching as she tastes heaven with her tongue and lips and inflicts hell with the nail against her skin. I slide my gaze to the small wooden cross, discreet and light on her buttoned-up blouse, heavy as a boulder on her heart.

It reminds me of seeing my mother lock my sisters in a motel room and then punish herself by praying for hours, kneeling on dried beans. Doing something wrong consciously and then punishing herself physically for fear of unleashing God's wrath.

A sour taste rises in my mouth, making my disgust palpable. I've always hated my mother and father for how they tried to atone for their sins before God, their hands still stained with the blood of those they had hurt. That attempt to silence their conscience before God without ever feeling repentant for their wrongdoing. I have always found them hypocritical, false, soulless. It is their fault that I stopped believing in God, because if he really existed and punished the bad guys, the two of them would already be in hell.

Faith is not allergic to food; she is not on a diet. She is just the victim of those who taught her to fear the Most High. I would like to grab her by those tiny shoulders and shake her until she realizes she's throwing away her life, but the way she's savoring that chocolate, I believe she has already tasted

a piece of hell and can no longer live without it.

***

"You did *what?*" Evan screeches, his tone choked by surprise, giving voice to the perplexity painted on the faces of everyone in the meeting room. Emily, Lilly, and Iris are wide-eyed and open-mouthed and holding hands as if, without support, they might just slip off the couch and fall to the floor—and then they say I'm the drama queen!

"I asked that Levi have the chance to finish serving the two months of his sentence in my care instead of in prison, and the judge ruled in favor, citing extreme circumstances to justify his decision."

Damian opens his mouth, looking for words, but he's empty of arguments for the first time. I know my decision was rash, but I have good reasons for it.

"Wait, let me recap," says Thomas, incredulous. "A month ago in prison, you saved a kid from a guard who was beating him up. In the infirmary, you ask the nurse to call you if something happens to him. After three weeks of silence, she calls saying they took the boy to the hospital. You rush there but they don't let you see him—because you're not a legal guardian—then you ask a judge to entrust him to you, and two days later he says yes? Who the hell was behind the bench in that courtroom, Spongebob? Is it even legal to entrust you with a child rather than send him back to prison?" He looks at me like I've just asked him to bury a corpse in the garden.

I shake my head and feel myself sinking a little into the armchair. When I left the courtroom a few hours ago, I immediately ran here because I thought they would be happy hearing the news. They know how crappy it is in there, so if I can

help a kid get out, why not? I need them, I can't juggle this mess alone, and they are making a huge deal of it. It's not the reaction I expected from my friends. I'm already terrified of screwing everything up.

I sit up taller in my chair and clear my throat to gain some confidence before responding. "The kids who are sent there are judged as violent and a danger to the communities where they could serve their sentences. But we all know that most of them are *not* violent—it's just easier to put them there than to try to rehabilitate them. The other facilities are packed, so they're simply turned over to juvies, and the problem of where to serve their sentence is solved."

I pause and let that sink in before continuing.

"Do you know when the director arrived at the hospital? At nine-thirty the next morning, taking his time after breakfast. And do you know what he asked? Whether the boy would need help or if he could fend for himself once he got out. He didn't even ask how he was doing or how long he would stay in that hospital bed. He didn't even care if the surgery went well or not."

Thomas shakes his head, and his gaze softens a little. "I'm not questioning that Levi is safer with you; I'm just wondering if it's even legal that in two days they'll give a kid to you."

I inhale deeply and try to sort through the information that has fallen on me in the last forty-eight hours, and that has completely turned my life upside down.

"Apparently, if there is evidence that the child's life is in danger, a judge may decide to have his sentence served in a different facility. With the three hours he spent in surgery and Faith's testimony that he was in the infirmary seven times in

six months with wounds from beatings, the judge ruled that he could serve his remaining two months under house arrest. Since he's been in the system for seven years now and has ended up in God knows how many different foster homes, I asked for custody of Levi. I may have thrown around some famous names, and the judge may be a close friend and golf partner of my lawyer... I mean, do I have to dot the i's and cross the t's?"

They all inhale deeply and look at each other a little disoriented, their expressions revealing the same thousand doubts I've had since making this decision.

It is Simon who gives voice to the doubts. "Okay, Michael, we understand your point of view, and it's definitely a generous gesture. But you can't just keep a kid under your roof. He's not a puppy to take to the park twice a day…you don't even have a house."

"Well, you're right about that. I have to find a house before he leaves the hospital. In about fifteen days."

They all burst out laughing.

"What's so funny?"

"Michael, you lived for eight years in a hotel with room service. Do you have any idea what it's like to live in a house?" Damian teases me.

"You're making it much harder than it is."

Evan intervenes and helps me. "Okay, you're right. If you've made this decision, it means you've thought about it, and we'll give you a hand."

"If Michael has decided to become a dad, we should be happy for him, not make fun of him."

I turn with wide eyes towards Emily's grin. "I'm not going to be a dad!" I hasten to specify.

“Do you really think it’s so different?” adds Simon sipping his coffee to hide his smile.

“Maybe the word is ‘legal representative,’ but that doesn’t change the reality.”

What the hell did I do? Until seventy-two hours ago, I had the life of a single rock star, plenty of women and zero worries. Now I find myself looking for a house, with a kid to look after, and friends who make fun of me by calling me a dad.

CHAPTER 6

Faith

I stare at the cardboard box in front of me, empty apart from my small bag. When the director made me sign the resignation, he told me to take my stuff and leave even before starting my shift, handing me the box. I didn't think I had so few possessions in this office.

I've never had anything entirely mine. In my parents' house, everything is shared with my siblings. Even the clothes we pass along from the oldest to the youngest. We never had many toys, and Christmas or birthday gifts have always been useful items for the family. According to my father, personal gifts are the devil's temptation to test our greed.

Do people really have so many personal items in their office they can fill this box? I could put all the things I have in boarding school in it. So focused on this thought, I don't notice Penelope in the room until she gently grabs my arm and makes me turn toward her.

"Don't cry, honey. We'll find a solution. I'm so sorry, I came as soon as I knew," she whispers in my ear as she hugs me.

I also didn't notice I was crying. "I don't know what to do."

But that's not true. I know what I have to do: pack my few things and call my father to pick me up. It's time to go home. Without a job, I have no reason to stay here.

“First, we go out and get some air. You would have had the night shift, right?”

I nod.

“Then you don’t need to go back to the boarding school. Come and sleep at my place tonight. I’ll take you back tomorrow morning, so no one will notice anything.”

I open my eyes and shake my head. I cannot lie to Mother Superior; it is a sin I cannot commit. Penelope looks at me and understands my discomfort.

“Faith, what did we say about lies? That they’re not lies if they are decisions that only affect *your* life. You can’t feel guilty because you don’t go back in to that place. At the end of the day, you pay the rent for the room. You’re not their student, and you have no obligation to come back when they tell you. You’re an adult, and the rules in there apply to minors under their responsibility. Was there a condition in the room lease about a curfew?”

“No, but my father requested it.”

“What did we say about the decisions your father made that affected your life?”

“That they’re right only if I’m a minor or can’t make decisions on my own.”

“But you are an adult and able to make decisions for your life.”

“Apparently not, since I got fired.”

Penelope inhales deeply and smiles at me, grabbing the box and leaving it on the desk, retrieving my bag and taking me by the arm.

“Let’s get out of here, so we can think about this more calmly.”

***

Penelope's house is a huge two-story building, beige with a gray roof, overlooking the Atlantic Ocean. Between the front porch and the beach there is only a tiny strip of a road that runs along the stretch of this coast. I've never seen anything like it. It's impressive, but not as lavish and tacky as so many of the houses I've noticed around here.

Entering the living room, we are greeted by warm neutral tones and a huge fireplace covered with stones that reach the ceiling at least twenty feet above our heads. It feels luxurious and also warm and cozy. A pair of shoes clutter the entryway and a stack of board games are piled high on a nearby bookshelf. There are a couple of novels on the coffee table and a pillow on the floor with a big black cat curled on top of it.

"Come with me to the kitchen and we'll fix something hot. Have you eaten?"

I shake my head and realize for the first time that my stomach is empty since lunch. Penelope goes to the fridge, pulls out a cake, and boils a pot of water. I will never get used to people who eat sweets for dinner, but I've learned not to contradict the psychologist on this point, because she makes me eat what she wants, whether I agree or not. Also, I discovered that I like sweets; we are not allowed to eat them at home.

"What did the director tell you today? Did he bring you into the office and fire you?"

"No, he made me sign a letter of resignation, effective immediately."

"He saved his ass. What a prick," she whispers under her breath. "And don't make that scandalized face. In this situation, both insults and swear words are justified. Since he

couldn't fire you without a just cause or risk of being dragged to court, he made you resign so no one could touch him. He's a slimy worm."

I look down, speechless. No matter what the particulars are, the fact is that I'm out of a job and will have to go home.

"I'm sorry I convinced you to testify. I didn't think that imbecile would fire you."

I look down and take a breath, trying to hold back the tears. My father would disapprove of crying, only people who have something to hide or a guilty conscience cry.

"I told the truth, and I didn't think being honest under oath would bring these consequences. They made me swear by the Word of God. I couldn't lie, you know?" In part, I feel guilty because if I had omitted some detail, perhaps, I would not be in this situation. But it is unthinkable to do so if you have sworn on God.

Penelope pours me a cup of tea and smiles at me lovingly. "You'll learn that often life isn't fair, but you still have to accept what comes to you because some things you can't change. The most you can do is manage the consequences and adapt the course of your future to what life throws at you. It doesn't help to cry, or despair, or break down, the only thing you can do is roll up your sleeves and respond to the best of your ability."

I nod and sink the fork into the soft dough of the dark red cake with the white glaze.

"What do you want to do with your future, Faith?" she insists.

"I'll have to go home. My father won't let me stay here without a job."

The woman shakes her head and smiles. "I didn't ask you what your father will tell you to do; I asked you what *you* want to do."

"I don't want to go home." It's the only thing I'm sure of. "I don't want to marry Jacob."

"Good. This is a good place to start. If you don't want to marry the guy your parents chose for you, you don't have to. The law is on your side, and they can't force you to marry someone you don't love and haven't chosen to live with."

I nod because I understand what she's trying to tell me. She explained that legally I can decide who to marry, but the reality I grew up with is so far from what she describes I find it hard to imagine my life being different from what I saw at home.

"What if Jacob doesn't find a woman to marry? If no one wants him because I reject him? It will be a scandal, and he'll suffer the consequences of my choice."

"If this happens, Jacob will decide how to react to what life has thrown at *him*. He is not your responsibility, or at least not until you decide that he's the person you want to share your future with. Don't take on the burden of someone else's life."

"But how do I stay here? I'll have to tell my dad I don't have a job anymore when I call him on Sunday."

Penelope is about to answer when the doorbell rings and she goes to answer it, leaving me hanging. Who shows up so late at someone's house? I don't have to wait long to find out because Michael's big frame soon appears in all its magnificence. I'll never get used to the beauty of this man.

He sees me and frowns, then he opens up with a smile. "Did they let you out of the convent?" he asks with a hint of fun in his voice.

I lower my head, trying to cover the redness blooming over my cheeks and the smile on my face.

"There are still women who blush?" He approaches me, perhaps hoping I'll raise my head or respond, but I feel my whole body on fire just from his presence.

"Michael, the modest women who get embarrassed when a man strips them with his eyes have not become extinct. You just never look above their nipples."

I turn to Penelope. I've never heard her talk so scandalously! But she looks at me and laughs, and I get the feeling this is one of those times when it's okay to talk about a person's private parts in front of others. I'll *never* get used to this.

Michael rolls his eyes and then sits on the kitchen stool next to me. The skin of his arm inadvertently touches mine, and a shock makes me move quickly. My heart skips a beat and I struggle to get a grip on my body's excited response to his presence—it makes me feel uncomfortable.

He doesn't seem to notice it in the least. He takes the fork from my plate, sinks it into the cake, and brings it to his lips. What an uncivilized, rude person! I follow his gesture with such disbelief that I realize my mouth and eyes are wide open only when he looks at me and grins. He sinks the fork back into the cake and brings it up to my lips.

"Do you want a bite, or does your religion forbid it?" he asks with a raised eyebrow.

I turn my gaze to Penelope, who is studying us with a smile, shaking her head.

"Michael, not all women want to exchange saliva with you," she teases, handing me another slice of cake.

"Really? It's usually just a matter of time before everyone

wants to exchange some kind of bodily fluid with me."

How arrogant and brazen! I look down on my still intact cake and sink the clean fork into my dinner. I feel Michael's eyes fixed on me, but I don't dare check to see if it's just my perception or reality. I'm afraid to read the expression on his face.

"Anyway, Faith, I wanted to thank you for testifying in court. The lawyer said it was crucial for making the judge give in, making him understand that the abuse was something that lasted over time, not just an occasional brawl between boys as the prison wanted him to believe."

His tone is sincere, and for the first time, I look up at him without feeling embarrassed. "You're welcome." The answer comes out much more confident than I actually feel.

"The testimony cost her a job." Penelope says what I have not been able to say.

Michael suddenly looks at her and then back again at me. "Really? I'm sorry."

"He asked me to resign," I admit with a half-nod of my head.

"What a son of a bitch. He's always been a filthy slimy manipulator, but I didn't think he'd go this far."

The vulgarity of his words makes me inhale loudly. "Please don't talk like that. It's vulgar and doesn't fit in Penelope's kitchen." I feel like I'm overreacting. I've never scolded a stranger, but his vulgarity makes my skin crawl.

"Is she serious?" he asks Penelope as if I weren't right here.

"Faith comes from a rigorous education and you are disrespecting her, Michael."

He turns around and studies me for a few interminable seconds. “Sorry if I used terms too…strong for you, but it doesn’t change the fact that he behaved like a...” He scratches a hand over his face then turns to Penelope with a desperate look. “Help me out here. I don’t know how to talk without swearing. I’ve never done it!”

Penelope laughs, and I smile, too, although I try not to show it. The despair on his face seems sincere. “Asshole, you can use the term asshole, Michael. Faith, there really are no other, less vulgar terms to describe what that man did, believe me.”

I smile at her and nod. If my path ever crosses Michael’s again, I’ll just have to expect to hear inappropriate language. He seems like someone who doesn’t mince words.

“Michael, let’s get to why you needed to see me so urgently?” Penelope asks with that loving tone she uses with people she genuinely cares for.

“I have custody of Levi from the time he leaves the hospital until he finishes serving his sentence.” He looks at her with a frown as if that explains everything he feels about this situation.

“Yes. And that worries you?”

“I have no idea how to look after a kid. Plus, he can’t leave the house until his sentence is over and I have to go to the studio or travel for concerts, and I can’t leave him at home alone. I have no idea how to raise a teenager. I haven’t had decent sex since I went to live with Simon…and I don’t even have a house for the kid stay in.”

Penelope smiles as I blush at his blatant admission. “You didn’t think too far into the future when you decided to make this heroic gesture, did you?”

“I didn’t really think of anything except that Levi couldn’t

go back to that place. I live moment to moment. Since getting famous, my life has always been planned by someone else. But I can't ask Evan to take care of this. That man already has his work cut out for him, now that we've dropped the record company and set up our own. I tried calling babysitting agencies, but when I mention Levi's age and the particulars of our situation, they all pull back, saying they're not specialized in dealing with problematic kids."

Penelope leans her elbows on the kitchen counter and stares at us for a few seconds.

"Yes, usually agencies don't want to take responsibility if something goes wrong and kids with Levi's needs aren't on their ideal client list. But don't say you don't know how to raise a teenager, Michael. You've bothered to call those agencies; you've realized that Levi can't stay alone despite being fourteen years old and being able to look after himself during the hours you're out. Michael, that's what every parent does, whether the child was born into the family or adopted: learn as problems arise."

"I'm not a parent! I didn't decide to be a dad, and I'll never stop reminding you all of that, okay?"

Penelope laughs, and I look at him curiously. Maybe he doesn't see it that way, but taking care of a boy in this way comes very close to being a father.

"Your three troublemaker friends have already called you 'daddy', haven't they?"

Michael grunts and looks at her sideways. "It's not funny."

I smile at his sudden shyness. It's the first time I've seen him really struggling with something. He's usually so self-confident, brash, and even arrogant. His facial features have softened a bit and it seems impossible that he could look more handsome than he does at the moment.

"Oh, for us it is, trust me," Penelope teases.

"Okay, laugh, but I don't know how to solve my problem."

"Faith." Penelope says my name but is looking Michael in the eye.

"You have to give me a few more clues. I'm not the sharpest knife in the drawer." He furrows his brows.

"Faith is your solution. She's been dealing with kids all her life because she has so many siblings. And she just lost her job and doesn't want to go home to her parents—she needs to find a solution as soon as possible. You need a full-time helper since you're often out all hours of the day or night, between concerts and recording studios. Basically, it seems like a win-win for both of you, right? She needs a place to stay, and you can set aside a room in your new house for a full-time nanny."

"Would I have to live with him? With a man who's not my husband?" I ask with my cheeks hot with shame.

"Just hearing her questions should tip you off that this solution is full of holes. You see that, don't you? She blushes and gets offended if I say 'son of a bitch.' By the end of the week, I'll have to take her to a mental hospital."

As rude as his comment is, Michael is right. He and I are opposites. We could never live together in the same house, not to mention that I just should *not* share my space with a man who is not my family. From his comments I can tell he's promiscuous with many women, and I couldn't live with that.

"My father will never allow me to do such a thing. Me? Move to Manhattan? The city of sin?"

I notice Michael widening his eyes and holding back a

laugh, but Penelope seems determined.

"Faith, you have to start living and making decisions on your own, not continue to base your life on what your father allows you to do or not. Do you want to go home and marry Jacob? Because right now, it's your only option. If you love him and want to marry him, alright, I won't stop you. But if you feel nothing for him, do *not* let yourself be influenced by your father's will."

Her words only tighten the vise-like grip in my chest. Of course I don't love Jacob; I don't even like him and feel repulsed by his smell when I'm near him. The mere idea of returning to my community, marrying him, and giving him children, makes me want to scream and run away. Maybe one day I'll change my mind, I'll see in him a loving father and a devoted husband, but right now, the thought of being with him for the rest of my life repels me.

Two months. It's only two months until Levi finishes serving his sentence and Michael finds another solution, provided that the child stays with him after the end of the sentence.

I turn to Michael. "Okay. I have to go and get my things at the boarding school, but it shouldn't take long."

He seems shocked by my decision. "Wait. Stop there, Bambi. I don't have a house yet. I'll pick you up when I have something more certain in hand, or at least after asking Simon if he can accommodate you. I have already swooped into his house without warning. I cannot take you there without his permission."

"Do I have to live with *two* men?" I ask Penelope, who is smiling.

Michael snorts and opens his arms, pointing at me but looking into my friend's eyes as if to say, *See what I'm talking about?* "You know this thing is going to end badly, don't you?"

"Or, eventually she'll open up a little and start to discover the world, and you'll learn to live with a woman who doesn't open her legs just because you wink at her," Penelope reproaches him.

My heart begins to hammer inside my chest. Since leaving the community and looking at the world from a different perspective, I began to want to discover new things, satisfying the desire for adventure I've had since I was a child. But I'm afraid that my life will become more than an adventure by going to live with Michael, even for just a couple of months. It scares me and makes me feel alive at the same time. It's as if I've lived a black-and-white life up to now, and Michael is that lens that makes me see the world in color. Vivid, brilliant scenes that are imprinted on your eyes, brain, and heart. I'm afraid of being dazzled so much by them that I can't live without them.

CHAPTER 7

Michael

"Simon, have you seen my iPad?" I shout from the kitchen, hoping he'll hear me in the room upstairs. It's only been three days since the court ruling, and I already have a headache at the thought of wandering another day around Manhattan to visit apartments for sale.

"Did you look in your room? Last night you went to sleep with it while you were looking at the new houses the real estate agent sent you," suggests Faith. She's sitting at the kitchen table having breakfast, eating fruit with a knife and fork and a slice of toast in front of her. Strictly black coffee because sugar or milk, God forbid, might attract the devil. In my opinion, the devil's already taken her because no one eats fruit with cutlery. She's cutting the grapes in half, for Pete's sake!

"Yes, miss Goody Two-shoes, I looked. Otherwise, I wouldn't have asked my friend, right?"

I like teasing her. She's always so composed and perfect I just want to shake her and make her scream. But I don't think she ever will.

The other day, I found her folding her breakfast place-mat perfectly in half, flattening the wrinkles with her hands. I couldn't resist and took it from her hands and balled it up, looking straight into her eyes and making her blush. She didn't get angry—she remained silent and took the placemat back, flattening it again and folding it like she was doing before. She didn't say a word, just kept on doing her task as if she had no right to speak. It made my blood boil so much that I grabbed that damn placemat, rolled it up, and threw it in the garbage, then crossed my arms across my chest waiting for her to get angry, to react, to do any damn thing. I would've even accepted crying at that point, but nothing. She was probably taught to hold back tears because crying does not suit a submissive woman. My mother always did it in her room secretly, when she thought no one could see her.

I hate her old-fashioned submissive attitude. Penelope told me she had lived in a community of religious extremists who never let her discover the world, so why she suggested Faith join me I have no clue. Penelope knows I hate everything related to religions and all of their unholy wars for what they deem a just cause. I grew up in an environment where corporal punishment in the name of God was the daily routine and I won't tolerate any of that bullshit anymore. That includes this wanna-be nun who comes from years of psychological abuse and accepts it with a smile in the name of God and the salvation of her soul. I'd rather corrupt her, open her eyes and let her taste those sins she thinks will send her to hell, but will actually allow her to experience heaven right here on earth.

I hear Simon grumble as he walks down the stairs. Entering the kitchen, he hands me my iPad with a glance that could kill me. "It was in your room, on the nightstand," he grumbles, annoyed.

I glance at Faith, who hides her smile behind a cup of coffee.

"It must have been hidden," I murmur, equally annoyed.

"No, it was in plain sight!" he replies, grabbing a cup from the counter and filling it with coffee.

I scroll through the emails to see any news and notice the umpteenth one from my lawyer. These days I'm making him earn his fees.

"By the way, Faith, I have an employment contract for you to sign. If you give me your email, I'll send it so you can check that it's okay and send it back to me signed." I look up when I don't hear any answer and find her staring at me with wide eyes.

"Michael, send it to me. I'll print it today in the office." Simon presses me with a look of reproach. What the hell did I do wrong this time? "Faith, I'll bring it to you tonight, and if you want, we'll take a look at it together if there's something you don't understand. Usually, lawyers have an obsession for writing big words for even the simplest things." He smiles at her, and I don't understand anything anymore.

"Thank you," she whispers as Simon casts another frown my way.

"Can you explain why you're angry with me? What did I do wrong?"

Simon spreads his arms as if surrendering to my stupidity.

"I have no idea what an email is," Faith murmurs, looking down and blushing with shame.

I feel like a perfect idiot. "Oh," is the only thing I can say as Simon shakes his head disconsolately.

"Have you decided on a house yet?" Simon's question is an obvious attempt to change the subject and a not-so-veiled invitation to find another place to live.

After more than a month of living together, we're not getting along at all. The fact that I asked him to host Faith, too, while searching for more stable accommodations, doesn't help. Fortunately, Simon seems to appreciate that she's quiet and causes as little disturbance as possible. She leaves almost no trace of her existence anywhere—I caught her flattening the folds of a pillow after getting up from the couch.

"Today I'm looking at an apartment overlooking the MET. It's not a very big complex, but it has all the privacy I need with a concierge and security service twenty-four hours, seven days a week."

"Are you going to see it too?" he asks Faith, who is already dressed for the appointment in her long skirt, shirt, and sweater so high-necked they're almost choking her. It's June. Why the hell is she wearing a sweater?

"Yes. Michael thinks it's a good idea to have a second opinion."

"Especially since he's only ever lived in hotels," he quips.

Faith's eyes widen in surprise. She's judging me, I'm sure, but doesn't dare to say it out loud.

"You can say I live like a spoiled rock star; you wouldn't be the first or the last," I tease her.

She blushes and looks down for a moment, then raises her eyes again to mine. "I don't think you're spoiled, just that it must have been very sad to live in a hotel. I've only stayed in one for a couple of days, when I first came to the city to look for a place to stay. It was very…impersonal, not very welcoming, a cold environment."

She caught me by surprise. I've never seen the hotel this way. I've always found it practical, with room service and

someone cleaning my room. After all, a home is where the people you love live. Otherwise, it's just a place to sleep. I've only felt at home in the homes of my friends.

***

"Do you like it?" I ask Faith, who is wandering around the living room with its view overlooking the steps of the MET.

She seems overwhelmed. "You must plan on having a very big family here. This place is immense. We'll only need three, and there are six bedrooms."

I noticed when she came in her eyes widened in surprise. I don't know what she's used to, but considering that her clothes are worn and look like they come straight from the early 1900s, though always ironed and clean, I doubt she has the kind of money to throw away like I do.

"Actually, when I asked the real estate agent to find me a place, he didn't show me anything with less than five rooms. When you deal with certain types of customers, you only show them luxury listings." I shrug my shoulders, not knowing how to explain this aspect of my life to her. I realize this girl comes from another planet altogether.

"I don't understand what you mean. For me, a house should be practical and functional for the purpose it serves—to put a roof over my head. Big or small, what difference does it make? If you have enough rooms to live comfortably, why have so much extra space?"

I observe her carefully and immerse myself in those blue eyes that, at the moment, lie below two furrowed, perplexed eyebrows. While I hate the way she was raised, I envy how nice it must be to live in an ideal world where everything is simple, where the complications of fame don't exist, where

you can choose a house without thinking about what the newspapers will write about you. Whether they'll paint you like a beggar because you choose to live simply, or if they'll crucify you because you have a pool while some people don't even have water to drink.

"You just have to live here a couple of months to understand what I mean. Being a rock star is not all parties, women, and the good life. Often you find yourself having to live by the rules of your environment: in this case, you have to buy a six-bedroom house and spend millions of dollars for a view of a staircase." I point out the museum in front of us and the famous staircase visible through the window.

"And why do you do it? Isn't it easier to do something you really like?"

The question surprises me, considering that she does nothing without her father's approval. She should know what it feels like to compromise.

"This job allowed me to escape the future that my family had decided for me. I'm willing to take some shit if I can afford to live peacefully. Do you love everything about your job as a nurse? Your life inside the convent?"

"It's not a convent. It's a boarding school," she replies, a little piqued. It's the first time I've gotten a reaction from her.

"But you dress like a nun."

"I don't like women walking around the city half-naked. Certain parts of the body should be seen only by the husband, not on display for all men to see."

"What if the husband becomes tired of his wife? Or the wife gets tired of her husband? Are they allowed to show their skin to someone else?" I've never had such a ridiculous con-

versation with another human being, let alone a woman! I feel the almost physical need to shake her. To provoke her, taunt her, and make her lose that robotic composure they've drilled into her with since she was a child.

"Divorce is a sin!" She rests her pale hand on her chest and appears scandalized.

"So is lying. And when you're with a person you no longer love, simply because God has imposed it on you, to pretend to love them would be lying to yourself and the other person. You're betraying an oath you made before God, because when your heart no longer belongs to that marriage, it's not divorce papers that cause you to sin. You've already done it—you're not married, you're just living under the same roof."

My words obviously strike a chord. As Penelope said, she's not stupid. She's actually brilliant, she's just been forced to live in a completely different reality from the one she's been immersed in until a few years ago. I watch her think about what I said, which is clearly in conflict with her beliefs. I didn't claim they were wrong, just showed them to her from a slightly different point of view, an unexpected one.

Good, because a brain like hers is a shame to keep inside such a narrow box. Watching Faith over these three days of forced proximity, on the one hand, makes want to scream at all of her self-imposed restrictions. On the other hand, I'm intrigued more and more by her continuous discoveries about the world around her. She doesn't talk much, but when she does it's always relevant and demonstrates her intelligent curiosity. She has a perceptive, naïve mind, pure as a child's, and is refreshing to be around because she's so transparent. There are no manipulations, double meanings, or deceptions. I have

to admit, I love this about her.

***

It took a week of signatures and phone calls to my financial advisor, but in the end, we managed to move quickly and get the apartment. The poor guy had to jump through hoops to raise seven figures in such a short time, but I pay him well, and after closing this deal so quickly, he deserves a big fat Christmas bonus.

"How do you like your room?"

Faith is finishing putting her clothes away and turns around when she hears my voice from the doorway. I don't dare enter. I know how embarrassed she is when someone invades her space, and I want her to feel comfortable here. This room is just for her, a small corner of paradise where she can find refuge when she needs it.

"This closet can hold ten times my clothes, and I have my own bathroom!" she exclaims in amazement. "I don't know what to do—having all of this to myself. It's huge!"

Obviously, she's not used to such luxury, but I can see in her eyes she appreciates it. "You'll see. When you have a fourteen-year-old around the house, you'll look forward to locking yourself in your bathroom, trust me."

She smiles at me and sits on her king-size bed.

"Speaking of fourteen-year-olds, I had some things brought to his room. Do you want to come and see and tell me if I missed anything?"

She nods and stands up, satisfied. When I first asked her to help me do some online shopping for this place, she looked at me like I was crazy. She dragged me out and into a supermarket to decide what to put in the pantry. I must say that despite

the first embarrassing contact with people staring at us and Max behind us snickering at each of my, "Do we really need this? And how do you use this?", it was a relaxing experience. It seems unlikely, but in this case, she was more comfortable among the shelves of food that looked all the same to me and had the exact same problem: you had to know how to cook it.

When we enter Levi's room, she approaches the huge desk that's stocked with every essential piece of equipment a kid of that age needs to keep up with his friends: a computer, gaming chair, iPad, iPhone, a stereo and speakers, television, and three different video game consoles. I doubt he had any personal belongings left after he ended up in jail.

"There's no bed." She frowns and turns around, perplexed.

I massage my forehead nervously, laughing. "Yes, that comes tomorrow. They didn't have time to deliver it today. But do you like the rest? I thought he needed a jump start to catch up with everything he missed while inside."

When she turns to me, the look of reproach in her eyes almost hurts me physically. It's been a long time since someone looked at me with such disappointment bordering on contempt. It's a look I promised myself I wouldn't see anymore, and what's worse is it's coming from a woman I just met a few weeks ago.

"Levi is serving a sentence. This should be a bedroom, not a playground. What message does it send to a fourteen-year-old boy who ended up in prison? That if you make a mistake, you get a prize? Where are the notebooks, the school books he has to study?"

Her words punch my gut like a personal attack—on me, on Levi, on anyone who has been in prison. "Do you even know *why* Levi ended up in prison?"

She shakes her head slightly but does not abandon her condemning expression toward me.

"Of course you don't. To you, we're just scum, right? You're only here because otherwise, you'd have to go home to daddy and you don't want to. Because no matter how much of a saint you are, you like living life outside of that hole you came from."

For the first time ever, she looks angry—her cheeks blaze and her eyes burn with indignation.

"I'm here because I testified to help Levi, and they fired me for it." Her voice is surprisingly calm, the tone low. I'll never hear her scream. "And if Levi is really as innocent as you like to make me think, he wouldn't have ended up in jail. No one with a clear conscience would be in his position, especially if he could prove his innocence. Levi was wrong, and he has to pay like everyone else who makes mistakes."

I have to clench my fists tightly to keep from shattering the new TV on the boy's desk. "Of *course* Levi was wrong, and so was I when I ended up in there. But do you know why he did it?" I hiss, moving a few steps closer to her petite figure, imposing my presence on her tiny one. "Because his foster family only took him in for the money and when that wasn't enough, what did they make Levi do? They forced him to rob stores and threatened to beat him to death if he didn't."

She arches her back to move away from me and for a moment, I feel guilty for having frightened her, but her sassy look sets me off even more, erasing every thought of giving in.

"You're just lying to justify the fact that he behaved badly. The truth is no one taught him discipline, and this is the re-

sult," she says sharply.

I move close enough to look her in the eye without being distracted by her lips.

"You've lived with your head buried under so many layers of sand that your brain has fossilized. You have no idea what real life is or how to get by in this world. You're a little girl who can't even tie her shoes without daddy telling her how to do it, but you're ready to judge people as if you were God. News flash, honey: God doesn't exist and he certainly won't save you from hell. Because hell is the world out there that people like you don't even know exists. Wake up from your fairytale, princess. Or some wolf will tear you to pieces sooner or later."

She says nothing. Her eyes become shiny, her jaw tightens, but her face shows no emotion, just as she was taught, no doubt. She leaves immediately and locks herself in her room. I already know she'll let go of the tears she wouldn't allow me to see.

My mother used to tell me that tears are secrets you have to keep locked up inside your heart. But she was never good at keeping secrets because at night I heard her, after my father beat her, crying alone in her bedroom, while he grunted between the thighs of a newcomer to the brothel. The important thing was to go to church in the morning, confess your sins, and hide the bruises.

***

I grab the girl by the hips and pull her to me on the couch. Her shirt and bra lay on the floor by the front door, her panties slipped down just before she straddled me and made me wear a condom. I love a girl who knows what she wants and has no

problem taking it—even better if what she wants is my erection between her thighs. I sink into her, grabbing her by the waistband of her hiked-up skirt. Her breasts tease and taunt me, drawing my lips and my tongue like a magnet.

I go in hot, not bothering to contain the guttural grunt of pleasure, appreciating for the first time that I can make noise in my own house. I channel all the frustration I felt this afternoon into my thrusts, all the anger at seeing Faith's judging eyes on me. Who does she think she is? Does she really think she's better than me, Levi, and all my bandmates? She's lived in a prison all her life and doesn't even know it, thanks to her father.

"Oh, yes. Yes, keep going." The girl's panting takes me over the edge, exploding into an orgasm that almost makes me scream.

"You're such an animal," she purrs, slumping on me and breathing deeply to catch her breath.

I don't say anything, just rest my head on the back of the sofa and close my eyes, enjoying the feeling of emptiness in my chest. It's better than the anger I couldn't shake before, but I feel completely drained: I can't even enjoy the pleasure of this blonde on my body. It's not like when I was a kid, when a fuck could made me walk around with a smile all day. Now sinking between a woman's thighs is not much better than pleasuring myself. A mechanical gesture, almost a routine. Every time I chase it, hoping it will make me feel something, even if only for a few hours, it leaves me indifferent instead. Yet I hope every damn time.

"Who the hell is that?" she snaps. "You didn't tell me you lived with your girlfriend. You didn't even tell me you had

one."

I look at the blond, confused, then turn to the kitchen and find Faith standing there, eyes wide, a glass in her hand. Her face is a mask of horror and embarrassment, but she doesn't look away. I throw her the kind of smile that makes most women melt and she only blushes more. The girl next to me doesn't even try to cover up, but I try to situate myself so Faith can see my naked chest but not the parts of a man she's probably never seen before.

She's so clearly shocked by the situation she doesn't even look away. Maybe because she actually likes me—I catch her stealing glances a few times and blushing. She notices my physicality, obviously, but it's not like she'll ever follow up on any impulse she might have. That would be obscene and sinful by her standards.

Shit.

She must've already been in the kitchen when we got here, probably to get a drink since she still has the glass in his hand. But we didn't notice her, we were too busy tearing off our clothes. If she'd wanted to run to her room, she would have had to pass right by us. So, instead, she stood there watching us, like a deer in the headlights, while we fucked like animals. It must have been quite the spectacle for her.

"She's not my girlfriend. Right, Faith?"

She doesn't respond. She remains frozen, swallowing with difficulty.

"What the hell is she wearing? Her grandmother's nightgown?" the blond asks, and it annoys me a bit because Faith suddenly looks down, embarrassed at her nightgown with its high neck and ankle length, and the blue fabric that brings out

her eyes in this dimly-lit room. She's always so damn proud of her clothes and now she's uncomfortable. I don't know why, but it bothers me.

The blond whose name I can't remember giggles, amused by the whole thing. "I'd ask you to join us, but I don't think you're the type who'd enjoy a threesome, are you? By the looks of you, you're still a virgin."

Faith curls into herself even more, slumping those shoulders normally so straight and proud. Of course she's a virgin; I don't need her to confirm it. Knowing how deeply rooted she is in her religious mindset, it's obvious she isn't one to open her legs before marriage.

"Maybe it's time to go home. What do you say?" I ask the woman without even looking at her face.

Faith looks up in surprise, and I don't move my eyes away from hers. I've never been someone who backs down when it comes to saying things as they are, but I'm not cruel. The way this woman made fun of Faith doesn't belong in my house, and neither does she.

The girl picks up her stuff, mumbling something that sounds like an insult. I don't care; I had no intention of seeing her again anyway. I put on my boxers without losing sight of Faith and when I hear the front door open and close, I approach the kitchen counter where she's leaning.

She doesn't move. She doesn't even breathe, though I approach slowly enough to give her time to go back to her bedroom if she wants. It's like she's paralyzed by the absurdity of the situation. I take the glass from her hands, touching her fingers. She inhales sharply, squinting her eyes and biting her lower lip, holding her breath. I take a sip from her glass, know-

ing how much it annoys her when I use her dishes, then place it on the counter behind her. Her hands are still clasped across her chest.

I bend down a bit to move a lock of hair behind her ear and whisper: "Good night, Faith, and sorry for the show."

I feel her shudder, holding back a small choked scream, the kind I'd like to hear as I sink into her and take her innocence. When I turn to go back to my bedroom, she's still standing there, frozen to the floor.

I just had sex with a woman whose fluids are still on a condom, yet I've never felt so intoxicated, thrilled, and content as I did the moment I discovered the power I have over Faith. She may have her father convinced that she'll keep her virtue for someone waiting for her at home, but she just watched me fuck another woman without being able to look away.

***

"What's with the funeral face?" Damian watches me as I enter the meeting room after an almost sleepless night of thinking about Faith watching me fuck another woman. I sit next to him while we wait for Iris, Emily, and Evan.

"The last time I was here, we ended up in prison again, and now I find myself with a new house, a nanny sleeping in the guest room, and I'm the legal guardian of a kid. Honestly, I've had enough changes for the next ten lives."

My mind goes back to Faith. Last night I made a titanic effort not to enter her bedroom and convince her to take off her panties. After the incident the other night, my desire to corrupt that puritanical armor she wears like a uniform has become an almost physical necessity.

My friends start laughing, but no jokes follow because Evan

enters, followed by the two women, smiling from ear to ear.

"When you wear that expression, you terrify me." Thomas voices what we're all thinking.

"Trust me, Iris has a brilliant idea. If we can execute it properly, you'll be back in the spotlight and even more famous than before."

"More famous than the most famous band in the world? That's a big challenge even for you," I tease him.

I know that Evan feels guilty for putting us in the uncomfortable position of signing binding clauses with the record company. But no one blames him for what they made us do; or, in our case, not do. It was a damn good contract, and Evan did the best he could for us at the time.

"You'll be back on tour," he announces, excited to be dropping the news.

We look at each other surprised.

"Did you magically find the money? Wasn't it too expensive for our pockets at the time?" Simon is the most perplexed of all.

"Not exactly. We decided to do a promotional tour a little different from the usual. We'll do *surprise* concerts." Iris lights up as she adds this confusing detail that we have no idea how to interpret.

"I'm lost," admits Damian.

"We'll do the concerts in clubs. I'll write a series of blog posts with clues as to where you'll be playing, and your fans will have to figure it out. The concerts will cost much less since the venues will be paying you to perform, and the novelty of not knowing where you'll appear next will create a buzz. Your fans will have to tweet and share information about you

to know where you are. We'll create special hashtags and, if everything goes as planned, you'll be a trending topic throughout the whole tour."

We look at her for a few seconds, surprised as much by its madness as its brilliance.

"We're going back on tour!" I let out a liberating cry. "We're finally going back on tour! I didn't think this day would ever come."

Emily is even more excited than we are. "It's not going to be a tour bus thing or organized like before with the old record company, but you can introduce new music out there sooner than you think. We'll also fit in some traditional concerts—like festivals, which we're negotiating now, but you'll be on everyone's lips the whole summer."

That woman is an organizing machine. She could set up an expedition to the Antarctic in five working days with just a computer, a notepad, and a pen.

"See? You don't always gain a family when you leave this room," Damian teases me, making everyone laugh.

PRESS *Review*

The Jailbirds Are Coming Back!

Hi, Roadies!

I'm back with news that will have you jumping out of your seats. Many of you have asked me if the Jailbirds will ever be back on tour, and the answer is: *Much sooner than you think!* You might then ask when the dates will be released and tickets go on sale. And the answer to that is, *There will be no dates or advanced ticket sales.*

You got that right, there will be no dates announced and tickets can only be purchased at the venues on the day of the show. Following this blog, I'll be leaving clues during the week before each show about which lucky city and venue the band will be playing.

Think of it as a scavenger hunt, and the reward is an evening with the Jailbirds in a much more intimate environment than the stadiums we're used to. Yes, you'll be able to watch them up close and very personal!

See you soon with more news from the Jailbirds.

Be kind and Rock'n'Roll,

Iris

463722 Likes 38942 Tweets 27832 Shares 9872 Comments

Rock Now

The Jailbirds are attempting an unprecedented publicity stunt. The surprise concerts they have planned will undoubtedly get people talking about them, but how long will it last? The decision to leave their record company was a gamble even for a world-famous band like theirs. We don't know how much longer they'll be able to hold on to the throne in the Olympus of rock without an organization with budgets as hefty as a record label has. We'll just have to wait and see if this will be the beginning of their end.

Live Stage

Risky move for the Jailbirds. While we can understand their desire to return to touring, they risk these small club concerts turning into flops. There is no advance notice for fans, no advertising for the event other than a "treasure hunt" where fans have to guess the venue. That can only end in two ways: no one shows up, or too many people crowd the venue, creating public security problems. In both cases, many fans will be left empty-handed and dissatisfied with the band's decisions. Sometimes, being too innovative doesn't pay off, and we're afraid this decision will permanently sink the band's already precarious career.

CHAPTER 8
Faith

Michael has either been standing or pacing around the kitchen all morning while sipping his coffee. I know he's nervous because this isn't the little routine we've established in the ten days since we've lived here. Usually, he sits at the counter with me and eats a different cookie from every single package he bought. His breakfast is typically a hodgepodge of things that don't have to be cooked because Michael can't prepare anything other than coffee.

Today, however, is the day Levi gets released from the hospital and we're waiting for the court-appointed officer to deliver him directly to our door. Michael wanted to pick him up, but the court ruled that Levi could not leave the house, so they will "tag him" by installing what they explained to me is a device connected to the police station that monitors the kid's whereabouts. Levi cannot leave this apartment without the device around his ankle alerting the police station. Michael didn't like this decision, but he kept his mouth shut for fear that someone would take the boy away from him.

It's admirable how he decided to take care of Levi. I don't think many people would have taken on this responsibility, even if they had Michael's money.

I watch him look out the window and frown. "What time

will they be arriving?" I put my cup in the sink, rinse it, and reluctantly put it in the dishwasher. I still struggle to use all this technology for something as simple as washing dishes.

"They should have been here half an hour ago." He's irritated and looking at his phone.

"There must have been traffic." One thing I can't get over is the number of cars in Manhattan. In the village where I grew up, my brothers could play ball in the middle of the street for hours without ever encountering a car. Here it seems everyone needs a car even to do the most stupid things, like going for a coffee.

"They should have left earlier. If they give me a timetable, I expect them to respect it."

Michael is not someone who throws tantrums, that much I know. He loves to joke around, but when it comes to serious topics, he weighs his words very calmly. I've witnessed several conversations between him and his manager and saw a part of him that I didn't know existed. The arrogance I noticed in the beginning disappears when it comes to discussing weighty issues.

When the doorbell finally rings, Michael is a bundle of nerves. I thought he would've rushed to the door but he remains still until I take the coffee cup from his hands. He gives me a look I can only interpret as frightened then approaches the door and opens it in a snap. Levi stands before him looking up, a half-smile on his face. Like Michael's, his blue, almost ice-like eyes have a light I've never seen before in them. Hope—the expectation of someone who is seeing something he's always wanted.

The policeman who accompanies him is out of uniform,

and while he puts the anklet on Levi and connects it to the device they installed earlier this week, the silence is almost surreal. Michael looks as if he is ready to kill him any minute. When they'd imposed the electronic device on Levi, he was enraged. He said it was for hardened criminals, not a kid who ended up in juvie. Looking at it now, the contraption looks enormous on the boy's slender ankle.

Levi is fourteen years old—that age when some kids already look like adults and others like children. He has the face of one of those cherubs you see in church paintings, with those blue eyes, blond hair, and delicate features. I wonder how a child who looks like the picture of innocence can think of running away and not finishing his sentence. Where could he hide if he's not even old enough to drive?

When the man finally leaves after having Michael sign many papers, the air seems lighter and it's easier to breathe. I realize that outside that prison, he's not as scary as I've always imagined. If I had met Levi anywhere else, I would have thought he was an ordinary kid who couldn't hurt a fly. Penelope's words come back to my mind – "they're not criminals" – and after spending time in Michael's company, I'm beginning to see what she means. Levi doesn't scare me. I don't feel in any danger without a guard when I'm in his presence. Pale, moving around weakly because he's still recovering, I see a fragile boy who has to carry the weight of an anklet too large for his slender leg.

"You have nothing but the clothes you have on?" asks Michael.

Levi shakes his head and lowers his gaze. I read the shame on his face.

"Don't worry, it's normal. When I got out, I only had the clothes they gave me. Now we order them online, and you can tell me what you like."

Levi nods and then looks at me. "Are you here to check on me? Will the director want to know if I'm being punished enough, like in prison?"

The question catches me off guard. I had never even thought that the director could ask me to do such a thing. My heart clenches at the thought that the boy assumes there will be punishments, regardless of how he behaves.

"No, I'm here to take care of you when Michael isn't at home."

Levi sends a suspicious look to Michael, who hasn't taken his eyes off him since he arrived.

"Don't worry, you can trust her. She's the one who testified in court to keep you from going back inside, and that asshole director fired her. She lives here with us now."

"Michael, you can't say certain words in front of a child," I snap, scandalized by his lack of regard for vulgar language.

Michael rolls his eyes, and Levi giggles. "We'll have to teach her how people talk these days. When she got here from the eighteenth century, they didn't give her an instruction manual." He looks at me and winks, the corner of his mouth slightly raised in an utterly mischievous grin.

I should be offended but the truth is, after catching him having sex on his couch, my cheeks go up in flames every time he lays eyes on me. My mouth gets dry and I can't control my heartbeat.

"So, what do we do now?" Levi's question drags me away from the embarrassment but puts Michael in a somewhat un-

comfortable position. I see his forehead wrinkle in a worried gesture. I don't think he thought beyond Levi getting out of the hospital. Michael is impulsive, but raising a kid involves making a schedule for him. You have to give him rules and make sure he follows them.

"Under normal conditions, you would be at school at this time," I intervene, trying to save Michael from the awkwardness. It's only noon, and he has no idea how to entertain Levi until the evening.

Levi's smile fades a little, and Michael looks at me as if I just insulted him.

"He's just come out of the hospital and you're already talking about school? You're heartless."

By now, I know this man enough to understand he's making fun of me. In fact, even Levi chuckles.

"Sooner or later, you will have to think about it," I insist.

"On this point, she's right: sooner or later, we'll have to think about school, but today give yourself a day off. Maybe a shower without fifteen other people in the same room, what do you say?"

Levi shrugs his shoulders and nods as he sits with Michael on the couch. "The shower sounds like a dream, but I don't know how you're going to enroll me in school. I haven't been there for at least three years."

Michael and I look at him, puzzled. "Not even before you ended up inside?"

"My last foster family didn't care much about whether we went to school or not, but they wanted us to bring home at least a hundred dollars a day." He explains it with a simplicity that almost hurts me.

"Didn't social services send people to check on you?" I ask in astonishment. "In our house, my father had to show that we had an education even though we were homeschooled."

Levi still shrugs his shoulders. "They knew when the visits would be because they had friends who worked inside. On those days, we had to get all cleaned up and iron our clothes and pretend to do our homework, and after a while, they didn't come to check anymore."

Michael seems to catch the note of embarrassment in Levi's voice and puts a hand on his shoulder to get his attention. "In this house, don't even think about escaping homework. You can enjoy a few days of doing nothing since you've just come out of the hospital, but Faith will help you catch up, so don't worry about not graduating. You'll have a diploma if I have to kick your ass until I get cramps in my leg. I may be open to negotiating about college, but there is no question about high school. Whether or not you stay here after the two remaining months of your sentence, I will not stop keeping an eye on you."

His statement surprises me. I always thought Michael would allow Levi to get away with anything, given his propensity for a wild and crazy career over a real job. In all honesty, I didn't think school was much of a priority. I know he was joking about actually kicking Levi, but the determined way he told him to study left zero room for arguments.

A rough knock on the door startles me. Michael wrinkles his forehead, looking at me with a questioning look as he gets up to go and open it. I shake my head; I have no idea who it could be at this hour. When he opens it, I recognize the tall guy with the long hair as part of his band, followed by other

guys and girls who I struggle to put names to. Each of them is carrying a pot or tray of food.

"Since we know that Levi can't leave the apartment, we decided to come here to meet him and welcome him," announces the girl with long red hair, while Simon approaches me and takes me by the hand, dragging me out of the kitchen.

If my father knew I was here in the company of the devil in person, he would kill me. Guilt creeps into my stomach. I haven't called him since they fired me, and even then I had lied to him, telling him my job was going well.

Everyone is sitting on the sofas and armchairs introducing themselves as members of the band, the manager, the partners, and another girl who, as I understand it, works for them. They're all comfortable and I feel like a fish out of water.

"You must be Faith, right? I'm Lilly, Damian's girlfriend," she says, reaching out to me and shaking my hand vigorously.

Silence falls almost instantaneously. Everyone turns to me, and I recoil with shame. Apart from Simon, who has a half-smile on his lips, all eyes are on me, looking intrigued.

"Is this the prison nurse?" Damian asks, his eyes wide, pointing a finger in my direction and looking at Michael in disbelief.

"Yes, who did you think she was?"

For the first time since meeting him, I notice Michael struggle for words.

Damian bursts out laughing so hard he bends over. A full, manly laugh, the kind that makes your belly vibrate and for which my father would have scolded us. Everyone seems to be hiding a smile, and I can't tell if it's out of embarrassment or for some other reason.

"Forgive me, Faith. I'm not laughing at you. I was expecting Ruth, and I'm just surprised," he explains when he catches his breath.

I don't know whether or not to feel offended by this. "Ruth retired last year." My voice comes out more uncertain than I'd like.

"Yes, no worries. I didn't elaborate, and Damian is a jerk," Michael says, trying to dispel the confusion.

Everyone holds their breath with an amused expression, while Damian rests a hand on Michael's shoulder and says, "Man, you're fucked," clearly amused by the situation himself. "Those lips? Perfect for blo..."

"Don't you dare finish that sentence," Michael threatens him good-naturedly.

There's an exchange of looks in the room that I can't read and it makes me uncomfortable.

"So I'm not the only one who's noticed Michael has the hots for Faith," Levi intervenes, and I almost feel my face explode with heat.

They all start laughing, and the atmosphere relaxes as they pat the boy on the back, his chest swelling like a pigeon.

"Ignore them; they're idiots," says the redhead who introduced herself as Iris. "They act like they've never seen a woman in their lives."

"I'm used to getting comments about how I dress, and I know I'm not like the other women they meet." I smile shyly and am a little happy Mother Superior isn't here to scold me for my lack of backbone.

"It's not your clothing, trust me," reassures the brunette, Emily, who's thrown a piece of rolled-up paper at Damian, hitting Evan instead, who gives her a look I can't decipher. I've only witnessed a couple of minutes of interactions, but I realize they have a secret language of their own, built on years of friendship and life together.

"So, Levi, ready to live the rock star life?" asks Damian, and I'm surprised by the heavy, frowning look Michael throws at him.

"Stop there. First, he has to finish serving his sentence. Then he has to think about studying and only then will I consider letting him come to the concerts with us. Do you want him to grow up and be like you?"

"A child can't go to concerts!" I exclaim without thinking about it, and the silence that falls is severe. Everyone looks at me like I've just said I want to go to the moon.

"And why not?" Michael challenges me with his words and his eyes.

We've never shared the same world view, and this is definitely one of those times. I just didn't want to have an audience for this conversation.

"Because I don't think it's a kid-friendly environment, that's all." I feel my stomach tighten at the disappointment that passes through Michael's eyes just before changing into a smile.

"You should know that the young lady here thinks that being part of a rock band means a life of sex, alcohol, and drugs. A life full of sins that lead you straight to hell. Basically, a corruption of the soul." He challenges me again with his gaze, and it seems like everyone else has disappeared from the room. One thing I'll never get used to is being the center of Michael's attention: there's no one else; you're alone with him and that

look of his that makes your stomach turn upside down and your face heat up.

"She's not all wrong. Until a few years ago, you were the perfect rock band, with all the aforementioned vices." Iris smiles, throwing a glance at the four of them. "But don't worry, now they've become couch potatoes. Just getting them off the couch is a miracle!"

They all burst out laughing, including me, because I just can't imagine Michael spending his days on the couch. At least not without a naked girl writhing on top of him. It took me days to stop thinking impure thoughts about what I witnessed that night.

Everyone goes back to their mundane topics as if the banter between Michael and me had never taken place. Still, I'm uncomfortable with the glances he's sending me from the other side of the room. He's not angry, he's disappointed, hurt, and I didn't expect to feel bad about provoking those feelings in him.

***

Levi has been sleeping for a while, and Michael disappeared immediately after putting away the leftover food in the fridge, forbidding me to clean up the kitchen because he says he pays a cleaning lady well to do it. What I'll never understand about rich people is why they feel the need to pay for something they can do themselves. I have two hands and the energy to clean. Why do I have to live with a mess until someone comes and does what I could do right now?

I look at the crumbs on the counter and am tempted to wait for Michael to go to bed to clean up.

"Don't even think about it." Michael's voice behind me

makes me jump out of fear.

I turn to look at him, and my mouth goes dry. He's standing, dripping wet from his shower, in the middle of the living room, completely naked except for a white towel knotted at the waist. Wet hair drips onto his well-defined chest; his abs could have been sculpted by Michelangelo. That body contains all the perfection and sin that leads women to hell. When I look up to his eyes, I find him smiling with that knowing grin: he's fully aware I can't tear my eyes away from him.

I should do it, I should shift my eyes to something other than the forbidden fruit in front of me, but I can't. I begin to understand what Eve must have felt when facing that apple: the awareness of not being able to have even a bite but the lacerating desire to taste a tiny piece of it. Try on your tongue the sweet taste of that juice that envelops your body and mind with a pleasure that sends you straight to hell.

I watch him approaching, knowing I should move from this counter, but I'm not capable of it. It is as if, since leaving the safety of my community, the devil has clutched my ankles and anchored me to the ground, making it impossible for me to escape these temptations. Because Michael is surely the most tempting morsel the devil has even put in front of me to test my faith. He can't be an ordinary mortal—his beauty sears into your brain impure thoughts so vivid you feel as if you've been branded with fire.

When he reaches me and rests his hands on the marble counter I'm leaning on, trapping me with no way out, my cheeks are engulfed in a heat I've never felt before, the same heat igniting my lower belly and making me tighten my thighs to keep from releasing my juices right here on the floor.

"Be careful where you put those eyes, Faith. You may wish to sin. You know we rock stars are famous for being damned souls," he whispers in my ear.

My skin feels shook by an electric shock that makes the hairs on my arms stand up. I can feel the heat emanating from his body, from his closeness. My breath catches in my throat so much that a small hiccup erupts out of me, and I try to suck in air. He notices and smiles, only to disappear again near my ear.

"You want me, Faith. I can tell from a mile away that you want me. But you're so scared of sinning that you're missing out on all the beauty of life. You can't ignore your body shouting at you right now. I see the chills covering your skin when I'm this close to you. I may be a corrupt person who you consider scum, but you know you want to get dirty by sinning with this low-life."

"I never thought you were scum." My voice comes out in a trembling whisper I struggle to even recognize. I can't keep control over my body, over my own will, but I don't want Michael to think I consider him unworthy.

His voice is still a whisper, his breath smelling of mint; the combination makes my head spin with desire. "Maybe not, but I scare you. You're afraid of all the emotions I bring out in you. Why are you squeezing your legs, Faith? What do you feel there, between your legs, that scares you so much?"

This man reads my body language as if he was born to do so. How does he know what's happening in my lower belly? How does he know that the chills stirring in my stomach are shooting up to my brain, clouding my reason? A small moan escapes my lips, and I realize I've closed my eyes and moved closer to the skin of his neck, inhaling the scent of soap that envelops him.

"You're a good girl, Faith, but you're not a saint. At some point, you'll want to taste the forbidden fruit, and once you do, you won't want to live without it. You've become my favorite prey, and trust me, even if you don't give in right away, I have infinite patience and endless ways to win you over."

I believe him. Right now, I'm well aware that the devil is offering me many temptations wrapped within this perfect body; it beckons me to give in and stain my soul with its pleasures. Michael will take my hand and walk me to hell, and I'll be happy to follow him, sacrificing myself on the altar of desire until he corrupts my soul.

I open my eyes and find him looking at me with such intensity I feel naked, helpless, vulnerable, but for a reason I can't explain, I can't look away. Inside those eyes I see something that terrifies me, yet I'm also aware of having access to his soul like he has access to mine. It's as if he's removed the veil and allowed me to see behind his gaze into the real Michael, with all his compulsions, his desires, his sins. What scares me the most is that I should be firm and walk away from this temptation, but instead I remain motionless, unable to resist the physical pleasure of his nearness.

CHAPTER 9

Michael

Simon opens the front door of his house, and right away his surprised expression makes me wonder if I should have come. Maybe Evan is better suited to give me advice about Levi. My friend doesn't say a word, just nods his head. I must look desperate because as we walk through the jungle that is his house and into the kitchen, the first thing he does is hand me a beer. "I'm doing everything wrong with Levi," I blurt out. No sense beating around the bush.

"It hasn't even been a week, and you're already throwing in the towel?" He smiles as he sips from his bottle. Sometimes I envy his angelic calm.

"I'm not throwing in the towel, but I don't have the faintest idea of what's best for him. I can't get him out of bed before ten in the morning. He spends his day either questioning what Faith teaches him or playing video games. I can't engage him in any activities because I have no idea what he might like. I'm not capable of doing any of this. I don't know how to raise a kid," I admit sincerely.

Simon studies me for a while with that wise look that frequently defines his facial expression.

"Is it crucial that he gets up before ten o'clock? He can't leave the house, Michael, let him sleep. Do you remember

how long the days inside the prison were? Let him adjust a little to this new life; you can't expect everything to magically fall into place."

"What if I can't help him? What if Faith was right and our life isn't compatible with that of a young impressionable kid? Let's be honest, how do you think a fourteen-year-old boy will grow up around concerts with half-naked women, alcohol, drugs, and everything that goes on? Faith thinks we're the children of Satan, and as much as I insist on opposing her, she may not be entirely wrong."

Simon sits next to me and puts his hand on my shoulder, squeezing slightly. It's a gesture he rarely uses and it draws all my attention. "First, Levi comes from such a dysfunctional foster family that you couldn't do any more harm than what's already been done. The important thing is that he feels wanted by you, Faith, and all of us. He doesn't give a damn if one day he's in a club with half-naked women and the next day he's in a recording studio. He needs safety, a home where he can return without fear. Undressed women are the least of his problems. The real question is, is the problem here Levi or Faith?"

I inhale sharply and take a generous sip of beer. It's the question that haunts me the most since we started living under one roof.

"I don't know," I admit honestly. "The problem is that she's lived her whole life in a box. She has these blinders as big as a house. All she sees is: rock bands are evil, possessed by Satan who came straight out of the earth's bowels. It's impossible to change her mind. According to her, Levi shouldn't be around an environment like ours, and as much as I keep telling her we don't perform human sacrifices backstage, she keeps looking

at me like I'm the devil."

I get nervous just talking about it.

Simon tilts his head and studies me for a few seconds. "Does it bother you more that she has a different idea of how to raise Levi or that she has a bad opinion of you?"

I shrug. "I don't know. I never cared what people thought of me, but the way she judges me is nerve-racking. I feel like I'm going to trip up. Whenever I do, she makes me feel the way my father made me feel: like I'm nothing."

"I don't believe that you don't care about what people think. It's just you've always had surface- level relationships, so you don't feel bad if that person doesn't like you for who you are, for your past, or your family. If Evan or one of us says you're a jerk, and not as a joke, you feel bad about it. You care what Faith thinks."

"No, what bothers me is that she doesn't know me and judges me."

"Michael, she's lived her whole life in an ultra-conservative bubble. You can't expect her to be open-minded out of the blue. And what worries me most is that you're like a bulldozer—trying to turn her whole belief system upside down just to prove her wrong. You risk ruining her if you try to convince her to see things your way. I already see your arrogant, smartass attitude as you explain to her how the music business works."

"I'm not arrogant, and I'm not doing anything to ruin her," I snap, indignant at the turn of this conversation.

"Really? Do you want me to believe you've never provoked her in any way? Not even a single time?"

"That's not the point."

"That's exactly the point. She's light years away from you, and you're losing your mind over it."

"That's not true. I provoke her because if she doesn't learn how to live in the real world, she'll be torn to shreds the first time she sets foot outside that apartment. I don't do it out of selfishness or because I'm bored. I do it because out there, the world is a den of wolves, and she's a lamb hiding in a cave. But sooner or later, someone will smell her and end up tearing her apart. For some stupid reason, this scares me almost more than not being a good example for Levi. I feel this need to build an armor around her that can defend her even when I'm not there. Because one day she will leave, and I want to make sure she doesn't end up like my mother, unable to defend herself—from men and from real life."

***

The conversation with Simon left me feeling nervous about Faith and guilty about Levi. I knew I had to go to Evan's. Simon has a way of reasoning that, in some ways, looks a lot like Faith's, so of course he was on her side. His warnings, however, did nothing to lessen my desire to get her out of her shell. If anything, I feel even more strongly that it's an urgent necessity.

I open the front door and find Levi in front of the television, greeting me with a smile while watching one of those crazy shows where they challenge people to eat the most disgusting things for money or prizes. Not even if I were starving would I do it.

"Doesn't it suck to watch this stuff after dinner?" I sit next to him and notice that Faith is busy in the kitchen putting dishes in the dishwasher. I feel guilty because I should have had

dinner with them instead of staying with Simon drinking beer and emptying his fridge of leftovers from the night before. But it's something I'm not used to. I've never had to wait for someone else. I've always eaten according to my own schedule, commitments, and restaurant or room service hours.

"Sometimes I feel like vomiting, yes." He laughs, amused.

I study him carefully, and he looks like another person than the frightened little kid I met in prison. Of course, he's not opening up yet, but I suppose it's because he's had to learn to weigh words and hold secrets his entire life.

"What did you eat?" It's such a trivial question I laugh at the very thought. I've never asked it to anyone.

Levi finally looks away from the TV and turns around with his whole body, paying attention to me. "Faith made a fantastic steak, but then she tricked me and made me eat cauliflower puree." He wrinkles his nose. "I thought it was mashed potatoes."

I burst out laughing. "Was it really that bad?"

Levi frowns as if thinking about it for a moment. "To be honest, no. I had to ask what it was to know she fooled me. It tastes good, but you can't give me something that looks like potatoes and then tell me it's cauliflower. That's how people develop trust issues!"

I laugh even louder and realize that I haven't felt this good with someone besides my bandmates for a long time.

"Do you know that she doesn't let me eat sweets? At least in prison, they gave you pudding on Sundays. She says sweets are unhealthy."

"I'm going to tell her to put a label on the cauliflower and give you a piece of cake after meals." I wink at him.

"Yes, go talk to her. All day long she looks at the front door hoping it will open. Kiss her, make up to her, do whatever you have to do to keep her from being in a bad mood because then she tortures me with homework."

He goes back to focus on TV, and my window for deepening my connection with Levi has closed. At least now I know I can trick him and make him eat cauliflower if I make it look like mashed potatoes.

I watch Faith at the sink for a while. She's been avoiding me for days after I came on to her that evening. I know I was an asshole, but I couldn't resist exposing the excitement she was trying to hide. I saw her tightening her thighs under her skirt and her nipples straining against her worn out shirt. She may not even have realized it, but I saw the desire in her movements. She stared at the drops of water on my chest as if she wanted to stick out her tongue and lick them like ice cream dripping from the cone on a hot summer day.

Maybe my methods aren't too tactful, but I like to push people to overcome their limits, and I don't want to see another weak woman as long as I live. I grew up with one who couldn't defend me; I don't want Faith's children to have the same fate as me.

I get up and walk closer to her. "Levi told me you made him eat cauliflower."

She smiles and rinses a plate in the sink. "He was almost offended when he found out."

I can't hold back a laugh. "You did the right thing making him eat it. He won't die if he eats some vegetables. Nor will he die if he eats a few sweets."

The smile disappears from her lips. "Sweets are bad for

you."

"Are they bad for the body or the soul? Because I've never seen anyone die from a piece of chocolate."

She straightens her back and tenses. "Sweets are just bad." It's a diplomatic response to keep her position while knowing what I think of the subject.

"Really? So if I give you a piece of chocolate now, will you die here on the spot?"

"You know what I mean."

"No, I don't. Because if you mean that they hurt physically, then you're right to keep Levi away from sweets, but if you say they hurt the soul, then I have to disagree."

She looks down and clenches her fists. I open a kitchen cabinet and grab a piece of chocolate from the bar I opened this morning. I approach her and hug her from behind, holding her wrists with one hand so she can't torture herself with some punishment. She is perfect in my arms. Her back molds perfectly to my chest, and I almost let out a moan of pleasure.

"Open your mouth, Faith. It won't kill you, I promise," I whisper in her ear as I place the piece of chocolate in front of her lips.

She pulls her head back to avoid it but slams into my shoulder. She's tense, I can feel her every muscle ready to snap, but she doesn't leave. When I'm nearer, she looks petrified. I put the chocolate between her lips, and I reach out with my fingers to touch her skin. She squints her eyes, and a small moan of pleasure escapes her when the dark cube sits on her tongue.

"See, Faith? It's not killing you, and God hasn't come down to earth to punish you. You can indulge in certain pleasures, and you can let others have them too. Nothing's changed from

five minutes ago, except that right now you feel a little happier." I wrap both arms around her waist and hold her close to me, unable to stop with her body that seems to call to mine. I gently touch her cheek with my lips, inhale her scent deeply, go down to her neck and kiss her slightly just below the ear.

I feel her inhale deeply and stiffen again, but then rest her cheek on mine, looking for contact I know she wants despite all her beliefs. It's the first time I've really touched her. The excitement is awakening parts in my pants that should be dormant, which is when I decide to stop. Playing with her, pushing her to overcome her limits and fears is one thing, but pressing my erection on her buttocks is forcing an intimacy she has never felt and for which she is certainly not ready.

I move away from her and kiss her lightly on the cheek before turning around and going to sit on the couch with Levi. When I turn to see if she is okay, I see her raise the sleeve of her shirt and press firmly with the prongs of a fork into her wrist. The anger that assails me is almost blinding.

The memories of my mother are still vivid in my mind: of her being forced to suffer the blows of my father's belt on her back because she allowed herself an afternoon at the home of one of our neighbors to get her hair done. According to my father, vanity is the work of the devil; as I saw it, it was just his fear that some man more decent than him would notice my mother and take her away from him. I remember the silent suffering, the words of repentance from a woman who had done nothing but felt guilty, the prayers whispered in front of the statue of Our Lady that never helped her to get rid of the monster within her house.

Maybe Simon is right. Maybe I'm just an asshole who

pushes Faith beyond her limits, but I'm the only one forcing her to take her life into her own hands and not to be a slave to a reality that is suffocating her.

CHAPTER 10

Faith

"If you stare any harder at that phone, it'll go up in flames."

Michael is at the door of my bedroom, just outside it, where he usually stands. I've learned that even though he often approaches me in the main living areas, he never enters my room without permission. This is my space, and he respects it. It's a big deal for me since there were no personal spaces in my house. If my father wanted to monitor what we do, he was allowed to enter without any argument from us. He says we only need to hide if we're committing a sin.

"It's Sunday." I beckon him to come in and sit down.

"And on Sundays you stare at the phone hoping it will ring?" he asks me, perplexed but teasing.

I smile and shake my head. "On Sundays at eleven o'clock, I always call my father."

"I've never seen you do that. We're usually busy with Levi or with my friends coming to visit."

I inhale deeply and try to find words to describe the discomfort I feel. "Before coming here, Penelope made me call home and say that I wouldn't be calling for a few weeks because I had to cover multiple shifts since one of my colleagues broke her leg. I've managed to hold off for a month and a half now, but I can't avoid a conversation with him any longer. No one

is that sick from a broken leg."

I look up and find him staring at me with wide eyes. "You lied to your father?"

My cheeks go up in flames. "It's a white lie!" I use Penelope's exact words though I don't really believe my own. The guilt is so intense it almost makes me vomit.

Michael starts laughing, but not out of mockery. He seems more amused by this whole situation.

"If that makes you feel at peace with your conscience, I certainly won't stop you. Do you want to call home? I'll leave you alone if you want."

I shrug and stop him. "When I called from the boarding school, Mother Superior was always there to listen to my conversations; the same at home when I answered for my father. I've always talked on the phone with someone in the room. It doesn't bother me. In fact, it seems strange to be alone." I smile, amused by this realization.

Michael gestures for me to call. It's ten minutes before eleven, but I try anyway. It rings at least four times before someone answers.

"Hi, Dad, it's Faith."

"You finally remembered to call."

"Sorry. It was a bit of a crazy time at work."

"I don't like what they make you do. You should come home and stop with all this nonsense." He's angry. He doesn't like not knowing what his children are doing at every single moment of the day.

"I know, but the more hours I do in the infirmary, the more experience I gain, and the sooner I can come home." How long will I be able to keep using this excuse before he comes to pick me up and bring me back to my community?

My father seems to think about it for a while. The silence lasts so long I start to fear he can see through the phone that I'm no longer at the boarding school and lying to him.

"Don't push your luck too much, Faith. Resign from that job. I'm getting tired of your whims. Do you think Jacob is happy with this situation? You should already be married."

"Dad..." I look for a way to tell him I don't want to marry Jacob, but what can I say? How can I convince my father I don't want to spend the rest of my life with him?

I look up at Michael and see his forehead is wrinkled, his fists clenched. Clearly, he can hear my father's imposing voice on the other end; he looks angry enough to grab this phone and shout at the man who raised me. I swallow hard and try to breathe deeply.

"Stop acting like an ungrateful little girl. If I say you have to come home, you come home. End of discussion."

My father hangs up without even waiting for an answer. Not that I had one. What can I tell him? That I don't even work for the detention center anymore? That I've been lying to him for almost two months? I put my phone on the bed and take another deep breath.

"I came to tell you it's time to eat." Michael gets up, annoyed every time the topic of my family comes up. He seems to hate the community I grew up in. Of course, we have such different backgrounds we may as well come from two different planets, but that doesn't justify his annoyance. I never asked him to be part of my life; he could just stay out of it instead of constantly judging my family.

"I'm going to make lunch for Levi." I get off the bed and

follow him out to the kitchen.

"Why don't you make it for all of us?"

I frown and look at him to see if he's serious. "Because you pay me to take care of Levi, not to feed everyone."

Hearing his name, the boy sits up on the couch and looks away from the television he's been watching since he got up. That kid seems to spend his entire life on that couch.

Michael bursts out laughing, sarcasm dripping from his words. "Why? In the cult you live in, isn't the woman in charge of making food, washing, and ironing for everyone?" His teasing has a tone that makes me angry.

"You're not my husband, and I have no obligation to take care of you. You can feed yourself, you're an adult man, and we are *not* a family." I shouldn't respond out of anger. I shouldn't even feel this resentment, but Michael manages to spark emotions in me that make me do things I would never do under normal circumstances.

A vein of pain runs through his eyes for a moment, but then the arrogant mask returns in its place. "I've never cooked a day in my life, and I'm not going to start now." That insolent attitude comes out again. It hadn't been peeking out for a while.

"You've never cooked? How have you survived so far?" I ask, puzzled. It's impossible to me that a grown man has never cooked anything.

"I've always had someone serve me food. First the 'housewife,' then the prison, and finally the restaurants and room service."

The way he says "housewife" with such bitterness, I assume he wasn't all that happy that someone was preparing his meals. I point to the stove. "Well, it's time to learn how to use the kitchen."

"You know you two look like an old married couple arguing over who should clean the house, don't you?" Levi's amused voice makes our heads spin at the same time. His smiling face and enjoyment ease the tension in the air.

"And in your opinion, who's right?" Michael raises an eyebrow as if daring him to blame him.

"I don't know; you both have a point. Faith is right—she's not obligated to feed you, but you're also right admitting you don't know how to cook. I don't know who's right, but you're the man of the house. I don't know—go out and hunt for food." He giggles, and a slight smile appears on my lips.

Michael's bewildered face is priceless. "Stay here, you two, don't move," he says before leaving the room like a tornado, grabbing the keys and disappearing behind the front door.

"Do you think he went to catch some squirrels in Central Park?" asks Levi, as amused by the scene as I am.

"I hope not, or we'll have to go and get him out of prison."

***

Half an hour later, Michael returns with two paper bags loaded with boxes that smell delicious.

"This is my way of hunting for food. If anyone complains, there's the stove, you're free to cook whatever you want."

"What did you get?" asks Levi, running to the table enthusiastically while Michael begins to pull out the boxes.

I, meanwhile, go to get the plates and cutlery.

"It's Chinese. I didn't know what you liked, so I got a little bit of everything."

Typical Michael. He always overdoes it with the buying. We have a fridge full of rice pudding since I gave up on not

eating sweets. I categorically refused to eat chocolate ice cream straight from the tub as Michael and Levi do, but I do indulge in vanilla rice pudding. Every now and then, I dare to alternate with tapioca, which I like the most, and if I really feel brave, I put a splash of cinnamon on it. And to think that until a few months ago I only ate what was prepared at home: vegetables, potatoes, meat once a week, soups. All strictly cooked according to the tradition of our family, certainly not the Chinese tradition. But I appreciate the effort Michael has made to please us, and I want to give him the benefit of the doubt about this lunch.

"We don't need these," he tells me, taking cutlery from my hands.

"Then how do we eat?"

"Have you never eaten Chinese? With these." He shows me a pair of chopsticks.

"But there's spaghetti and rice. How do we eat that with those?" I ask, seriously worried. I can indulge him this exotic food, but this? It's too much even for Michael's quirky ways.

"Have you really never eaten Chinese?" asks Levi, completely stunned, as he stuffs himself with dumplings that he first dips in a dark sauce.

"No, it's not something you can find where I grew up."

Levi frowns but asks nothing else. It would be hard to explain where I come from to a kid who has no idea what's outside of New Jersey or Manhattan.

"Wait, I'll show you how to use them." Michael approaches, wraps me in a hug from behind, and puts the two chopsticks in my hand, placing them between my fingers. He teaches me how to make movements, but I'm so awkward that one of the

dumplings that Levi grabs so dexterously slips off the plate. Michael chuckles behind me, I feel his chest vibrate on my back, and I turn around to cast a reproaching look at him. I try again. This time I can raise it from the plate in a somewhat unstable way before it slips again and, flipping upside-down, ends up in the glass of water.

"Michael, let her use a fork or she'll starve," Levi chuckles.

Michael moves away and looks me straight in the eye. "This time, I'll let you eat with a fork because Chinese is new for you, but don't think about getting away with it forever."

I blush. The insinuation that there will be other lunches like this makes my stomach tighten in a vise. It's strange how the balance of my life has shifted in just a few months, from being afraid to go home to looking forward to taking part in something intimate like lunch with people I love being around. I feel such contentment right now that I almost forgot the conversation with my father. Almost.

He hands me a fork, and finally, I manage to skewer the pale dumpling. I put it in my mouth, and immediately an explosion of taste makes my eyes widen. The texture is a bit strange: the outer dough is slimy while the inside is like a meatball of vegetables and meat, but the whole is good. I didn't expect something so tasty, given how bland it looks.

I look up and smile as Levi and Michael stare at me, waiting for the verdict. "It's good," I admit when I finally manage to swallow.

"You have to taste it with soy sauce," Levi suggests, and immediately Michael stops eating and gets me a bowl with the dark liquid inside.

It's strange to see Michael so excited to have me try some-

thing new. He points the dishes out to me, pronounces names I'll never remember, explains where they come from, how they cook them, the differences between the two spaghetti dishes—which I learn are called noodles—that to me look perfectly identical.

"You like to teach." The observation comes to me spontaneously after he explains that traditional soy sauce is dense and has to mature for years in wooden barrels, but that tradition has now been lost.

"I like to introduce people to new things."

"You've obviously studied a lot."

I see him look down and a veil of sadness passes across his face before revealing his usual smile again. "As a child, my grandfather made me read many books about how to build things, and I was left with a passion for learning how everyday objects work. I once took apart a calculator at the motel my parents run and couldn't get it back together. My mother screamed so much while scolding me that I think her vocal cords were torn apart. The number three is still missing."

He smiles at the memory.

"Are you close to your parents?" I ask him. It's rare for Michael to talk about his family and usually, what I gather is that it's not positive. I wonder what his life must have been like for having led him to end up in prison so young.

"I haven't seen them in years." It's all he says before his mood goes dark.

Levi glances at me to feel the pulse of the situation. Michael turns as prickly as a cactus, and the festive atmosphere melts, giving way to bitterness. I feel guilty for bringing it up.

"You should teach Levi to play the guitar," I suggest, changing the subject.

Michael looks at me first and then the kid with a frown.

"Yes, please. I'd love to learn how to play it."

"Really? You spend all day in front of the television."

"It's not like I can do anything else. I can't go out, use the Internet, meet my friends, or skate. Basically, the only thing I can do is the homework Faith gives me and watch TV. I'd love to come to the recording studio with you sometime. I've never seen a musician at work." He's clearly enthusiastic about the proposal.

Michael seems caught by surprise. He wondered what to get Levi to do, but he didn't think about the most obvious thing: music. There are more guitars than people in this apartment, but I've never seen Michael play, maybe because he does it all day for work, but I admit that I'd like to see him play, and not just in the videos my colleagues showed me.

"Okay, this afternoon, let's start with something simple."

"Can you teach me one of your songs?" Levi's eyes are bright with enthusiasm.

With his blond hair and blue eyes, he could be Michael's son, and the image of the two of them doing something together feels like what a family would look like. I told Michael this morning that we're not, but the truth is we look a bit like a real family here, sitting around this table having lunch and making plans for the afternoon.

"Maybe let's start by holding a guitar, what do you say? There's no need to make Faith listen to 'Sex on the Beach' or she'll be calling an exorcist," Michael teases me as Levi chuckles.

"I've heard that song, actually, and I agree that it's not ap-

propriate for innocent ears like Levi's."

Michael widens his eyes and turns his attention on me. "Did you watch the videos? Miss Faith, I didn't take you for such a rebel," he teases.

"I was forced by my co-workers," I point out as the other two traitors laugh.

"Yeah, that's what they all say." He winks at Levi who is cracking up.

I feel ashamed, but happy that the atmosphere has lightened again.

"If you want, I'll play it for you later. A private concert just for you, since you like it so much."

He winks at me and now I'm totally embarrassed as he bursts out laughing, though I can't help but smile too. Michael teases me mercilessly, pushes me to try things I've never done, and mocks me, but in this whirlwind of newness, one thing I do more and more often is smile—without being afraid someone will reproach me. The freedom is intoxicating.

***

"Is he sleeping?" I ask Michael as he approaches the fridge and pulls out a bottle of wine and two glasses from the cupboard.

"Yes, he finally collapsed. I had nightmares too, the first few months when I got out of there. They'll go away with time and the help of a good psychologist." He sits next to me on the couch. Too close for my taste.

I want to ask him how he ended up in prison, what his life was like in there, but I'm afraid he'll close up like today at lunch, and I don't want to spoil the atmosphere again.

"Since you're in the mood for experiments today, do you

want to taste some wine?" He smiles and studies me carefully.

"No, I don't drink alcohol."

He shakes his head and emits that exasperated laugh that I now recognize. "You don't really do anything outside the rules, do you? Do you know that Jesus turned water into wine? I don't think he'd punish you if you drink it. It would be a bit hypocritical of him. What do you say?"

"You're blasphemous, you know that?" I try to reproach him, but the smile on my face when I look at him cancels all my efforts.

"You grew up in a world that revolves around the Bible, and you don't know it's one of Jesus' miracles, and *I* am the blasphemous one?" He raises an eyebrow challenging me in his usual way.

"True, Jesus transformed water into wine, but that doesn't mean we can abuse it. Wine removes the inhibitions God has set in place to keep our souls pure."

"Or maybe God has put wine in our lives because it's not actually a sin to follow one's own impulses." He sips from his glass and studies me with a look so charged with heat it makes my skin vibrate.

It's already tempting enough to have him in front of me day after day without adding something that could alter my decision-making abilities. I lower my gaze, unable to maintain eye contact.

"How does life in your community work? Are there gates? Can you go in and out freely, or do you have to ask someone's permission?" he asks, perhaps sensing my embarrassment and changing the subject.

"There are no fences or anything. It's just a small village

in the countryside. We are just over six hundred, and we are self-sufficient. We have our own farms, crops, and, if we need anything, once a month some adults from the village go buy it in a city a hundred miles from where we live. It's not that we're a cult or anything like that. We just live a simple life; we enjoy the little things."

"But you can't get out," he insists.

"We can go out, wherever we want, but not having a car or much to see around there, we don't really have anything to do."

"Which is a bit like being in prison."

"It's not like that. It's just, when you don't know what's out there, our whole world becomes our community. We don't need to go out looking for something if we don't even know what to look for."

"You know this is wrong, don't you? To keep a person in a position of not being able to choose their own life is to keep them prisoner."

"Or maybe it's protecting them from what might happen to them given their naivety and inexperience."

He thinks about it for a while, still drinking wine. "You can't learn without making mistakes. You don't grow that way."

I don't know how to answer him. I honestly don't have the tools to argue.

Michael puts the glass on the table in front of us and comes closer. "Do you trust me?" he whispers.

Do I trust Michael? Until now, he has never given me a reason to believe he's a bad person. The problem is I don't trust myself in his presence.

"I suppose so…" My answer is hesitant.

He leans forward without giving me time to react, places one hand behind my neck, and draws me to himself, sinking his face into the hollow of my neck and kissing my bare skin. The shiver that assails me is so violent it makes me tremble. I close my eyes and hold my breath.

His lips run up my neck until they get under my ear, kissing that tiny patch of skin that makes me groan. How is it possible that so much pleasure is so wrong?

"You see, Faith? If you don't know what pleasure feels like, how do you know it's wrong?"

I can't answer. It's like he's reading my thoughts. My fingers squeeze his shirt so tightly I'm afraid I'll tear it off, my body is pressed against his, and I'm not sure if it's Michael's hand on my neck that draws me to him.

"Is it so wrong to feel pleasure? Answer me, Faith. Is what we are doing so wrong?"

My mind wants to answer that what I feel right now is a natural pull towards him, the same one that attracts animals to mate, but my heart knows he's not the man I'm going to spend the rest of my life with.

"Yes. It's wrong." I rest my hands on his chest and push him slightly. He doesn't resist. "You're not the man I'm going to marry. That's why it's wrong." My voice comes out breathy, panting, a victim of my body that can't regain composure.

I can hardly breathe, my heart is beating so hard it's bouncing off my ribcage. I have to get up from this couch and put an end to this moment of weakness. I must go and atone for my sins as my father taught me. I try to free myself from Michael's grip, but his hands around my wrists stop me. He's not hurting me, but in his eyes I see a determination not to let go.

"Don't go to your room to punish yourself, Faith. Commit this sin, stay here and learn that the pleasure you feel is not wrong. Nothing will happen if you don't punish yourself. Nothing will happen at all. God will continue to torment the earth with disasters and wars, and you will live with the knowledge that physical pleasure is part of life. Giving it up won't make you live a better death."

I don't answer. I want to escape, take refuge away from him, but I can't because for the first time in my life, physical contact with another human being doesn't burn inside with the weight of guilt. I feel the tears threatening to come out, but I can't let them. Years of holding them back because crying wasn't allowed, and now I can't let them slip in front of the only person who could understand them.

Michael pulls me into a hug, the first one I can remember, and the feeling is so shocking I can hardly breathe. No one has ever held me so tight in my entire life, and the line between right and wrong fades into a whirlwind of feelings I can't control.

CHAPTER 11

Michael

Seeing the amazed faces of Faith and Levi when we boarded the private jet that took us from New York to Los Angeles was the most fun I've had in a long time. Levi had never been on a plane and was so excited he didn't even open his mouth—a true miracle, since this kid usually talks nonstop about everything, including stuff he knows nothing about.

His sentence is over and the judge has decided that, since there were no problems, he can stay with us temporarily, at least until they find an ideal adoption candidate. I doubt there will be. For years this kid has been in and out of foster families. He wasn't adopted at age seven when they took him from his drug addict mother, I doubt he will be at fourteen with an eight-month sentence in a juvenile prison on his record. The truth is my lawyer convinced the judge to let me keep him until they find someone to take care of him, in order to help him make up for the years of school he lost. After the last foster care home ended up putting him behind bars, it wasn't difficult to convince the judge Levi was safer with me than in many other places. At the end of the day, the system is so jammed with adoption paperwork and with so little money they're happy when a solution like this falls into their laps without them having to lift a finger.

"Wow!" Levi's mouth and eyes are wide open when we get out of the car and approach the mansion we rented for the week.

Finally, it's time to get back on stage. Tomorrow's charity concert in Santa Monica is the breath of fresh air I needed after this particularly stressful time. I didn't choose this career because of an innate passion for music, but I soon discovered that I love being on stage, having thousands of people singing our songs at the top of their lungs. Some may consider me egotistical or self-absorbed. I'm just proud to have pulled myself out of the crap and built a career that people admire me for. I like to be noticed for what I do well, not just when I screw everything up.

"Did you rent this whole mansion just for us?" Faith's voice is almost dreamy, and looking at her, I see the same amazed expression as Levi's. It's a constant surprise to see the innocence on their faces, the sincere amazement at things I'm so accustomed to. In some ways, Faith seems almost the same age as Levi. They're discovering the world in the same way, and I feel a little sadness for how much life that's been denied her so far.

"It costs less than renting hotel rooms for everyone. Plus, we have a private beach where we can rest without being hassled by fans and paparazzi. It's great to stay in Malibu, where life is a little easier to navigate—as long as you have money." I take the bag from her hands and accompany her to the door while the others catch up.

"Faith, you'll room with me!" Emily approaches and takes her by the arm.

Faith stiffens for a second and then relaxes again, and I can

tell she's still getting used to the freedom with which people touch each other. But I'm happy my friends welcome her as one of the group and do everything to make her feel comfortable.

"Levi, you and I will share a room, so hurry up and go choose the best one!" He scrambles inside the house like a rocket fired into orbit. Less than two seconds later, he disappears up the stairs. I look around and take a deep breath of the sea air wafting through the sliding glass doors of the living room that lead to the patio surrounding the pool. The stretch of grass that separates it from the cliff overlooking the beach is so well-kept it looks like a golf course. The kitchen, living room, and dining room make up a single great room dotted with light furniture that reflects the warm California sun.

I hear a loud laugh over my shoulder and turn around to find Damian, Thomas, and Simon doubled over.

"So, you're sleeping with the kid? You'll have a hard time finding a woman," Damian teases.

"Don't remind me. I haven't fucked anyone for weeks." I rub a hand over my face. In that department, my frustration is at levels I've never been before, what with Faith walking around the house all day with those lips I want to devour.

"That's a record for you," says Lilly, who, together with Iris and Evan, is putting bottles of water in the fridge.

"I rented a hotel room nearby in case I need it." I wink at her, trying to save face, but I don't think I'll use it. The truth is my concern for Levi absorbs all my energy, and I don't have as much time to think about finding a woman for a quick fuck. Besides, after Faith caught me on the couch, it became a bit embarrassing. At the time I strutted around with my usual bra-

vado, but the following day I felt the weight of my actions. I've never lived with anyone after the band began to earn enough to have a place of our own, and I forgot how to respect other people's boundaries in that way. Taking someone home and having to sneak into my room to keep quiet is enough to deter me from going looking for a woman.

"Since we don't have any appointments until tomorrow, how about going to the beach and relaxing for today? All phones in this basket!" proclaims Emily, as she comes down the stairs with Faith. While Emily is tucked into a micro-bikini that leaves little to the imagination, Faith is covered up in her usual long-sleeved shirt, skirt down to her ankles, and the inevitable boots that I've wanted several times to throw in the garbage. We all put our phones in the basket, but when it's our manager's turn, I see him go pale and tighten his grip like he's possessed.

"Evan, the phone." Emily's tone scares me, but not as much as the murderous look she's giving our manager.

"I can't. I'm waiting for important phone calls," he stammers. I've never heard him stutter in my life.

"That's not true," she informs him. "I manage your life and that of the four troublemakers here. I know what phone calls you are waiting for and what emails you are receiving. You can leave your phone in this basket because I have freed up your whole day from appointments."

We all hold our breath at this head-to-head. Evan has found a woman who manages his life—it's nothing short of a miracle.

"So that's why I have no appointments." He seems almost scandalized by Emily's brazenness for having forced him to

take a day off.

At that, she rolls her eyes and slams the basket in his chest. Evan turns greenish and squeezes his fingers around the phone so tightly his knuckles turn white. When Emily reaches to pull it out of his grip, he raises his arm above his head with wide eyes.

"Evan!" hisses Emily with a look that scares me too.

A cry of pain escapes his chest as he reluctantly gives in against his will, dropping the phone into that damn container. "Don't think this is over. We'll talk about this when we get back to New York."

Emily shrugs her shoulders, annoyed, and stores the phones in a cabinet in the living room, which she then locks.

Our manager turns to us with a threatening look. Needless to say, we all burst out laughing.

"Do you want to put on your swimsuit?" I ask Faith when everyone else disappears to change clothes.

Her eyes get big and she blushes feverishly. "I'm good with what I'm wearing."

I inhale sharply. "No, I refuse to let you come to the beach like this. It's late June and eighty-six degrees out there. If you're covered from head to toe, you'll end up in the hospital with heat stroke. It's not about how you look. If you go to the beach dressed like this, you'll collapse," I explain, exasperated. Her stubborn commitment to this straight-laced lifestyle makes me crazy.

Faith looks down. "I've never worn a swimsuit; I don't even have one."

I should've known. I bite my tongue for assuming she was equipped for a trip to the beach.

"Let's go buy one."

"No, Michael. I don't want to put on a swimsuit. I feel embarrassed." She puts her hands on her belly, and I feel a twinge of guilt.

I grab her chin between my fingers and force her to look into my eyes. "There will be many things you'll be embarrassed about in life, but you can't give up a day at the beach with your friends because of shyness. We don't need to buy a skimpy bikini like Emily's; we can buy a one-piece swimsuit if it makes you feel less naked. If you don't go, the others will feel obligated to stay with you and not leave you here alone all afternoon."

She doesn't look convinced by my speech, but she also doesn't dare say no. Maybe because she feels guilty and doesn't want to ruin the day for the others. I'm an asshole, counting on her good heart in wanting to make my friends happy, and I drag her out the front door towards the SUV where I find the keys that Max left.

We drive silently along the main road as I check out the shops. When I see one with beachwear in the window, I slip into the parking lot and get out, taking her by the hand and dragging her into what looks like a luxury boutique. Faith sticks to my side like glue and grabs my hand, intimidated by all the glitz and bling.

A saleswoman in her early twenties approaches us with a smile that almost blinds me. Her outfit—elegant black shorts and a pink silk top that falls softly over her generous breasts—perfectly fits the environment. I notice her holding her breath when she recognizes me and devours me with her eyes. But when she looks at Faith, her face goes from a not-so-disguised look of jealousy, to disgust, pity, and finally relief as she moves her gaze from her face to her clothing. Faith is beautiful, but she has no clue about how to dress in a way that shows off her strong points. The saleswoman doesn't consider her a threat. If she only knew how wrong she is—I'd prefer Faith a thousand times over the fake eyelashes, plastic surgery nose, and perfect waves of the saleswoman's hair.

"How can I help you?" she squeaks dramatically. Even her Californian accent sounds fake.

"We'd like a swimsuit for my friend. Not a bikini, something more modest, maybe a one-piece." I take the liberty of speaking for Faith as she doesn't seem to be able to open her mouth at the moment.

"Oh, unfortunately, we don't have those kinds of swimsuits. Ours are made to show off the perfect bodies of our customers, to enhance and play to their strong points. But she can try a sporting goods store; maybe she'd find something there that better suits her style." Her tone reveals that she doesn't think Faith is worthy of this store, and it makes me smoke with anger.

I glance at Faith, who, after a quick overview of the bikinis on display, looks down and blazes with shame, gripping my hand even more tightly.

I feel like an idiot because I understand this is a real humiliation, not just a slight embarrassment. I'm about to respond badly to the bitch in front of me when a woman in her fifties approaches us, wrapped in an elegant sand-colored dress.

"Amanda, you can go. I'll take care of the lady." Her tone is calm, the smile never leaving her lips, but her order is so authoritarian the girl straightens her back and lowers her gaze,

mumbling quietly and moving away.

"From what I've heard, you're looking for a swimsuit that is less flashy than what we have here. I have something I think you'll like, but not in this shop; it's a couple of doors down." She beckons us to follow her.

We leave the shop and enter a second building not even a block away—a high-end clothing store, but with much more elegant clothes. We follow the woman who I'm guessing is the owner, given how nervous the sales assistants seem in her presence, and we slip into a section a bit more sheltered, with a huge white counter and a row of vintage style swimsuits behind her. She takes one off of the mannequin, red with white stripes, and shows it to Faith. It's as if I don't exist, she devotes all her attention to Faith and speaks directly to her, and Faith seems to relax slightly.

"See?" she explains, pointing out the features. "This short completely covers the bottom and upper thighs. The ruffles at the bustline enhance it without leaving it too exposed, and the wide straps help keep everything in place when you lie down to sunbathe or go into the water. The back covers up to the shoulder blades, and doesn't ride up when you get out of the water, and the weight of the wet fabric tends to cover the rear discreetly."

Faith nods, not quite convinced, but no longer as tense as before. The woman has put her at ease, and I can never thank her enough for it.

"Try it and see if it suits you," I suggest, but she turns to me with wide eyes.

"No." Her voice is firm.

"Faith, you can't know if it's the right size if you don't try it." I smile but I really want to wrap her in a hug. She looks as frightened as a lamb in front of a hungry wolf.

"No!" she repeats even more forcefully.

"If I may…," the woman intervenes. "It's a bathing suit; it's not difficult to guess the size. I can measure your hips and chest over your clothes, and find you the right size." She smiles reassuringly, and I see Faith's lips bending slightly upwards.

Ten minutes later, we leave with a swimsuit, a short white tunic to wear as a cover-up, a pair of heelless sandals, and the promise that I would do a lot of publicity for that place, considering the miracle she performed.

"See? That wasn't so hard, right?" The atmosphere is definitely more relaxed as we return home.

"You didn't have to spend all that money on me. When we get home, I'll pay you back," she hurries to clarify.

"Don't even think about it. I forced you to buy yourself a bathing suit; the least I can do is pay for it."

"Thank you."

I glance at her and wonder what she's thinking. She's staring out the window with an indecipherable expression on her face. Given the choice, she would never have bought that swimsuit, yet she's sitting here holding the paper bag in a vice grip. This woman is a living contradiction.

Entering through the front door, we bump into Emily, who runs down the stairs in her skimpy bikini that highlights all of her curves. Before meeting Faith, that would have been the clothing I'd do anything to see a woman in. Now, I'm more curious to see what's hidden under those long skirts and high-cut blouses. Living under the same roof, I'm finding it's not so bad to imagine what's under her clothes instead of having

everything on display. Waiting to take a peek makes things more exciting.

"There you are! We've looked everywhere for you."

"We went to get a swimsuit for Faith." I turn to her. "If you go change, we can head down to the beach together."

Faith looks away, embarrassed. For a moment, I'm afraid she'll refuse to wear the bathing suit.

"I...don't... I don't..." She lacks words and looks for help from Emily.

I swear, trying to follow what she's saying, I'd need a GPS. The women I'm used to dating are much more straightforward and much less complicated. She gestures at Emily's legs with one hand, but I don't understand. The girl, however, seems to have figured it out.

"Michael, change and go to the beach; we'll join you there. Because as much as you are used to smooth and silky women, I can guarantee that we are not born without hair from the neck down," she scolds. "Come on, honey, I have everything we need in the bedroom." She takes Faith by the arm and pulls her up the stairs.

***

The beach is small and cozy, connected to the house by a steep wooden staircase that descends from the cliff. As soon as I reach the base of the stairs, I take off my flip-flops and look for Levi. He and I have to have a word about respecting others' spaces and his messiness: when I opened the bedroom door it looked like his suitcase had exploded, shooting clothes everywhere. Bathroom included.

I watch my friends and laugh. Damian is throwing Levi into the water with such force that I'm afraid he'll send him

into orbit. Lilly is warning him not to hurt the kid, but Levi is laughing like a madman. Simon watches them grinning, with his usual calm and arms crossed over his chest. Thomas takes pictures of Iris, who cooperates for a while, but she begins to grumble and threaten him with death glares at the millionth pose. But most comical is Evan, a lost soul who walks in a circle on six square feet of beach, his hands tightening rhythmically along his hips. Take the phone and the work from that man and he breaks down.

"Do you want me to pick up your computer, or can you hold off until tomorrow?" I tease him, approaching him and putting a hand on his shoulder to stop his pacing.

"I swear I'll kill her. I swear this time I'll suffocate her," he mumbles without much conviction.

"No, that's not true. You keep her because she's one of the best assistants you've ever found. She is organized, knows how to do her job very well, and above all, thinks outside the box exactly like you do. More than an assistant, you have found a partner who could easily replace you."

He looks at me and smiles. "True. But she didn't have to plan my vacation without telling me."

"If she had told you, would you have let her do it?"

"Of course not!" he replies, scandalized.

I raise an eyebrow when I notice his expression change; his eyes get huge as he stares at a point behind me. I turn around and almost have a heart attack. Faith has just come down with Emily; she is wrapped in the gauzy white tunic that reaches her mid-thigh, leaving a glimpse of the red swimsuit on her slender figure. Her face is partly hidden under a huge wide-brimmed straw hat, but I can see she's looking down and her cheeks are

pink with embarrassment. Did she really hide those long legs and gorgeous white skin under all those clothes? She's an almost mystical vision, and I struggle to swallow while I see her take off her sandals and walk barefoot on the beach.

I turn to Evan, who is still bewildered, then I look at the others who are all looking at her with their mouths wide open. It's hard to tell my brain to get a grip, to move my legs and go to her to make her feel less like a fish out of water. But the girls beat me to it. Lilly and Iris reach her, take her by the hands, throw her sandals at me and reach the shore.

Meanwhile, the guys walk briskly towards me, and when they catch me, they cross their arms to their chest.

"You want to explain why you never told us she looked like that under all those clothes?" Damian invites me to give an explanation.

"I swear I didn't know. She has never shown up like this around the house. Ask Levi."

"It's true. She's always dressed like a nun," says the kid, continuing to stare at her.

"Levi, if you want to live to see your fifteenth birthday, stop staring at her ass," I warn.

"But you look at it! Why can't I?" he asks indignantly.

"He has a point," Simon teases me.

"Because you're still a kid, and you don't need to be looking at women's asses." This is the only excuse that comes to mind.

The others burst out laughing because they know I'd already been between the thighs of older girls at his age, but I glare at them to make them shut up. I have to maintain some semblance of rules around Levi.

"I heard Iris and Lilly organizing a girls' night out." Damian tries to divert the topic. "What do you say we all go out to dinner to celebrate the end of your sentence?"

Levi looks up at Damian with a mixture of disbelief and reverence. "Seriously?"

"Of course, you're one of us now, and we celebrate the achievements of our friends." Damian looks up and winks at me.

I appreciate his attempt to include Levi in our group. It hasn't been easy to try to make him feel part of my life, not just a burden in our house or the charity case of a bored rock star. I genuinely care about Levi, but I have no idea how to deal with kids because I never was one. All four of us grew up too fast to really understand what it felt like to be a teenager.

"I've already booked a place in Beverly Hills," Evan announces.

"Where did you find a phone?" asks Simon intrigued.

"I told Max he could have the evening off," he candidly confesses, "if he could sneak my cell phone to me so I could get a quick look at my emails and then bring it back upstairs."

We all burst out laughing.

"Have you been in prison too?" Levi asks, bringing the attention back to himself.

Evan looks him in the eye and smiles almost lovingly. I didn't think a no-nonsense guy like him could have a soft spot for a kid. "No, I'm the one who stays out of trouble, so I can get them a good lawyer."

"Cool! You're like Alfred getting Batman out of trouble."

I smile. Only Levi would compare us to superheroes, and looking at my friends' surprised faces, I understand their mix-

ture of disbelief and gratitude at being thought of as the good guys.

"Yes. I'll have to ask to have a Batcave built for me," laughs Evan, ruffling the boy's hair.

I glance over at Faith laughing with the girls, putting her feet in the water, running away from the waves like a child. If someone had told me a few months ago that I'd consider this a perfect day, I would have called them crazy.

***

Dinner with the guys turned out to be much more fun than I had imagined. The place is a current hot spot in Los Angeles, with frequent comings and goings of famous people. Outside, the paparazzi go wild at every car that stops in front of the place. Levi spent half the evening pointing at people and asking me if they were really famous actors or singers. Basically, it's the type of place we usually avoid, but Evan booked it for two reasons: to get the media talking about us and to give Levi the VIP experience. Even the entrance from the underground garage seemed extraordinary to him, with the four of us being photographed on the red carpet. I don't want to feed the kid to news-hungry vultures, but Levi seemed to enjoy playing the role of the spy who travels incognito.

I even managed to give my hotel room key to our waitress, who's waiting for me there after her shift. They're playing live music, the food is good, and we're relaxing after a day at the beach, half of which I spent in the water dampening my erection after Faith took off her tunic and showed off her new bathing suit. What I need tonight is a good fuck before going home. Two weeks of abstinence was a long enough torture.

"Levi, you go back with the guys while I stay out a few

hours, okay?"

"Where are you going?"

He always surprises me with these questions—I'm not used to being accountable to anyone about my plans, but I soon realized I can't just do what I want: the kid depends on me, and I owe him an explanation. Even if it gets uncomfortable.

"I have an appointment that I can't miss."

I hear the others snickering.

"With who?"

"Yeah, Michael, who do you have an appointment with on Thursday night? It must be super important," Thomas insists, as Levi's eyes focus on me.

I glare at my friend before bringing my attention back to the kid. "With the waitress. I have a date with the waitress."

"Oh, okay." He shrugs his shoulders, unimpressed, and sinks his spoon back into the cup of ice cream in front of him.

I look back at the guys who are watching me, amused.

"I think this exchange is called 'fatherhood,'" Simon teases me as I throw the napkin at him.

"Jerk."

"Look at it this way: at least he's already grown, and you don't have to go through the diaper phase. I can't really see you with your hands in poop," Evan adds, making everyone else laugh.

The mere thought disgusts me.

"Don't rejoice over victory too soon," Thomas teases me. "If Faith continues to live under the same roof, sooner or later, he'll impregnate her with his thoughts alone. This is Michael, after all, who manages to take three women to bed and satisfy them all,"

I turn to Levi and find him observing the room without paying too much attention to our talk.

"Can you please keep it above board around him?" I glance at my friend and gesture toward the kid with my head.

Another round of laughter envelops the table, except Damian, who seems confused by a message on his phone. "Speaking of Faith. Lilly says you should probably come home because she's apparently sick."

Suddenly the good mood drains from my body. "What do you mean, sick?"

"I don't know, but she says it's best if you come home." Damian seems worried, and it makes my heart squeeze inside my chest. "Call an Uber and go. We'll pay and catch up with you."

The trip to the house takes an eternity. I tried to call the girls, but none of them answered. When I enter the front door, I find them all around the sofa where Faith is lying, her skin a grayish hue that scares me.

"What the hell happened?" I ask, kneeling next to her.

"She drank too much and felt sick. Just in the last ten minutes, she can't seem to keep her eyes open. We think we'd better call an ambulance," Emily explains quickly.

"How did she *drink too much?* She doesn't drink alcohol at all—never had it in her life," I say accusingly as I pick her up and take her to the nearest bathroom.

"We found out too late," Iris says. "We had some fruit cocktails but she didn't know they were alcoholic, and I think she drank three or four."

I glance back at them from the bathroom door a few feet away and see they're more frightened than I am.

"I'm going to make her throw up. It won't be pretty, so I

suggest you stay there," I say in a less aggressive tone than before. The guilt is written all over their faces.

I lay her on the bathroom floor and hold her head over the toilet bowl.

"Come on, Faith, you have to vomit. You'll feel so much better afterward," I whisper in her ear as I move her hair out of her face and try to open her mouth. Kneeling behind her, I use my body to keep her straight and my hands to open her mouth, then I gingerly stick two fingers in her throat to try to make her vomit. At first she resists, but then she seems to gain some awareness of the situation. She moves my hand, which is absolutely useless and not working, and tries to get up, and the effort suddenly opens up the dam.

I hold her hair as she clings to the bowl and pours out the contents of her stomach. The spasms are so violent that I have to keep her forehead from slamming on the edge.

"Good girl, you'll feel so much better after this."

After endless rounds of retching, she finally manages to open her eyes and inhale large amounts of air. Tears stream down her cheeks, and when another gag makes her bend over the toilet, a hoarse cry escapes her throat.

I feel helpless, scared, and like I might be losing my mind. I didn't think you could worry so much about another person. I've seen my friends wasted on the floor of several hotel rooms, but I've never held in my arms a small body as helpless as hers.

"I'm going to die."

"No, you aren't going to die," I sigh, glad to hear her speak.

"I hate you, Michael..." she cries.

Her words hit me like a slap in the face.

"It's your fault. You're the devil. You're..." She can't finish the sentence because she's assaulted by another retch. I hold her hair with one hand and massage her back with the other.

"The devil. You tempt me, and you make me commit sins. Satan himself has possessed you to make my thoughts impure."

I can't hold back a smile. "Really? I've been sent by the devil?" I whisper when I see she's finally calming down. The worst is over, she's rid of most of the alcohol in her body, and I can start breathing again. Fear slowly leaves my body.

"Yes. He put you inside a beautiful body and sent you to me to make me commit sins…impure thoughts…beautiful," she keeps repeating, and I can't hold back a smile that fills my face and my heart at the same time.

"*Beautiful,* you say? I swear I'll use this against you forever." My chest shakes with a slight chuckle.

"Yes, beautiful. Your chest is beautiful. Your smile is beautiful. Your butt is beautiful."

"Even my butt? You look at that too?"

"Yes, every time you bend down to pick up something."

I'll have to do that more often. I hold her close while another gag shakes her.

"And what else have you noticed about me, hm?" As long as she's talking I know she's conscious and recovering from this colossal hangover, and we won't need to take her to the hospital.

"Your smell. Your smell is beautiful."

I laugh. "That's beautiful too?"

"Yes. But inside, you're a demon that makes me commit sins."

"Impure thoughts?"

"Yes."

"And what are those thoughts?"

"Kisses. Kisses are impure thoughts."

"Do you dream of kissing me?" I'm touched to know her most indecent thoughts involve a kiss. Something I don't often do with the women I sleep with. Too intimate.

"Yes. Your lips. And your chest. Your chest is beautiful," she barely whispers as her breathing becomes more regular and seems to calm down completely.

I smile, sitting on the bathroom floor and holding her against my chest. She is so petite she almost disappears into my arms. I reach for a towel hanging next to the sink and use it to clean her lips, face, and hair. I pause to watch her as she falls asleep snuggled up next to me and realize how much I worry about her. Aside from my friends, I've never cared so much about anyone like I do her and Levi. I feel the need to protect her, but at the same time, I want to encourage her, to see her take flight and grab hold of her life, her future, her happiness with her own two hands. I want to see her smile and laugh like she did today on the beach, try on a bathing suit, or dance under the stars. I don't care what she does with her life, but I want her to do it for herself and not to please someone else. I want her to discover pleasure, happiness, be light-hearted and free.

I get up and take her carefully in my arms when I'm sure she won't suffocate in her sleep. When I enter the living room, I find everyone there looking at me, half smiling.

"So, you have a beautiful chest, huh?" Damian teases.

I smile. They all stayed here, silent in the dim light, worrying about her. "Shut up, idiot," I scold him good-naturedly.

"Can one of you girls come and give me a hand? I have to undress her and put her to bed, but I don't think she'd like me to do it."

All three follow me at a brisk pace as I climb the stairs with Faith in my arms. I can still hear my friends chuckling downstairs.

"Do you think he's salvageable, or have we lost Michael too?" Simon jokes.

Normally I would have shouted something sarcastic, but I don't care tonight. Faith is okay, and that's all that matters. I'm not lost or too far gone, as my friend insinuates. I'm just worried about a person living under my roof. That's completely normal, right?

PRESS *Review*

People

The Jailbirds are back in the limelight. Finally, after months of silence, they were spotted last night having dinner at SoBeh, the trendy LA restaurant. As you can see from these photos, the band seemed relaxed, smiling, and accessible to photographers. Rumors say a young boy was with them, but we have no evidence to confirm this. Is he their new musical discovery? Maybe a young rock star for their new record label? If so, we look forward to an announcement soon.

At one point in the evening, Michael left the restaurant in a different car than he had arrived in. Was he escaping to meet a new flame? With Damian and Thomas settled down, we can only hope that Michael will give us some much-needed rock star gossip.

Gossip Now

The Jailbirds are back to showing themselves in public. In advance of their concert tonight in Santa Monica, the band arrived in Los Angeles a few days ago to enjoy the sun and sand of California. Last night, after a short dinner for men only in

Beverly Hills, they ran off in a hurry, perhaps heading to an exclusive party to which we were not invited.

As you can see from these pictures, Michael left the restaurant before his bandmates. Was he going to meet a new flame? No one knows where they ended the night, but knowing their bad boy past, it's no surprise we lost their tracks.

CHAPTER 12
Faith

The effort it takes to open my eyes is unbearable. My brain is throbbing with a headache worse than anything I've ever felt in my entire life, the nausea and dizziness are indescribable. I try to stand up, but the movement alone makes me tremble like a leaf.

"Dear Jesus, help. I'm dying..." Only divine intervention can save me.

I don't know what's worse: the rancid taste in my mouth or the horror of trying to figure out what happened. Truthfully, I remember almost nothing from last night. I went out with the girls to a place where they served delicious fruit juices. It was crowded with loud music. I've never been anywhere like it, but it was fun, especially hearing the girls talk about their crazy adventures with the band. But then came the void—a massive hole between the venue and five minutes ago when I woke up.

I look over at Emily's bed and it's undone, so I assume she's already up. Michael. I remember Michael holding me in his arms and placing me on the bed. Was he the one who put me to sleep?

I lift the sheet and find my nightgown twisted around my legs. Did Michael undress me and tuck me in the blankets?

The embarrassment is so overwhelming I feel tears start to fall to the side of my head. No one's ever seen me without clothes. Not even my mother since I've been old enough to take care of myself. That's reserved for the man you decide to spend the rest of your life with, not for a rock star who goes from bed to bed casually, like it's nothing. Even if he has behaved like a gentleman in recent weeks, it doesn't change the fact that he's seen more skin than any man from my community.

I grit my teeth and finally find the strength to sit up. A note from Emily on the nightstand tells me that the girls are at the beach, to join them as soon as the hangover allows. So that's why I feel this way this morning: that fruit juice was not as harmless as it seemed. But it was good, sweet, colorful. I suppose the devil puts something inviting in front of you if he really wants to tempt you. I get a little angry with Michael. This whole environment is filled with temptations to sin. Even though the girls are kind to me, they drink alcohol and have promiscuous relationships with men they're not married to. I'm not used to all this, and I'm not sure I want to learn anything else about their ways. If my father knew I got drunk, I can't even imagine the punishment he'd inflict. Never in my life have I committed such a horrible sin.

I struggle to get dressed in my usual clothes. I can't bear putting on the bathing suit Michael bought me—one embarrassment at a time, and this hangover is more than enough.

I walk down to the kitchen and find a plate on the counter covered with a plastic lid, three glasses of water, two pills that look a lot like painkillers, and a note folded in half with my name written on it in Michael's handwriting. I open it curiously as I sit on the stool.

Steps to recover from the hangover (trust me, I've tried many and this is the magic recipe):

1. *Take a sip of water to wash the dead mouse taste out of your mouth. Just a sip, otherwise you will not be able to eat anything more because you will vomit.*
2. *Eat everything on your plate. Without discussion and taking all the time you need.*
3. *Drink all three glasses of water. You need to rehydrate your body after everything you vomited last night. Don't cheat. God sees you!*
4. *Take both Advil pills. I recommend doing it after you have eaten. Your stomach is already quite shaken up after the night you had.*
5. *Stop feeling ashamed and guilty. It happens to everyone; you waited a lifetime before getting drunk. Cross it off your bucket list. It was a colossal hangover; I congratulate you. You should be proud—it's not easy to almost get alcohol poisoning without ending up in the hospital.*

The girls are at the beach, we're at tonight's concert venue, Levi is with me, you have the whole day off. Stay with them, avoid alcohol, and above all, have fun.

Michael

P.S. We need to talk about my beautiful chest, but I'd prefer to do it in person.

Talk about his chest? Why do we have to talk about his chest? A hot flash sets my cheeks on fire and I'm not sure I

want to find out what he means by that. But I am pleasantly impressed by his care. It's sweet of him to worry about me, and I feel my anger fade.

I follow his instructions to the letter, although it scares me to eat everything on the plate: eggs, bacon, toast, even a grilled tomato cut in the shape of a flower, mushrooms, and two mini-pancakes. Michael can't cook. How did he put all this stuff together? I smile as I sink my fork into the eggs and take a bite, looking at the ocean in front of me.

My father would call this place the devil's house, but all in all, I don't feel particularly guilty about enjoying the sun coming in through the windows, the sound of the waves in the distance, and the heat warming my bones. Maybe it's the alcohol's fault, or perhaps my father never experienced life outside the community where he grew up. I can understand why he's afraid of these things; it's different and it scares me a lot too, but the others live this way and I've seen with my own eyes that they're good people. Maybe it's because they've been exposed to so much temptation all of their lives that they seem stronger than me and more prepared to face life.

I begin to understand what Michael means by trying experiences in my own skin to really understand the difference between good and evil. Surely the hangover I got is wrong, and maybe God's punishment is to make me feel like a rag this morning. But God also decided to allow me to live, go through the headache with this meal, and not make me feel nauseous anymore. If God wanted to punish me severely, I would have ended up in the hospital, right? I don't know if these are excuses to justify something I've done wrong or reasons why none of the bad things my father feared has happened to me since I left the community.

I don't punish myself anymore for the little pleasures I feel, for the chocolate I have a weakness for, or for the Sunday Mass I've been skipping for months. Of course, I pray every day, and on Sundays, I take time to do penance, but God has not yet punished me. I kept watching and waiting for weeks for some big awful thing to happen to me, as payment for my sins, as my father always predicted, but until now, Michael's been right: nothing has changed.

***

I walk down the stairs leading to the beach slowly, regretting not putting on the swimsuit that Michael bought me. The heat is stifling, and I'm sweating already. At least I allowed myself the straw hat Emily lent me that protects my head from the scorching sun.

"Finally, you got up! We thought you were going to sleep until late afternoon." Iris runs towards me, hugging me while the other two reach us.

My heart hammers in my throat, and the shame for what happened makes my cheeks burn.

"Sorry for last night. I don't even know how I got drunk, but I must've been a lot of trouble. I don't know how I'm going to make up to you. I have no excuse for what I did," I say all in one breath trying to find words for how bad I feel.

They giggle, amused, but hug me.

"Don't feel guilty. It was our fault. We didn't know you're a teetotaler, and we ordered alcoholic fruit cocktails without telling you." Lilly seems genuinely mortified by what happened, and I feel even worse.

"I should have known. They were delicious, and after the

first one the others went down easy."

They burst out laughing.

"Yes, we know how it works," Emily says. "You go out one night saying, 'I won't drink tonight, and I'll come home early,' and then find yourself at four in the morning clinging to the toilet hoping to die because you can't bear another retch."

"I don't remember that. I remember Michael taking me to bed, and this morning, I woke up in my nightgown." I cover my face with my hands, but Iris's slender fingers force me to remove them.

"Michael asked us to change you because he knew you would feel embarrassed. We were the ones who put on your nightgown," she reassures me, and a wave of relief hits me, making me smile.

Michael is a braggart, sometimes arrogant, but more and more often, he gives me a glimpse of that side of him I like the most. Little courtesies like the note he left me this morning, asking the girls to change me, or the milk chocolate bar he always buys me, different from the dark one he likes—things he minimizes with a shrug of the shoulders if I point them out, but that make me smile and feel happy.

"Did he cook my breakfast?" I ask, perplexed. I've never seen him touch the stove in the house.

"Oh, no. Michael would not be able to boil two eggs. He made Damian and Thomas cook everything on that plate. Luckily, it meant we all had a decent breakfast," Lilly explains as we approach the stairs back to the house. "But now we have to go and change. We'll be going to the venue in a while, and we need to put on something comfortable. Do you have something shorter? Because you might die of a heat stroke all day in the sun."

I look at my long skirt and shirt and realize she's right. Just coming down here to the beach almost made me faint. I could stay at the house instead of going to the concert, but Levi's with Michael, and when he goes on stage, he'll need someone to watch him. Because as much as we all took it a bit like a vacation, we are still here to work.

"It's not like I have anything much different than this," I admit with embarrassment.

The girls smile at me, and Iris takes me by the arm. "Don't worry, we're about the same size. I definitely have something to lend you, and when we go back to New York, we'll go shopping." She winks at me.

Apart from yesterday's outing with Michael, I've never been clothes shopping for myself. Everything I wear comes from my mother and other hand-me-downs from my community.

I'm surprised to notice that Iris and I really are the same size, though I'm a few inches taller, and the jean shorts barely cover more than the suit I wore yesterday. My skinny white legs stick out like a flamingo's. The shirt is a simple white T-shirt with the word 'Jailbirds' in large black letters on the chest. The other girls also wear it and, since they are men's sizes, we knotted them at the waist. When I move, the air conditioning hits the skin on my naked belly. Just a few inches but too much for me. I've never worn anything showing so much skin in public.

Nor have I ever coordinated my outfit with others before. "Is there a particular reason why we're branded with the name of the band like cows in a pasture?" We're all in shorts, sneak-

ers, white T-shirts, and backstage passes around our necks. I have no idea what a backstage is, but I assume I'll find out soon.

The girls laugh.

"I never thought of it that way, but it's more like tagging the ears of cows. It marks the territory, lets everyone know who we're there for and that we only have eyes for them," Emily explains, but I don't understand much.

"If he could," Lilly jokes, "Damian would brand my ass to show ownership."

I really hope the guy doesn't do something that cruel, but I get the impression it's a joke I don't quite grasp.

"He should just scorch the earth around you, the way he looks at other men who dare approach you—as if he wants to rip off their heads with his bare hands," Iris adds.

I smile because I've noticed it too. I've never seen a man so jealous of his woman. Watching them and comparing them with the married couples I know brings home a reality I'd never considered before. Lilly and Damian are happy and they show it: hugging and kissing in public, exchanging explicit looks, all those demonstrations of affection that my community warns couples who are about to get married not to do because it goes against the teachings of modesty.

Seeing the two of them, however, I doubt that my community refrains from this kind of intimacy out of fear of God but rather out of lack of love. I've always heard girls say: "I will learn to love my husband"; never: "I love my husband so much that I can't contain myself even in public." But if God teaches us above all to love, shouldn't we show it like Damian and Lilly do?

***

When we finally arrive near the venue, the crowd is indescribable. From what I understand, the Jailbirds is not the only band playing today. At least a dozen bands will alternate on the stage set up on the beach. It's a charity concert with the proceeds going to a hospital in Los Angeles that treats children with cancer and is involved in preventative research. It's a wonderful cause, and I'm happy to make my small contribution, even if it's just babysitting Levi.

Max, the driver, shows a pass to a guy standing next to a barricade that completely blocks the road. People are walking in the direction of the beach, girls are wearing microscopic and colorful clothes, smiling, laughing, and having fun. Thinking back to the few celebrations in my community…no one ever showed this kind of joy. They usually took place after church in an old converted barn used for gatherings and meetings. Large tables are set up, each family brings food, and it's the only time we ever eat together as a community. We're dressed in our church clothes, and there's no music or chatter, only the pastor's voice raised in prayer before lunch. The younger children whisper, but there's no laughter or yelling or any of the joy that's in the air here.

The moment we manage to get to the road that runs along the beach, I'm amazed at the sight before us. The stage is immense, with tall scaffolding and spotlights moving in sync with the music we now hear rumbling inside our car. There's no one playing at the moment, but the people on the beach are dancing to music I've never heard before, and I can feel the rhythmic pulses way down in my belly. Behind the stage extends a massive pier with a Ferris wheel and other rides I

recognize from pictures Levi showed me.

"That's the Santa Monica Pier," Emily points out with one finger when she realizes I'm looking out the window with my mouth wide open.

"I didn't think it was this impressive. The photos don't do it justice."

"I know, I love coming to these shows. I have fond memories of this place. I got my first kiss on that Ferris wheel." She smiles, and I blush. I wish I had something like this to share, but the more I'm with them the more I realize the number of things I haven't experienced is astronomical. Resentment starts to creep in—not for them, but for a community that has always condemned me for being a curious little girl.

We arrive with difficulty in front of another gate where Max shows the pass again, another guy checks it, talks into a radio around his neck and waits for the answer from a headset pressed against his ear with one hand. He beckons us to enter while someone inside opens the gate. It's my first time ever at an event like this, my first concert, my first live show—other than the church choir—and the butterflies in my stomach have nothing to do with last night's alcohol. I'm excited and surprised to discover I'm not worried about someone scolding me for it—a pleasant feeling I'm not used to yet.

"You'll have to get out here and walk to the others. I can't go any farther," Max says, getting our attention. Immediately we thank him and get out of the car.

Around me, men dressed like the guy at the entrance are wandering around the parking lot setting up for the show as if they owned the place. Their faces are concentrated, sweat covers their foreheads. The heat is stifling, and it can't be easy pushing those heavy crates in these conditions.

My senses are on overload. A general chaos of people wearing the same pass as I am are coming and going, having quick conversations in their earpieces or with others. While the men are dressed casually or in work clothes, the women are a whole different story. Even though they're in shorts and T-shirts like us, most of it looks very expensive, like the clothes I saw at the boutique where Michael took me to buy the swimsuit. The fabrics are sleek, sparkling; some embellished with stones I didn't even know could be sewn on a shirt. Some women wear necklines all the way down to their navels, and I blush at the thought of a slight gust of wind exposing their breasts to everyone. Emily's bikini, which was scandalous enough, covers more than much of what I'm seeing here. These girls' feet are clad in sky-high heeled strappy shoes, with an opening at the top revealing brightly colored toenails. Jewelry, microscopic bags, and cell phones with sparkling cases are practically a uniform.

I keep looking down, embarrassed at so much skin on display without a shred of modesty. When I raise my eyes again, I try to remember that I'm the one discovering the world for the first time, that most people in the world don't live like me.

"Give me your hand, or we'll lose you," Emily laughs, then grabs me by the arm and drags me with her. "If your eyes get any bigger, they'll come out of your sockets!"

I'm in ecstasy staring at all this newness sparkling around me. My head feels light, and a smile breaks out across my face. For the first time in my life, I feel excitement for something that's about to happen, a sense of expectation that makes my heart beat faster, and my mind imagines a thousand dif-

ferent scenarios. I feel part of something bigger than myself, huge compared to what I'm used to, and I realize how lucky I am to be here. Out there is a river of people flocking to see the show, but I'm in here with a tiny percentage of people who are privileged to see it up close.

"Finally, you're here! We thought you were running away with someone else," Damian teases us, approaching Lilly and kissing her passionately.

I look away from their intimacy and find Levi watching them, disgusted. I smile because he's just a kid and doesn't understand that one day he'll want to do those things too—or so they told me; I've never felt the need to kiss a guy in my community. But since living with Michael, I've found myself staring at those lips and having those same impure thoughts several times.

"We needed to change." Emily points to our T-shirts, then turns to their manager. "Evan, we have to talk about merchandising. Seriously, seventy percent of Jailbirds fans are female, and you don't have women's shirts?"

Their manager shrugs. It's the first time I've seen him in a work environment without his elegant suit, although he's wearing linen pants and a white shirt with rolled-up sleeves, not as casual as the others. But it's how he carries himself that makes him elegant.

"I know, but the record label thought it was a waste of money to invest in different types of clothing when girls can 'wear anything they want and still look sexy.' Their words, not mine. It was a losing battle."

Emily turns bright red, the anger on her face almost indescribable. "Sexists, exploiters, misogynists…I don't even

have words to describe them. That has to change. When we're back in New York, I'll make a list of potential suppliers for new merchandise. I have a friend who could help us with the graphics."

"Don't forget Trisha, who's studying to become a fashion designer," Iris adds. "She can give us a hand with the clothing line. Band merchandise doesn't have to look like PE uniforms."

Evan seems impressed by the proposal. "You have my blessing. When we have the merchandising in place, we'll put together a marketing campaign." His face lights up like he's thinking of at least ten brilliant ideas to make it happen. I wonder if that man ever rests.

I'm so immersed in the conversation and confusion around me I don't even notice that Michael has approached us from behind. I stiffen when he leans his chest into my back and wraps his arms around me, pulling me into an embrace. His scent envelops me and inebriates me as the others throw curious glances at us, but no one dares to speak. I'm so caught by surprise I can't move, and stand there like a dead fish. Penelope explained the idea of butterflies in the stomach to me once, but she was wrong: these are eagles, and they're turning my entire digestive system upside down.

"Relax," he whispers in my ear while I struggle to maintain mental clarity. "I see the looks you're getting around here. Sooner or later, someone's going to hit on you. If you want that, I'll leave you alone. But if you don't want to be bothered, let them think you're with me. Do you want me to go away?"

It takes longer than necessary to understand that he asked me a question I have to answer.

"No, stay." I don't know what it means for someone to 'hit on me,' but I know for a fact that I don't want him to leave.

"Well, because otherwise, I would have had to smash some faces. Unless you've become completely uninhibited after last night's hangover and want male company," he teases.

His lips near my ear and the vibrations from his laughter make my skin explode into goosebumps. "Please don't remind me. By the way, thank you for tucking me into bed. I don't think I could have walked upstairs on my own."

"Don't feel embarrassed. You had fun, you did something out of the ordinary for yourself, and you let yourself go. Be proud of that. By the way, we need to talk about my beautiful chest."

I try to extricate myself from his grip and turn around to look him straight in the eye, but he holds me tight in a hug that is not at all unpleasant. "What do you mean? Why do you keep saying that?"

"Not here, honey. We don't talk about certain things in public."

I hear a mocking note in his tone that sets my cheeks on fire. "Please, what is it with your chest? Have I done something?"

"No, why? Would you like to?" This time the teasing in his voice is obvious.

I hate not remembering what happened—it makes me feel vulnerable. "Michael, what did I do?" It comes out almost like a plea.

"Nothing to be ashamed of, I swear to you." His tone is serious, but I have a feeling there's something I *should* feel embarrassed about.

I rest my head on his shoulder and enjoy the sense of calm

being in his arms brings. I begin to understand what people get from the demonstrations of affection I've been denied since I was a child. Michael's physical closeness feels nice. Almost like I'm stronger, protected by the bigness that envelops me, leaving the rest of the world outside.

***

The day passes in a whirlwind of emotions and events that make my head spin. I am dragged from side to side holding Levi's hand, so I don't lose him, but I don't feel much like an adult. We're like two children trying to keep up with their parents. I don't even have time to get frustrated because there's always something new needing my attention.

I always thought the life of a rock star was simple: show up at the venue, get on stage, do the show, get off the stage. The reality is much more chaotic. Interviews, photos with fans, chats with industry insiders, colleagues, and influencers working for brands they're sponsoring who have to be photographed with famous celebrities at major events. Emily explained this to me as I was trying to figure out why an extremely handsome man talking to Damian kept resting his hand on his chest every time someone from the press took a picture. She said he's a Hollywood star who just signed a million-dollar contract with a watch brand, so he has to get photographed wearing one of the pieces worth hundreds of thousands of dollars.

I was so shocked by her explanation I had to ask three times if she was kidding me. Are there really people who do this for work? She explained that it's a very effective way of advertising products, and I stared at her open-mouthed for several seconds before she burst out laughing.

I saw dozens of celebrities walk by who looked as important

and well-dressed as the people in the magazines Emily leafed through on the plane. So beautiful they take your breath away, with their bodyguards a step behind them, but none that I recognized. The girls have named endless TV shows or movies these people are from, but since I was never allowed to watch anything, the names don't ring a bell. Only one guy looked familiar—from a show Levi watches, who's usually squeezed into a dark green costume and walking around the city with a bow and arrow catching bad guys. I must say, in person he's a lot shorter than he looks on TV.

But the best part of the whole day is when the bands start to take the stage. More or less famous groups alternate for several minutes, doing their best to entertain the crowd. What strikes me most are the low, thumping vibrations that go straight to my belly and make me gasp. The rhythm is so infectious my head starts moving up and down following the beat.

"Are you enjoying the shows?" asks Iris, who seems entirely enraptured by her surroundings. Looking at her face, you can see what it means to be happy doing what you love for a living. I've no idea what that's like. For me, it's always been about dedication, commitment, sacrifice. I've never loved my job, but I didn't think a job was supposed to be loved. I chose this path because it was a way out of the community, one that my father reluctantly accepted, and, in hindsight, an excuse to delay my marriage with Jacob.

"Yes. It overwhelms you almost on a physical level. I love the energy it exudes."

She smiles at me. "Just wait until you hear the Jailbirds..." She winks at me but doesn't add anything else.

Ten minutes later, it's their turn: the final act in a full day of

shows. When the two hosts leave the stage after announcing the amount of money raised and congratulating the audience for its generosity, the lights go down and the roar that rises from the crowd makes my stomach tremble.

We're right in front of the stage, a few feet from the band, along with the security team that keeps an eye on the people who push, scream and jump behind us. I turn to the girls, and their faces are baked by the sun and tired, but wearing the same expression of ecstasy that can only be described as bliss.

The first to take the stage is Thomas, followed by Simon. The clamor is crazy, but when Michael goes on, the volume rises even more. When Damian makes his entrance, the roar is so deafening it reaches the sky.

At the first note, the audience goes crazy, begins to jump and shout even louder, becoming an animal that roars behind me, entering my belly, tearing my bowels in the grip of excitement, fear, and adrenaline as Michael starts playing, running from one side of the stage to the other.

He is a force of nature, a concentration of skill, sensuality, and erotic charge I've learned to recognize. For most of my life, I've been unaware of the sexual dynamics between men and women. Of course, I studied it, I'm a nurse, but I never fully understood the attraction until I met the Jailbirds. They exude sensuality, eroticism, maybe some sort of invisible testosterone wave that draws women in without letting them escape. But it is Michael who attracts every cell in my body like a magnet.

Every small surface of my skin is hit with electric shocks, even below my belly, where everything should be still. Instead, Michael awakens sleeping synapses there and makes

them pulsate with bolts of pleasure I didn't know I could feel. When he approaches the corner where we're standing, I see him search for us in the VIP group with backstage passes, and when he sees me, he smiles mischievously and winks at me.

The moment is charged with all the tension that's been building throughout the day. I've remained still and composed like a good girl, in spite of how energetic the music and bands have been, but I can't hold back any longer. This is the straw that breaks the camel's back. I feel the shout going up my throat and let out a scream like the thousands of people around me and begin jumping to the rhythm of the music.

Michael bursts into laughter, and out of the corner of my eye, I see Emily, Lilly, Iris, Evan, and Levi do the same. I don't even care. For the first time in my life, I feel free to express my excitement without being scolded and it's such a liberating sensation it makes me light-headed. If my sisters saw me now, they'd think I was crazy and help my father lock me up in the basement as punishment. I spent the whole day holding back a desire to dance so strongly that it made my legs quiver, but with the Jailbirds, it's useless to try to stop. They are passion, freedom, life that I am savoring, and I like how it feels so much I'm not going to let guilt ruin them.

***

I open the door of the house to let Michael in with Levi asleep in his arms. It's almost one o'clock in the morning, and after such a tiring day, he collapsed during the car ride. The others are still out partying, but Michael and I came home right after the mandatory interviews. I told Michael he should stay out with his friends, that I would take care of putting Levi to bed, but his response was that when he took responsibility

for the boy, he knew he would have to make some adjustments to his life. Which made me smile because even though he still gets mad when his friends call him daddy, he's actually behaving exactly as a father should.

"Do you want to eat something after I tuck him into bed?" he whispers before climbing the stairs.

"There are leftovers from this morning's breakfast. I can make a couple of sandwiches," I suggest.

When he comes back to the kitchen, I've fixed the two sandwiches and put them on a plate. He grabs it and gestures for me to follow him. He heads towards a section of the deck out of the kitchen's light and makes me lie on an oversized deck chair overlooking the sea. He lies next to me and puts an arm around my neck, resting the plate on his legs. I feel the warmth of his body through his clothes, and the spot where our skin touches seems to ignite. He's so close I can smell the soap he used to shower right after the concert. I look at his profile in the dim light. I didn't think a man's neck could be so sexy. His face is relaxed, with barely a hint of a smile curving his lips. I want to reach over and caress his cheek, but the mere thought is so indecent it makes my heart jump in my throat. I squeeze my hands tightly in my lap to make sure I don't do anything rash.

"Relax, I'm not making a move on you. It's just that it's going to be cold out here in a while, especially if you've been in the sun all day and got a little sunburned."

"I'm not used to being in such close contact with a man," I candidly confess. I'm tired of always being careful about what I say for fear that people will think I'm crazy. Michael doesn't judge me for my past.

"I gathered that, you know?" he jokes as he grabs the sand-

wich with one hand and lightly tickles my arm. He's relaxed and completely comfortable in this deck chair and I wonder how many women he's stroked like this after making love to them.

"I enjoyed today's concert. Seeing you on stage stirs up emotions I didn't think I could feel."

Michael chuckles and I feel his body vibrate next to mine. "I saw you screaming like a madwoman when I winked at you."

"Don't make fun of me." I jokingly nudge him. "It was liberating. I'd never done anything like that before."

"I know, kiddo, everybody knew that. You're beautiful when you lose control and let go. It was an adrenaline rush for me to see you like that too." The last words come out as a whisper as he gently kisses my hair.

My cheeks burn and the eagles in my stomach take flight, throwing my insides into turmoil. I'm so agitated my arms go stiff, like two trunks resting on my belly. Michael stretches to the side to put the plate on the ground, then grabs my hand and places it on his belly, trapping it with his.

"You won't die if you touch me. You know that, right?"

Easy for him to say. Does he not feel my heart exploding in my chest? "Do you ask every woman to touch you like this?"

His chest and belly vibrate with laughter, tickling my fingers. "No, not in such a nonsexual way. No."

"Michael!"

He pulls me closer, and when I raise my head to look into his eyes, he places his lips on my forehead with a kiss so light I'd swear I'd dreamed it if I wasn't seeing it with my own two eyes.

"Don't worry, Faith. I'm not trying to corrupt you. I just

want to enjoy the sound of the sea and some peace here with you. You realize you were at your first concert today, don't you? That you jumped, danced, screamed. When was the last time you felt so free?"

"Never." My voice comes out in a whisper. I'm so nervous.

"See? This is something we should celebrate. It's your own little victory."

"Why do you care so much about making me try new things? It's almost like you enjoy making me live in sin."

Michael looks down and studies me for a few moments. "Because these are not sins, Faith. It's called life, and you're too smart to spend it locked in a box."

His expression is intense and I'm confused by it. It's not defiance, or reproach or mockery. For a moment, it feels like his face is slowly moving closer, but then he closes his eyes, wraps both arms around my body, and draws me in, closing any distance between us. My torso is glued to his, and when I rest my head on his chest, I feel his heart pound furiously against my ear.

I allow myself to relax on him, lulled by his breathing that becomes longer and more regular, letting the darkness hide my blushing cheeks. Today was full of many firsts, including being embraced by a man who will never be my husband. I'll worry about this sin tomorrow, along with all the others I've committed today. Wrapped in his scent, I close my eyes and listen to the sound of the sea.

CHAPTER 13

Michael

"Can I come to the studio with you? Can I see how you record an album?"

Levi has been pestering me with these questions since this morning when I told him that he and Faith could join me at the record company. The truth is I need them with me. I've gotten so used to having them around, it's hard to walk out the door in the morning and let them live the day without me. I like to go home and hear Levi's stories, but I like it better when we do things together, and he asks me to explain things to him. He's a smart kid who wants to learn. He reminds me of myself as a young boy, before my grandfather died and left me in the hands of my rotten parents.

"Evan, can Levi come into the studio with us?" I ask him as we enter.

Our manager studies him for a few seconds with a serious face, but I already know what his response will be. I'm grateful my friends let this kid into their hearts.

"Can you operate a mixer?"

"No." Levi is a little perplexed, almost intimidated by the question.

"Then come in, we'll show you how." Evan smiles and winks at him, beckoning to follow him.

Levi lights up and trots behind him. "Really?"

"Of course, I never joke about these things."

"Yeah, but am I too young?"

Evan casts a tender glance at him as they take the hall leading to the recording studio. I glance towards the conference room and find Damian, Simon, and Thomas watching us amused.

"If you're old enough to be punished as an adult, you're also old enough to use a mixer." I hear Evan's answer fading out as they lock themselves in the studio, and Levi's nonstop questions start in again.

"He should be at home doing his homework. You know he's behind the other kids his age," Faith cautions. She didn't agree to this day off from the beginning. Faith and her sense of duty. We've got a long road ahead of us, but I swear I'm going to make her enjoy her life. I grab her shoulders and make her look at me.

"He missed years of school. One day won't make a difference. And today he *will* learn something—how to make music. Remember? That saved our lives."

She doesn't seem particularly convinced but says nothing. It isn't in her nature to make a scene like a stubborn child. I kiss her on the forehead and smile when I see her blush and look down.

"Go up to the top floor. Emily and Iris are there working today. They'd love for you to keep them company," Thomas suggests with a smile.

Faith looks at me as if asking permission. I hate how this girl was raised to not make a single decision on her own. Does she really think she needs my blessing to take that damn ele-

vator and go chat with the girls?

"What if Levi needs me?" Her voice is undecided, her sense of duty outweighing the desire to spend time with people she enjoys. Friends might be too strong a word yet, but certainly they're people she seems to like being around.

"There are six adults with him; I think we can get by. Don't make me play the boss card and force you to take the day off."

She smiles and nods. "Just don't fire me."

"I'd be lost without you, and you know it."

I watch her take the elevator to the top floor of the house where Iris's apartment is located. Or at least the one where she insists on keeping her clothes—she actually lives at Thomas's place since leaving the apartment she was renting before they met.

"Can I talk to you privately?" Simon's voice calls me back to reality, and when I turn to face him I'm met with an expression so grim my smile instantly fades. I glance at Damian and Thomas, but they shrug their shoulders. I follow Simon, who is already outside the door, and join him on the bench in the corner of the garden.

"Do you want to tell me what the hell you're doing?" he asks evenly, as though trying to contain himself.

"Can you be more specific? I do a lot of bullshit."

"With Faith. What the hell are you doing with her?"

"She works for me. Have you missed the fact that I pay her?"

"And do you always put your hands on your employees?"

The turn this little talk has taken annoys me. "If by *putting my hands on her* you mean being friendly towards her with the occasional platonic touch, yes. I do."

"You just gave her a kiss on the forehead. Last week at the concert in Los Angeles, you were hugging her and whispering sweet nothings in her ear. Don't try and bullshit me, please."

Sticking his nose in my business and judging my behavior annoys the hell out of me. "Did you see how all those guys looked at her? They were devouring her with their eyes and would've hit on her all night if I didn't mark my territory. And you know what I said in her ear? I explained why I was hugging her the same way I'm explaining it to you. I wasn't being coy, I know she's not like other girls—she needs that kind of thing explained to her. She's smart but very naïve when it comes to people. Stop preaching to me when you don't even have all the facts."

"It's obvious how she looks at you, Michael. She has the dreamy eyes of a woman in love. Don't give in to the temptation to fuck her just because she has two beautiful legs. You'll ruin her."

Anger rises in my stomach. As if I'm some kind of animal. Sure, I'm usually one to fuck a girl and not look back, but they're all consenting. I don't force anyone, I don't deceive, and most importantly, I have no intention of slipping into Faith's panties and then breaking her heart. I didn't suddenly become a monster.

"Do you know why my mother married my father?"

Simon frowns, not understanding where I'm going with this. He shakes his head but says nothing.

"When my mother was sixteen and my father thirty, their parents met and arranged the marriage. My father had already been married, but his first wife had died during childbirth along with the baby. No one bothered to mention at the funeral, in

a church before God, that the baby was born prematurely at seven months because my father beat the poor woman so violently he almost killed her. Technically, she died in childbirth."

Simon looks at me without speaking, but I see the sorrow in his eyes.

"Anyway, my father goes to church, makes a good confession, is absolved of all his sins. Meanwhile, his parents discover a poor man in debt up to his neck with their family, and they force him to give his daughter in marriage to cancel the debts. So in fifteen days, they organize a nice wedding. Invite lots of guests, get the church set up for the celebration, the priest congratulates the new couple, and my father rapes my mother on their wedding night, stealing her virginity and innocence. During the day, he sends her to do the cleaning at the brothel—sorry, motel—he manages."

Simon looks down, unable to continue the conversation, but I don't care. I lived for fifteen long years with those monsters; he can survive ten minutes.

"A month later, after thirty days of continuous assaults on a girl who was barely more than a child, my mother discovers she's pregnant. Nine months later, a daughter is born. My father goes on a rampage because women are useless, but he can't kill her because everyone has now congratulated the newlyweds for this blessed pregnancy. So my father continues to do what he always did: abuse my mother until she becomes pregnant again, four months after giving birth. Second female, a second baptism, and my father's fury continues until he gets her pregnant again. Finally, six months later, she becomes pregnant for the third time, and, thank God, a boy is born. Michael, one of the archangels, one of the most powerful angels

in heaven. That's why I never wanted to change my first name. I want my father to remember every day that I will never accept the path he chose for me."

Simon stares at me in silence for a moment, and the compassion in his gaze turns the lump in my throat to a boulder. "Is this why you have nightmares?" he asks me finally.

I raise my shoulders but do not answer his question. Many things have triggered the endless nights of terror and tears. My family, prison, the violence that has always surrounded me. If you add them all up, they're traumatizing. Too much to contain.

"My father always hid behind priests and confessions to do the most disgusting things. My sisters had barely developed breasts when my father locked them both in brothel rooms and forced them to make a living. When I was twelve, he decided I needed to become a man, so he locked me up for a night with one of the girls who worked for him—thank God at least he didn't put me with one of my sisters. And do you know what my mother did? She cried and punished herself for everything."

I inhale deeply and get up from the bench, too agitated to sit, and notice Simon swallow with difficulty.

"If you ask me if I know anything about relationships between men and women, I'll admit—I know nothing. The only healthy relationships I've seen in my life are Damian's and Thomas's. But if you ask me about Faith…I believe that girl has every right to make her own decisions. She grew up in a community where they decided everything from birth, preventing her from making the most basic choices. Does she want to marry the man her father found for her? She's free to

do so, but only if it's her choice. Does she want to eat chocolate? She's welcome to it if she likes it. Does she want to get drunk during a night out with her friends? I'll be there to keep her hair out of her face while she vomits as many times as she wants me to, because if that's what she wants, she should do it without asking permission from anyone.

"I want Faith to have the chance at a life my mother and sisters never had. I want her to be a strong woman who doesn't need a man to survive. I want her to be able to make all her own decisions by evaluating what is best for her, not based on what others expect of her."

I turn away without waiting for my friend to say something and, before returning to the studio, I leave through the gate and go grab a coffee. I need to recover after pouring out to Simon what I've been keeping inside all these years. I don't know if it was God, fate, or chance that put Faith in my path, but I was given a second chance to save someone from a life I know all too well.

On one thing Simon is wrong about: Faith has the most beautiful legs in the world, but they're not what I want most from her. I want her smiles, her carefree screams, her happiness. I want her to have the life she's been denied, and I want to see her grab it with all her might.

***

"Guess what? Evan and the sound engineer, Greg, taught me how to mix audio tracks!"

Levi is thrilled as he enters the house and jumps on the sofa, bouncing with his knees on the pillows. One minute he's conversing like an adult and the next he's jumping on the bed until he touches the ceiling.

"Really? They let you do it?" I ask, putting down the pizza we bought coming home. Faith grabs plates and cutlery, and I smile—she'll never get used to eating pizza with her hands right out of the box. I take them from her and put them back in the cupboard, and she grumbles but says nothing.

"Yes. I mixed Simon's track for the song you did today. The one about sex," he explains wide-eyed and full of excitement.

I glance at Faith, who gives me a disappointed look. I agree with her that there's far too much explicit language in our music for a kid, but he has been in prison, after all; he's experienced much worse things than a song where we talk about having sex.

"All their songs are about sex," she mumbles. I smile, amused.

"It's 'Swing,' the one where she sleeps with two men." Levi's explanation is so straightforward I don't immediately register his words, but Faith's face is priceless. She's horrified, to say the least, and throws me a disgusted look.

"Does it really say those things?" she asks, and I struggle to hold back a laugh.

Levi chuckles, amused. He is less naïve at fourteen than she is at twenty-four.

"What did you think we meant when the chorus says: *She smiles choosing both, rocking in pleasure like a swing*?"

"I thought…I thought…but at the same time?" she asks, scandalized.

Levi is now cracking up.

I try to keep a straight face while explaining it to her scientifically. "Yes, at the same time. You can sleep with two or more women or two or more men. The woman, as this song

says, can be penetrated by two penises at the same time." I know I shouldn't be so outspoken in front of the kid, but better to talk openly about sex than drugs or prison.

The resulting silence is so absolute that time seems to stop as I watch her face trying to process what I've said. Then she frowns, red as a tomato. "But how?" Clearly, she's struggling to understand the dynamics of the act. I should seriously start making her watch some porn.

"Vagina and anus, or vagina and mouth, or anus and mouth. There are lots of ways to penetrate a woman's body at the same time during the sexual act." It's now becoming impossible to hold back a laugh.

"Michael!" She shouts while Levi laughs. That kid *really* knows a lot more than she does.

"Relax and eat. You and I will have to have a little talk about the birds and the bees." I nudge her chair because she's so shocked she doesn't move a muscle.

She sits quietly and bites into a piece of pizza, trying to hide her embarrassment with a lowered gaze. Levi sits next to her and looks at her, smiling, genuinely amused by her lack of knowledge.

I take her chin gently and raise her head so she looks me straight in the eye. "There's nothing to be ashamed of. If they're all consenting adults in the bedroom, people can do what they want. If a girl is comfortable with three men at once, she should be able to do it without feeling ashamed because she's doing nothing wrong. It's only wrong when a person is forced to do what they don't want. Sex becomes violence and rape when one of the parties is not consenting and the other forces the act. But if a woman or a man wants to enjoy one or more people, they're free to do so. We need to stop sticking our noses into other people's bedrooms, judging, and start minding our own business."

"And what does everyone think of all this freedom? It goes against what they teach us in church."

"For one thing, not everyone is religious or believes in the same God as yours, so that's not a problem. Second, what you are taught in the church is to be submissive to your husband and his decisions; it's not exactly at the top of the list of teachings."

Faith seems upset. "And what about procreation? Sex is just for this purpose, and there's only one…um…,"

"You can say *hole*—it's a normal word." I poke fun at her inability to be specific.

"Okay, hole. Only one of those you listed actually conceives children, and it's a sin to use…the others," she concludes indignantly.

"Faith, sex is also for pleasure, and I can guarantee you that not everyone wants children. When you understand that your body can give you pleasure, and it's not just a machine to churn out babies, then you'll realize that certain songs are not so obscene."

"So what do people who don't want children do? You're expected to have them at some point in life. It's the natural consequence of being in a relationship."

"It's stupid to base your choices on others' expectations. It's you that has to live with the consequences of your choices. You should decide what's best for you, not for others."

She gets quiet, not even chewing on her pizza. She knows I'm talking about her father and that I don't like what he im-

poses on her.

"Sometimes, you almost sound wise." Levi breaks the silence, lightening the atmosphere, and I grin at him.

"I *am* wise. And you start eating because I want to teach you how to do something."

"A new song on the guitar?"

"No, something different. Something that helps you stay focused."

"That sounds like a lot to learn." He looks suspicious, his initial enthusiasm quickly fading.

I laugh, amused. "I'm the one who let you skip school here. Give me a little more credit."

"So what is it?"

"I'm going to teach you how to carve wood."

Levi looks at me, frowning for a few seconds, but then his face opens in an enthusiastic smile.

"Cool!"

"You want to give a knife to a kid? He could get hurt," says Faith, all talk of sex gone now.

"He's fourteen, not five!" I answer exasperatedly. Is there *anything* she's allowed to do?

Levi laughs like a madman as he snatches another piece of pizza. "You two look like a grumpy old couple."

I wink at him as I bite into a slice of pizza under Faith's scrutinizing eye. We really are a weird mix of roommates.

***

Teaching Levi how to carve wood makes me nervous. My grandfather taught me when he saw all that energy boiling inside me and no place to channel it. I hated sitting still and doing my homework, so one day he put a piece of wood and a knife in front of me and began teaching me how to create shapes, first simple, then more and more complex. It gave me a purpose to sit for hours focused on something I liked, and this helped me learn to focus on what I didn't like to do.

"My fish sucks," Levi complains after hours spent working on the piece I gave him.

"It's your first attempt. It's good!" I tell him as I carve the scales on mine.

"It's tailless!" He gives me the side-eye.

"You'll see, your next one will be better. But first, finish that, use it to learn how to carve the details. Learn to ease up on the force of your knife, so next time you won't cut off the fins."

Levi gives me another side-eye, but in the end he does what I tell him. I like his attitude, he doesn't give up at the first difficulty. A lot of kids his age would just give up as soon as the tail came off. Levi frowned, got angry, cursed, but continued, first looking for a way to reattach the piece, then focusing on something else.

"Who taught you how to carve?" Faith wants to know while she is embroidering intricate designs on a handkerchief with a needle and thread. We look like we've come straight out of the nineteenth century. If my friends saw us now, the teasing would never end.

"My grandfather on my mother's side." I look up and find her huddled in the armchair, studying me with interest.

"Were you close to him?"

I inhale deeply and place the almost finished wooden fish on my knees. "He was the only one who protected me somewhat from my family. Yes, I was very close to him."

Out of the corner of my eye, I see Levi resting his hands on his lap and looking up at me.

"Why did you need to be protected from your family?" he asks with the naivety of his fourteen years.

"My father is a criminal, and my mother helps him. My grandfather tried to keep me away from that environment or, at the very least, to make me study and do something better with my life so that growing up, I'd have other choices than following in my father's footsteps."

"But you ended up in prison anyway," he points out, and I see Faith's forehead wrinkle in sadness.

"My grandfather died when I was a little younger than you, and my father forced me to rob rich people's homes when I no longer had someone to defend me." It costs me a lot to admit this.

"Is that why you're teaching me how to carve wood? To keep me from going to prison again?" asks Levi with a mixture of hope and fear in his voice.

I know how he feels. As if he's broken, as if somehow he'll make mistakes again and end up in prison. Because that's what they made him believe: that he was a rotten apple, someone who can't become a good person. They did it with me, with Thomas, Damian, Simon, and with hundreds of kids locked up in there. It's hard to believe in yourself when everyone tells you you're worth nothing.

"I'm teaching you how to carve wood because it helps your concentration. It teaches you to focus on something and not to be distracted by your surroundings. You'll never end up in jail again because you're a good kid. You made a mistake once and learned from it. I'm sure you won't do it again because you're smart and have a heart of gold. That's why you won't end up in prison, not because you're learning to carve wood."

Levi lifts the corners of his mouth in a half-smile but keeps his gaze fixed on the piece of wood he's torturing. I reach out my arm and pull him in for a side hug and, after tensing up at first, he reciprocates with a firm grip around my waist.

"You're a good guy, Levi. Never forget it," I whisper before kissing the top of his blonde hair. How I wish I could inject him with the self-confidence they took from him when they stole his innocence.

I look up at Faith and find her staring at me silently, her eyes shining and full of affection. She doesn't express her feelings aloud, but a glance at her is enough to see all the affection she can pour on a person.

***

"I feel like I'm living with a newborn, not a fourteen-year-old kid." I sit down next to Faith on the couch, exhausted after spending the last two hours in Levi's room trying to help him fall asleep without nightmares.

"What does the psychologist say?"

"To keep doing what I'm doing, that he needs time to process what's happening. Sooner or later, the nightmares will disappear, I'm sure. I just feel so helpless, and it's exhausting." I had to sleep next to Simon when we were teenagers because my nightmares wouldn't leave me alone. Now I understand what he must have gone through, and I can't thank him enough for being with me every night.

"I wish I could help, take your place for a few nights, but you've seen how it's not the same when I'm there." Faith seems as frustrated and helpless as me.

"I know, don't worry. He feels safest with me because I've been there too."

Faith looks down. I realize our situation is so far from the norm it's difficult to find a way to help us, even for her.

"I'm sorry if I embarrassed you talking about sex," I say, breaking the silence.

She blushes and smiles. "You don't have to apologize. It's me who's just clueless sometimes. I feel stupid because here I'm, a nurse, having studied the human body, and know how the sexual act works, technically, from textbooks, but I don't know how to have sex. I don't know all the nuances there are in a relationship. It's inconceivable for me to think that a woman can have more than one partner during her lifetime; and even if she becomes a widow, I don't see the point of remarrying. And then you tell me there are women who have two men together in the same bed. It's…" She leaves the thought hanging for a moment, searching for words. "I mean, you can't conceive children if you put it in…in the mouth or…behind. What's the point?"

Her face is completely flushed, and I feel a rush of tenderness to see her struggling. Struggling against her instincts, utterly unaware that they are entirely natural drives. Even talking about it is torture for her.

"For pure pleasure."

She wrinkles her forehead. "So, it's pleasurable to slip it in…behind?"

I burst out laughing. "In certain circumstances, yes. Trust me."

She shakes her head smiling. She doesn't seem wildly convinced by my statement.

"How can you not know these things? You're a nurse; you went to college. You must have had contact with other people, with fellow students."

She shakes her head and lowers her gaze. "No. I went to college online. My father would never let me study away from home. I consulted sometimes with the doctor in our community—he explained things to me when I didn't understand them. He's the one who pushed me to practice outside the community, in a larger facility. I needed internship hours to be qualified as a nurse. But my father would only allow me to work in a prison, nowhere else. He didn't want me working in a hospital with other doctors and nurses and far too many patients for him to keep track of. He found that juvie job for me, through the nun of the boarding school where I lived. It was in the middle of nowhere, and I was under the supervision of the Mother Superior."

"Have you called him again since that time when I was with you?" I never see her picking up her phone to call him. I never see her on the phone at all, honestly.

"No. I've been avoiding it for weeks. I told him I had to pick up Sunday shifts. He told me to quit and come home."

"Does he have your cell number?"

She widens her eyes, horrified. "No! If he knew I had a cell phone, he'd come and get me himself...if he knew where I was, that is. I never told him I left the boarding school."

"I'm not going to find the police at my door one day, will I? I mean...won't he go to the police to report your disappearance?"

She smiles at me. "There's no police in our community, no firefighters either. We make do. Plus, I keep sending my

paycheck home. Penelope sends it every month so he doesn't suspect the change of address."

I look at her, confused "You send your paycheck home? An actual check? What era do you live in? First, there's digital transfers, and secondly, the money's yours. You shouldn't send it to your father."

"Not the whole amount. Just what's left over after living expenses. Or at least, until I came to work for you. My salary is significantly higher now, but I always send him the same amount, so he doesn't get suspicious," she hurries to explain.

"This is crazy—I feel like I'm living in another dimension, I swear. Can't you just transfer the money to him without going through Penelope?"

She looks down, ashamed. "No one in my community has a bank account. It's considered the devil's trap. They cash their checks once every two or three months when they go to the city to buy what the community can't produce."

"You're kidding, right?" I'm beyond shocked.

She shakes her head and smiles. "No, my father doesn't know I have a bank account. The prison would never give me a check, but Penelope helped me out by sending one to my father and one to the Mother Superior for the room."

"And here I thought those dystopian movies were just make believe," I laugh, but she frowns and gives me a confused look. I need to add some current films to my list of things to show her.

"What else did you never do before leaving that community?" On the one hand, I'm fascinated by how these people live. On the other hand, it makes me angry. How do you raise your

children like that? How many kids are there who have never seen the world?

"I don't know. So many things, I suppose. I'd never been to a mall or a movie theater, and I'd never had coffee in those huge cups with whipped cream on top."

"You've never been kissed, have you?"

I see her blush as I turn on the couch towards her. "I suppose that will happen after my marriage."

I smile and watch her. "What if you don't like it? What if you don't like the husband your father chose for you? When you got drunk, you said some things... Let's just say you got very honest."

I see her stiffen and widen her eyes.

"Calm down, nothing outrageous, but you said you dream of kissing me."

Her hands fly to her face in shame. I reach out and force her to remove them to look me in the eye. "There's nothing wrong with that, Faith. You're attracted to me, so it's normal to have certain fantasies. It's not the end of the world."

She doesn't say anything, but I can tell she's nervous.

"How does it happen, in your dreams? Do you take the initiative, or do I?"

For a moment, I think she won't respond, that she'll get up and run to her room, but then she bites her lip to hold back a smile, as though reliving the fantasy in her head. "You."

"Is it a friendly peck on the lips or more passionate—with the tongue, maybe? Have you ever seen someone kissing with their tongue?"

This time she lets the smile break open. "I've been around Damian and Lilly, and Thomas and Iris, remember? It's im-

possible *not* to see a kiss with tongue." She laughs.

"True, theirs is more like a scene from a porno than a display of affection. But kissing doesn't have to be like that. You can go slowly…or was it like that in your fantasies?" I raise an eyebrow and tease her a little.

She smiles and shakes her head. "A little less…passionate, but with tongue," she whispers slowly, embarrassed but determined to keep the conversation going.

"And would you like to try it?" I venture.

She widens her eyes, straightening her back. "We're not a couple. You don't do certain things if you're not a couple."

I roll my eyes. "Would you like to do it? Don't think about what you should or shouldn't do. What do you *want* to do? What does your gut tell you? I'm here in front of you. If I kissed you now, would it make you happy or not?"

"Without thinking about what I should or shouldn't do? Yes, I'd like to. I like it in my dreams."

"So, do you want to try?"

She hesitates. "I don't..."

"What does your gut tell you?" I insist, without letting her dwell too much on her insecurities.

She nods at me, and that's all I need to scoot closer to her. I put my hand behind her neck and draw her towards me until my lips touch hers. I see her eyes close, and I, too, let myself be carried away by the moment. But she's as stiff as a corpse. I hear her inhale quickly and then hold her breath.

I barely run my tongue over her lower lip, though, and she gives a little. She slowly opens her mouth for me, and with a slowness I've never experienced, I savor the sweet taste of her tongue. It's a clumsy kiss, but the slight groan that escapes her

throat tells me it's just inexperience, not disgust. I take all the time I need to make her first kiss worth remembering.

And it tastes like the first time for me too. I know I won't take her to bed, that after this there will be no follow-up, not even a quick grope, but I feel in my gut the importance of what I'm doing. I'm giving her the memory and feeling of her first kiss, something I've never given to anyone, and I want it to be perfect. I want her to smile every time she remembers this moment, every time someone asks her: "Do you remember your first kiss?" And I want to never forget the sweet taste of vanilla and the softness of those lips that almost make me lose control.

When I pull away from her slightly, her eyes are closed and her lips ready for another kiss, but I don't do it. I watch her hold her breath and, when I touch her lower lip with my fingertip, open those blue eyes that for a moment seem dreamy. When she focuses on me, she blushes violently and pulls back, slipping from my hands.

"Was it what you expected?"

She nods vigorously, biting her lips, never looking up at mine. I approach her again, and this time she doesn't stiffen like before. "Goodnight, Faith," I whisper in her ear before kissing her on the cheek.

I walk away without turning around, closing the door of my room behind me. I lean against it and take a deep breath. An erection that almost hurts presses into my pants.

"What the hell am I doing?" I whisper to myself, licking my lips and enjoying the taste of a woman I shouldn't be attracted to for a million good reasons. Simon's words to not to ruin her, not take her to bed echo in my chest like the voice of a conscience I want to silence. While I know for a fact I have

no intention of slipping between her legs, I've crossed a dangerous line tonight.

CHAPTER 14
Faith

I toss and turn in bed for the umpteenth time and watch the minutes of the alarm clock on the bedside table change slowly. Two thirty-four in the morning, an hour and a half after going to bed, and no hope of falling asleep. I'm so shaken by Michael's kiss my stomach is upside down. He kissed me! And I let him do it—that's what has me the most shook up.

I knelt by my bed at least ten times intending to ask forgiveness for what I did, but no words came. There are images of that kiss in my head, butterflies in my stomach, the memory of his delicate tongue on mine, but no sense of guilt anywhere. How many prayers do I have to say to make up for this sin? Ten, fifty, one hundred? How many times do I have to apologize to God for kissing a man who's not my husband? And the real question: how long do I have to kneel in prayer if I don't feel any guilt for what I've done?

My father may know all the answers to these questions, but a part of me doesn't even want to think about asking him because it would ruin the sweetness of the moment by making it dirty and indecent. I want my memory of my first kiss to be exciting, something that makes me feel alive, not guilty or ashamed.

Michael is a good kisser, or at least, I think he is. I have no

one to compare him to, but it was delightful. The eagles in my stomach almost made me gasp out loud with all that flapping and somersaulting. On the outside, though, I was as still as a stone, not knowing what to do with myself. His hand behind my neck guided my head towards his, but otherwise, I might as well have been in a full-body cast.

What an embarrassment! I wish I could have a second chance at participating in something I enjoyed at least as much as savoring chocolate. Michael and his sins, me and my first times. He's the one who convinced me to eat my first piece of chocolate, which led to eating Chinese, then pizza, and now my first kiss. First times I'll never forget, but I'm afraid I'll regret them when I have to go back.

Tossing and turning in bed makes no sense—I won't be able to keep my eyes open tomorrow—so I get up to go and make some chamomile tea. That usually helps me calm down. Stepping into the kitchen, I'm surprised to see the fridge light on and the door open with Michael bending in front of it. The rest of the room is entirely dark; only the street light through the windows outlines the shapes in the room and Michael in particular. His bare back, the silhouette of tight boxers that emphasize his toned rear and long muscular legs.

He hasn't noticed my presence, I could turn around and go back to bed, but I can't. I'm glued to the shape of his body that's awakening every single cell in mine.

When he straightens and closes the fridge, he jumps and puts one hand on his chest. "Holy Christ, you look like a serial killer over there in the dark."

"Sorry, I didn't mean to scare you."

"What are you doing out here? Do you need something?"

"I wanted to make myself some chamomile tea."

He gestures for me to come in. I grab a pot, fill it with water, and put it on the stove. He taught me to use the microwave, which is far more convenient, but I like the ritual of the old-fashioned way that seems to have gotten lost in the rush of city life. Plus, waiting for it to boil means I can stand near him a little longer, and that's not a bad feeling at all.

"So you know how to prepare yourself a meal!" I joke when I see him spread peanut butter and jelly on some bread.

Michael smiles and gives me a side glance. "I know how to assemble ingredients into something edible. Preparing a meal is a whole other story."

I grab a teaspoon from the drawer and hand it to him. "Use this for the jam. If you use the knife you used for the peanut butter, it gets in the jam jar," I explain, and he smiles, putting the knife in his mouth and licking away the sticky, salty layer—a gesture I've seen my brothers do thousands of times, but never seen it look so sensual.

When he's finished making his sandwich, he turns to me and folds his arms across his chest, making his biceps stand out, which I notice much more than I should, but he doesn't make any jokes. He looks intrigued.

"I'm sorry if I forced you to kiss me earlier. I didn't think you'd go to your room to punish yourself for that. I should have thought it through before doing it, but I'm not exactly famous for my ability to think ahead." He seems ashamed, sincerely sorry for making me do something I actually wanted too.

"You didn't push me into anything I didn't want. I was aware of what was going on, and I don't regret it. And honest-

ly, I didn't punish myself when I went to sleep. I couldn't feel that sense of guilt that usually pushes me to overcome the pain and accept suffering."

The corner of his mouth rises in a satisfied smile. "Did you like it?"

"Yes, even if I wasn't entirely participating. I was a little tense."

His smile widens more, and he nods. "Would you like to try again and see if it's better?"

His proposal takes me by surprise. I haven't thought of anything but that kiss all night. I'm dying for a chance to try it again. No guilt is big enough to overcome the feeling his lips bring me.

"Can you teach me how to do it?" I find myself asking in a trembling voice. As much as I want this second kiss, the anticipation of it awakens the even more restless eagles in my stomach.

Michael puts a hand on my waist and draws me towards him, making me lean on his chest. My arms turn as stiff as two boards. He takes one, then the other, and brings my hands behind his neck. With my fingertips, I caress his warm skin and soft hair.

"Let's start with something simple. We'll put our hands in safe areas and avoid the embarrassment of groping. Sound good?" He winks and smiles at me.

I nod as I get lost in his intense eyes.

"You can put your hands in my hair," he whispers in my ear, covering my jaw with light kisses that make me close my eyes and sigh. "Men like it when you play with our hair. It's even more sexy if you grab a handful in your fist and pull lightly,"

he explains softly as he slips a hand into my hair and demonstrates.

The shiver that runs from my neck to my lower belly makes me almost faint. I didn't think you could experience physical pleasure by pulling a person's hair. I try it on him and hear him utter a small guttural noise reminiscent of an animal: wild and dangerous.

With his free hand, he grabs me by the waist, and with the other in my hair, he draws me to himself, sinking his tongue between my lips in a much less controlled way than before. An explosion of pleasure pours into my stomach, making me groan. That sound seems to ignite him. I press myself against his body, my hands clinging to his hair. My tongue responds to his, caressing it and savoring the salty taste of peanut butter that tickles my senses.

The pressure of his hand on my back is warm and possessive, becoming one with the light fabric of my nightgown. My breasts pressed against his chest give me a shiver of pleasure that jolts me, and I feel like a shaken can of soda ready to explode. Never in my life have I experienced something like this. Never in my life have I let my body take over, and instinct leads me to reciprocate a kiss with every fiber of my body. One hand stays in his hair and the other frantically looks for his skin, his shoulders, his arms, that face so perfect it almost hurts. His beard tickles my fingertips, the veins of his neck pulsate under the pressure of my fingers. My eyes are closed, but it's as if I'm discovering his body for the first time. I've seen him often without a shirt, I know every muscle in his chest and belly, yet I'm learning to feel him as if I were meeting him for the first time. The warmth of his body is consuming me and the choked

sounds from his throat are sensual, surprising me with a small moan making its way between my lips.

I don't know if our kiss lasts hours or just a few seconds. Time is mixed up and utterly irrelevant in the whirlwind of emotions that overwhelm me. Michael leaves my lips reluctantly, leans his forehead on mine, and we take a few seconds to catch our breath. I feel him panting at least as much as I am. Is he really as into it as I am?

"See? It's not that difficult. You learn quickly," he says a little breathlessly as he smiles at me, kissing me lightly on the lips, the tip of my nose, and my forehead.

We're still in each other's arms and neither of us seems to want to step away first.

"You're a good teacher. You've had a lot of practice."

He raises a corner of his mouth in a smug smile. "But now I have to go back to my room, or I may not be able to control my instincts to teach you more than just how to kiss." His tone is light but I hear the effort in his voice, as though he's fighting a battle against himself.

He reluctantly steps away from me, grabs his sandwich, and heads to his room. I turn off the stove with the pot of water that has been boiling for a while now. It's useless for me to make chamomile tea at this point. I could fill a tub and take a bath in it, and I still wouldn't be able to calm the turmoil of emotions that shake my heart and stomach. Penelope told me that you never forget your first kiss, but I believe the second will remain etched in my memory as long as I live.

***

Breakfast is a succession of yawns on my part, a grunt of disapproval on Michael's, and curious glances on Levi's.

"With those dark circles under your eyes it looks like you've punched yourself in the face," the boy notices after my umpteenth yawn while sipping coffee.

I look up at Michael, who hides a smug smile behind his cup.

"Eat your breakfast, and don't worry about our dark circles. This morning you have a literature test if I remember correctly."

"Did you two have sex?"

I almost spit out the sip of coffee I just swallowed.

"No!" Michael and I respond in unison.

Levi raises his hands with an innocent look. "Just asking. You look like two animals in mating season. The male struts around inflating his feathers, and the female avoids him by turning the other way. It's fun to watch you. I figured you'd finally given in last night."

I'm running out of words. Do Michael and I really behave like this? Of course, after last night, I'm not sure I can be alone in the same room with him. I don't know if I could resist a pair of lips that I've tried to forget but can't. Eventually, last night I collapsed from exhaustion, but with a burning desire to kiss him again, again and again. Is this what my father meant by the devil tempting you—that once you've tasted, you can't stop? That a kiss becomes two, then three, and eventually the clothes slip on the floor, leading you into an even worse sin?

"I didn't think I'd ever say this, but you need to stop watching documentaries. They're bad for you," Michael says to lighten the conversation, but not before throwing me a couple of worried glances.

"They're amazing! Did you know that there's a forest in

Mexico where every November it's completely orange because millions of monarch butterflies migrate there? They travel about thirty-eight hundred miles from Canada and the United States to spend the winter where it is warmer. Isn't that amazing? Three thousand eight hundred miles, can you imagine that?" His enthusiasm is contagious.

That's Levi for you. He can ask if you've had sex one minute and then, ten seconds later, shift his attention to butterflies.

I watch Michael smile and look at him, genuinely interested in his explanation. "Really? We'll have to go there one day. Would that be cool?"

"Seriously? You'd take me to see the butterflies? You'd do that for me?" Levi's eyes become misty.

"Sure, why not? Let's go and see these butterflies."

Levi gets up and hugs Michael, taking him by surprise, and then runs to his room. Michael looks at me, his eyes and mouth wide open. "Did he just hug me? He's never done that without me initiating it first," he whispers, and my heart is filled with warmth.

The dance between Levi and Michael has been complicated. They never argue, but there are intense moments. Sometimes, Michael is the only one who can tune into Levi enough to calm his nightmares; other days, it seems that neither of them can find a way to approach the other. This is the first time Levi initiated a gesture of affection that's not linked to a moment of weakness. I understand why Michael's emotional about it, he's been very frustrated by his inability to get close to this kid.

"You made him happy." I smile at him as I help him clean the table and put the breakfast dishes in the dishwasher.

When I turn around, Michael is directly behind me, reaching up to put the bread back into the cupboard above my head. I stiffen when I hit his chest, and he instinctively grabs my waist. My cheeks are on fire with embarrassment. How do you behave in daylight with the guy you kissed at night in a dark kitchen?

"Relax. I've seen you avoiding me since you got up."

"I'm not avoiding you…it's just…yes and no." I don't know what I'm saying.

Michael laughs and backs up a step, allowing me to breathe again. "You don't have to be afraid I'll kiss you again, okay? Now, if you feel like doing it, I won't back down, but you don't have to feel awkward around me. I won't kiss you in front of other people, and I won't do it when we're alone if you haven't given me clear signals that you want it."

The seriousness I read in his eyes convinces me he's telling the truth. Michael is impulsive, throwing himself into things without thinking it through, but he's also a person who always keeps his word.

"Clear signals? I've never kissed anyone until last night. How do I give you clear signals?" I joke a bit to lighten the mood and shake off the embarrassment.

"Well, telling me clearly is one way, but don't worry—I'm an expert in these things. I understand when a woman wants to be kissed." He struts, winking at me. "And if I'm ignorant and read the wrong signals, just say no when I move in, okay?" he laughs.

I laugh with him too.

"Okay, that's fine. Now go call Levi because he really needs to take that literature test this morning, and your butter-

fly promise is distracting him."

"Goodness! You're way too strict with this homework," he teases as he leaves the room and goes to retrieve the boy.

I lean on the kitchen counter with a smile I can't contain. Was that an invitation to ask him to kiss me? How many kisses are allowed before the guilty feeling creeps into your stomach? The more I stay away from home, from the protected environment of the boarding school, and live among people the whole world considers normal, the more I forget what it means to live with the fear that God will punish me for everything. I kissed a man who's not my husband twice, but I'm standing here, alive, well, and…happy. Wouldn't God want this in a marriage? Wouldn't he want happiness between two people who unite in his presence? So many questions follow one another in my mind I don't even notice that Levi has entered the room until Michael approaches me.

"Faith, is everything okay?" I look up and find Michael's worried gaze.

"Yes, I was just lost in thought."

His lips form a knowing smile, and it almost seems like he wants to say something, but he shakes his head and remains silent. He grabs the house keys and heads towards the front door.

"Ladies and gentlemen, I am going to hunt for food. Or at least the money we need to buy it. If anyone needs me, I'll be in the studio. And you, Levi, I want a report of your test as soon as you've finished it, okay?" He points a finger at him.

Levi nods vigorously and smiles from ear to ear. When Michael walks out and closes the door behind him, the kid turns to me. "Do you really think he'll take me to see the butterflies?"

"Of course he will," I answer with conviction. If there's one thing I've learned about Michael, it's that he does exactly what he says. "But for now, sit in front of that computer or you'll never pass that test."

Levi snorts but sits and puts his cellphone in the basket I place out for him every morning on the other side of the dining table. No distractions while doing homework. Michael always makes fun of me for my strictness, but he agrees with that too.

At least two hours pass in which Levi's smile turns into a mask of concentration. When he takes these tests, I can't do much except stay nearby to make sure he doesn't pull out a textbook or grab his cell phone to check the answers. This morning, however, he could've stood up and started dancing on the table and I wouldn't have noticed. The images of my first kisses fill my mind and leave room for little else. They're so vivid that I relive the emotions, awakening that agitation in my chest that is less scary than the first time I experienced it and has become more and more pleasant. It's as if I'm addicted to it and looking for a new, ever-increasing dose.

"I'm finished!"

I move my gaze from the view out the window to his smiling face. "So? How did it go?" I study his face reddened by concentration, and his hair disheveled from running his hands through it.

"I got only three out of a hundred answers wrong," he says proudly.

"Really? That's outstanding! Did it seem difficult for you?"

He shrugs his shoulders and grimaces. "At first, I could only think about the trip to Mexico, but then I was able to focus on the questions."

"Shall we look at the three questions you got wrong tomor-

row? For today I think you can relax."

"Really?" His eyes widen in surprise.

I nod. Michael made me promise that I wouldn't stress Levi out with other tasks after the test, and I agreed. The truth is I wouldn't be able to concentrate enough to teach him anything right now. It's unnerving how strong emotions can make even a simple activity difficult.

I watch as Levi takes his phone out of the basket and starts texting with his friends like he does most days. His smiling face turns into an expression that seems almost disappointed. The more I live with him, the more I realize how different he is from his peers in that he experiences much more somber moods than most kids. Maybe my brothers and I grew up in such a sheltered community that we never felt real disappointment or moments of deep sadness, but sometimes Levi seems crushed by emotions even an adult would have difficulty managing. Michael seems to be the only person who can break through that gloom that takes hold of him.

"Can I go get a muffin at the coffee shop on the corner?" he asks with a smile that lacks the excitement of earlier this morning.

"Yes, you deserve it. Do you remember the rules?" I ask as I go get the credit card Michael leaves for Levi in case he wants to go out and buy something.

The kid rolls his eyes. "Don't talk to strangers and come back home right away."

"Good. Enjoy your reward." He doesn't smile at me as he grabs the credit card. Most likely, the stress of the test has caught up with him and he's feeling tired. He disappears into his room and then leaves a few minutes later through the front door, waving goodbye but never raising his eyes from the phone. I'll never understand how people can walk without stumbling with their eyes glued to that contraption.

As soon as the door closes, I sit on the couch and go back to thinking about Michael's lips on mine, immersing myself again in that little bubble of happiness I can't seem to get out of today.

CHAPTER 15

Michael

I whistle the refrain of the song we've been recording since yesterday. It's upbeat with catchy lyrics and a guitar solo that hits you right in the gut. It's been a long time since I've wanted to move my fingers so fast across my guitar fretboard, and I'm sure our fans are going to love it. I'm convinced this album will reach the top of the charts because we've stretched ourselves creatively, no longer constrained by the limits our old label imposed on us. I hand a coffee to each of my bandmates in the studio as I make my way to my guitar gear.

"Why is he whistling like a Disney princess?" Damian puzzledly asks Thomas, who is sipping his coffee watching me.

"I don't know, but unless he starts talking to birds, I don't want to know what it is."

Simon, on the other hand, studies me with a stern face and guilt grips my stomach. I loved kissing Faith, and I hope she'll give me the signal to do it again as soon as possible—that is, open the door of this room and shove her tongue in my mouth. I'm as excited as a pre-teen kid. I haven't had sex in weeks, and I'm worried about a kiss I promised Simon I would never give. His look makes me fry on the stool I'm sitting on.

"What the hell are you so happy about?" he asks me finally.

I look up and smile at him. "I promised Levi I'd take him to

Mexico to see the butterfly forest."

He looks at me like I've just confessed to a murder. "Fatherhood is a bad influence on you. And also, why is a fourteen-year-old boy interested in butterflies?"

I laugh and shake my head. "I don't know, man. He discovered them in one of those documentaries he always watches. He's like a sponge, that kid, whatever he watches he learns and assimilates. He's fascinated by how things work, by the strange mysteries of the world."

"You'd better make sure you don't download any porn. At that age, they look for everything online." We burst out laughing, and I'm relieved Simon seems to believe my story.

"Can we start by going through 'Moonlight' and then record the tracks?" I try to divert the attention away from my smile and my good mood.

"Why so fast? Do you have to go home to your wife?" Thomas jokes, and I give him the side-eye.

"No, because I can't wait to release this album and go on tour. I haven't fucked anyone in weeks, and I'm going crazy. So move your fat asses and let's get to it. My dick is wasting in my pants."

They smile and shake their heads but finally hurry to their instruments and nod to Greg on the other side of the glass. The song starts with a spoken first verse by Damian. No music, just his gritty voice full of sensuality. Then Simon joins in on bass, slowly Thomas begins and finally me. A rush of pleasure flows through me as my fingers touch the strings, and the vibrations expand deep inside me. Like sex, but with more emotion. I move my fingers along the neck of the guitar like I would on the body of a woman, only with music I make love; with wom-

en, the pleasure is only skin deep. The image of Faith, eyes shut and lips open and waiting, fills my mind, along with the sound of her moans and her shaky breathing. God, the woman is drop-dead gorgeous with that clean, natural face and that hair tousled wild by my hands. I'm so caught up I didn't even notice my bandmates have stopped playing.

"Michael!" Simon's tone is impatient. How long has he been calling me?

I open my eyes and see Evan in the doorway with the receptionist's phone in hand. "It's Faith; she's upset. She can't find Levi."

It takes several seconds to shake off my blissful state and register what Evan is telling me.

"What do you mean *she can't find Levi*? Let me talk to her."

Her voice is frightened, trembling. "Michael, he didn't come home. I let him go and get a muffin at the corner coffee shop because he got a good grade on the literature test. But after an hour and he hadn't come back, I went down to look for him and couldn't find him. I looked everywhere, asked the barista, but she didn't remember seeing him. I don't know where he is, Michael. I don't know where to look for him or if something's happened to him."

"An hour? You didn't notice for a whole hour?"

The silence on the other side makes me feel guilty. She must be terrified.

"Did he do or say anything strange? Did he seem agitated?"

"No…I don't know…I don't think so? I don't remember, exactly." It sounds like she's crying.

"Don't panic, Faith, and think. Because this morning he was excited about butterflies and three hours later he disappeared. It doesn't make sense."

"I don't know, Michael. I didn't notice anything."

"And why did it take you an hour to notice? Didn't it seem strange to you that he didn't come back right away? What were you doing?"

"I…I wasn't doing anything. I don't know how an hour passed."

She wasn't doing anything and didn't notice an hour had passed? How the hell is that possible?

"I'm coming, don't move. We'll go look for him."

I give the phone back to Evan and realize everyone is staring at me tensely, waiting for news.

"So?" Simon is the only one who speaks.

"Faith gave him permission to go down to the café, and he never came back. Damnit! It was me who said to give him some space, that he's old enough to go out a bit on his own," I snap as I look for my phone. Ten unanswered calls and all from Faith. Nothing from Levi.

"We'll help you look for him," Damian suggests, and I'm relieved my friends are with me. I've never been so scared in my life.

"Should you call the police?" asks Thomas worriedly.

For a moment it crossed my mind, but what would I say? That I've lost a kid that a judge entrusted to me to take care of? I did the impossible by getting him to stay even after he'd finished serving his sentence. My lawyer convinced the judge to give me temporary custody without going through the whole process with social services. He went out of his way to bend the rules and I lose the kid? What kind of responsible adult am I?

"First, let's try to find him ourselves. I don't think he'd react well to being approached by the police."

Thomas nods.

"Where do we start?" I ask desperately as I head out the door with the others following.

I feel a hand grab my elbow, and then Evan puts both hands on my shoulders, nailing me to the spot. "First, take a deep breath because you're only making it worse when you're this upset. You go home to Faith and try to figure out if Levi said anything that can help us. In the meantime, we'll start looking for him in the most obvious places in Manhattan. You're just a stone's throw from the MET or Central Park. We'll find him, Michael, don't worry." He smiles to reassure me, but I see the tension on everyone's faces.

I turn around to leave the building and get in the car with Max and find Simon next to me.

"I'm coming with you." It's not a question.

"Thank you," I whisper as I sit in the back seat of the SUV.

***

Faith is pacing the living room when I get home. As soon as she hears me, she runs to me.

"I don't know where he is, Michael. I don't know where he is. I tried to call him, but he didn't answer."

"I know, I tried too," I tell her, taking her by the arm and drawing her towards me. I feel her hesitating but then wrap her small arms around my body, resting her head on my chest.

"Did he say anything that sounded off?" Simon breaks the silence, reminding me of his presence.

I let her go reluctantly and turn to my friend's serious expression. At least he has the decency not to preach at me for hugging her.

Faith shakes her head. “He was so excited about the butterfly conversation that he struggled to concentrate during the test. But then he nailed it with an excellent score. I saw him texting on the phone with someone, and then he asked if he could go out and get a muffin.”

“Did his mood seem different than usual? Maybe stressed out about the test?” insists Simon in a firm voice, and I thank heaven he’s here.

Faith wrinkles her forehead and thinks about it. “He was tired from the test…and now that I think about it, after he got off the phone his mood turned more serious. His smile looked almost forced when he asked me to go out. I should’ve realized something was going on...” She throws a look at me, full of remorse. “I’m sorry I panicked on the phone.”

“At least you’ve calmed down and remembered some important details,” I say through gritted teeth, unable to apologize for behaving like an asshole earlier on the phone.

“It wasn’t your fault, Faith,” Simon reassures her, casting a scolding glance at me. “Do you know if he has any friends or someone he talks to regularly?”

“I know he’s always texting with a guy, but I didn’t want to be nosey. I don’t think he’s from juvie…maybe someone he knew before ending up in there. I don’t know. Since he’s been out, he hasn’t had many opportunities to make new friends besides us adults.” I rub my face, cursing myself for not asking him for at least one name. I wanted to trust him. I wanted him to feel free to live without me breathing down his neck, but maybe a kid needs an authority figure more than a friend.

“Do you have the address of the foster home where he

lived?" asks Simon.

I frown and look at him, surprised. "Why should he go back there? He ended up in jail because of them."

Simon gives me a bitter smile. "Because sometimes the other foster kids in the home are the only family you've ever known."

Simon never talks about his time living with a foster family. I don't know if he even kept in touch with them. When we got out of prison and changed our names, we burned all our bridges to the past. Some voluntarily, some not so much, but we've built a new life trying to forget the past.

But Simon's right to bring it up. I didn't think about it because I assumed he didn't want to go back to that house, but he's been through it and certainly understands the situation better than I do.

I pull out my phone and call my lawyer, explaining everything. Ten minutes later, we're in Max's car heading towards a New Jersey address.

***

After more than two hours in the car, we arrive in front of a nondescript white house in an equally forgettable neighborhood, and we notice people peeking out from behind their window curtains to see who drove up in this luxury car. The barbed wire atop the fence convinces me it's an unsafe neighborhood, but I wonder if it's there to keep the criminals out or to keep those who live there from escaping.

I inhale deeply and walk up the concrete driveway that's covered in cracks with tufts of grass growing through it. The gravel in place of a lawn in front of the house, along with the peeling paint, gives the run-down property a sad, depressing air.

I climb the three steps to the small, covered porch and look for a doorbell that I can't find. I turn to Faith, Simon, and Max, who look at me with apprehension, and my stomach tightens in a vise. What if he isn't here? Where the hell am I going to look for him?

I open the screen that separates me from the door, knock on the dark wood, then close it again and take a step back. I see a kid about Levi's age peeking out the window, scrutinizing me for a few seconds, then disappearing again. A few seconds later, the door opens by a few inches.

"What do you want?" he asks, putting his head out.

"Hi, my name is Michael. I'm looking for Levi."

"I know who you are."

"Is Levi here? I need to talk to him. I'm worried about him." The tension that's been building since he ran away is wearing me down.

The thin, almost skeletal boy, with black eyes and hair, throws a nearly imperceptible glance behind him. Levi is here, and the relief I feel makes my lungs expand until I breathe again.

"Why do you want to see him?"

"He left home without telling me, and I'm worried about him."

"Maybe he doesn't want to see you."

I nod and try to push down the lump that forms in my throat. Maybe it's my fault he ran away, something I did.

"Okay, but I'd like him to tell me in person. I want to make sure he's okay." The voice comes out almost in a prayer.

He seems to think about it for an eternity—I'm afraid he'll

slam the door in my face—but he finally opens it just enough to reveal Levi's face, streaked with tears.

"Are you okay? Are you hurt?"

He shakes his head, then glances behind me where Simon, Max, and Faith are standing motionless, holding their breath.

"Do you want to talk to me?" I ask him.

He glances at his friend, who gives him a slight nod. "I'll be here if you need me. Just call me, and I'll let you in, okay?"

Levi reassures him with a nod, then walks out and sits on the low wall surrounding the porch, with his back to the gravel yard. I sit next to him.

"Have I done something wrong? Did I hurt you in some way? Is that why you ran away?" I ask, trying to muster a calm I don't feel.

"No." His answer is a faint whisper.

"Is it the house? Don't you like where we live? Do you not like school, or the way Faith teaches? You can go to a regular school if you want. We can find a solution..." I'm trying to come to terms with whatever it is.

"No."

"Please, Levi. Help me understand what's wrong. You know I'm too dumb to comprehend hard things."

His lips bend slightly into a smile, but his gaze remains fixed on the worn wooden floor. "You won't really take me to see the butterflies," he whispers, and I'm even more confused.

"What? Of course I will. I promised you."

I see tears falling down his cheeks again and I want to hug him, but I hold back. He doesn't trust me now, and I can't force myself on him, even if my intentions are only to comfort him.

"Because you're famous. When you get tired of the newness, when you realize that a kid backstage at a concert is just a burden, you'll turn me back in to social services and forget about me."

His words cut my heart in two like a blade through my chest. I look down and take a breath.

"Do you know that you're the only person who's ever come to dinner with us, with our small group of friends? In Los Angeles, when we took you out to celebrate—we've never done that for anyone."

Levi looks perplexed, frowning. "There are always pictures of you on the internet, partying at fancy dinners."

My lips form a tired smile. "Those are business dinners. We go to maintain relationships with people in the industry, sign contracts, schmooze the judges who nominate us for awards, but they're not friends. The Jailbirds and their spouses are my friends, Evan, Emily, and the Red Velvet Curtains in the last few months. Never anyone else until you came along."

"Why? I'm nobody special."

I smile and look him straight in the eye. "You are, Levi. You survived that hell, like us, and now you're one of us. Right now, Damian, Thomas, and Evan are walking around Manhattan looking for you. Simon, Max, and Faith drove two and a half hours to come here—for you. You're part of this odd and kind of crazy family, whether you like it or not. It's your decision whether to stay in this house or come back to Manhattan, but we'll always have your back. When you need help or even just to talk, you can count on every single person you've met these past few months. Maybe you'll decide to take a different path and not live with me, but you can always count on me whenever you need me. And I *will* take you to see the butter-

flies."

Levi wipes his eyes with the sleeve of his shirt, then throws himself on me and we hug each other with what feels like all our might.

I pull back for a moment. "Can I ask who told you I would get tired of you?"

Levi looks down at the floor again. "Jay. He said November was a long ways away and you'd get tired of me sooner than that and send me back to a foster family. He was chosen for adoption a couple of times, but they always sent him back."

My throat tightens in a grip, trying to hold back the tears his words elicit. How the hell do you adopt a kid and then return him like a defective product? Don't they do checks before allowing people to care for a child?

"Levi, you're not a postal package. I won't send you back because I get tired of you. Sometimes we argue because you're a kid growing up and I'm the adult who has to teach you things. It's normal that we'll disagree about some things, especially when we live under the same roof. But I won't ever send you back just because we hit rough spots. They're part of life, and I guarantee that it won't always be like that. There will be many more good times, and that's why it's worth enduring the bad days—they make living worthwhile."

Levi looks up at me, and a slight smile appears on his face. "Can I also ask how you got here so fast? You didn't take the train. You didn't use the credit card I left at home, I didn't receive any notifications." The more I think about it, the more this thought scares me. Did he ask someone I don't know for a ride? A person old enough to have a car that I don't even know exists?

"I took a taxi."

"How? It must have cost you a fortune to take one here."

"I used the money I saved. That you give me every month for my expenses."

"That money was for you to buy whatever you like. Why did you save it?"

Levi shrugs his shoulders and avoids my gaze. "I don't know…for emergencies. You never know."

My heart just about breaks at a fourteen-year-old boy thinking he has to save money to cope with the uncertainties of life. "Levi, look at me." I wait for him to look up. "That money is for fun stuff, like toys or tech gadgets or whatever a kid your age likes. I'll take care of the emergencies. I'll take care of *you*. And I'll save money to handle anything unexpected, understood? You do not have to worry about not having enough funds to cover expenses of any kind. I promised to take care of you and that means the whole package. If you need clothes, something for school or if you want to come visit your friend, I'll take care of it. Just ask me, and I'll consider your request. Is that clear? I don't want there to be any doubts about this."

Levi nods.

"Do you want to come home with me?"

He still nods but doesn't say a word. I get up and take him by the hand, approach the door, and knock. The kid I assume is Jay comes to open the door, and when he sees Levi's hand in mine, the hope in his eyes dies. I would like to grab him and bring him with me, but I can't take on a child abduction charge, so I do the only thing that comes to mind.

"Jay, thank you for keeping Levi safe. I really appreciate your help. Do you have a cell phone?"

He looks confused, but after a moment of hesitation, he nods. I reach out my hand, and he hands it to me.

"This is my private number. If you're in trouble or even just if you feel like talking to Levi or me, call me, okay? For anything. Don't be shy. At any time of the day or night. If I don't answer immediately, it's because I'm in the studio recording or during a concert, but I'll call you back, understand?"

He remains still, just staring at me.

"Do you understand?"

He nods, and an emotion passes through his eyes, though his face remains blank. Hope, gratitude, maybe even a little fear? I turn around and walk to the car with Levi's hand clutched in mine.

"Let's go home," I say to Max, as everyone breathes a sigh of relief without saying a word. Stuck between Faith and me, Levi snuggles into my shoulder when I wrap my arm around his side, and Faith squeezes his hand in hers—no doubt for fear of losing him again.

I hadn't realized, until today, how empty my life would be without the two people I have by my side.

***

"Is he already asleep? It's only eight o'clock!" Faith is shocked when she sees me coming back from Levi's room so soon.

"He was exhausted. Five minutes and he was already sound asleep. Or he found our conversation particularly boring." I try to smile, but I don't quite feel it as I sit next to her on the couch and rub a hand across my face. "I'm not fit to raise a kid," I whisper as I shove my hands in my hair.

"No one knows how to raise a teenager. You learn as you

go."

"I don't have time to learn. Did you see what happened today?"

"I didn't say it's easy. I said, you learn. You're doing a good job, Michael. You'll see, over time it'll get easier."

"He ran away today. How can you say I'm doing a good job? He thought I would abandon him!"

"No, Jay *told* him you would abandon him, and he let himself believe it—it's the only reality he's ever known. If two years ago you'd told me the world outside my community is not teeming with demons and Satan himself, I wouldn't have believed you because all my life they've made me believe the opposite."

I shake my head and try to convince myself she's right, but I can't shake the guilt that grips my chest. "You're so much better with him than I am. You get him to study, you know how to prepare a meal for him. If it were up to me, we'd be living on pizza and Chinese."

"I was forced to look after my three younger brothers when I was only thirteen. I know how to do certain things because I was forced to learn. It was either that or let them starve, and I learned over time. I made mistakes many times but things turned out okay. Like today with Levi."

"You're a wise soul, you know that?"

Faith smiles, amused, and shakes her head. "I have no idea how to do the most basic things to survive in this world!"

I shrug my shoulders and smile at her. "You'll learn. You're smart; you learn quickly."

"I have a good teacher." She smiles at me.

I study her, caught by surprise. The only thing I taught her

was how to French kiss. I wouldn't really call myself a life coach.

"Do you want to practice again?" I make fun of her, but she blushes and nods.

I bite my lip so as not to smile like a kid. I was hoping she would ask me again. I draw her to me, grabbing one of her hands. She rests her hands on my shoulders and then around my neck like I taught her last night.

"See? You've already learned where to put your hands."

"Stop teasing me, or I'll leave," she threatens, but only with words.

"Come here and kiss me," I whisper to her lips before sinking my tongue into her mouth.

Immediately her fingers go into my hair as I take her face in my hands and draw her to me for a passionate kiss. I've always been delicate with her for fear she'd get scared and run away, but I think she wants more intensity now. She wouldn't have asked me to kiss her again, otherwise.

With one hand on her back, I pull her against my chest, making her moan softly with pleasure. Her fingers squeeze my hair, and I feel her let go. Her chest presses against mine, and when I feel her struggling to sit up straight, I grab her leg and pull it over my lap, making her sit astride me. For a second, I'm sure she'll tell me to back off; instead, a sexy groan leaves those innocent lips, and I struggle to restrain myself from taking off her shirt and feasting on her breasts. I don't think she realizes how close she is to my erection.

I grab her hair and force her to raise her head. A sound of disappointment escapes her when I pull back from her lips, but it's replaced by a small groan of surprise and pleasure when I

savor the skin of her neck with my tongue. I return to her lips again, and this time it is she who sinks her tongue urgently into my mouth, gently and casually stroking mine. She's learning quickly to follow that pleasure growing inside her.

I move my hand to her lower back, and I'm surprised to feel her pelvis circling slowly, as though searching for an orgasm I don't think she'd even recognize. I'm not even sure she noticed that she's swaying on me. I slide gently to the edge of the sofa to give her full access to my erection, without moving my hips, without pushing it against her most sensitive part, forcing something on her she may not be ready to handle. I give control over to her instincts and movements that sometimes lose their rhythm but still drive me crazy.

Her brain must be on autopilot, letting her hormones take command, because her small circles become wider and wider until she finds my erection and presses her pelvis against it, letting out a groan of unmistakable pleasure. I go back to kissing her neck, from her shoulder to her ear, dwelling on that little piece of skin just behind the lobe that makes her gasp. Her pelvis now presses rhythmically against mine. It's not an overtly sexual movement like the uninhibited cougars I usually take to bed, and I make a titanic effort to stay still, to use only my lips to tease those sensitive parts on her neck I manage to discover, to pleasure her at her pace, without groping, without embarrassing her.

I feel her breathing getting faster, her hips swaying faster. She clings to my shoulders, resting her lips on mine and pressing her core hard against an erection that strains against my pants almost to the point of pain. Her hips work at rubbing the thin fabric of her skirt against the rigid seams of my jeans,

trying to eliminate the annoying barriers between our skin and our pleasure. I let her discover and ride that pleasure, sinking my tongue into her mouth and swallowing her moan when she reaches the peak with an orgasm that makes her entire body tremble.

I feel her stiffen, pull away from me, and bring a hand to her mouth. Her eyes widen in a silent question.

"Yes, that was an orgasm." I smile at her and try to kiss her on the nose, but she snaps to her feet. Her cheeks turn red, and the tears begin to flow. My stomach churns with uneasiness as I watch her back away from me as if I were the devil.

"Faith, wait..." I reach for her and take her by the arm, but she wriggles out of my grasp.

"Stay away from me, Michael," she sobs as she turns around and heads to her room, closing the door behind her. I hear the metallic noise of the lock, and a knot forms in my stomach.

"Fuck," I hiss with gritted teeth as I reach the kitchen.

I pushed her too far and scared her. Anger consumes me—for myself because I shouldn't have forced her to this point, and for her because she could've told me to stop and she didn't. Since when am I that guy who doesn't notice when a girl is uncomfortable during sex?

I grab the keys and walk out of the front door before doing something stupid like unloading my tension on her.

***

"Yeah, honey, keep it up," I say to the blonde I approached at the hotel bar five blocks from the apartment.

When she talked to me, I didn't think twice about booking a room and fucking her. Blond bob, blue eyes, and the desire to ride me until I lose my senses. But the makeup on her face is too heavy, she's too curvy, those round, firm breasts I used to like so much no longer drive me crazy. I prefer a natural-looking face and legs for days. She's not Faith, and acknowledging that is painful.

"You're not really in the right mood, am I wrong?" she asks me, and I didn't even realize she'd stopped. I look down and realize my erection is just a distant memory.

"Sorry..." I don't even know what to say.

She smiles and begins to cover herself with the pink skirt still rolled up around her waist. "Don't worry, I got it the fifth time you called me Faith."

Did I really do that? "I'm not sure how to apologize."

She shrugs, sitting on the bed and putting on her sandals. "I don't know who this Faith is, but she's a lucky woman if she can handle a sex machine like you. Or your reputation is a bit inflated." She winks at me and smiles.

I rub my face and watch her fix her makeup before leaving the room. I'm so ashamed I want to crawl in a hole and stay there. I treated two girls like crap on the same night. Not bad for someone who prides himself on being a ladies' man.

***

Simon opens his door at ten in the evening and lets me in. "What the hell are you doing here? Is Levi okay?"

"Yes, he collapsed at eight o'clock. The problem is me. It's me who's a jerk."

He makes me sit on the couch but doesn't say a word.

"I kissed her."

He remains silent.

"Don't you want to say anything?"

"Michael, what do you want me to say? You did the one thing I specifically asked you not to do. What do I do now? Ground you?"

I shake my head and sigh. He's right. I don't know why I came here, maybe to be told I'm a jerk. I don't know. I'm so confused I don't know if I want him to punch me, hug me, or kick me out of the house.

"I tried to fuck someone tonight, and my dick went limp inside her. While the girl was riding me like a madwoman."

"You kissed her and then left her at home to go fuck another woman?" he asks incredulously.

I leave out the fact that I caused her first orgasm.

"Holy Christ, Michael. That's a dirty move—even by your low standards."

"Thank you." Sarcasm drips from my words.

"Oh, don't be offended. You're the one who's been a jerk. What do you want me to say?"

"I don't know! Maybe it's because I haven't had sex for weeks. I get hard kissing a girl like a teenager, and then I go limp when I literally have a grown woman sitting on my dick."

"Do you really need me to spell it out for you? Isn't it obvious?"

"Yes, I need you to tell me what's going on. I'm too dumb to figure it out, apparently."

"Maybe you actually care about Faith? Maybe you've realized that being in a relationship with someone, living together, is better than a careless night of sex?"

"A relationship? I have no idea what a relationship is or how to navigate one, just like I have no idea how to raise a fourteen-year-old."

Simon smiles at me kindly, and it makes my stomach tighten up even more. What the hell did I get myself into? "Welcome to adulthood, Michael, where you spend half your time fucking everything up and the other half Googling how to fix it."

I groan, trying to hold back a laugh.

"Seriously, we're all just flying blind here. We try, we make mistakes, we fix them. I just want you to be careful with her, don't push her too far and then leave her to fend for herself. She doesn't deserve to get her heart broken, even if you do have good intentions."

"I never forced her to do anything she didn't want."

"I know, it's just that sometimes you jump on things like a speeding train, carrying everyone else with you, before realizing you have no idea how to stop."

"Christ, thanks for the vote of confidence!"

Simon smiles and gives my shoulder a shove. "Go home and try to clean up that train wreck of a mess you made."

***

It's midnight when I open the front door, and I'm surprised to find Faith sitting on the couch.

"It's late. Shouldn't you be in bed?" I give her a half-smile.

"Levi woke up with one of his nightmares. It took me a while to calm him down. I tried to call you, but you didn't answer."

My heart sinks into my stomach. I hadn't even thought that Levi might need me. I assumed they were both fine without me here.

"Sorry…I…I was with a woman," I confess with a sense of fear and liberation I've never felt before.

I have no idea why I felt the need to tell her the truth, maybe because her pure, honest nature makes me feel like a coward every time I lie. I don't know why I feel this desire to be a better man when I'm with Faith, but I know sincerity is essential to her, and it feels like a double betrayal trying to hide where I've been.

I watch her go pale, lowering her suddenly darkened gaze and then raising it hesitantly towards me. The despair I feel at seeing her so vulnerable and on the verge of tears shakes me to the core. I move towards her, but she gets up and walks away to her room.

"Faith, sorry, I..." What? I didn't want to have sex with that woman? I didn't know what I was doing? What the hell kind of an excuse is that for being such an asshole?

"You don't have to explain yourself to me, Michael. I'm not your wife or your girlfriend, and you're free to do what you want." Her voice is choked, as though a lump in her throat prevents her from speaking.

I watch her hurry to her room and close the door behind her. I follow her, raising my hand to knock and enter, to try to explain what a jerk I've been, but I hear her sobbing. I stop, overwhelmed by a sense of guilt that's unfamiliar to me. Does Simon really think Google could solve this big of a mess?

CHAPTER 16

Faith

My eyelids are so swollen from crying I can hardly open them. I must have fallen asleep while I was still sobbing. I don't know what I was thinking letting Michael kiss me. I knew he was a womanizer, it's always been obvious, yet I gave him a part of me I should have saved for my husband—an orgasm. My first moment of pleasure and intimacy with a man, so intense it sent shivers of pleasure from my belly through my whole body and made my heart pump so hard I felt it echo in my ears. And I gave this moment to a man who will never share the same values as mine. This time the guilt has settled in my belly and shows no sign of leaving. Not even after the razor blade etched the skin of my thigh five times, numbing my feeling of emptiness and discomfort.

I look at my cell phone on the bedside table and rub my face. Maybe it's time to call my father. Perhaps he's right; it's time to go home. Before I can overthink it, I grab my phone and dial his number.

"Hello, Mom. Is Dad there with you?"

"Faith, is everything alright? Why are you calling so early on a Wednesday morning?"

"Yes, Mom, don't worry. It's just that my shift keeps changing, and I wanted to call before I started work to tell you I'm

fine."

I keep telling myself it's not a lie. My working hours have indeed changed, and I'm certainly about to start my work day. Still, I don't even recognize myself anymore. I've never lied so easily to my parents and it scares me. Who have I become? A woman who kisses strangers and betrays the trust of her parents? Exactly what my father predicted. The feeling of humiliation grips my heart painfully.

I hear her send one of my brothers to call my father in the workshop behind the house, and then she sighs. "Faith, when are you coming back? Your father isn't at all happy with this whole situation. Did you know that our doctor was told to leave the community? His ideas were far too liberal, and convincing us to let you do your internship outside the community was the last straw."

"Really? And who replaced him?"

"Mary. She sews well, and knows just a little disinfectant is enough to keep a wound from festering."

Mary is a seamstress, not a doctor. I feel guilty because the doctor, though old with outdated methods, was the only one who considered basic science and a foundational knowledge of the human body when treating people. They can't even get antibiotics if a wound becomes infected unless a doctor in the city prescribes them. Worry and a growing sense of guilt for the consequences of my choices grips my stomach and leaves a sour taste in my throat. But I don't have time to respond because I hear background noises and then my father's thundering voice.

"Young lady, it's time to stop being so stubborn and come home."

"I know, Dad. But it's not that simple. First they have to find someone to replace me."

"Faith, don't fight me on this. Otherwise, I'll be forced to come and pick you up."

A shiver of fear runs up my back. If he shows up at the boarding school and finds out I'm not living there, there will be hell to pay. "No, Dad. I've already warned them that they have to find someone soon. Please trust me."

And this is an actual lie, not an omitted truth or a different way of describing my job. A pure and simple lie that makes the sour taste rise up even more in my throat. I hear him exhale loudly and then give in.

"Don't test my patience. Your next phone call better be to say that you bought a return ticket—with the exact date of when to pick you up at the airport!" He hangs up without giving me time to say goodbye or explain.

I take a deep breath and drop on the bed. Depression and helplessness consume me, torturing me with thoughts of everything about this life I don't want to leave, including the people. I have to tell Michael and especially Levi. That boy does not deserve to have me disappear overnight, confusing him at a time when he's already struggling to find stability.

***

"Michael, can I talk to you?" I look at him through the open door of his room as he slips on a pair of sweatpants.

He gestures for me to enter. I hesitate for a moment, then set foot in what feels like his kingdom with its massive bed in the center of the room and black and glossy closets that reach the ceiling. I wonder what the mirrors covering a large part of the wall are for. The recessed ceiling lights are useless given

how dimly lit the room is, with thick curtains drawn across the huge window that faces out the back of the building. One thing, however, is certain: its modern, dark elegance perfectly represents Michael: no-nonsense luxury.

He studies me for a few seconds, frowning as he lingers over my swollen eyes, and I look away.

"It's important." It's not a question. He's not stupid; he can see something is tormenting me.

"I called my father. It's time I help you look for someone to care for Levi. I have to go home."

He clenches his jaw so hard his teeth grind, his sharp look not wavering from me for a second as his breathing becomes shallow. He's angry but trying to contain it. "Is it because of what happened last night?"

I think I finally realized last night that a kiss is not just a kiss with him, at least not for me. I care deeply for someone who doesn't feel the same, and because of that he'll make me suffer, leaving me stained, humiliated, and without the possibility of finding a husband.

"No. You knew this arrangement had an expiration date. It's just time to go back to my family."

A bitter smile crosses his face as he shakes his head. "You haven't figured out yet that you don't *have* to go home, have you? That you're an adult and don't have to do what your parents tell you?"

I inhale deeply, tired of having this discussion with Michael. "What should I do? Stay here and look for work as a nurse? Sooner or later, Levi will go back to school, graduate, and go his own way. I don't know anything about this world, and I'm not used to this life."

"That's bullshit and you know it. Do you want to go back to them? Fine, but don't let them treat you like property. You're a slave in your own house, you know that? You have no say in your own life! Tell me one thing you like about the man you're supposed to marry."

I look down, speechless. Not much attracts me about him, and I have to think hard to find something positive. "He has his own business and will be able to provide for the family."

He smiles and shakes his head. "I said *something you like about him,* not whether he can pay for your meals. If that's your criteria, I also have a job and can guarantee you a much more luxurious life than him. I asked you to tell me something you like, something that makes you smile if you think about it. Are you in love with him?"

"I'll learn to love him." As my mother did with my father.

"What if you fall in love with someone else? What then? Would you leave him?"

That's why I have to go home before my heart is irreparably tied to someone I can't have. "No, marriage is sacred," I whisper, feeling the grip on my stomach tighten.

"By your logic, then, you could learn to love me too. Why him and not me? Why did your father choose him for you? Introduce me to your father, then. I have everything you need: a job to support you, the desire to have sex and get you pregnant to keep the bloodline alive, and I'm also Catholic and baptized. You can learn to love me too, right? Why him and not me? There's no difference."

His words are hard, sharp. They penetrate my belly like a hot blade. I feel my blood boiling inside of me and my voice reaches my throat, enraged. "Because you'll never make me

an honest woman! You'll take what you want and then leave me to go seduce your next conquest—just like you did last night, making me feel pleasure and then slipping into another woman's bed because I didn't fulfill your desires. *That's* why it's him and not you. Because he's as safe as the ground under my feet, but you're a fire that'll burn me alive and take me to hell!" I shout the words at the top of my lungs, caught up in a wave of anger only Michael can stir in me.

Immediately, I cover my mouth, shocked. I've never shouted like that. Never. Not even as a little girl.

Michael looks at me, surprised either at my words or the way I said them—I don't know. I'm equal parts embarrassed and…relieved. Shouting those words I've been wanting to say was so liberating I feel intoxicated.

Michael smiles and shakes his head, looking almost pleased. "Finally, a reaction. Finally, you let go, and I can tell by your expression it felt good, didn't it? How many times have you been able to be yourself like that with the man you have to marry? With your father? With your family?"

More quietly now, he closes the distance between us and continues. "I certainly can't promise you a future. I don't even know what I'm doing tomorrow. But you can be sure that if you stay here, in this house, you can shout as much as you want, dress the way you want, and feel pleasure as often as you want it. I won't clip your wings, I won't stop you from flying, but I guarantee I'll catch you if you fall. If you stay here, you won't be alone. You'll have yourself, you'll have Levi, and you'll have me."

His last words are as close as a whisper on my lips, and all my anger melts into the desire to encircle my arms around his body and immerse myself in his warmth that both scares and comforts me.

And I do it. I reach out my arms and wrap them around his waist, getting lost in his eyes when he lifts my head and forces me to look at him. He rests his lips on mine tenderly, seeking approval he doesn't need. He can take my lips as often as he wants. They're his, like all my firsts. Michael can make me doubt all my decisions, make me believe I can do this life alone, without my family. No one has ever had as much confidence in me as he does.

I was always told I needed a man to survive. Someone to take care of me, my needs, make decisions for my life. And then I met Michael, who doesn't tell me what's right or wrong. He lets me choose for myself what I want after I've experienced it in my own skin. And while it's scary because I don't know if I'm capable of making my own decisions, I find myself wondering if it's really so wrong to want someone like him.

He gently pushes me on the bed without ever interrupting a kiss that has become more urgent and hectic. He slips between my legs and towers over me as I lay back on the rumpled sheets that smell of him, my head starting to spin. I don't know if it's his cologne, his tongue seeking mine with desperate urgency, or his erection that presses on my lower belly, making me gasp with pleasure at every little movement, but my hands desperately need to find his skin. I touch his back with my fingers and it's smooth, delicate, hot. His muscles contract under my touch as he kisses my neck, uncovering a small piece of shoulder, but not going any further.

He presses his pelvis against mine, making me groan,

ashamed, but Michael dampens it with a kiss that leaves me breathless. His belly presses against mine, his thrusts become more insistent, and my pleasure grows with the friction of our clothes. Two thin pieces of fabric are all that keep my purity intact—and make me feel dirty at the same time.

"Come, Faith," he whispers in my ear between kisses on the neck. "Do it for yourself and for me. Come."

He presses against me again, again and again. And I reach the peak of my pleasure with a moan that makes my back arch in pleasure as I press my chest against his. I squeeze him tightly, dig my nails into his skin, and cling to him with all my strength as I keep finding higher peaks and then fall back down into free fall.

But Michael is there, as he promised, to catch me when I feel the out-of-control emotions overwhelming me. He holds me tight, covers me with kisses, sinks his head into the hollow of my neck and breathes deeply. His heart hammers against his chest as fast as mine as he holds me tightly, both of us slowly calming down and letting reality sink in.

Leaning on his elbow, he looks at me with emotions in his eyes I've never seen. Fear, perhaps despair, uncertainty. "If you decide to go home and marry that man, make sure he gives you this and much more," he whispers. "Never settle, Faith, because you deserve to be happy, to smile every day of your life, and to moan every night. Don't settle because you're afraid to say no to those who think they can choose what's right for you." He kisses me on the lips and gets out of bed, heading for the bathroom.

I hear the water from the shower running on the other side of the closed door, and I lay there grasping the sheets tightly, inhaling his scent, thinking back to the phone call with my father and wishing more and more desperately that I never had to go home again.

***

Later, I enter the living room and find Levi on the couch doing his homework. I look at him, surprised as it's the first time I don't have to beg him to settle in and start his school day. I sit down next to him and pick up one of the notebooks he's not using.

"Did you do all your math problems already?" Again, I'm surprised. It's the subject he likes the least.

He just nods but doesn't look at me. He's serious, gloomy, and after what happened yesterday, I'm worried he might run away again.

"Did something happen?"

He shakes his head no.

"If there is something wrong, anything, would you tell me?" I insist worriedly.

Levi exhales deeply and puts his pen down on his notebook. "Do you really want to leave?"

His words catch me off guard, and I don't answer right away.

"I heard your conversation with Michael."

"My father wants me at home," I try to explain, and he raises his blue eyes on me.

"Why do you have to marry another man?"

I inhale and try to explain. "My family needs me."

"We need you too." It's not an argument, just a simple observation.

"And what should I say to my future husband?"

"That you made up your mind and you like Michael better."

I can't hold back a smile. "It's not that simple." It definitely isn't for me, what with the state of confusion my mind is in right now.

"Yes, it is simple. You like Michael, and he likes you. You always smile when you're together, and you already live under the same roof. Do you even know the other man? Is he cooler than Michael?"

I sigh and run out of words. No, Michael is everything I could want, apart from stability and a future, things I didn't think I could have without a man. "No, it's just that..."

"Am I the problem? Don't you want to live with me?" he asks in a whisper.

His words slam straight into my chest so hard it hurts, and without thinking twice I hug him tightly to me. "No, Levi. Don't even think of such a thing. You've never been a problem and never will be. I like living with you. I like helping you with your homework and watching documentaries together. You're fun and smart. You're the perfect person to live with."

"So why do you want to leave? Are the others more perfect than us?"

I shake my head no, but I don't know what to say. I don't want to leave. I always thought it was my duty to give him a rational explanation for things, but this time I don't have one.

"And you'll leave me alone with Michael. You know he can't even make a sandwich, right?" He frees himself from my grip.

I have to laugh because it's true. "But he does know how to hunt down good food. He knows all the best takeout restaurants."

“That’s true.” He smiles at me, and I can’t help but get lost in the sweetness of this boy.

I look down the hall and see Michael watching us in his sweatpants, his hair still wet, arms folded across his chest, an indecipherable expression on his face. I expect him to make a few jokes about his cooking skills, but he turns around and goes back to his room, disappearing behind the closed door. My heart tightens in my chest.

PRESS Review

The Treasure Hunt is About to Begin!

Hi, Roadies!

Are you ready for the first treasure hunt? Remember, if you figure out all the clues, you'll discover the date, time, and place of the next Jailbirds' show!

If I say "Cadillac Ranch" and "barbecue," what state comes to mind? The first clue is pretty straightforward, but you'll need to follow the blog to find out the rest. In the next few days, I'll be adding more. #HuntDownTheJailbirds

Be kind and Rock'n'Roll,

Iris

522734 Likes 42683 Tweets 33289 Shares 10732 Comments

Twitter:

@Rocknow The @Jailbirds_official seem to have lost their

minds since leaving the marketing department of their old record label. Why retweet a six-year-old tweet from us? #HuntDownTheJailbirds

@TheRocker First a treasure hunt to discover their concert whereabouts, then the retweets of our tweet from seven years ago. The @Jailbirds_official needs to update their press office that it's been years since their early interview with us. #HuntDownTheJailbirds

@Rocklive The @Jailbirds_official struck again. Our interview from six years ago was also retweeted from their official account. What are they doing? #HuntDownTheJailbirds

CHAPTER 17

Michael

Evan's hotel room is almost stuffy with all of us locked in here. We're finally in Austin, Texas, for the first of our surprise concerts. At first, I was a bit confused by the whole idea and worried no one would show up. But since this morning, when Iris finally posted the clue about the venue's name, about thirty people have been wandering around the place asking for information. At least it won't be completely empty.

"Can you explain why you've been retweeting tweets from several years ago on our Twitter account all week? They think we're idiots!" Damian asks Emily what we've all been wondering for a few days. When we asked Evan, he said it's a guerrilla marketing technique she discovered. I have no idea what half the terms mean that they use, but she seems pretty savvy in the Twitter world.

"What's the name of the venue you'll be playing tonight?" Emily's smile is diabolical.

"Vintage." Damian seems as perplexed as we are.

"That's right. Tonight, ten minutes before the show, we'll tweet a photo of the venue's sign with the caption: 'This isn't the only vintage thing tweeted this week. #HuntDownTheJailbirds'. It won't bring people to the club, but all week the media have been talking about you, about your show, and made the

hashtag ‘hunt down the Jailbirds’ a trending topic. They created all the hype around this event, and it cost us zero. Iris’s clues on the blog helped your fans figure out which venue you were going to play, but we needed the media to take an interest in this treasure hunt to run the story, and we couldn’t rely on the usual articles that cost us money and have little engagement. So we tricked people by retweeting old articles about you without giving any explanation. They took the bait and began to tweet the hashtag #HuntDownTheJailbirds, wondering why, hypothesizing theories, looking for answers from their followers. So, we’ve not only reached your most loyal fans but their entire audience. Even people who don’t follow you know about the treasure hunt ...

“The media has helped create a buzz about a show that won’t make much from an economic point of view, more or less a hundred tickets, but it will keep you on everyone’s radar. For the next shows, Twitter will be exploding with anticipation and news about you,” she finishes with a satisfied smile as we stare at her in awe.

I turn to Evan, who’s watching her with a smug smile.

“You are an evil genius!” laughs Damian.

“It’s a brilliant idea,” Simon adds.

“It’s not my idea, it was first used by a fast-food chain, but it’s tricky to find the right opportunity to use it without being discovered. The name of the place was a good hook to lure them into the trap. It could have been a huge flop, but it worked, and it didn’t cost us anything.”

“Do you understand now why I hired this woman?” gloats Evan.

“You hired her because you were desperate, and I told you

I had a friend who would do this job for free." Iris raises an eyebrow.

"But I kept her!" defends our manager, and we all laugh.

"Sorry to interrupt with a stupid question." Faith's calm voice makes us turn in unison towards her. "What is Twitter?"

We pause, perplexed at her question, and then laugh again. I hug her. "I'll show you and explain how it works."

She raises a wary eyebrow. "Is it something vulgar?"

"No! Not everything that comes out of my mouth is vulgar!" I protest while the others keep laughing.

"Michael, just give it up. She already knows you. Nothing you say can change her mind," Thomas jokes while Levi giggles uncontrollably. I give him a stern look, but the kid's not afraid of me. I have the authority of a goldfish as far as he's concerned.

"Are we done? Can we leave this hotel, or are you going to tease me for the rest of the day?"

Evan gets up from the desk he's been leaning on and gestures for us to leave as he follows us.

"The club said the instruments have arrived. Let's go and get set up for tonight. And Levi, you'll help the guys at the club run the mixing board for the show. You remember how it works, don't you? Keep an eye on them and make sure they don't do any damage."

Levi's chest puffs out a bit, and I send a look of gratitude to my friend.

***

"I look like a ninja!" Levi exclaims after being let in through the back entrance thanks to a diversion Evan created to distract fans in line at the main entrance.

The moment the van arrived with our gear, word spread that this must be the club where we'll be playing. The news is traveling at lightning speed, and so many fans are showing up we decided to start selling tickets early and notify everyone when they're sold out. I must admit, I like this strategy. It's nice—the mystery of not knowing how many people will be there and what the expectations are of those who do show up. It's definitely not like one of our usual shows, and it will be more intimate and entirely new for us.

"Glad to know *someone* enjoys sneaking through filthy alleys, trying not to attract attention," laughs Damian, amused at Levi's comment. He's wandering around a bit disoriented at the number of instruments on stage that aren't set up yet. It's been years since we personally set up our gear, from the instruments to the mixer to the lights, and I must say it feels somewhat nostalgic.

I look around to my right and see an open door that leads to a room with a sofa, where we'll probably have to change, and to my left, the bar counter with a guy in his thirties, long beard and flannel shirt, who's cleaning glasses. He nods at me when we enter, but otherwise, the place is entirely empty.

"Where's Evan and the girls?" I ask worriedly when I don't see our manager, Faith, Iris, and Emily.

"I texted Evan to go ahead and let them in. They were waiting in the van parked out front until we could get access from the back door," Simon says.

I'm a bit anxious. Faith is not used to crowds and wild fans. We never talked about what happened last week after her phone call with his father. We've just returned to a comforting routine: she no longer hints at wanting to leave, and I'm not

looking for anyone to replace her.

I'm totally against her moving away from Manhattan, but I realize I'm not sure where we are in the big picture. Obviously, she feels guilty about leaving Levi, especially after what he told her that morning, but I'm afraid all the confusion, shouting, and madness tonight might scare her away. This world really is light years away from the one she grew up in, and I can't assume that just because I like it, she will too. I'm afraid she'll leave not out of obligation to her father, but because she doesn't see a future in my world, which frightens me even more. It would be her choice, not forced on her by her family.

When I finally see them come in, all smiling, the weight I've felt on my chest since this morning lifts a little. The moment her gaze meets mine and I see an excitement I've never seen in her eyes, I can't help but smile. At the show in Los Angeles, she was happy but completely disoriented; today, she seems excited about being part of this adventure. Her face has that anticipation I see in the girls who wait for hours in front of the stage to see us play. Seeing it now, my heart swells with happiness.

"So? How does it look out there?"

"I'm in a happy daze. Lots of girls are in line, sitting behind the barricades with numbers on their hands to show who arrived first for tickets. Backstage in Los Angeles, all those famous people had nothing like the emotion I see in these girls' eyes. When we got out of the car and they thought it was you, they started screaming and crying…I mean…they're all here just for you. It's incredible!"

My eyes are locked on her face, her hands waving excitedly at what she's experiencing. "Are you glad you came?"

"Yes. I didn't realize how much people loved you until I saw them out here—tired but so happy. I've gotten used to the fact that you're a very famous band, but I never understood how much people adore you until seeing all of this."

She's almost breathless when the speech ends. I pull her in for a hug and rest my chin on her head. I feel her hesitating, but then her arms wrap around my waist in a soft but firm grip, and all my fears fade. Not disappear completely, but become background noise that I can ignore.

"I'm sorry to bother you two lovebirds, but the stage isn't going to set up itself." Damian's voice behind me makes me almost grumble in disappointment.

Faith pulls away from me, and immediately Emily needs her help to set up the merch table they've placed next to the bar to prevent access to the backstage area. No longer having the record company's security team behind us, we have to find alternative ways to guarantee a minimum of safety protocol. The venue, fortunately, has called in reinforcement bouncers to keep the crazy fans at bay. In the last few minutes, I've seen at least three new faces—men as big as a door and dressed in black t-shirts straining under the pressure of their muscles.

"If you keep looking at her like that, she'll catch fire," Evan teases me, grabbing me by the arm and dragging me to the stage.

"I'm just worried she'll freak out with all this chaos. She's lived in a protective bubble all her life."

He looks at me and lifts a corner of his mouth. "Well, Damian said the same about Lilly."

"Damian's testosterone flowed out in waves whenever he was around her. It was obvious to everyone how much he

wanted her."

"And you don't want Faith like that?" He raises an eyebrow in defiance.

It's not that simple. Of course, I would slip between her thighs instantly if she were like any other girl who was shy and had limited life experience. Faith is more than just a virgin from a sexual point of view, and the weight of not only having sex but taking such an essential part of her scares me.

"It doesn't matter what I want."

Evan puts his hand on my shoulder. "You're finally growing up." He winks at me before stepping over to the mixer and asking Levi how the setup is coming along.

I turn to the stage, the amps and instruments still not hooked up. I watch Thomas assemble his drum kit with a mixture of nervousness and melancholy stirring in my stomach. We haven't done a gig like this in a lifetime. Even the small tour we took around Manhattan with the Red Velvet Curtains wasn't loaded with so many emotions.

It's like we're starting all over, having to set up the stage, afraid something will go wrong, and no one to step in and solve the problem if it does. I missed all of this, the tension before going on stage that makes the adrenaline of the show that much more exciting.

I'm coated in dust and sweat, trying to secure the cables to the floor with duct tape, Evan helping next to me, when Emily walks up to us, interrupting our work. "I want Faith."

Our manager and I look up at her, frowning.

"I want her to come and work for us. She's a natural organizational machine. Did you know that she and her mother oversaw the weekly grocery orders for her entire community?

And that she had been the doctor's secretary since she was…I don't know, thirteen years old? Do you have any idea how well she's now organizing our merchandise table?"

Evan and I shake our heads no.

"Let's just say that she's numbered all the bags we'll be using to put the purchased merch in, to avoid any confusion about who bought what. She numbered the bags! I want her!"

Evan laughs at her explanation, but I'm not so amused. "Besides the fact that I hired her to look after Levi, so you'd need to find me a replacement nanny who's also a great teacher, I'm not sure she wants to stay in Manhattan."

They look at me, both confused.

"The family wants her to go home and marry the guy they chose for her, pop out a dozen children and die in that damn community," I explain, mumbling bitterly.

"And you'll let her go?" Emily says, shocked.

I frown and study her. "Emily, what can I do? Kidnap her and lock her in the house? The whole point of my role is to give her the freedom to make her own choices and not behave like her father. Doesn't that sound a bit hypocritical?"

Evan gets up and smiles at me, wiping his hands on a napkin he found. "No, but you can always convince her that this life is better than the one that waits for her at home."

"You make it sound so easy. Do you know how chaotic and messy this life is?"

"Have you ever wondered what *she* really wants? Have you even asked her?"

To tell the truth, no, I never specifically asked her what she wants in life. Maybe being a wife and a mother is everything she's ever dreamed of.

"It's not that simple," I answer, getting up and going to Levi, who's been driving the mixing guys crazy with chatter for at least two hours. Emily and Evan study me but seem to understand there's nothing more to say.

"So, have you learned how to do it? And next time you can run it by yourself?" I tease him.

Levi's eyes widen, terrified by my suggestion. "It's very complicated. I'll never remember everything. Will there be someone with me? If I do something wrong, I'll mess up the whole show!"

Seeing the seriousness of his reaction, I immediately regret joking with him. Sometimes I forget that he didn't grow up like a normal kid and that everything he was told to do was followed by a beating if he couldn't complete it. He's only fourteen, but I'm sure some of the things he was "asked" to do were totally over his head.

"There will be someone to give you a hand, don't worry. And if you're unsure of something, you can always ask me, Evan, or any of the guys for help. We're a family, remember? And families help each other."

I look over at Faith laughing at something Iris told her, and I wonder if this will ever be her family. I asked her to stay, to take care of Levi, but after Levi grows up? Can I be that selfish to ask her to leave her community for a position that has an expiration date?

Damian distracts me from my thoughts and doubts. "Can we do a soundcheck and then eat something? The bartender is making us sandwiches and doors open in a few hours."

I nod, take the headphones off the mixing board and make Levi wear them, though he looks at me with disappointment.

"You know the rule: concerts mean protecting your ears from music that's too loud. If you don't put these on now, you'll be deaf in your twenties and regret not listening to me. You can't ever get your hearing back if you damage it." I'm so serious that even the two kids at the mixer immediately put their earplugs in.

Levi grumbles but nods. He's a smart kid, and he knows it's for his own good. We talked about it at home, and after asking me for a scientific explanation of how the ear and our hearing work, which Faith was more than prepared to give him, he agreed that he should protect himself.

I head to the stage and put on my guitar. It's time to get back to playing live, and like every time I walk on the stage, big or small, my heart comes back to life.

***

We're quiet in the room backstage with the patched sofa and beat-up coffee table littered with bottles of water. Damian, Simon, Thomas, and I are all listening to the buzz on the other side of the door that will turn into a roar when we get onstage. This is the moment that most electrifies me: the moment just before going onstage, when the blood pumps fast in your veins and your gut clenches, making you want to run to the bathroom at the last minute. Once you're onstage, the logical part of your brain turns off and the primal animal that entertains the crowd lights up. Everything depends on the audience's reaction, and the more you can energize them, the more powerful you feel.

But this is the moment when fear and tension keep you on the razor's edge: do you go up and face the audience or bail? Ultimately, you know you have to do it, but I get fired up by the conflict raging inside of me just before the door opens wide

and the crowd comes into view.

Damian makes the first move, getting up from the couch, followed by Simon. Thomas hops off the table he's been sitting on and I move away from the wall where I've been leaning. We converge in the center of the room and hug as we always do before a show. Our heads unite in the center of a circle which no one else can enter. Us against the world, as it's always been since the beginning of this adventure.

"Let's go drive them crazy!" Damian laughs as we raise our heads and look into each other's eyes.

It's the one thing we've been telling ourselves for ten years, every single time, just us and the world outside. We don't answer him. We don't need to, it's our battle cry, and no one can take it from us.

Thomas opens the door, always the first to go out because he has the most difficulty getting behind the drums, and for the first time in years, we all follow immediately behind him. No big stage entrance, no lights going down. We simply go up and grab our instruments.

It takes people a few seconds to process what's happening, but when they see us, the roar shakes the walls of this place. Ninety-two paying tickets, the venue is sold-out for the evening—the fewest tickets we've ever sold since becoming pros, but the warmest welcome we've ever received. The stage is small, the air warm and stale and smells of sweat and alcohol, and my heart hammers against my chest like a teenager's first time.

That's what I love about making music: people's energy. It doesn't matter if it's ninety thousand in a stadium or ninety in a club. The voices rising in here tonight are all that matter. We

start with "Swing," the new song no one's heard except for a few small clips Emily and Iris posted online, but people recognize it, scream even louder, jump to the beat, and my fingers devour the guitar with the same hunger as when we were kids.

The millions of dollars in revenue from world tours doesn't matter anymore; we have enough money that we don't have to work for the rest of our lives. What saves us from despair every day is this: the music that flows inside you, the energy that brings you to life and makes you breathe like a fucking oxygen tank when you're buried in the middle of the ocean.

I look over at the bar where Evan, Levi, Iris, Faith, and Emily are gathered near Max and a new security guy. Levi is speechless; Faith is bobbing up and down to the rhythm, happy and euphoric, her eyes wide and dreamy: I've reached paradise.

Suddenly, it's clear that everything I want is inside this room: friends to make music with, a kid to help guide and teach that life isn't all crap, and a woman to show the chance for a better life. She may not be my woman, but—Christ!—she makes me feel like a god when she looks at me with those trusting eyes.

She trusts me, the Michael who's always ready to party, who doesn't commit, who risked dying of an overdose, who faces nightmares and demons. She trusts me, and that makes me feel worthy of being called a man for the first time in my life.

I turn to my friends who are dripping with sweat, more intense than I've ever seen them, and smiling as wide as the Pacific Ocean. Christ, this feels great! This show will go down as one of the all-time best moments ever, for us and the fans,

and who gives a damn if my fingers are bloody.

We play several new songs mixed with old hits, but none from the album we released just before giving up all the certainties we had with our record deal. That music is part of a past we've cut ties with. We never had time to play them live, bond with our fans, and listen to the crowd sing them. We detached from those songs, technically perfect but arriving at a time when our hearts could not embrace them.

We play for two hours without stopping, without catching our breath, giving our best and getting back just as much from the audience. The venue owner holds up a sign saying he'll turn off the power if we don't stop, but we laugh and keep playing. I search the crowd again for Faith and Levi, but I don't see them; they're already in the dressing room waiting for us. It's really time to leave this stage.

I look down at a girl in the front row who screamed the whole time. Purple hair, red face, a crumpled tank top, and a dreamy smile on her lips. Sweat has glued a few dark hairs to her forehead, she's exhausted out of her mind and it's beautiful because she experienced the show with her whole being. She'll take home the memories of this night we all shared forever.

I move towards her after taking off my guitar. The stage is so close to the crowd I just have to crouch and stretch out my arm to reach her and put my guitar pick in her hand. She looks at me in shock as her friends squeak excitedly.

"Thank you for coming tonight! We really appreciate your support," I tell her, and she bursts into tears, covering her mouth with her hand.

An entire day of emotions reach their peak and explode—for her, but also for me, it's a moment to remember. I get off

the stage, approach the barrier and stretch my arms out to hug her. She hesitates and then lets go, sobbing in the hollow of my neck.

"Thank you," I hear her whisper between hiccups, and I have to smile.

"Thank you," I tell her before I walk away and reach out to grab the hands of others who are watching me curiously.

That's what I like about these intimate concerts, the contact with the fans, the genuine ones, without hidden motives. They're here for our music, not to take us to bed, not to have a piece of us. They're here because they share our same passion. In the arenas, we're the gods of rock. But in these places, we're emotions given and received. Everything is amplified, exceptional, and the electricity is felt not only by me but by everyone around me. Damian has an erection you can see from a mile away, Thomas has an idiot smile splattered on his face, and even Simon has a dreamy look.

We enter the same small dressing room where we started the evening, Max and the other guy guarding the door. Inside, Evan, Iris, Emily, Faith, and Levi are waiting for us with smiles that cover their entire faces. I don't say anything, don't look anyone in the eye except Faith, who's looking at me like I'm a fucking god, and I can't resist. I stride towards her, grab her waist and pull her towards me, my hand in her hair, my mouth devouring her lips in a kiss that makes her moan. I'm so sweaty it's gross, but she doesn't seem to care because she gets on her tiptoes and grabs my hair, reciprocating the kiss with a tongue that seems to want to fight with mine. When I move away to catch my breath, I find her special smile for me. I look around and see everyone staring at us in shock.

Levi's voice breaks the silence. "I knew the mating season had started! For weeks he's been walking around, puffing out his chest and showing off like a peacock when she's around."

Damian breaks into a full-belly laugh. "Kid, you're my hero, I swear," he says, ruffling Levi's hair with his giant hand.

***

We take the elevator; it's half-past two in the morning, Levi has fallen asleep in the car and, rather than drag him like a zombie through the hotel, I carried him in my arms and am taking him to bed.

"Did you like the show?" It's just the three of us. The others stayed at the venue with the owners to chat a bit, like the old days when Joe kicked us out at dawn.

"It was amazing. Much more engaging than the one in Los Angeles. That wasn't bad, just there were too many people and so much distance between you and the audience. Tonight it felt like I was right there on stage."

I smile at her knowingly. I felt the magic too.

When we enter the suite, I breathe a sigh of relief. Carrying a fourteen-year-old boy in your arms is a bit too much, especially when the exhaustion from the show is kicking my ass.

"I'll put Levi to bed and then take a shower. If you want to use the bathroom first, go ahead," I say as I head towards one of the two rooms in the suite.

She hesitates for a moment and then nods. She looks at me with those eyes that make me want to pick her up, take her to her room, and make love to her all night until she shouts my name. But I put the idea aside and go put down the sack of potatoes I have in my arms.

When I come out of the bedroom, the living room is still

dimly lit and I don't hear any noise coming from the bathroom. I turn to the sofa and find Faith sitting there gazing out at the lights of Austin with a look that seems conflicted.

"Did something upset you?" I whisper as I sit next to her.

"Is it really so wrong to want a man who's not the one you're supposed to marry?"

Her question surprises me, especially since she doesn't have the courage to look me in the eye when she asks it. "It's wrong to marry a man you don't love. But desiring someone isn't wrong. It's human nature, and as long as you feel comfortable with that desire, there's nothing wrong."

"Even if you know that man will never marry you and make you an honest woman?"

This time she turns around and looks me straight in the eye. The struggle I read in her face leaves me breathless. I know she wants to kiss me at least as much as I want it, and I hate seeing her in such torment over something I can't give her. I'm not marriage material. I'm not even suitable for relationships longer than one night, but it kills me not to give her all the certainty she needs.

"It's how you live your life that makes you an honest woman, not if you sleep with the person you're going to marry. Being a good person, helping others, and staying true to yourself make you an honest woman. If sex is consenting and gives you pleasure, you shouldn't be ashamed to do it, even with a man you don't marry. You should be ashamed if you hurt someone, not if you feel pleasure."

Faith stares at me for a few moments, and I don't know if I said something wrong because I see her frowning, torn, but then she surprises me. She throws her arms around my neck

and kisses me, sinking her tongue into my mouth. It takes me a few seconds to react, to wrap my arms around her body, and to hold her to me. I hear her moan as she presses her pelvis against mine and tries to drag me over her onto the couch.

I don't know how I managed to stop—I'd love nothing more than to be dragged down on this sofa—but my rational side, the one that wants to protect her, hits the brake. "Not here; Levi might wake up and surprise us," I whisper to her lips as I lift her in my arms and get up from the couch.

I lay her on the king-size bed and close the door of the room, watching her look at me with wide eyes and a mixture of desire and fear runs through that intense blue. My legs tremble every time I see it. I kneel in front of her and reach out my hand to caress her cheek, feeling her shiver under my touch.

"You know we can stop whenever you want, right? You don't have to do anything that doesn't make you feel comfortable. If something embarrasses you or you're not sure, tell me, and I'll stop. Okay?" I'm more nervous than she is. I want this to be her choice; I want her to decide how far to explore without feeling any pressure. Realizing the power I have over her makes my heart pound in my chest with so much force that, while I feel like a superhero on one hand, I'm also doubting all the choices I've ever made in my life.

"Yes, I know. I trust you." Her voice is little more than a whisper.

She trusts me. She's the first woman who's ever placed the responsibility of such magnitude into my care. I take her face in my hands and kiss her, trying to convey all the sweetness I feel for her. This woman deserves all my time, my consideration, my attention.

Her fingers sink into my hair and tighten in a grip that sends a wave of pleasure through my body. A small groan escapes my lips, and I feel her pressing against my body, searching for the contact I've been craving since I first saw her in the infirmary. I lie her down on her back and concentrate on the delicate skin of her neck, tasting her with my lips, tongue, nibbling gently with my teeth until she pants. My hands slip under her shirt, stroking the skin of her belly and hips, never pushing further, giving her time to get used to my touch. I go back to her mouth, kiss her, savor every little groan she emits and feel intoxicated by her emotions. It's not like being in bed with other women; we're not just going through the motions for the sake of pure pleasure. It's a discovery of the senses, of hers but also of mine, which have never been so alive as in this moment.

"Can I take this off?" I ask her, grabbing the hem of her shirt.

She nods yes as she props up on one elbow to help me. I slowly pull off her shirt, and she leans back into the bed, her hands covering her chest, blushing in embarrassment. She's the sexiest woman I've ever seen, with her small breasts contained in a simple white cotton bra. No lace, no silk or frills. Only her pale skin and the veil of embarrassment that adds to her sensuality in my eyes.

I don't move her hands away; instead, I kiss her neck and then descend on her long fingers, savoring them with my lips and tongue, one by one. Her palm moves, resting on my cheek. I give her all the attention she deserves, kissing every single inch before going back to her chest, that pale stripe between her breasts that's driving me crazy. I kiss a trail to her navel

and feel her hold her breath. I look up at her watching me with excitement and fear. I kiss her again, going up towards her breast. I linger just above the white tissue and place my lips on it, feeling the nipple harden under a touch that makes her pant.

I look up at her while my fingers slip under the shoulder straps of her bra. She bites her lip, blushes, gives me a slight nod of her head, and I let the strap slip to unveil the perfect breast, with that pink nipple now begging me. I run my tongue over it without ever looking away from her face. I don't want to miss a single moment as she experiences this pleasure for the first time. She widens her eyes slightly then narrows them, emitting a moan of pleasure while arching her back until she's pressed her chest against my lips. I suck, nibble her skin, and the nipple gets hard. Small shivers cover her arms.

I pull her other bra strap down and bring my mouth to her nipple, taking her breast in my hand and squeezing it gently. Her eyes are shut, her lips open, and she is panting. I go down with my mouth on her belly, causing a sigh of protest from her lips.

"There are other places where it feels good to have my lips and tongue. Do you want to try?" I ask with a smile as she blushes.

She bites her lip again and nods, holding back a smile. I unbutton the jeans she's begun wearing recently and pull them off slowly. I kiss her feet, ankles, making my way up to her knees calmly, savoring her skin. When I get closer to the inside of her thigh and she understands where I want to go, she squeezes her legs and covers her face.

"What are you doing?"

I move up towards her, lying between her legs and kissing

the back of her hands until she moves them. “There are lots of ways to enjoy sex, and making you orgasm with my mouth is one of them. You don’t have to say yes if you feel embarrassed, but I promise it’ll feel amazing.”

She looks me straight in the eye, embarrassment covering her entire face, then sinks her head into the hollow of my neck and giggles nervously.

“Okay, but you have to take off some clothes too. It’s not fair that I’m the only one naked,” she whispers, her shyness evident in her faltering words.

I kiss her on the lips before kneeling, taking off my shirt while she looks at me and then sliding my pants on the floor. I leave my boxers on; my erection is too much for a moment so soaked in a feeling I can’t describe. It’s never taken me so long to have sex with a woman, and I’ve never been more aroused because of it. I could come in my underwear, just leaning on her body.

I slip between her legs to kiss her inner thigh and discover her skin is studded with small scars like the ones on her arms. How many times has she punished herself for something she’s not to blame for? How many times has she inflicted pain after feeling pleasure?

I go back to kissing her and savoring her with my tongue, trying to make the wounds disappear. I feel her tense and relax in a continuous cycle while I approach her opening with my lips, still covered by a pair of white cotton panties. I touch them with my fingers before resting my mouth on them with a light kiss. I hear her let out a small moan, her arms grabbing the bedspread. I touch her, kiss her, and then slip a couple of fingers under the elastic of her panties, raising my eyes to

her for approval before pulling them off. Her eyes are wide, a mixture of emotions across her face, but she shows no sign of stopping me as I pull them down to reveal the blonde hair that covers her and then all the way to the floor.

I go back to where the little piece of cloth was and kiss her, intoxicated by her smell and her slightly salty taste. She looks at me then closes her eyes, arching her back and moaning when I start licking and sucking the most sensitive part of her body. She mumbles nonsense while I savor the softness of her skin, aware that no one before has had the honor—a thought that makes my head spin. Her taste whets my appetite for her, her body, her femininity. I've always been with perfectly shaved women, comfortable in any situation, all so similar I couldn't tell them apart. Faith, however, has a touch and feel so unique that from now on, no woman will ever be able to compete. All of those past experiences disappear in a faint and confused memory. It's only Faith now.

I keep licking, kissing, sucking, and nibbling. With one hand, I reach for her breasts, playing with her nipples, and when I feel the muscles of her legs contract, I focus only on her. I don't stop. I don't give her a moment of breath until an orgasm seizes her, arching her back, pressing her against my mouth and stretching out her legs. The sight of her in the throes of an orgasm is so sexy I almost come in my boxers.

I kiss my way up along her belly until I reach her breasts and her panting face, inebriated with pleasure, her cheeks flushed with embarrassment.

Beside her now, I kiss her neck as she caresses my face with one hand. "Did you like it?"

"Yes..." Her voice is still trembling.

With one hand, I descend along her body, touching her breasts, belly, thighs, until I dwell on her opening, wetting my fingers, playing with her pleasure. “If you want, we can stop. If you don’t want to go any further, you don’t have to.”

I look into her eyes and have never seen such determination. “Don’t stop, Michael. Don’t stop.”

I kiss her on the lips before getting up and taking off my boxers. Her eyes widen and she blushes more but never looks away from my erection. I grab my wallet from my pants pocket and slip on a condom without ever losing sight of her face, trying to read every slight change of thought. I feel the burden of this responsibility—I’ve never taken anyone’s virginity—and the equally competing emotions of power and fear are new to me. I’m shaking like a teenager during his first time.

I slip between her legs and soak in the comforting sensation of her fingers stroking my hair. I kiss her again, stealing her breath, letting her know how important this moment is to me. She tenses when my erection presses on her opening, so I pull back, kiss her again, and lower myself to kiss her breasts while unhooking her bra and removing it altogether. Skin against skin now, I savor her neck, press against her bundle of nerves until I hear her moan again, her eyes closed, searching for a new wave of pleasure. I push a little, slide into her slowly until I feel her stiffen, and hold her breath.

“Try to relax; it will hurt less,” I whisper in her ear.

She inhales deeply a couple of times. I don’t move until I feel her muscles relax. I push slowly until I get into her completely. The feeling is so overwhelming my heart beats wildly inside my chest, rumbling in my ears. Her eyes shine as she stares at me with no sign of regret. I begin to sink into her with

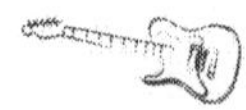

slow thrusts, not rushing. I continue without looking away from her eyes, kissing her lips from time to time, chasing my own pleasure only when I feel her circling her hips to meet mine.

She closes her eyes again, her breathing speeds up, and when I hear her moaning against my ear, all my fears vanish and culminate in an orgasm that shakes me so profoundly I tremble. I've never come so forcefully inside a woman's body, and the power of it almost makes me collapse on her.

I roll to one side, wrapping my arms around her body and drawing her into an embrace that almost suffocates her. I move aside her hair stuck to her forehead and study her expression, terrified of seeing remorse for what we've done. But my chest expands with a new breath when I meet her gaze and find a little embarrassment mixed with a smile.

I kiss her again, holding her close, and wonder how my life ever made any sense before meeting her.

PRESS *Review*

Rock Now!

The Jailbirds should be high-fiving whoever devised this recent brilliant marketing campaign. We all fell for it. Who expected the name of the place to be “Vintage”? Their return to the scene, however, was not just a well-designed advertising move. Even more than that, it was a return to their roots.

What a show, guys! What a show. The venue’s atmosphere was so vibrant the fans lingered for hours before leaving the neighborhood and returning home, drunk on music we haven’t heard in years. Forget the big stadiums and the roar of the crowds. At Vintage last night, our bellies positively reverberated with the absolute perfection of the show. The Jailbirds are stage animals, and when they let go of the reins, you’re overwhelmed with their unbridled energy and humanity.

We look forward to knowing where the next gig will be.

People

The return of the Jailbirds certainly didn’t go unnoticed, and while on stage the band unleashed an unprecedented show, it was behind the scenes that caught our attention. While Lilly’s absence from Damian’s side was noticeable, fueling rumors of their breakup, a mysterious blonde made an appearance with a

child who could have been her son. Is she an old flame of one of the Jailbirds coming back to surprise them with a paternity test? Witnesses confirm there was no intimate contact with any of the guys, but did say the woman carried herself with the confidence of someone who's known the band for quite a while. We're waiting for confirmation from the band, but in the meantime, we'll keep our eyes open for another possible public appearance of the mysterious woman. Who knows? Maybe a romantic date with one of the band's members.

CHAPTER 18
Faith

Light filters through the windows, and when I open my eyes, it takes a few moments before remembering we're still in Austin. I feel Michael's heavy arm encircling my waist, and the whole night comes back to my mind and I smile.

"Good morning," he whispers in my ear, drawing my back against his chest. The warmth emanating from his body feels comforting and safe.

What Michael makes me feel the most is protected, a sense of belonging. I experienced it every single moment last night when I gave him all of me. I still blush at what we did, the pleasure he made me feel, the emotions that still overwhelm my chest.

"Good morning." My voice is raspy from sleep.

He kisses me on the bare shoulder and then climbs towards my neck, and only now do I notice his erection pressing against my backside. I blush at the idea of making love to him again.

"How do you feel?" He gently turns me to look in my eyes, not simply making conversation or breaking the ice, but wanting to know.

"Sore but good."

He giggles and kisses me on the lips. "I know, I'm a sex machine." He acts cocky but it seems more like a way to hide

his embarrassment, perhaps for fear of my reaction.

"I guess the women who wake up next to you are tired after a night between the sheets with you." I tease, but my heart sinks a little thinking about all the women he's been with and all the ones yet to come.

"To tell the truth, I never wake up next to anyone," he admits, lowering his head into the hollow of my neck.

I'm a little surprised by his confession. "Michael, I know you've been with other women. You don't need to protect me."

His head pops up again, and he moves a lock of hair from my forehead. "I'm not kidding. I've had sex with them, but haven't slept with them. After we're done, everyone goes their own way. No awkward conversation, no need to exchange phone numbers. Friends as before. It's the first time I've woken up next to a woman."

My heart skips a beat. I'm happy to have been a first-time for Michael. "So you also lost your virginity tonight."

He frowns for a few moments and then laughs. "Yes, in a way." He kisses me again. "How do you feel? Do you regret it?" He seems almost intimidated by the question, as if afraid of the answer.

"Regret it, no. I don't make this decision lightly or in the heat of the moment. But I'll have to talk to my father and tell him I can't marry Jacob. I don't have any feelings for him, no physical attraction, and thinking about spending the rest of my life with him makes me miserable.

"I thought you could learn to love a person, but the more I live in the outside world, the more I realize this isn't going to happen. I can't learn to overcome a total lack of physical attraction towards him. After meeting you, I can't deny anymore that attraction isn't something you can learn. It's either there or not, like a switch. With you, it happened immediately, as soon as I saw that video. I didn't need to convince myself. I just felt it."

I turn to Michael and find him thoughtful. I can't understand what's going through his head. "How do you think he'll take it? Your father, not Jacob."

"Very badly," I answer without thinking. The thought of his explosive, irate reaction has loomed over my head from the moment I made the decision last night in Michael's arms. "But I hope in time he'll understand. I've never said no to his rules, and I don't know when and if he could ever forgive me."

"Do you think anyone in your family will support you?" He seems worried.

"I don't know. Maybe my sisters will take my side, but they'll never understand me. They didn't when I insisted on studying and leaving the community. They never fully comprehended my choices; they just didn't express their opinion."

Michael seems to think about it but says nothing, drawing me into an even tighter embrace and kissing me on the cheek. He's never been this affectionate, but then we've never been so intimate, so I don't know if this is normal for him. This is all so new to me I'm struggling to grasp it. How do you behave the next day? What do you say? The nagging doubt that this is just a one-time thing becomes more and more insistent, wrapping my chest in a grip I can't even articulate.

"What will happen now?" My words come out in a whisper; it's hard to keep a steady voice when your chest is in turmoil.

"If you're asking if what we did last night will happen again, that depends on you. I'd do it a thousand times, but if

you don't want to, I'll accept your decision. If you're asking about the future, the truth is I don't know. Waking up next to you is already a whole new experience for me. I'm experiencing it for the first time, just like you are."

I smile. "At least you're honest."

"I've never been one to hide behind lies to save my ass. I'm not capable of that. Lying doesn't change our reality or solve problems." He's so serious it's impossible to argue with his logic. "Now, if you ask what we're going to do in five minutes, I'll tell you that I don't have a condom for a second round." We both laugh. "So I guess we get up, have breakfast with Levi, and then meet with Evan and the others to go home."

The Michael I'm used to, who jokes about everything, re-emerges in a flash of normality that lightens the heavy air around us. My mind, however, goes back to what happened last night, and my sore muscles are a reminder that this morning I woke up different. A change I feel inside so profoundly I'm almost afraid it'll show on the outside. Will the girls realize I'm no longer as pure as yesterday when I left them? And their boyfriends? Most of all, will my father notice it the next time I see him? The mere thought that he could read it in my face makes me want to stay locked up in this room for the rest of my life.

***

The drive from the airport home is punctuated by Levi's constant chatter about Texas, concerts, the mixer, and the private jet no one will ever believe he flew in. I glance at Michael and find him looking at the boy with a level of engagement I've never seen before, even when talking to his closest friends. At first, I thought his interest in Levi was just the whim of a rock

star who harbors resentment towards the place that made him suffer. I've come to realize that he loves this kid unconditionally, like a son. I've never seen him once express regret at welcoming him into his house, even when he ran away or when he screams at night because of his nightmares.

We arrive at the apartment entrance, grabbing our bags and heading quickly towards the lobby, ready to take a shower and shake off the exhaustion of the flight. As soon as we set foot inside the building, however, the tense frown of Matthew, the day-shift concierge, alerts us that something is wrong.

"Is there a problem?" Michael asks, approaching him almost conspiratorially.

"Those gentlemen, " he gestures towards the corner of the lobby, "have been here since early this morning, asking about Miss Faith, and don't want to leave. I tried to convince them to give me a phone number I could call if you returned before this afternoon, but they weren't interested. They haven't been disruptive or anything, but I don't know…maybe I should have called the police?"

Michael responds but I don't hear it. My gaze has rested on the three figures who are getting up from the chairs in the corner of the lobby and approaching me. My father, along with my two older brothers, Joseph and Peter, are wearing expressions that make the blood freeze in my veins. All the courage I had this morning is lost, frozen in a grip that tightens my insides and doesn't let me breathe.

"Pack your bags." My father's voice is as harsh as his expression, and the disgusted looks of my brothers pass from me to Michael to Levi.

"Dad..." My whisper comes out faintly; my voice betrays

all my fear.

"Go pack your bags!" he thunders louder. My father has raised his voice only a few times in the presence of people outside our family, adhering to the belief that you don't air your dirty laundry in public.

From the corner of my eye, I notice Michael move in closer to me, Levi behind him peeking around his back and grabbing my hand to hold it tightly.

"Did you really believe that after weeks of not communicating, we wouldn't look for you at the boarding school? The Mother Superior said you've been gone for months," he shouts again as my brothers' gaze becomes even darker.

"Dad, let me explain," I say in a trembling voice.

"Shut up! You lied to me. What have you come to do here with this man? Have you become his concubine? Jacob is at home waiting for you to become your husband. He has already been all too lenient with you. Do you have any idea of the rumors going around in the community? You are the shame of our family. Your brothers had to search the Internet to see what had happened to you. And they found you attending concerts of the devil's music. Now, pack your bags and come home. We'll try to convince Jacob not to disown you before the marriage."

The lump in my throat is as big as a baseball, but I don't let the tears fall as I look my father in the eye. "I'm not going to marry Jacob, Dad. I'm not in love with him."

My brothers' eyes go big with rage, and they look ready to grab me like a sack of potatoes and load me on a plane. But it is my father who takes a step forward and hisses, "Stop being a tramp and put on some decent clothes before you come

home. I will not tell your mother I found you dressed like a prostitute."

"Enough is enough!" Michael's steady voice reminds me he's still by my side. "You may be her father, but I won't allow you to talk to her like that. Faith is an adult: she has an honest job and is an independent woman. She's decided not to marry that man, and if she doesn't want to go home, you have to respect her decision."

His passionate defense of me makes me turn my head to look up at him. He's so intense my heart almost jumps out of my chest. Whether he really cares for me or just can't stand my father's bullying, having someone defend me, stand by my side and listen to what I have to say, feels like a boulder being lifted off my chest.

My father is undaunted by Michael's words. "Who do you think you are? You're a crook who lives in sin and corrupts a girl just for your own carnal pleasure. You have no right to speak. You're nothing but scum that this liberal society can't keep locked up because it's too lenient with its criminals."

Michael's face is a mask of anger, resentment, and pain at my father's words. A hiccup shakes Levi and I look down to see him watching the man with eyes full of tears, shame contorting his face. The poison from my father's lips, acidic and corrosive, has pierced this kid's chest and made his heart bleed. Michael's an adult with thick skin, but Levi's just a boy with a heart of gold and as much intelligence as shyness. He's alone, helpless, and struggling to trust people and a society that branded him a criminal at only fourteen years old.

I realize, after months of living with the two of them, how wrong my father's teachings are; how limited his worldview

is compared to the reality around him. He's never experienced life in a way that allows him to understand people for who they really are: human beings who make mistakes but can be redeemed.

"Stop!" My voice is firm, and I see my brothers look up sharply, stunned. "You don't know what you're talking about, Dad. Don't judge Michael if you've never even tried to get to know him. You have no right."

The slap comes like a bolt out of the blue, followed by Michael pushing a hand on my father's chest to keep him at a safe distance. I haven't been slapped like that since I was a child, and it's clear now that my father never stopped treating me like one. To him, I'll always be a little girl who doesn't know how to make decisions.

I look at my brothers, who haven't opened their mouths, and they won't. They never have. It's my father who bosses me around—I'm *his* property—just like they order around their wives and children. They're only here because they understand technology, and he needed them to find me.

"You've become a slut, impertinent, unworthy of being part of our family. Don't you dare come home again. You're dead to us. I'll try to convince Jacob to marry your sister Grace and save the honor of the family you have stained with your insolence."

My heart clenches in my chest. I didn't think he had a contingency plan to save his reputation.

"She's only sixteen years old," I plead.

"Plenty of time for her to start behaving like a good devoted wife!"

Michael looks at me, scandalized: "Is that even legal?"

"In our state, the age for consent is sixteen," I say with a lump in my throat.

All the women in our community regard their sixteenth birthday as a sad day. While not many of us marry at that age, all of us are introduced to the man who will be our husband then. Grace will turn sixteen in a few months, and I'm sure my father will marry her off shortly after that, avoiding the scandal of another daughter escaping marriage.

"And would Grace actually consent?" insists Michael, with the anger and frustration of someone who's witnessed such a thing before.

"Dad, please. Don't make her marry that man."

"You are no longer part of our family. Never dare to contact any of us again. Not your mother, not your sisters or brothers. You have decided to live in sin, and you will do it alone." My father's words reach my heart like a sword. He's serious; he's disowned me as a daughter. I no longer have a family. I no longer belong to anyone. Not now. Not ever.

"Father..." For the first time Joseph says something, his eyes wide with disbelief, a mirror of Peter's expression.

My father says nothing, just gives him a stern look that shuts down any conversation. Joseph closes his mouth and looks down, while Peter's eyes plead with me, a tacit request to ask my father for forgiveness. But I can't do that. As miserable and guilty as his decision makes me feel, I can't go back. I can no longer go back to being unhappy in a life I don't want to live.

I watch them walk out the door, Levi's arms tightened around my waist, Michael's sad eyes watching a man I no longer recognize, or perhaps see for the first time. A man who

doesn't care about his family but only the image it projects to the outside world.

"I have to call Grace, warn her of what my father wants to do," I whisper without ever looking away from the now empty door.

"Will it give her a chance to escape? Does she have a place to go if she decides not to marry that man?"

I look at Michael, his worry, shake my head, and try to swallow the knot forming in my throat. My sister will never leave home because she has nothing and no one. She doesn't have a decent education to get a job, and she has no idea that a woman outside the community can work and support herself, just like a man. She doesn't know there's a whole other life out here because no one's ever taught her that. It's too late for her.

"Can we go home?" I plead softly as he takes me by the hand and walks me to the elevators, Levi clinging to my waist as if afraid my father will come back and take me away.

When we finally get inside, I head to my room and barely get my shoes off before curling up on the bed and letting the tears finally fall. I hear Michael's heavy steps followed by Levi's lighter ones, and then Michael stretches out behind me, holding me in a hug while Levi makes room inside my arms and encircles my waist. Despite being scared to death by what awaits me in the future, their arms give me comfort, holding together what's left of the only life I knew, and that's now crumbling before my eyes.

CHAPTER 19

Michael

Walking into the record company offices, I notice the phone is ringing and there's no one behind the counter.

"Where the hell is the receptionist?" I ask Emily, who seems tense as she enters the elevator to join Iris on the top floor.

"She went home due to an urgent problem with her dog-sitter. She says Molly's not eating her new vegan diet and the guy who looks after her dog threatened to give her chicken nuggets," she explains through gritted teeth as the doors close.

"Is she serious?" I ask Damian, who has just come out of the recording room and is ducking into the conference room. "People actually put their dogs on a vegan diet? Christ, only in Manhattan!"

"Look, I don't even want to know. Emily's furious," Simon says as we all take a seat in the conference room to discuss the next stages of the tour.

"How are Faith and Levi?" asks Thomas as he takes his seat next to Evan.

"Fine, I think... But I have to ask you for a favor."

Everyone looks up from what they're doing to give me their full attention. I don't often ask for favors, and when I do, I'm either in trouble or having a hard time doing something on my own.

"You've got me worried." Evan breaks the silence when he sees I'm taking my time, searching for a way to say it.

"Yesterday, Faith's father came looking for her, along with her two brothers. To say it was a tense meeting is an understatement."

"Does he want to take her home?" Simon frowns, worried.

"He tried, but when she told him she doesn't want to marry the guy they forced on her, her father told her she's a whore and disowned her."

For a moment, complete and utter silence falls on the room as they all stare at me with horrified expressions.

"Wow," Thomas says. "Just when I thought I'd seen the worst of the dysfunctional families, I'm reminded it can get even worse."

"That's not all. He plans to marry that Jacob guy to her sixteen-year-old sister to save the good name of the family."

"How old is this guy? Is that even legal?" Damian is more angry than surprised.

"I don't know, I think about twenty-five, thirty. And yes, Faith says the age for consent in their state is sixteen, so it can't even be considered rape!" I admit this with a taste of bile in my mouth that's been sickening me since yesterday afternoon.

"In those kinds of communities, they keep to the letter of the laws to prevent social services from taking their children away," whispers Simon disgustedly, and I can't blame him.

"How can we help?" Evan catches my eye.

"Faith is suddenly without a family out of the blue. I think she's scared about her future. She's always assumed she would go back to live in her community—kind of kept it as her lifeline when she launched herself into the world. Now she has nowhere to go, and even if she tries to pretend everything is fine, I know she's afraid of what might happen down the road."

"She has you, she has us... She shouldn't worry about that, we're her family now." Simon is almost anxious.

I smile at him. I know him enough to know that he wants to make everyone feel safe and welcome. "You don't need to tell me. We're a family, I know I'll have you all for the rest of my life, but it's difficult for Faith and Levi to understand this. I think they're afraid at any moment things could change and they'd have nothing, no one. I have no idea how to help them understand that even if we don't spend the rest of our lives together, they can always count on us."

"At first, we had a hard time trusting too. And we weren't sure we'd all stay together once we got out," Thomas admits.

"Exactly. That's why I was wondering if we could spend a weekend together somewhere, maybe in Connecticut. To show them that we're really a family, even if a rather unconventional one."

"I'll send a message to Emily and tell her to book a place." Evan steps in without even asking if we're all agreed because my friends' faces show that they're one hundred percent in.

***

I watch Faith and Levi, full of surprise and admiration at the huge colonial-style house with its gray stone façade and stately white entrance columns. It's impressive, surrounded by a vast lawn, and big enough to accommodate the ten of us and maybe even a few more.

"There's even a swimming pool," Evan announces as he opens the front door.

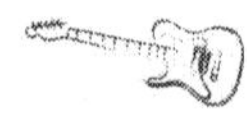

Faith lingers in the entryway, enchanted by the white marble and massive staircase and dominated by a crystal chandelier hanging above our heads.

"Do you like it?" I ask, feeling a little anxious. I asked my friends to plan this weekend for her and Levi, but I'd be hurt if she wasn't completely won over. This realization confuses me, as I've never been one to think too much about what a woman might like, yet here I am with my heart slamming in my chest, waiting for her answer.

"It's…it's…I don't even have words to describe how beautiful this place is."

I smile, relieved. "You'll see, it'll be relaxing too."

Faith looks up at me, and the smile on her lips seems to lighten a little of the pain she's been carrying for a couple of days. "Thank you," she whispers.

I hold her in a hug and then lead her upstairs to choose her room and put her suitcases down while I look for one with two beds to share with Levi. It's strange how it's become a habit to share my spaces with the kid, giving Faith privacy. I've gotten used to it, and it doesn't bother me at all. Before they came to live with me, I was annoyed to death at having to accommodate someone else.

"Okay, this is not a room. It's not possible; it even has its own living room!" she exclaims when I pull her into one of the double bedrooms overlooking the back garden.

"Prepare to be stunned by many other luxuries these troublemakers enjoy regularly. My old Manhattan apartment would fit comfortably in this room." Iris's voice comes from behind us, and we turn around to find her leaning against the doorjamb.

"I don't know if I should get used to it. Once Levi has private teachers, I'll have no reason to stay in Manhattan." She looks down, perhaps to hide that veil of fear that runs through her eyes.

I was right. Her desire to return home has always been about security, out of uncertainty for what the future holds for her. Now that her father doesn't want her back, there's nothing left to make her feel safe. I can't imagine how difficult this must be for her. She has no idea what's out there, the possibilities she has. Starting from a disadvantaged position, despite being intelligent and having studied, she has no clue about any of the world's opportunities. I hate her father even more for clipping her wings and making her so dependent on her family.

Iris approaches and embraces her. "You don't have to think about that. Not only will Levi still need you, even if you don't keep working full-time for Michael, we'll help you find a job, a place to stay. We won't abandon you just because you no longer work for Michael. Now you're part of our family; you can't get rid of us so easily."

The mere thought that she could leave our house makes my heart beat wildly. That apartment isn't mine; it's ours—Faith's, Levi's, and mine. True, I paid for it, but the idea of one of us leaving it is so frightening it almost suffocates me.

"You don't need to look for any other home. That room is yours. No one will take it away from you, whether or not you want to continue to take care of Levi." The words come out in a single breath, hurried, with that vein of despair I feel and can't seem to hide.

Faith looks at me with relief in her eyes. Iris, on the other hand, has a smug smile.

"Also, judging from the way Michael kisses you, I don't think you're going anywhere soon." She chuckles as she walks to the door. That girl has spent too much time with Thomas, she's becoming just like him.

Damn that time I let myself go and kissed her in front of everyone. "Iris!" I give her the side-eye as she leaves.

"Don't blame me, I just came to warn you that we're all in the kitchen preparing dinner if you want to join us…but if you want to stay a while on your own, no problem. Just close the door." She laughs as she walks away.

Faith is red with embarrassment. "She's joking," I clarify before she comes up with any strange ideas.

"I know. But you know what's funny? The temptation to stay here locked up with you for the rest of the weekend isn't all that bad an idea."

I look at her for a few seconds, stunned, and then burst out laughing. "I created a monster." I pull her in for a hug, and she stretches her arms around my waist. What the hell am I doing? I should stay away from her, but I don't even try.

She looks up, and I lower myself to kiss her on the lips, enjoying the taste when my tongue touches hers. She's no longer as shy and awkward as the first time. In fact, she seems to want me with the same intensity that I want her.

"Let's go downstairs before they think we've gone missing," I whisper, leaning my forehead against hers. My words are in stark contrast to the burning desire to lay her on that bed and make love to her until I lose myself in her. Making love... I never thought there could be anything but sex with a woman, yet here I am, after tasting the forbidden fruit only once, wanting more. This thought terrifies me. I've already known what it's like to depend on something to make me feel good that, in the end, almost killed me. Faith isn't a drug; she's not toxic to my health. But I'm scared that if she leaves, I *will* die.

***

"Where did you learn to make this?" Lilly turns to Faith, grabbing yet another piece of bread she made while Thomas and Damian were busy with dinner.

We're all seated around the long table on the back deck. Ivy-covered beams obscure the starry sky above us, and the rows of tiny lights give a soft glow that makes this summer evening almost magical. The dim radiance from the pool reflects small ripples that dance slowly across our faces. Only the sounds of crickets keep us company, immersing us in a reality so different from that of Manhattan that all our problems seem to disappear. Even the air seems to smell like freshly cut grass tonight.

Whenever I came to the area to visit Simon, it always seemed like something was missing, that the air smelled like nothing. But now, I could imagine buying a house around here like the others did if this feeling of peace could last forever.

"It's something my mother does when she needs sourdough for some other recipe. This doesn't need yeast and can be made in a few minutes in a pan without using the oven. If you want, I'll teach you."

"No, please," we all shout in chorus, with Faith remaining stunned by our reaction.

"Lilly is so bad at cooking she could set fire to the building," Damian explains, and Faith looks shocked.

"Shut up! I'm not that bad." Lilly rolls her eyes, pretending to be offended.

"How long have we lived together?"

"Almost a year," she mutters.

"And how many pans have we had to replace because you ruined them after just one use?"

"Six," she whispers, and we all burst out laughing.

When Faith turns to me stunned, looking for confirmation, I nod. "Yes, she's terrible in the kitchen."

"Then who cooks at home?"

"Damian," Lilly replies, grabbing the hand of her partner and clutching it as she looks at him with such intensity I know what it means to be willing to die for another person.

"Really?"

We all turn to Faith's incredulous gaze. She blushes and looks down. "Sorry. I didn't mean to be rude. It's just that I'm not used to men cooking. In the community where I grew up, women take care of the children and the family. Men work the fields or take care of the animals... For me, it's strange to think of a man in the kitchen."

"What's it like to live in that community?" Emily expresses everyone's curiosity. "I mean, you have no contact with the outside, so what do you do? Do you have a TV? Do you read books?"

"We have a TV, but we're not allowed to watch movies or anything. Usually, my father follows the news with my older brothers to know what's happening in the world, but the younger ones are not allowed to. He says there's too much evil in the world, and it's not necessary for us to see it. We have some books we're allowed to read, and we find some in the church library. We get up around four in the morning and by nine at night we're already in bed." Her voice is uncertain, and

I don't know if she's ashamed or feeling nostalgic.

"So basically, you work all day and then after dinner you don't do…anything?" asks Emily, perplexed like the rest of us.

Faith shrugs as if she doesn't know what to say.

"Boys spend time talking with their friends, chewing tobacco, and just hanging out. Girls over the age of sixteen are mostly busy preparing their dowries, and that takes a lot of time."

We all look at her with wide eyes.

"Dowry?" asks Iris incredulously.

"Yes, the sheets, tablecloths, and embroidered towels to take to the new house when you get married. Most girls also embroider their entire wedding dress for the day of the ceremony. Don't you do that?" she asks uncertainly.

"I think that custom's been out of fashion for two centuries now," Emily admits.

I think back to my mother, to the white sheets with the embroidered edge that she laid out so carefully in the room where we had the boiler, and about how Faith is more like my family than me.

"Really?" Faith finds this hard to fathom. "Then what do you give as a gift to your husband when you get married?"

"Mostly debt." Lilly laughs. "Whether it's from college or the house you desperately try to buy, usually when you get married, you're up to your eyeballs in debt."

We all laugh, because modern society really is like that. You leave your parents' house and start fighting for every single penny. In some aspects, Faith's community protects its children from these struggles. But it's such a high price to pay I don't know if it's worth it.

"The guy you were going to marry... Is it true your father wants to marry him to your sister?" asks Iris worriedly.

Faith gives me an embarrassed look. I told her my friends know all about our meeting with her father, that I tell them everything and she can trust us, but I don't know how much she wants to revisit that day.

I reach out and take her hand, trying to reassure her. "You don't have to answer if you don't want to."

She smiles at me and clasps my hands tightly. "No, it's okay," she reassures me, then turns to Iris. "Yes, it's true. In a few months, she'll be sixteen, and as part of the birthday celebration they'll present her to Jacob."

A worried look passes between Emily, Iris, and Lilly.

"Do you have something to say?" I ask, feeling protective of Faith.

"No, it's just that we wondered if there was a specific reason why you don't want to marry him... Like, if he's…violent. Maybe we can call the police or social services, and your sister won't become his prey," Iris explains.

While I appreciate the gesture, I don't think we can take care of everyone who lives in that community.

"No, absolutely," Faith is quick to specify. "Jacob is a peaceful man, and he would never hurt a person. No one in our community has ever raised their hand to anyone else. As much as it seems like a cult, as Michael calls it, we actually cultivate the ideals of love and mutual respect. And protection for anyone who lives with us."

She inhales deeply as if looking for the right words.

"The reason I don't want to marry him, apart from the fact that I'm not in love with him, is that I don't feel attracted to him. Specifically, I'm…disgusted by his smell. I know it's a selfish motive, but Jacob and his family have a pig farm and he works all day on it. So, partly because hygiene is not a priority with him, and partly because that smell permeates everything he wears, every time I'm close to him, the nausea makes me almost throw up. My mother says I'll get used to it by living with him, but I don't know if I want to. I'm ungrateful, I should appreciate the fact that he wants to start a family with me, but I just can't."

"Don't even think something like that." It's Evan who speaks, surprising everyone. "It's already crazy that you can't choose the person to be with. Feeling guilty because you don't like someone is ridiculous. You have every right to fall in love and be attracted to whoever you want."

He normally doesn't comment on anyone's lives but his friends', so to make this statement about the community where she grew up means he thinks of her as one of us. Faith smiles, but it's hard to convince her that she's made the right choice.

"Incense," I say without thinking.

Everyone turns to me with puzzled looks.

"The smell of it nauseates me. When I lived with my parents, my father would force me into houses to steal and then drag me to church to confess my sins to a priest, his friend, to be absolved. He did the same every time he beat up my mother or one of my sisters. The church always smelled of incense and it nauseated me. Or rather, it nauseated me to go to church and be made to confess sins I never wanted to commit. To this day, incense reminds me of that feeling of shame and anger," I confess as everyone looks at me with an understanding expression.

"Alcohol," Damian says, in the absolute silence that has fallen around the table. "As crazy as it sounds because I drink it regularly, whenever I enter a room where there's a drunk, the first thing I notice is the smell of alcohol. When my father lost his job, that smell was the first thing I inhaled every morning when I got up and went to the kitchen for breakfast. Usually, there were broken plates in the trash can, and my mother tried to hide the bruises under layers of makeup. I always associated that smell with the way my father treated my mother."

"Cookies," begins Thomas. "Even though I keep churning them out regularly, the scent reminds me of my mother, and that wound in the center of my chest begins to bleed again. When I smell cookies, I remember every time I'll never see my parents or my sister and nieces or nephews again."

Iris extends her hand to his and squeezes it tightly. "Disinfectant," she then whispers. "The smell of disinfectant in clinics or hospitals drives me crazy. It's the first smell that hits me every time I enter the clinic where my mother is hospitalized and reminds me that she'll never get out of there. God, I hate it so much I don't even keep it at home!"

The silence that follows feels like respect for the confessions we've made. I'm surprised that it's broken by Levi, who's spent the evening playing with his phone. I thought he was bored with our adult conversation, but I was wrong; he's listening to every single word.

"The smell of people..." He looks up from the phone and passes his young gaze around the table. "Before my mom died and social services came to pick me up when I was seven, I lived with her in an abandoned house with other junkie friends of hers. Even more than the dirty mattresses, what I remember is the stink of people who never washed. We didn't have running water or even doors on the bathrooms, and the guys smelled so bad. Of sweat, vomit…I don't know…smelled. I hate smelling people who don't bathe," he confesses before returning to play with his phone, as though he hadn't just dropped a bomb that none of us will be able to forget.

I struggle to swallow as I stretch out a hand to his shoulder and squeeze it, letting him know I'm here for him. I look around at my friends' faces and realize they're gazing at him with such tenderness and care, as if they want to erase those memories from his mind. I knew he'd had a hard life in the foster care system, but I had no idea his life before that time was even worse.

The need to protect him is so strong there's no doubt in my mind that I'll never let him go again. He *will* stay with me, even if I have to flee from the country and hide him from anyone who will come looking for him.

***

"If you need anything, we're just across the hall, okay?" I say to Levi as I help pull his pajamas out of the bag he brought for the weekend.

"I know, you've already told me. You'll be back in a while, but if I need it there's a glass of water on the nightstand and no worries if I sleep with the light on. I'm not a little kid!" he exclaims dramatically.

I smile. I know he's not a child; he never was, he had to grow up too fast, but I tell him those things because they reassure me more than anything else.

"Listen, I spoke to my lawyer..." He freezes immediately, eyes wide and pajamas tight against his chest. "I'd like to for-

malize the fact that you live with us, and officially ask for guardianship from social services. But first, I wanted to ask you if you want to live with Faith and me. I don't want to make that decision for you." My heart hammers in my chest. I've never been so anxious about an answer. If he tells me he doesn't want to, I think it would break my heart.

"Are you kidding right now? Because if you are, it's not funny, okay?" His eyes are veiled with tears.

"I'm very serious. We may not be the most normal family in Manhattan, but I don't think we're so bad, are we?"

Levi throws his arms around my waist and squeezes me tightly.

"Do I take this for a yes?" I hold him in an embrace.

He nods as he wipes away his tears. "Of course, it's a yes. And if you're taking me to see the butterflies, I'll have to stay at least until November, right?"

"I want you to stay much longer than November, but yes, if we have to go and see the butterflies, it's better if we live under the same roof."

"Good." He smiles at me, and I can't help but stretch out my hand and ruffle his hair.

"Do you promise to call me if you need anything?" Why is it so difficult to leave this kid's room?

Levi rolls his eyes and lets out an exasperated sigh. "Yes, I promise! Can I go to sleep now?"

I smile and nod. "Yes. I'm leaving."

When I turn around, Faith is at the doorjamb smiling. I follow her to her room, and when she invites me to come in, my heart squeezes in my chest.

"It's wonderful what you're doing for Levi. He needs stability, and as absurd as it sounds given the work you do, I think you're the most solid thing he's ever had in his life."

"It wasn't a hard decision. In fact, I think it was the easiest one I've ever made. And when I say there's room for you in our lives too, I'm not kidding. Right now, the future seems uncertain and frightening, but you can stay with us as long as you want until you find your way," I whisper as I hold her face tightly in my hands. I want her to look me in the eye. I want her to understand that I mean it, that I would never lie to her.

"And when I find out what I want to do in life?"

"You can decide then whether to stay with us or whether you want to continue on your way."

I silently pray this will never happen. Not that she doesn't find her calling in life, but that she decides to leave us. Faith rises on her tiptoes and kisses me on the lips. A gesture as innocent as it is sinful. I can no longer live without her, her body, her lips, her taste. I tasted her, and she's become my favorite drug. I hold her close and put my hand in her hair, savoring her lips again, her tongue, her every sigh. I make her lie on the bed then slip between her legs, feeding on her moans, her hips looking for mine.

"Please tell me you have a condom," she whispers in my ear when I kiss her neck.

I look up at her and find her charged with palpable desire. I can't hold back a smile. "You love to live in sin." I make fun of her a little. "I like the influence I'm having on you."

She laughs, amused. "Don't pretend you haven't thought about repeating the experience. I don't believe you suddenly took a vow of chastity…or you have several other women who satisfy you..." The smile dies on her lips along with the words.

I take her chin in one hand and force her to look into my eyes. "As absurd as it sounds coming from me, there's no one but you I'd rather go to bed with—now and forever." The words slip from my lips with such simplicity it sobers me. I hadn't noticed until now that I'm no longer interested in women, not in the sexual sense, at least. I've been blaming Levi for the fact that I can't go out every night to party and find myself a different woman, but the truth is everything I need to satisfy me is at home with Levi and Faith.

She smiles and kisses me on the lips. "Is that a yes or a no?"

"It's in my pants pocket," I confirm before lowering myself again and kissing her with a devotion I haven't felt in a long time.

"Get it!" She pushes me on the chest, and I laugh like an idiot.

"Whatever you say, boss."

She looks at me as I get up, grab the condom from my wallet, and throw it on the bed, and then watches while I take off my shirt, pants, and boxers. I remain naked, enjoying her eyes sliding over every part of my body, blushing but never looking away. I love the naivety in her look and the desire she tries to hide when lingering on my awakening erection.

"What should I do now?" Her words catch me by surprise. I look up at her face and find her biting her lower lip, unsure of what she should do lying on that bed.

"Would you like to undress?" My question is more insecure than hers. We're both in uncharted territory here. I've never taught a woman to have sex.

Her cheeks flush with embarrassment, but she doesn't let it stop her. With slightly clumsy movements, she pulls the floral

dress over her head and then stretches out again, waiting for me to give her other directions. Another woman would have sensually stripped herself, playing it up, seducing me. Faith just looks at me with such innocence it makes me lose my mind. I put the condom on my overbearing erection and kneel between her legs, helping her pull off the bra and cotton panties I didn't think could tease my imagination as much as they do.

I move up to kiss her and then down to savor the skin of her breasts, her belly, until I reach the area that makes her orgasm and blush with embarrassment at the same time. I look up at her, her eyes are wide, biting her lip. With a mischievous smile, I wink at her and then sink my tongue into the folds of her pleasure and make her sigh.

"Michael..." Her whisper is like a melody I'd never tire of hearing in her moments of pleasure.

With one hand, she pulls up my head and I look up, trying to figure out if I'm doing something wrong, but her smile reassures me.

"I like to feel you inside me." She blushes as she says it. Any other time, I would have made a joke, but she says it with such innocence all my cockiness slips away, leaving me dry-mouthed and short of words.

I slip between her legs, spreading them, press against her opening, and slide into her with a slow but continuous movement. I feel her inhale deeply, stiffen, and hold her breath. But when I kiss her and start moving, her muscles relax, and I guide her legs until they're wrapped around my waist.

"Michael," she whispers again when I begin to sink into her more eagerly, no longer able to hold back my desperate desire

for her.

I meet her gaze and get lost in those blue eyes so full of pleasure. Her hands cling to my shoulders and when she comes, closing her eyes and moaning, her beauty takes my breath away. The orgasm that shakes me after a few lunges is so intense it seems to never end. My heart gallops in my chest, the air struggles to reach my lungs, and I'm almost afraid to pull out of her perfect body. I'm worried that if I separate myself from her right now, I may lose my soul in the folds of these sheets.

CHAPTER 20

Faith

"Where the hell did the receptionist go?" asks Michael as we walk through the door of Jail Records. The phone is ringing, but no one answers, which seems to be a pattern lately.

Evan throws us an exasperated look while talking on his cell phone, and Emily approaches just as the phone stops ringing. "I fired her. She was never at her desk, she went out to get coffee without ever telling anyone, and to top it all off, she hit on every one of you. Do you know she 'accidentally' left a pair of panties in Evan's bag?"

I'm not exactly used to the rock star life, but it can't be appropriate in any job setting to find your employees' underwear in your personal belongings. Evan seems to have lost all hope of finding someone who can run this office. Since I've known them, five girls have come and gone from this counter.

Michael glances at me resignedly while Levi waits in the conference room for our appointment with the school that provides private tutors for home study. Michael has realized that if Levi wants a chance at getting into college, he'll have to work hard with suitable teachers to make up for the school years he's lost so far. I can get him to do the homework assigned by private schools, but I'm not prepared to help fill the increasingly apparent gaps in his school curriculum. Levi's brilliant.

He can catch up, but he needs professionals, not a nurse who's been improvising as a teacher.

Emily returns to the conference room with her computer just as the phone starts ringing again. She lowers her head in frustration. It can't be easy to do your job while constantly being interrupted. Evan leans his forehead against the door jamb and closes his eyes, the exasperation evident as he answers his own cell call.

Without thinking, I lean over the counter, take the notepad and pen and grab the phone. "Good morning, Jail Records. This is Faith. How can I help you?"

"Hi, Faith, I'm Rachel from *The Times*. I tried calling Iris, but she didn't answer. Can I talk to her for a moment? I really only need to steal five minutes."

I write the name on the notepad. "Iris is in a meeting now and isn't available. If you leave me a message and the phone number, she'll contact you as soon as possible."

I hear the person on the other end sighing then giving in. "Iris has my number. Tell her to call me back as soon as possible about the interview we talked about."

"Of course, I'll give her the message. Have a nice day."

The journalist mutters something I can't understand and hangs up the phone. I finish writing the message on the pad and look up to see them all staring at me with wide eyes: Evan, Emily, and even Michael are silent, incredulous. I'm suddenly struck by the fear that I've done something wrong. I just wanted to help Emily, but maybe I overstepped my bounds.

"I'm sorry. I thought it was a good idea to give you a hand. It was a message for Iris. Should I have said something different?" Insecurity seeps through my voice.

"Where did you learn to answer the phone like that?" asks Emily incredulously. "I thought you were isolated from the world."

"From the outside world, yes, but not from my community. I spent several years in the doctor's office, and he taught me how to answer the phone and arrange appointments. He preferred to prepare his bait for fishing rather than answering calls from people who often just wanted to chat."

Michael bursts out laughing, and Emily runs to hug me while Evan slips his cell phone into his pocket.

"Please tell me you enjoy that work," Emily pleads. "You can organize a merchandising table *and* answer the phone? I can't let you go."

"Michael, you'll have to find another nanny because she's working here," says Evan resolutely.

Levi, hearing everything, gets up from his chair in the conference room and says anxiously, "Don't you want to stay with me anymore? Is it because I'm too far behind in my homework? I swear I'll work harder. I swear I'll make up for all the years I've lost." He almost struggles to breathe while saying the words.

I walk closer to him and take him by the shoulders, forcing him to look at me. "I'm not going anywhere, Levi. You know I'm in the room next to yours. We've already talked about it, remember? You need real teachers, and I won't be able to stay with you all day because you'll be working with them."

"So you won't leave?" He looks calmer. Since Michael proposed formalizing the custody, he seems to have even more insecurities. At first, he seemed resigned to the fact that no one wanted him, but once he began to hope, every little change

ruffles him much more than necessary.

"She's not going anywhere," Michael says. "Emily and Evan's offer is only a proposal, but even if Faith did accept it, she'd come home every night. To *our* home." He says the last words looking me straight in the eye, as if afraid I'll change my mind and find another place to stay.

It's strange how a man who supposedly hates committing to long-term relationships is now mainly concerned about raising this child in our peculiar little family. And as much as he pays me to look after Levi, the truth is, I would do it for free.

"Okay," Levi whispers, a little embarrassed. I can't imagine what it means for the kid to try to trust adults. The only people he's ever known, who should have cared for him with unconditional love, have let him down so many times. How could he possibly believe in promises? Not having anyone who wants you is heartbreaking even for an adult, for a child, it destroys all their dreams and hopes.

"Are you coming with me?" Michael says. "We need to make some adjustments to my track before meeting with the school principal. You stay at the mixer with Greg, what do you say?"

The smile opens again on Levi's face, and I see Michael breathe a sigh of relief. For someone who says he doesn't know how to deal with kids, he's behaving like any good parent would: with patience and love. Living with him, I've seen that all the women, the so-called rock star lifestyle, the cockiness on stage are just a facade hiding a man who manages to love in one way: unconditionally.

Penelope's words come to my mind about Michael having so many layers he can no longer find himself. It's true.

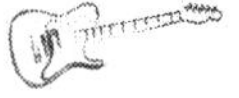

His cocky facade hides an insecurity I've slowly discovered, which is his fear of losing what he truly loves. Michael does everything with his whole heart, and he shows it every day with Levi, loving him like his own son, even knowing he may not stay long. He's the same with me, making me feel more loved than I've ever been.

And yet, even that can't erase my feeling that all of this must have an end date. I wish it wasn't there, but how trustworthy can a man be if he doesn't want to commit in front of God?

I watch them close the door of the recording studio while I enter the conference room and find Evan and Emily looking at me like two wild animals viewing their prey. I sit in the armchair and they sit on the sofa in front of me, never looking away.

"You're scaring me," I say frankly, and a slight smile appears on Evan's face. Emily, on the other hand, remains impassive.

"Our proposal wasn't a joke. Come and work with us," Evan says.

"I only know how to answer the phone," I admit with a bit of embarrassment. "I don't know how to redirect phone calls, how to use your complicated computer programs. I learned to use a cell phone only because I've been living with a fourteen-year-old boy for months who taught me tricks. I don't know anything about how to run an office."

Emily smiles, finally. I almost wondered if she was angry with me. "Computer tricks are the easiest part to teach you. What the girls we've had so far lacked is maturity and exceptional organizational skill like yours. After the concert in

Austin, I'd already told Evan that no one organizes a merchandising table like you did, unless they have a clear idea of how to do it. I don't know if your logistical expertise is innate or learned in your community, but it's a rare gift difficult to find in the girls who apply for this job. Using a computer is the easiest part, like using a phone or printer. The hardest part is knowing how to filter a call gracefully, as you did. You didn't know Iris was avoiding that journalist's calls, but you bought her some time without offending the person on the other end of the phone. That's the most difficult thing to teach a beginner at this job."

Her words almost embarrass me. I'm not used to receiving compliments for what I do, and it makes me uncomfortable. "I can't leave Michael and Levi alone out of the blue. I need time to find them a replacement."

"Can I talk to Faith for a moment alone?" Michael is looking at us from the door. I didn't even hear him coming.

Emily and Evan get up from the couch, smile at us, and walk out, closing the door behind them. Michael takes me by the hand, pulling me up gently from the armchair, then sits on the couch and sits me on his legs. I cuddle up to him, as I've been doing lately. More and more, I crave physical contact with him.

"I never asked you why you decided to be a nurse. You agreed to work in a prison, where most of the time you see people with bruises, and every now and then stitch up a wound. Nothing compared to what a nurse does in a hospital. But since getting out of there, you haven't even touched a Band-Aid. Did you know I have a first aid kit prepared at home? Did you notice it's in the bathroom cabinet near the living room?"

I look down at my hands nervously playing with the hem of my skirt. "I hate being a nurse," I admit in a whisper, and a weight lifts from my chest. I've never confessed it to anyone.

"Why did you decide to do a job you don't like?"

"When I was a child, I was curious. I knew there was a whole world outside my community, and I wanted to know more. I read books, I was constantly asking questions, but none of the adults in my house gave me answers. In fact, they scolded me because the devil was out there, and asking questions was a direct path to him. So I stopped."

I feel Michael stiffening under me. I know these issues are a source of tension between us. He's never understood my family, and recently I'm beginning to understand why.

"Why do you become angry every time I talk about my past? I understand you don't like my family, but they don't think for me anymore."

Michael seems torn and looks down. "I grew up in a house where my father used religion to control us, forcing us to do what he wanted. Your situation sounds a lot like the one I grew up in, and I don't want you to get trapped. I want to help you live the life you deserve."

His confession leaves me bewildered. Is that why he is breathing down my neck? Out of a sense of duty? Am I just an experiment for him, or does he really feel something for me?

Michael takes my chin and lifts it up, forcing me to look into his eyes. "You didn't tell me why you chose that job."

"When I was about thirteen, my grandmother started to suffer from kidney failure, so once a week, we took her to the community doctor because he was the only one who had dialysis equipment. I stayed with her during these sessions un-

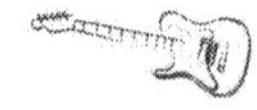

til it was time to go home. She slept most of the time, and I was bored to death, so I started wandering around the doctor's office and discovered his fishing magazines one day. For me, it was like discovering the world again, all those photos of beautiful places in the United States. One day I got brave and began to ask him questions. He saw that I was chomping at the bit to know more and suggested I become a nurse, so I could do an internship outside the community. He convinced my father that having a person with professional skills would help the whole community. My family would never allow me to become a doctor, too many years of study, but as a nurse, I could study from home and then do my internship in an outside facility. So my father found me a place in prison through the Mother Superior."

I look up at Michael, who is frowning. "So you didn't choose to be a nurse because you felt called to it, or good at it."

I shake my head, ashamed of how I ended up doing a job that's supposed to be for the sole purpose of helping other people. "No. It was my only chance to get out of the community and avoid marrying Jacob on my eighteenth birthday. I was so desperate I accepted any solution. He simply understood my anguish and suggested a way out."

Michael holds me tightly, almost taking my breath away. "And now that you don't have to go back to the community, you don't know what to do anymore, I guess."

I shake my head again. "The girls there don't think about what job they want to do when they grow up. No one teaches us that there are any options besides taking care of the family. I don't know what careers I can even have as a woman."

"Did you like organizing the merchandising table at the

show?"

I nod.

"And you don't have trouble answering the phone, right?"

"That's right."

"So why don't you give this job a chance? You'd have the opportunity to do something you like with people you like. We're all familiar faces, but the record company is still a small entity. You'd be able to learn a job, as well as things about the new world you live in, without the pressure and competition that these environments can sometimes have. Plus, we already know where you come from, so we can help you."

"And you'd be around the studio, I guess..." The part that most attracts me is being able to see Michael, the part I regret the most is being away from Levi.

Michael smiles and kisses me lightly on the lips. "Let's just say it's the selfish part of me that wants you to accept a job where I can see you all day." He winks at me, and I melt with embarrassment. The closer we become, the more I see him behaving with me like Thomas does
with Iris or Damian with Lilly…just without all the groping of intimate body parts in front of everyone.

"What if I'm terrible at it? I would disappoint you and your friends."

"Faith, if there's one thing I know about you, it's that you're smart, have a good head on your shoulders and are very willing to learn. If you don't know how to do something, I'm sure you'll figure it out. There's nothing you can't do. Of course, I could make things easy and support you financially for the rest of your life, because you know money has never been an issue. But that's just exchanging one prison for another—from your

community to my home. I want you to find something you like and become independent, even financially. And if one day you get tired of living with me, I want you to have no problem packing your bags and leaving because you're a strong and independent woman in every way."

My heart hammers madly into my chest. "Putting it like that, you make it sound like a long-term situation…very long-term, even though you're not the type to commit. I'm inexperienced but not stupid, Michael. I know that however long we may talk about living under the same roof, sooner or later it will end." I may have lived away from modern life for most of my existence, but I know that two people who don't have a familial, emotional, or employment bond don't plan to live under the same roof for years. The situation between us is very confusing.

Michael clears his voice. "I'm not one to make long-term plans. Situations can change drastically at any moment, without giving you time to think or clean up your mess. Marriage is an institution that binds two people together for the rest of their lives. You don't need a piece of paper to be happy. A person should feel free to get out of a relationship without having to call a lawyer. How can anyone know they'll stay in love with someone for the rest of their life? Or if that person will feel the same way? But I *have* learned one thing: to enjoy what makes you happy right now. I don't know if in ten years all three of us will still live in that apartment, but I know that now living with you and that boy makes me happy, peaceful. I've never been calmer in my whole life, and I'm not going to give it up for fear that all this will end sometime in the future. We live in the present, Faith. We've already fucked up the past,

and the future is just a great unknown."

Leave it to Michael to be so down to earth, telling it like it is, brutally honest about having no idea what the future holds for us. I've always been someone who needed certainties, to know what I'd be doing for the rest of my life. Yet here I am, in the arms of a man who doesn't make promises but who makes me smile and who makes my heart feel like I can be satisfied with what he gives me. I've never felt as alive as I do right now.

"Okay," I whisper as he kisses me again.

He seems to exhale in relief. "But now we're going to find teachers for Levi because although I don't know what the future holds, if that kid doesn't catch up academically, college is nowhere in sight."

Smiling, we get up and open the door to find Emily, Evan, and Levi busy examining their toes.

"I guess I don't have to tell you that we'll find a solution for Levi and that Faith will start working here, right? Clearly, you all heard everything." Michael pretends to be angry but struggles to hold back a smile.

The muttering chorus of "Not true," "I was just passing by," and "I just got out here" is not at all convincing. Michael extends his hand to Levi, and we all head towards the front door, ready to embrace a future full of uncertainty, family, and happiness—at least, as long as it lasts.

CHAPTER 21
Michael

I didn't feel as much nervousness that grips my stomach now even when we had our first stadium concert, with the noise of the audience penetrating the walls so loudly we heard it in the green room. I squeeze the white marble of the kitchen counter tightly, staring at the cup of coffee in front of me without drinking it.

"Do you think if you stare at it harder you could absorb it without drinking it?" Faith's voice makes me smile, but I don't look up.

"I'm undecided. I'm so nervous I'll probably stain my white shirt, but if I don't drink it, I might puke my guts up."

Faith grabs the cup of coffee and, without saying a word, pours it into the sink. "You shouldn't drink it if you're nervous. But you know it's going to be fine, right?"

Yesterday, my lawyer called me to let me know that today is the social worker's first scheduled visit to proceed with the paperwork to get custody of Levi. Apparently, our situation is unique, or at least our judge friend has defined it that way. We don't have to go through all the red tape that most people who request custody have to endure, but we can't completely avoid routine visits from social services checking in on him. Visits I highly doubt were made when he was at the old foster

family's house.

"This person will decide whether Levi can stay with me or not. I have the right to be nervous."

Faith smiles at me and caresses my face until I turn my whole body towards her. "Look around, Michael. This apartment is wonderful. You are wonderful with Levi. They have to give you custody of that kid."

I breathe deeply and draw her into a hug. Inhaling the smell of her coconut shampoo I like so much always relaxes me. She looks beautiful in her yellow summer dress with tiny white daisies. It doesn't show too much, typical of Faith, but at least it's not the nun's clothing she wore when I first met her. I'm glad the girls take her shopping every now and then, showing her a more or less normal life.

"Michael!" The scream coming from the hall makes my blood freeze. "I think I have a problem." Levi walks towards us, rubbing his shirt with a towel.

I glance at Faith, who's trying to hide a smile behind her hand.

"I stained my shirt with chocolate, and when I tried to wash it, the stain got bigger." He points to the enormous dark patch in the middle of his chest.

I don't have time to say anything because a firm knock on the door makes me shoot like an Olympic runner towards the door. I open it wide and a middle-aged woman with a gray bob, a suit of the same color, and an intimidating red folder in her hand enters. Matthew, standing behind her, greets me with a nod. I appreciate that our concierge has accompanied her all the way up. The social worker passes a quick glance around the room and a faint grimace of disappointment appears on her

lips. It's subtle, but to me it stands out like a big flashing neon sign.

"Hi, I'm Michael. This is Levi, and this is Faith." I give her my most charming smile, the one that tears women's panties off, while I stretch out my hand to shake hers. Her serious expression doesn't crack even a little: a bad omen. My smile is a weapon of mass destruction that works every single time, on every single woman.

Her gaze rests on Levi's shirt, then on me, and finally on Faith.

"Levi, please, go and change your shirt?" I try to maintain a confident demeanor while the woman offers not even the hint of a smile.

"Shall we sit at the table so we can have a chat?" She makes this declaration then heads to the dining room without invitation. I'm almost afraid she'll pull out a lamp and point it in our faces for the questioning.

"Of course," I stutter, and Faith grabs my hand, squeezing it slightly and then releasing it again. I wish she'd keep squeezing it, but I don't know what this woman walking in front of us might think.

We barely have time to sit down; Faith and I are on one side of the table and the "warden" on the other. Levi comes out of his room wearing the Iron Maiden T-shirt I gave him—the one with the zombie soldier holding the British flag and the bloody sword—and I clearly remember telling him to put it in the dirty laundry two days ago because it smelled. The social worker raises an eyebrow but says nothing. Marks something on that damn folder I can't read.

"You're the person asking for custody, right?" she asks.

"That's right."

"And you are?" She turns to Faith.

"Faith, my name is Faith," she whispers, terrified by this whole situation.

"Are you Mr. Wright's girlfriend?"

"No," is all she manages to say.

"The nanny?"

"Not exactly..." she stutters.

I try to intervene, but the woman waves her hand in a way that silences me immediately. I've never been so afraid of a woman in my entire life.

"What do you mean?"

"I was hired by Michel to look after Levi when he was serving his sentence, and then after that, to help him with school, but now he has qualified teachers getting him caught up with the school he's missed."

"So you don't work for Mr. Wright anymore?"

"No."

"But you live in this house?"

I don't like her inquisitorial tone at all.

"Excuse me..." My voice is firm. "What does our relationship with Faith have to do with whether or not I'm fit to have custody of Levi?" I start to get nervous.

"Mr. Wright, I don't care what relationship you have with the young lady, but if you're running, for example, a prostitution ring in this house, I can't leave Levi with you." She doesn't flinch even once during this explanation.

I wrinkle my forehead in confusion. "Does she *look* like a prostitute?" I ask incredulously.

"Do I look like a prostitute?" echoes Faith, offended.

Next to me, Levi inhales deeply, clearly more practical than the two of us in this situation.
"You two are gonna send me back to a foster family," he mumbles quietly.

The angle of the woman's mouth curves slightly upwards. Ah, so there is a way to melt that icy heart: a little blond angel with naïve blue eyes.

"Let me talk to Levi for a bit alone, then we'll take a tour of the house, okay?" Finally, a smile.

I turn to Levi and look him straight in the eye. "If for any reason you feel uncomfortable and want us to come back, just call, and we'll be here right away, okay?"

I wait for him to nod before getting up and casting a stern glance at the woman. She may be here to do her job, but I won't make her life easy if she wants to take Levi away from me.

***

It took her two solid hours to determine that our house was not the worst place Levi has ever lived. Two hours in which she nit-picked every detail. I'm almost sure it's because I used my name to push the system to entrust me with the boy, first when serving his sentence, then keeping him at home. She was wrong if she thought I'd feel guilty for using my status to save Levi from the streets.

"Finally, you're here! I thought I had to find a new guitarist," Evan teases when we get on the plane he booked for the band.

"That social worker was relentless." I roll my eyes.

"Levi is still with us, so I assume the visit went well." Simon gives me a half-smile. Of all my friends, he's the only one who doesn't think I'm a fool for deciding to ask for custody of Levi. The others help me, but they think it's one of my rush decisions. It's hard to explain to them that I've become so attached to this boy that I'm willing to completely change my life to fit his.

"For now, we're safe. We'll have other meetings, but I hope they're less invasive than this. She wanted to know exactly what each room in the house was for. What else could a bathroom be used for?" I complain as Levi and Faith chuckle.

"She asked Michael if he was running a prostitution ring," the kid laughs.

Simon, Damian, and Thomas look at me for an explanation.

"She wondered if Faith was a prostitute."

Simon frowns. "How could anyone assume that about Faith?"

"Don't ask me." I rub my face, still upset about that visit that just about cost me a nervous breakdown. I'm so exhausted after the meeting that I sleep like a log all the way to our destination, ignoring even Simon's panic attack during some turbulence.

We finally arrive at the hotel after making our way through downtown Chicago in our limo. Levi and Faith are at my side when we get out in the underground parking lot and head towards the service elevator that will take us to the room. A text from Evan says to go straight to the top floor, where he's waiting with the keys for our suites.

Ours has the usual layout that feels comfortable and familiar: a central living room, a bedroom with two beds and bathroom on the left, a king bedroom with private bathroom on the right. Since tasting life in an apartment, it occurs to me how

similar and impersonal hotel rooms are. After living in a house that I love, these places just feel sad to me now.

Levi, however, runs to his room and dives into the bed, bouncing several times face down, more like a five-year-old than a teenager. It breaks my heart. I don't think he had many opportunities to just be a kid.

"Would you like it if we both slept in the master bedroom?" I ask Faith, a little awkward.

I've been thinking about it for a while. After all, I almost always sneak into her room to spend the night, and she's fine with it. Why still pretend not to be attracted to each other?

Her forehead, however, scrunches up in a way that makes me think she's not going to make it so easy. "You don't even take me to dinner once, and you want to go straight to sharing a hotel room?"

I'm speechless. I realize this is exactly what I do with women: I head straight for the sheets without ever seeing the shadow of a tablecloth. So far, it's never been a problem, and it was always clear what we wanted from each other.

"Do you want to go out on a date?" I ask, following her into the master bedroom and closing the door behind me.

She sits on the bed and sighs. "It's not that I want to go out on a date, but I would like to know what this is. I don't know how to be in a relationship. I don't even know if you and I are *in* a relationship, but the fact that we sometimes make love makes me hope we're more than just roommates. Last night Thomas and Iris went out, just the two of them, like a real couple. I know we're not a couple, but you're taking what you want from me…and, in a way, it's fine, don't get me wrong, you didn't force me to do anything I didn't want. It's just that sometimes it seems like I'm your dirty little secret, the one you don't dare show the world because you're ashamed."

I walk closer to her and take her face in my hands, forcing her to look at me.

"You're not my dirty little secret, understood? I don't care if the world knows I'm sleeping with you. The only thing that matters to me is that the world doesn't ruin what we have. I don't know exactly what it is, but it makes me happy. In this business, they tend to take something beautiful and turn it into something scandalous and dirty. I don't want that. I don't want them to take your innocence and ruin it."

Faith looks at me with a smile. "Michael, I let you do things to me that are nowhere near innocent. It's not the world that has stolen my innocence." She laughs, and I join her.

"If you want, I'll teach you something else that's not innocent at all," I whisper in her ear as I kiss the skin of her neck.

I feel her inhale deeply and then hold her breath. "Michael, I'm here to work. Evan bought me an iPad for email and redirecting calls to my cell phone. I can't…let you teach me things right now!"

I smile and touch her nipple visible under her light dress. "Lesson number one. This is called a quickie, and you do it when you don't have time for foreplay, but you're so excited you don't need it."

I put my hand between her legs, under her summer dress. I love that she's started wearing knee-length dresses and skirts, giving me a glimpse of those gorgeous legs. I move up, stroking the inside of her thigh, continuing to kiss her neck. Her hands are resting on the bed, her fingers clinging to the sheet in an iron grip.

"You're wet, Faith, see? You're already learning the lesson."

"Shut up, Michael," she pants.

I smile and quickly pull out a condom from my pants pocket, unfastening my belt and unzipping my jeans without ever looking away. She's torn between a sense of duty and the desire to have me between her legs. She bites her lip, smiles shyly, and she is so sexy and innocent at the same time that I could come without even touching her.

I put on my condom, lower down to take off her panties from under her skirt, then sit on the bed and pull her to me, forcing her to straddle my legs. I watch as she blushes at our skin rubbing and the desire that makes us almost tremble. I grab her hair and draw her to me for a kiss that she reciprocates with the same urgency, circling with her hips on my erection and letting out a small groan that melts on our tongues.

"Fuck me, Faith. I want you to fuck me, take all the pleasure you want without thinking about me. I want you to go after your orgasm."

I drive my erection towards her opening, but then I let her take control. She moves towards me timidly until she meets my pelvis, a disarming slowness that almost drives me crazy and come like a kid for the first time. I sink my head into the hollow of her neck and enjoy her little moans of pleasure when I grab her butt in my hands and squeeze. She begins to move on me, first with hesitation, then taking a steady rhythm. I hear her panting, trying to hold back moans coming out of her throat, clinging to my shoulders, and pressing her core against me.

When I feel her coming with an orgasm that makes her legs

tremble, I sink a couple more times into her and join her pleasure. I've never been so excited about a quickie in my life. Her head is resting on my shoulder and she covers my neck with small kisses.

"See? You learn quickly. This was a quickie. You don't take off your clothes, it doesn't take long, and comes in handy when you have a fifteen-minute lunch break and the desire to fuck like a teenager with raging hormones."

"Michael!" She laughs and slaps my shoulder just as her phone starts ringing.

She tries to get up, but I grab the phone and give it to her.

"Michael, it's Evan..." she begs me.

"Answer, it's not a video call. And besides, you're dressed," I challenge her with a grin.

She looks at me, begging for a few more seconds, then finally gives in under the weight of responsibility for her work. "Evan." Her voice is trembling and short of breath.

"Hi, Faith, we're down in the garage waiting for you to go to the club."

"Yes, I'm coming…I mean, we're coming."

I smile, seeing her so overwhelmed and trying to keep her shit together. Evan's voice is faint on the other side of the line, but I can still hear him.

"Is everything okay? You seem…agitated."

"Yes, everything's fine. I was just…finishing a few things."

I watch her blush, and my smile gets bigger. I love seeing her so innocent and inexperienced.

"Okay. We're waiting for you," I hear him say, then he hangs up.

I burst out laughing as she gets up, grabs her panties, and

puts them on in a hurry. "You will pay for this," she threatens without much force.

I grab her by the wrist and draw her in for a kiss. "When two people want each other, Faith, no matter where they are or how much time they have, they'll always find a way to be together."

She kisses me gently on the lips. "Was that lesson number two?"

I nod. "Do you want number three as well?"

"We don't have time for the third one now, but I'm ready to learn later."

I laugh and kiss her again before getting up, making myself presentable, and running out of the room to reach others.

***

The second concert is a bigger success than the first. After Austin, the word spread about how great it was, and when we arrived to set up the stage, the line of people almost reached around the block. Even journalists who didn't get a press invitation lined up to get a ticket and write a piece about this somewhat bizarre way of doing business. When we announced the project, the industry thought we were crazy. They were sure we'd fail and people would never show up. Instead, this time we had to send home a lot of people. Evan is already looking for bigger locations for upcoming shows.

I watch Faith behind the merchandising desk, focused on managing the fans and directing Iris and Emily, who gave her complete control of the situation.

"If you stare any harder, she'll catch fire," Simon teases, putting his hand on my shoulder.

"I was just observing that she's really very good at what

she does. I can't believe that no one has ever appreciated these qualities."

Simon laughs. "Holy Christ! Only you could snatch a girl from a cult, still so pure and naïve,

and slide her into the world of rock stars and concerts without a second thought."

"What do you want me to say? We all have our superpowers." I laugh.

"Of course, and yours is to make sure that no adult woman within a one-mile radius is still a virgin," Damian teases.

"Shut up." I glare at him, but I find it difficult to hold back a smile at his joke.

"We thought Simon would bust your balls for making her suffer," Thomas laughs. "But you're so lost to those doe eyes I think she's the one keeping you on a leash."

"She doesn't keep me on a leash." My defense is not very convincing.

"Sure, whatever you say, Michael," Thomas replies.

"Let's just say we've noticed how you'd gladly gouge out the eyes of every man who lays them on her."

"Because, Simon, they're all disgusting pigs who fantasize about her in every position."

"Oh? And you don't?" asks Damian, raising an eyebrow. "Ah, no, that's true. You actually make her try all those positions."

They burst out laughing, and I can't hide an embarrassed smile. I'd let her try the whole Kamasutra at least five or six times until she knew what her favorite position was. The mere thought that someone else could put their hands on her makes me foam with anger.

Evan calls our attention from the other side of the club where he's keeping an eye on Levi, scrutinizing the mixer, and gesturing that it's time to start. When we all go out together from the hall leading to the stage, the roar of the crowd makes the place tremble again. The adrenaline running through my veins is so powerful my hands shake. I squeeze my guitar tightly and settle to the right of Damian, ready to start. I glance at Faith and find her looking at me with adoring eyes and a smile. The explosion of emotions in my chest is so overwhelming I want to hop off this stage, run over to her and kiss her until she's out of breath.

The chimes of Thomas' drumsticks, however, call me back to reality. I glance at the others who are waiting for me, grinning. I smile, get my shit together and join others for the first song. My eyes shift to our fans jumping, dancing, tossing, and turning to the frantic rhythm of the new song, "Jailed."

The energy they give us is indescribable. If we didn't have our earbuds in, we couldn't hear a single note of what we're playing. Damian looks possessed, his hair covering his sweaty face, and during the third song he's hit in the face with a bra thrown by the audience. Simon and I laugh as he picks it up and slips it into the back pocket of his jeans. We're usually thrown teddy bears, notes, T-shirts, but never a bra, mainly because in the stadiums, the stage is so far from the audience it's almost impossible for the lighter objects to reach us.

Halfway through our show, someone starts throwing balloons in our direction. I watch Damian's confused look directed towards the far end of the room, but we realize they're not balloons but condoms when they get closer. He can't resist at the end of the song and doubles over in laughter, while Simon

tries to grab one and throw it back to the audience.

"I hope they're not used," Damian thunders into the microphone, and people burst into laughter. "And if they're not used, what the fuck are you doing? It costs a kidney to buy them, so don't waste them on dicks like us. Find someone and use them!" he laughs.

The audience is in a frenzy, and someone from the first row shakes a silver wrapper that we know well. "I have a closed one. If you're interested, we can open it together!" shouts the boy who holds it in his hand.

The people around him laugh, and Damian lowers himself to look him in the face. "You have too much beard for my taste, but if you want, we can sing together." The rising roar hits us like a punch to the gut.

The kid doesn't think twice. He makes his way to the stage, and a security guy helps him up. He's slender compared to Damian, with a few days' beard and a smile from ear to ear. We start with the first notes of "Swing," and the guy begins jumping with us on the small stage. When he starts singing, we realize he's not that bad. Sure, he doesn't have Damian's hoarse voice, but he does well with the whole song. When he finally gets down, he's so overcome with emotion he almost falls on the floor.

I cast a glance towards the back of the room, where Evan stands watching us, and the smile I see on his lips says a lot about what he thinks of this treasure hunt idea. Every show is a new adventure, but the media will undoubtedly have a lot to report after this one.

I can't help but be happy for our manager. When we left the record company, he took on the responsibility of upholding

our status and reputation, but it doesn't take a genius to understand it was a risky move. Without the stellar budget of a label, we have to make do with what we have, and sometimes it's not enough to do big, attention-getting things like a world tour. Evan took on a big responsibility, and we all realized the stress is eating him alive. He always keeps his spirits up, but more and more we see, in his eyes and in the wrinkles on his forehead, a growing concern that is crushing him.

The success of these concerts is a huge reward for the incomparable work he's been doing.

***

"Where are we going?" Faith looks puzzled when I press the elevator button that leads to the terrace and not to our floor.

"I have a little surprise for you. I know it's two in the morning, and tomorrow we have a plane to catch, but this is what I managed to organize at the last minute."

"And Levi?"

"I asked Evan to keep an eye on him until we got back to the room. I swear we won't stay that long up there."

Faith seems perplexed but remains silent. She is tired, I read it in her face, but curiosity takes over. When we get to the top, the elevator opens onto the restaurant on the hotel's terrace. At the moment, it is closed. There is only one guy behind the bar that I asked to reopen just for us. A single table is prepared and overlooks Grant Park and the spectacular Lake Michigan at night. On it are two plates covered with a silver bowl and a bottle of sparkling water.

"I couldn't find much at such short notice and especially at this time. But I ordered a couple of burgers with fries."

She smiles and looks with wonderment at the guy behind

the counter who gives us a nod. "Did you keep this place open just for us?" She can't believe it as I pull her chair out for her.

"You'll soon discover it's not so easy to go out to dinner with someone like me. Usually, paparazzi are stationed everywhere, and often in order not to be disturbed halfway through the meal, we have to reserve a private room. But using our name has its advantages." I gesture with one hand the deserted restaurant around us.

"Like opening a restaurant at two in the morning," she smiles.

"If it keeps you from the front pages of gossip sites and doesn't scare you away, I'll do anything. It may not be easy to live with someone like me." The anxiety in my voice is almost palpable. I know she wants Prince Charming, but I'm not one to ride in on a white horse wearing brightly-colored tights.

She looks at me with confusion. "Michael, until Iris explained to me a month ago what gossip sites are, I didn't even know they exist. I've never seen one in my twenty-four years, and I certainly won't start now. I don't care what they say, and I'm not worried about it."

I smile because I really hope so. Sometimes I wish she'd never come out of her bubble of naivety. "Good."

"Anyway, I'm glad you took me out to dinner. Even if it's two in the morning…and you're only doing it to get into my bed," she laughs before sticking a fry in her mouth.

"It's all part of my plan not to move my suitcase from your room to Levi's." I wink at her and she laughs.

God, I could stay here for hours listening to her laugh at my idiotic jokes. I watch her as she turns her head, staring at the lights of the city with an almost melancholy expression.

"Do you miss your family?" My voice comes out in a whisper. I'm afraid that sooner or later she'll tell me she wants to see her parents and siblings again, and that she's decided to return, in spite of everything.

"I was thinking that my sisters will never see a show like this. They'll never see the world, and that makes me sad."

"Do you want to go back to them?"

Faith looks back at me, and a veil falls over her eyes. Guilt. "In my family, we were never taught to be affectionate, to show love for each other. Everyone always kept feelings to themselves. There's loyalty between us, and many secrets, but we've never shed a tear for each other. When I left the community more than a year ago, I was afraid of the world outside, but I've never missed what I left there, including my family. I discovered what it's like to feel affection when I saw Damian and Lilly together, or Thomas and Iris... You and Levi. Now I understand what it means to love."

I watch her playing with the fries on her plate.

"When someone gets married and leaves their parents' house, do they no longer have contact with their family?" I know what it means to no longer want to be around the family you're born into, but I chose that out of resentment and disgust towards them. She seems to have almost no feeling towards her own people.

"We meet within the community, we see each other in church and in public places, but we don't visit each other's homes like you do. My parents would never come to my house like your friends did when Levi couldn't go out. Even the holidays are spent just with immediate family, the ones you live under the same roof with."

"But you're sad for your sisters because they have no future."

Faith shrugs her shoulders. "I feel sadness and anger because now I understand what we've been denied. I wish they could have the same opportunities as me. Maybe if they had an idea of all the possibilities the world offers, our relationship might be different. I could possibly even learn to love them."

I stare at her for a few moments before returning to my plate and dinner, as she does.

"Am I a bad person?" she then asks me, with a half-smile and doubt veiling her eyes.

"No. You are not. You're just a person whose life was messed up by others. There's nothing wrong with you." And I believe that. We all come from messed-up family situations, but I think hers is the worst I've seen. And the cruelest thing about her entire existence is that she lived by the teachings of a religion based solely on loving each other. Yet she was denied affection to the point of not shedding a single tear when she abandoned her family forever.

"When I got out of prison, I didn't even think about going back to my family, and I never felt sad about the separation," I confess. "Perhaps certain blood ties are not supposed to make us happy, but to make us understand which people we really want to bond with and which we don't want to be like."

"Have you talked to them since you got out?"

"No. I asked my lawyer to pay them to silence them about my past, but I no longer wanted to have anything to do with them."

"And sooner or later, will those conflicted feelings go away?"

"I don't know, but if they ever do, you'll be the first one I'll tell."

Faith looks down with a smile but says nothing more. She bites into her dinner, but that veil of melancholy falls even heavier over her gaze. She's looking for certainties I can't give her because I'm still chasing them too.

CHAPTER 22

Faith

Down in the hotel lobby, we join the others ready to board the shuttle taking us to the airport. Michael has huge dark under-eye circles that match mine in an almost embarrassing way. The only one looking rested is Levi. It was almost dawn when I finally fell asleep in Michael's arms.

I think they're staring not just at the exhaustion on our faces, but at the way Michael squeezes my hand as we approach them. He's never been one to show affection in public, and I don't even think he noticed it when, coming out of the elevator, he intertwined his fingers with mine while absent-mindedly scrolling through the news on his phone.

"Evan, I have the Miami flight and hotel reservation information in my bag, if you need it," I say to break the ice and divert attention from our hands more than anything else.

"You know there are emails, right? That you don't need to print out all our travel itineraries," Michael teases as we get into the shuttle van.

"Of course, I know that. In fact, Evan has an email with a summary of everything we need, but what happens if his phone stops working? Or the Internet connection doesn't work? Or if this horrific technology just breaks down?" Actually, my biggest fear is making some huge mistake and blowing up the

whole tour.

"If all the technology were to suddenly stop working, I think catching a plane wouldn't be our biggest problem," he chuckles, and I see his friends smiling.

"Michael, stop teasing her," Evan reprimands him. "She's doing an excellent job and has learned to run an office in record time. Hiring her was like a Christmas miracle in July."

"Thank you, Evan." I smile as Michael draws me to himself and kisses me on the head.

"I like teasing you. Let me do it while I still have an advantage over you. In a few months, you'll be a career woman, and I'll go back to being just a shallow rock star you're ashamed to show your face with."

His friends laugh, and I lightly pinch his side without ever leaving the comforting warmth of his embrace.

"I doubt that, Michael. You're a tech genius. I'm pretty sure none of us will ever be able to compete with you," Simon jokes.

"Really?" Levi beats me to the question. Neither of us knew this about Michael, and we're both intrigued.

"Of course, he ended up in jail because they caught him after countless burglaries of rich people's homes where he managed to turn off the alarm," continues Damian, but I feel Michael tense beside me and darken his gaze.

Iris and Lilly explain that during one of the burglaries the homeowner had woken up, and while Michael was trying to escape, he accidentally pushed the man down the stairs and he ended up in a coma for a week.

"Really? How cool! Could you teach me how to do that?" asks Levi in his total naivety.

Michael leans towards him and gives him a scolding glance. "Wasn't eight months in jail enough for you? Do you want to end up in there again?"

Levi makes himself small in his seat. "No, I mean…just the part about the alarm, not ending up in jail," he mumbles, folding his arms across his chest and making the others laugh.

I feel the change in Michael's mood. I know his family forced him to steal, and he's never made a secret of how much he hated his life. That episode continues to torment him, or maybe a part of him has never stopped thinking about it. After all, if you steal for years, a part of your soul remains stained by those sins. You can compensate for evil deeds with just as many good ones, but you can never completely erase them from your heart.

***

Florida is exactly how Iris and Emily described it: hot, humid, and crowded. It took us forever to get from the airport to the hotel. Luckily, I remembered to call and make sure the underground garage was open. I felt proud, and even a bit cocky when, getting off the private plane, I immediately got on the phone with the hotel to arrange our arrival. When we entered the garage, there were already two valets ready to take care of the suitcases and one to accompany us to the lobby for check-in. Evan, unlike in Chicago, also let me handle the hotel registration, including Lilly's arrival later this afternoon from New York; she'll need to get her room keys after Damian.

"Levi, do you mind if I sleep in the room with Faith and leave you alone in the one with the two beds?" I hear Michael ask the boy with a bit of hesitation.

I turn to find Michael with his hands in his pocket, his ex-

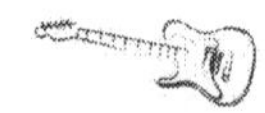

pression a bit awkward. I don't think he's used to reporting to anyone about where he sleeps at night, not even when he was a teenager.

Levi frowns in response. "Isn't that what you already do? I know you slip into your bed early in the morning and pretend you've been there all night. Please, I'm fourteen years old. I can sleep alone in a hotel room." His observation is so blunt it leaves Michael speechless while I can't help but giggle.

"Couldn't you have told me this before? It's annoying to get up at the crack of dawn just to change beds and get into cold sheets."

Levi shrugs his shoulders and ducks into his room. When Michael turns around, he still has an incredulous expression on his face. "Did you know this?"

"Michael, he's fourteen, and he's smart."

He rubs his face, shakes his head, and smiles, changing the subject. "Put on that swimsuit we bought in Los Angeles." He seems to think about it. "Or, if you want, we can go and get a new one." He moves in and puts his arms around my waist, drawing me in for a light kiss on the nose.

Butterflies wake up in my stomach, and I feel my cheeks flare up. I'm not used to all these demonstrations of affection. "I don't need a new bathing suit. We're only staying one day."

"I know you don't need it, but you went out a couple of times with the girls and bought just a few dresses. You know if you need money, you can ask for anything you want, right?" His frown tells me he's serious, that he really is worried that I can't survive on my salary.

I smile at him and kiss him on the lips to make him shut up. "Michael, you don't even charge me rent or for groceries.

I've never had this much money. I've been used to dressing in second- or third-hand clothes, sewing them when they tear up and washing them carefully so they don't wear out. It's just a force of habit."

He takes my face in his hands and kisses me on the lips with a sweetness that makes my legs tremble. What I love about Michael is that he can be so passionate you catch fire or so sweet you melt. He has so many layers and nuances a lifetime wouldn't be enough to learn them all.

"When we get home, I'll teach you how to invest the money you're setting aside. It's unwise to keep it in a savings account with interest so low it doesn't even cover expenses. Help me feel useful. If I can't buy you clothes, at least I can teach you how to save for your future."

"You'll need a lot of patience with me. I still don't know the difference between a debit card and a credit card— I didn't even know they existed until I came to work for Jail Records."

He bends down to kiss me again and this time lets his tongue slide over mine, holding my face in his hands.

"Can you two stop kissing? I want to go to the beach!" Levi's complaint brings us back to reality.

Michael gives me another light kiss on the lips and then locks himself in the room to put on his swimsuit, covering the bulge in his pants. I smile, embarrassed. I'll never get used to the effect I have on him.

***

The beach is crowded with people who look like they walked right out of a magazine. Perfect physiques, shiny hair, and bikinis that leave very little to the imagination. The up-side to all the chaos that surrounds us, however, is that while

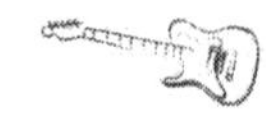

a lot of people recognize the Jailbirds, no one comes up and asks for photos or autographs. Emily told me this place is so crowded with famous people that no one notices it anymore, including actors, singers, and show business people. The paparazzi I spied on the road that runs along the beach are having a field day.

“Don’t worry about photographers. As long as they take pictures of us here, they’ll leave us alone everywhere else,” Iris reassures me as she takes me by the hand and diverts my attention from a man with a giant camera.

“You did that work in New York, right?”

“I’ve been in this field for years,” she confirms as we walk to the water. “But now that the Jailbirds have hired me, I don’t need it anymore.”

“I guess they only take on desperate cases,” I chuckle. “A paparazzo, a bartender, a nurse... No one who has actually prepared for the job.”

Iris laughs and nods. “Yes, they have a tendency to pick up strays and give them a home.”

I laugh at just how right she is. We couldn’t be more different, yet we somehow work together. And it is exactly this diversity and openness to accept everyone that keeps the ideas fresh and the solutions creative in this group.

“Ready for a dip in the water?” Michael sneaks up from behind me and takes me in his arms.

I cling to him as if my life depended on it, and maybe it’s a little bit true: I have never swum in the ocean. It terrifies me.

“No, please! I’m scared.” I sink my head into his neck.

“Well, it’s time to face it,” he says, starting to run until we both end up tumbling into the water like two sacks of potatoes.

The warm water pulls me under me completely, and when my nostrils fill with saltwater, panic takes over and I start kicking to resurface, hitting Michael's legs. When I emerge to catch my breath, with my eyes still closed, I feel his strong arms around my waist.

"Calm down, I'm here. I won't let you go, okay?" His voice is firm but sweet.

My arms cling to his neck as my legs tighten in a grip around his waist. "I'm scared…I'm scared," I whisper in his ear.

His arms don't leave me even for a second, and his lips kiss my neck slightly, just below my ear, before whispering again that he won't let me go. The waves lull us and, when I finally manage to let go of my iron grip and relax a little, I allow them to push me at a slow pace towards his hips. I move away just enough from him to look him in the face.

"See? It's not so bad, right?" He asks before lifting his hand off my back to move the hair covering my face.

"I had no choice." I raise an eyebrow, pretending to be angry.

"If we'd waited for you, it would've gotten dark and we can't stay that long. I just gave you a little push."

"No, you're just an asshole who couldn't wait to prank her," Damian chuckles. He's joined us with Lilly, clinging to his back like a monkey.

Michael grins amusedly but then holds me in a hug that sends electric shocks down my spine. My entire core is in contact with his private parts awakening inside his swimsuit. I look around, embarrassed, and see the others have also reached us.

"So? Have you decided to make it official?" Emily asks Michael, nodding her head to a small group of photographers

crowding near the beach.

Michael turns around and watches them, then turns back to us and shrugs. "They would've found a way to take pictures anyway. If you're okay with it, I am."

"I don't care what strangers say. What matters is what the people I love think of me," I confirm. "I don't understand all this anxiety about the media. What they write isn't true; I know it, the people who know me know it, I don't see any reason to worry about the rest."

The others giggle in amusement.

"Woman, I adore you!" exclaims Lilly. "We should use the conference room sometime to do a group therapy session where we tell you about our front-page anxieties, and you demolish them with your iron logic."

They all laugh again, and this time I join them.

"Only after working hours. That conference room is always busy," says Evan, who I see for the first time in a swimsuit, his hair wet and messy. Underneath those elegant clothes, he hides a physique that turns many heads, and I notice Emily eyeing his abs when she thinks no one is looking at her. I smile at her discretion.

"There's an opening on Tuesday from three to four in the afternoon, if you want," I suggest more as a joke than to organize the meeting.

"Damn. You're too good. Now I can't use the excuse of office mismanagement to skip meetings," Evan jokingly says. We all know it takes more than lousy organization for him to miss a meeting. That man lives for his work.

We all burst out laughing, and I bask a little more in Michael's arms. After all, it's Saturday, and I can allow myself a

day away from the iPad, checking emails.

Michael, meanwhile, throws continuous glances over at Levi, diving with Simon, who seems to be having almost more fun than the boy. Everyone calls Michael "daddy," but each of them treats Levi like a son. They're always ready to include him in whatever they're doing, showing him what a family really looks like.

***

Tonight's concert is in a larger venue than the previous ones, with a capacity of at least eight hundred people, so we can't set up a merchandise table next to the stage. It's too dangerous, and security can't guarantee us enough protection if people start pushing towards us. The merchandising is left to the guys behind the bar, which has a reserved area for this purpose.

The eight hundred tickets were sold at an actual box office this time. Before entering, people are checked with metal detectors and searched—a necessity when there are so many people at an indoor event.

In addition to the larger rooms where the Jailbirds can change and relax before the concert, the stage is bigger, and there's a balcony upstairs where you can watch the show in private.

While Lilly has disappeared with Damian to help "ease the concert tension," something I have no idea about or how it gets resolved, Emily is with Evan at the ticket office figuring out how many people are left without a ticket. Levy, Iris, and I occupy the chairs in the balcony area that overlooks the stage and the audience. Levi is focused on his phone, while Iris seems particularly relaxed, waiting, with her notebook in hand. She explained to me once that this is the job she has al-

ways dreamed of doing.

"So…are you and Michael together? I know it's a direct question, but there aren't many other ways to ask it."

I turn to her, smiling, and open my mouth a couple of times but no answer comes out. The problem is I don't know what we are. Of course, we kiss, we make love, when we're on tour we sleep in the same bed, but we've never talked about a relationship. I don't even know if it's normal to talk about it. "I don't know."

"They kiss all the time and sleep in the same room," Levi adds, still playing with the phone from which he never looks up.

Iris bursts out laughing, amused. "Thank you for the gossip."

"You're welcome."

I feel embarrassed when Iris looks at me again. "I didn't mean to embarrass you with my question. You can do whatever you want with him without feeling guilty or judged."

"I don't feel judged. Not from you, at least." For a moment, I remember my father's words and my brothers' disgusted faces. "We just never talked about it. I don't really know."

Iris curves her lips and shrugs. "And you probably won't talk about it. I don't think Michael has ever done anything like this. He's never gone this far with anyone."

"You mean I'm his first time?"

She chuckles again. "You can say that again! Michael lives like a switch: on, off. There is no middle ground with him. Either he goes from one woman to another on the same night, or he lives with her and adopts a kid before even kissing her. I don't think he even knows what it's like to date a girl, take her out to dinner, woo her. Basically, this is all new for him. So don't be scared if you feel like you're going from zero to a thousand miles per hour in the blink of an eye. It's Michael. He's not a bad guy. It's just with him it's all or nothing."

I look down and nod. "Actually, I don't know how to behave in a relationship either. I've never been in one, and I haven't even been around them, so for all I know this could be normal. Michael can sometimes be…intense…but I've never not felt safe. I mean, look how he acts with Levi. He'd throw himself into the fire for him."

"Yep, you just described Michael to a 't'. I'm glad he's met you. I don't think I've ever seen him so happy. He's always been the clown who entertains everyone. But lately, it's him that's always in a good mood. His presence in a room, his smile is enough to lighten it up. The two of you made that happen."

My heart fills with joy. I never thought hearing those words could make me so happy. But I don't have time to answer because Lilly joins us with disheveled hair, a crumpled tank top, and her shorts pockets inside out.

"What happened to you?" I ask, wide-eyed.

Lilly blushes and passes a hand through her hair.

"You don't want to know, trust me," Iris laughs next to me, and I don't dare ask any more questions.

***

The room is dimly lit, and Michael is taking a shower after returning from the concert. I pull from my suitcase the pearl-gray silk nightgown Iris made me buy the last time we went out in New York, promising me that sooner or later, I'd wear it. I put it on and look in the mirror. It feels silky against my skin, covering enough not to make me feel embarrassed but empha-

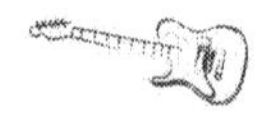

sizing my breasts and hips, making me feel like a woman and no longer a girl.

"You are a heavenly vision..." Michael's hoarse voice gives me a start. I was so caught up in the new version of myself I didn't hear the water stop running. I look over to see him wrapped with a towel around his waist, the moisture clinging to his chest and sculpted abs. My mouth suddenly goes dry, and the shock that starts from my lower belly makes me go weak in the knees. Dressed or completely naked, this man makes me want to do indecent things. Now I understand why my father kept us away from sex—once you try it you can't live without it. I want to touch my lips to every single inch of that perfect body. I want to feel him inside me, move until I reach the intense pleasure that only Michael can give me.

"If you keep looking at me like that, though, I'll devour you in one bite." His tone is sensual, full of a nuance I've never heard. I see in his eyes an almost animalistic desire that I've come to know and need more of.

"Teach me how to please you." My voice comes out in a whisper, almost uncertain, full of fear mixed with excitement that I can't control. He's always given me pleasure, but I want to devote myself to him this time.

He seems surprised by my request, slowly approaches, and then bends down until his lips are close to my ear. "Be careful what you ask, Faith. So far, I've been kind to you, but if you ask me like that, I could make you very, very sinful."

His threat seems more like a promise, and I'm amazed to discover that rather than scaring me, it electrifies me. "Make me whatever you want." The words come out whispered, infused with a rush of excitement, making me feel dirty and reckless. When I'm with him, I want to try everything, stain myself with whatever sin makes me feel good, alive, euphoric.

Michael studies me for a few seconds. I feel naked under his gaze, then his face opens up in a mischievous smile. "If you say so..."

He pulls off my nightgown, making me raise my arms. I'm tempted to cover myself, but I force myself to keep my hands away from my breasts and lower belly, waiting for him to tell me what to do. He takes one step away and looks at me like a wolf with a lamb, ready to take his time devouring me. He unties his towel knot and lets it drop to the floor, his semi-erection welcoming me, making me blush. He walks around me once slowly and sits on the edge of the bed.

"Kneel here." He points to the floor between his legs with a firm command.

I hold my breath and go along with his will. When he gently takes my hands and brings them to his erection, I feel my face flush with fire. The warmth of his intimate body part matches the heat in my cheeks.

"You can squeeze. You won't hurt me." That earlier tone of command gives way to a sweetness in his voice.

I do as he says, and I feel him inhale in an almost violent way and then hold his breath. His hand wraps mine and guides me up and down with slow movements.

"Use your lips, your tongue to wet it." His instructions come out like a hiss. I look up, trying to figure out how to do it, and his eyes are full of more lust than I've ever seen in them before. I taste it first with my tongue in a clumsy attempt. The smell of soap mixing with the salty taste of his skin is a little overbearing, but I'm too hypnotized by his eyes fixed on my

face to know if I like it or not. It's as if he's been waiting for this moment all his life, and I don't know what to do.

"Wrap it with your lips, please." His plea comes out almost in a whisper, and when I do, without ever taking my eyes off his, I see him widen his eyes and tense, moving his hand even more and increasing the pace.

I use my tongue to wet it while I sink it a little deeper into my mouth. Michael closes his eyes and throws his head back, breathing deeply. I take it as a sign that I'm doing the right thing, and continue following the rhythm of his hand still wrapped around mine. He lowers his gaze again, and I feel him panting. His perfect and sculpted chest rises with faster movements. He puts his hand in my hair and, with a slight pressure, dictates a slightly quicker rhythm without ever forcing how deep I should go.

"Christ, if you continue like this, I'll come in your mouth." He gently pulls me back until he's freed from my lips.

"If that's what pleases you, okay." I quickly wonder if I've done something wrong. After all, before meeting Michael, I'd never even seen a penis, let alone tried to please him with my lips.

But Michael smiles at me and lowers down to kiss my lips gently. "No, Faith. As a first time, it's better than I imagined. Let's leave something for the next few weeks, okay?" He kisses me, sliding his tongue across mine, erasing the salty taste of his skin with the sweet taste of his mouth.

"Get a condom from the bedside table," he orders me.

I move quickly to please him, feeling a rush of pleasure anticipating what will come later. I watch him slip it on and then he guides me over to the bed and has me kneel in front of him, with my hands resting on the mattress and his fingers sunk into my hips. Michael is behind me, I don't see him, but I feel his erection press on my opening and sink slowly in without ever stopping, filling me up, taking my breath away. With one hand, he caresses my back but no longer moves. I look over my shoulder and see him staring at me as if seeking my approval.

"Michael, don't treat me like a porcelain doll. Show me what you like."

"I won't be as patient and attentive as the other times, Faith."

"Stop treating me as if I could break at any moment. Fu... fuck me." I stumble on the term that has never left my lips before.

Michael doesn't seem to notice my inexperience because his gaze gets dark, his lips curl up, and his hips start slapping against my buttocks at a pace I didn't think was possible. He pulls almost all the way out and then sinks quickly and slams into my butt. With one hand, he holds my hip tightly while he grabs my hair with his other fist, pulling it in a mixture of pain and pleasure that almost makes me gasp. He continues with his assault, filling me more deeply than I've ever felt. My breasts swing with a force that almost pushes my face onto the mattress. The rhythmic noise of skin against skin, flesh against flesh, his breath getting shorter and shorter until it explodes in a guttural grunt that vibrates in my bowels. He stops inside me for a few moments, panting and resting his forehead on my back, then pulls out and helps me lie on the bed, makes me turn around. Out of breath, he kisses my belly then sinks between my legs and kisses me, sucks, stimulates me with his

tongue until I reach the peak of an orgasm so intense I think it won't ever end.

When I finally relax my back and stretch my legs, he gets up and stretches out next to me, pulling me into a hug.

"I swear if you say 'fuck me' again with that innocent face, I can't be held responsible for my actions anymore," he whispers in my ear, kissing my neck. "Where did you learn to talk like that?" He raises his head to look me straight in the eye.

"Damian is always talking about fucking, a good fuck, getting fucked. It seemed like the right word." I bite my lip.

Michael looks at me stunned for a few seconds, then bursts out laughing, sinking his head into the hollow of my neck and making me smile too. "You spend too much time with my friends."

I cuddle his chest and bask in his breathing that becomes heavier until it sinks into sleep. I watch him sleep, relaxed, with a serene expression. Iris's words come back to my mind, making me feel that perhaps there is hope for our future. These are the moments when my heart holds on to the illusion that someday he'll make me an honest woman.

CHAPTER 23
Michael

I enter the record company offices with my keys. It's dawn, and no one's here. Thomas doesn't have the lights on yet. I doubt he's already up. He usually takes advantage of the fact that he lives a few steps away to sleep until the last minute, and then he comes down wearing only a T-shirt, sweatpants, and bed hair.

I walk to the coffee machine and realize it's ready. Water and coffee are inside; I just need to turn it on. I smile: Faith. Since she's started working here, I recognize her presence in these small gestures. They're small acts that make me appreciate the presence of a woman in my house. I didn't think that a simple meal eaten together could be so nice, even if we're quiet.

The door behind me opens; I turn around and see Simon surprised to see me here. Since we met, I've never been the first one to arrive for rehearsal. I take out a cup for him and place it on the cabinet.

"What are you doing here already? Did something happen?"

I roll my eyes and shake my head. "Good morning to you too, Simon. No, nothing happened.

It's not like if I wake up early, something bad must have hap-

pened."

My friend raises an eyebrow as he pours coffee into both cups. "You usually go to bed around this time, Michael."

I sip and sit in one of the armchairs. "Not since Levi. I stopped going out and discovered that if I go to bed at midnight, at five o'clock, I'm awake."

Simon sits on the couch. "Fatherhood makes you do strange things," he chuckles amusedly before making a disgusting face at his coffee. He stopped putting sugar in it for a while now, but I don't think he's gotten used to it yet.

"So does the monogamy, if I'm being honest," I admit in a moment of sincerity.

Simon studies me for a few minutes in silence, and I wait, already knowing that the sermon will come. "Speaking of which, what are your intentions with Faith?"

Straight to the point as usual.

"I don't know, but I haven't slept with anyone but her. For a couple of weeks now, we've been sleeping together every night without necessarily having sex. I think there's only one option: monogamy."

"The problem is, Faith likes to plan her future, and you're forcing her into a situation that makes her uncomfortable," he reprimands me.

"Did she tell you this?"

"No, but you can assume it from her background. She had an arranged marriage, for Christ's sake!"

I raise an eyebrow at the intensity of his exclamation. He lowers his gaze, ashamed at this sudden outburst defending the honor of a woman who, until proven otherwise, is still asleep in my bed.

"Faith knows I'm not good at putting a label on this, but she also knows she can trust me. If there's one thing I can stand by, it's my honesty with women. If it's just sex, I call it. If we live together, it's because I'm sure I don't need another pair of boobs to be satisfied. Holy Christ, I've taken her virginity. That must count for something. Do you think I'd do that lightly?"

Simon sips from his cup, but I see he's hiding a slight smile. "And we didn't even get a description of the deed."

"I don't want you to look at Faith and imagine her... No, I don't even want you to think about it." I'm irritated by just the thought.

Simon bursts out laughing. "Michael, you're the one who was evicted from a hotel room with your dick hidden behind a vase of flowers. We've come to expect all the details from you. But the fact that you've never once talked about it is proof that you care." He gets up from the couch and heads to the studio. "Did you come here early for a reason or because you were bored at home?"

I watch him curiously as I get up and follow him. "With a woman like that sleeping in my bed, I'd stay in for years without going out even to eat. But I wanted to finish the song I started writing, and I didn't want to stay too late tonight. I have dinner plans."

Simon chuckles and nods, satisfied. "I'm glad you started writing again. I've always liked your songs."

It's the first time Simon has openly admitted this. I stopped writing after the overdose and the period in the clinic. I didn't feel I had anything more to say. Before, I wrote songs to keep my demons at bay, but after I almost died, I felt utterly drained. I filled my days with parties and meaningless sex, trying to fill

the void drugs had left. Now, that emptiness has been filled without me noticing and I need to write again, pull out what I have inside, the difference is this time they're not demons that haunt me but feelings I can't identify.

"I don't think they'll be as gloomy as the others."

Simon keeps the door open and lets me into the studio. The guitar is waiting for me on the rack next to an iPad that's been collecting my emotions for days.

"Love songs are good."

"They're not corny," I want to clarify, and Simon laughs.

"Between you and Damian, I have no doubt there'll be at least a couple of references to sex in every chorus. Calm down; I wasn't thinking you'd suddenly become pure and holy. Faith may be a good girl, but she can't work miracles."

I think back to Faith's lips around my erection, the innocent way she asked me to teach her about sex and fuck her, and I can't hold back a mischievous smile spreading on my lips.

Simon looks at me and closes his eyes. "I'm stopping there. I want to keep imagining her naïve and virginal for a while longer before she starts sneaking into bathrooms like Lilly. That girl thinks she's sly, but you can hear her moans from miles away."

We both laugh.

"So you're in love?" he asks me after a long silence.

"No."

Simon smiles and shakes his head as I get back to focusing on my iPad. "You sleep with her, right?"

"Yes."

"But you don't always have sex."

"That's right."

"Do you have plans with her tonight?"

"It's just a dinner."

"Like the ones you two have every night when you leave here, hugging and kissing?"

"That's right, nothing special."

"She's not looking for a new apartment, right?"

"No, why should she?" I look up at him.

"Because she no longer works for you. I thought she'd find a place of her own."

"No! We like living together. Why should she look for another place?"

"Just a guess. I didn't want to insinuate anything." He smiles. "But you're not in love with her."

"Correct."

He shakes his head and looks down on the bass he's grabbed while we've been talking. "Right, of course you're not." He chuckles before sitting down and playing part of a song we'll be rehearsing today.

I observe him for a few moments before looking back at my iPad, not able to concentrate now that I'm thinking over his words. Damn him and his Jiminy Cricket questions!

***

"Okay, see you tomorrow?" I get up from my stool with a sore butt and tired hands after a full day of playing.

Damian looks up bewildered. "Where are you going? It's only six o'clock."

"Yeah, I've been here for twelve hours and I want to go home to take a shower before dinner with Levi and Faith. I have plans tonight."

Thomas and Damian wrinkle their foreheads.

"I can confirm that when I arrived here this morning at six, he was already making coffee," Simon says.

Damian shakes his head and laughs. "Couple's life. I didn't even think you could open your eyes before ten o'clock."

"Can you stop making fun of me? I just stopped staying out all night and coming home at dawn. That's all."

Thomas shakes his head and throws me a drum stick I barely avoid. "Let us enjoy this novelty a little. It's nice to finally see you without the dark circles and hangovers."

I smile as I grab the door handle. "I leave you to your wild nights. I'm going home to my family."

"Look at him! Adulting so hard. No matter how much you try to be a good guy, you'll always be our dick," Damian shouts after me, laughing and making me chuckle too.

Out in the reception area, I lean over to Faith and kiss her on the lips, surprising her. I know I'm embarrassing her, but the room is empty, and the phone isn't ringing.

"Are you ready to go home? I wanted to take you and Levi out for dinner tonight."

"Really? I'm not dressed to go out."

"No worries. I have to take a shower myself. We can pick up Levi and go home before going out."

The advantage of having Thomas and Iris's house upstairs is that we can have the teachers come straight to Iris's apartment to work with Levi. We can keep an eye on him and, if he wants, he can join us in the studio, without having a nanny who looks after him all day in a big empty apartment. I believe a family should be together as much as possible. That's how it was before my grandfather died: I always had a refuge when I felt alone. When my parents left me at home for days, with no one to check on me, I would run to my grandfather's small shoemaker's shop and sit on the stool carving wood while he told me stories of when he was young. He's the only person from my past that I really miss, and sometimes I wish he was still here, especially now, to show him that I, too, in my own way, have built a family for myself.

***

Our SUV arrives in front of the Mandalay where I booked reservations, and immediately I realize there's a buzz in front of the restaurant. Someone famous must be inside because the paparazzi are already stationed nearby. The driver turns to me, not quite knowing what to do.

"Do you want me to call the restaurant and let you out in the underground parking lot?" he proposes when it's clear the photographers have noticed the luxury car that has just pulled up.

I look at Faith and Levi and notice that they're not worried.

"It's fine with me," Faith reassures me.

"Okay, let's go. If you want, you can try to cover your face."

"Why? I can show my friends, they'll see us online. I'm not covering my face!" Levi is clearly attracted by the notoriety and fame my job entails. I look up at the driver, who's smiling.

"And here I thought they stayed with me because of my charm and my mad musician skills!"

The driver chuckles, and Faith slaps my arm, amused. "Are we getting out of this car or not? I'm hungry." She urges me to open the door.

When I set foot on the sidewalk, the rapid series of shots is almost deafening. Hearing my name murmured in a low voice tells me they did not expect to see me—I'd booked under a

fictitious name so it's impossible they knew about our arrival. I reach out to let Levi out of the car, guide him in front of me, and then help Faith. She fusses at the hem of her dress to keep it to a suitable length, and I like how she's always careful not to show too much skin in public, a noticeable difference from the women I used to date.

I put one hand on Levi's back, the other on Faith's. The kid is smiling with all thirty-two teeth, making the victory sign. Faith, however, walks with back straight and eyes forward, her cheeks a shade of pink that reveals her shyness.

"Michael, is this your son? Are you the mother?" The questions follow one after another, and I realize that sooner or later, I'll have to deal with this topic. It was nice living in our bubble, away from the media hype, but going out with me also means being in the crosshairs of public opinion.

I decide to take the bull by the horns and face them head-on rather than feeding the gossip machine. I turn around and give them a forced smile. I don't want them to see me as the enemy.

"They're my family. I ask that you respect the privacy of the boy, who's a minor." My tone is courteous but firm. The flashes are unleashed for a few moments on me, but then slowly, they die. I look them in the face, and they already know they'll have to blur out Levi's face to put him online. It's a half victory for me and a half victory for the paparazzi because the websites and gossip magazines will download their photos for their front pages, and they'll earn their living.

"Thank you and good night," I greet them before turning around and meeting the smiling look of Faith and Levi.

"Are we going to order? I'm hungry." I push them into the restaurant.

“You think they’re going to leave us alone?” asks Faith. I look to see if there’s concern on her face, but I see only curiosity.

“No, but at least I was courteous and honest, so the manhunt will not be unleashed. They also know I could sue for publishing photos of Levi. He’s still a minor. There will be other times when it’s inevitable they’ll take pictures of us, but they won’t go so far as to follow us inside the house.”

She barely nods before looking at the hostess, who, with a huge smile, invites us to follow her to our table. I tried to reassure Faith about the paparazzi story, but I’m not so sure my request tonight will be followed. It’s too juicy a news story to let slip away without exploiting it a bit. I just hope they don’t make our life hell.

PRESS *Review*

People:

A secret son of Michael's! Apparently, the Jailbirds don't just hide a past in prison. Last night, in front of the well-known Mandalay restaurant in New York City, Michael confirmed that he had a family. Sources close to the couple said the mysterious woman appeared at the door of the famous rock star requesting a paternity test for the boy who could be his son. However, blonde hair and blue eyes seem not to be the only resemblance between father and son.

As you can see from the photos, it doesn't take a laboratory test to confirm the relationship between the two. Still, Michael will rightly want to protect his economic interests since the mysterious woman seems to have no past. No social media, no public appearance except the one on the beaches of Miami next to the guitarist of the most famous band in the world.

Will she be able to snatch a hefty child-support sum from Michael? We're waiting for confirmation from those directly concerned. Meanwhile, we like the kid's enthusiasm for the spotlight. Hair color is not the only thing he got from his father.

Gossip Now!

Apparently, the rumors that were already circulating before the Los Angeles concert are true. Michael has a son by a mysterious woman. Judging by the boy's age, the two have known each other for more than ten years. We still don't know if the woman was his high school sweetheart, but the guitarist's protective attitude in front of photographers leaves no doubt that there is a strong bond between the two. We await confirmation from those directly concerned, but we don't need a paternity test to see this boy has the same enthusiasm for the spotlight as his father.

CHAPTER 24
Faith

"Levi, have you brushed your teeth?"

The kid throws me a bored look from the couch. "Yes."

"And have you cleaned your room?"

No answer, as if a wall between us prevents him from hearing me.

"Levi, did you hear what Faith asked you?" Michael says, looking up from his iPad and frowning.

Levi turns to us, exhaling. "Someone comes three times a week to do the cleaning. Why do I have to clean my room? It's a waste of time."

Michael sits up straight and arches an eyebrow. The best thing about his relationship with Levi is that he doesn't treat him like a kid. Michael doesn't know how to deal with children. He himself had to grow up quickly, and, as much as he loves Levi, he's never allowed him to get away from his responsibilities: whether it's finishing to serve his sentence or picking up clothes from the floor of his room.

"That's no reason to disrespect the person who comes here to clean, leaving the house looking like a pigsty, and there's no reason to live in filth. Before you start playing online with your friends, go and pick up the clothes scattered on the floor, change the towels in your bathroom, and especially tidy up your desk. There are computer parts everywhere. I'm glad you want to learn how to assemble the perfect computer, but you're going to find rats' nests in all of it if you leave it lying around." His voice is calm but firm, and Levi, rolling his eyes, walks out, mumbling something we don't understand. "And if you keep rolling your eyes like that, they'll get stuck in the back of your head," shouts Michael with an amused grin.

He places the iPad on the kitchen counter where he's leaning and comes over to hug me and gently kiss my lips. " Levi's being a pain-in-the-ass teenager today. Do you want me to stay home? It's Saturday; I don't need to go to the studio."

"No, don't worry, I'll get by. He's a kid, he's allowed to throw a tantrum every now and then."

Michael raises an eyebrow. "Did you ever do that?"

My mouth forms a grimace. "No, but I've never had a normal life, you know?"

Michael kisses me again and then leans into my ear. "We could go to our room to fix this," he whispers maliciously.

"I just made the bed."

Michael frowns, looking at me. "I could get you on your knees in the chair and make you scream my name. The sheets would remain intact."

I burst out laughing. I've discovered with Michael you don't need a bed to make love. Any surface will do, and even standing up works.

"Michael, your friends are waiting for you. You have an album to release as soon as possible if you want your record company to stay afloat. You're the only artists currently under contract," I remind him. I've noticed the tension around those rooms over the last few weeks, with Evan trying to make ends

meet and the Jailbirds having far too many songs still to record to release an album. I've seen how the pressure for selling an album does not go hand in hand with the creative process.

"Damn, why didn't I choose a shallow woman instead of one who talks like my conscience?" he teases me, chuckling.

"Because you like it when we talk about serious topics. Because you like to teach me complicated things and brag about being a good teacher because I understand them immediately. And because I have a nice butt. You tell me that all the time, especially in bed."

He laughs. "It's true, but I never said you have a nice butt. I think my exact words are: 'You have such a perfect ass I want to make a mold to carry around so I can touch it and bite it even when you're not around.'"

I blush at his frankness. I'm still not used to his uninhibited way of speaking. "Yes, I think those are the words, but I'm not as vulgar as you to repeat them."

Michael kisses me before taking his iPad, the keys, and saying bye to Levi from the hall. I watch him as he leaves the apartment and leaves me here, with the desire to make a mess in that bed, rolling between the sheets with him.

***

One of the things I like about life with Michael is that I can enjoy a few luxuries that I couldn't before. Like long hours immersed in the bathtub, soaking in the coconut scent of the bubble bath Michael bought me. A pleasure I'll never be able to give up again. With my eyes closed and my head resting on the back of the tub, I'm enjoying the relaxation of a lazy Saturday morning.

"Faith! Faith, come here!" Levi's shaken voice reaches me

from behind the door of my bathroom.

My heart bolts in my chest, not so much at the sudden interruption, but that Levi is in my room. He never does this. We each keep to our own space. We leave the door open when we're available, but we close it when we need some solitude. If he's knocking on the door of my bathroom, it must be urgent.

"I'm coming! Give me a minute to get dressed."

"No, you have to come right away."

The panic in his voice makes me jump out of the tub without even rinsing off and grab my white bathrobe. I open the door and go check his room but he's not there, so with my feet still wet, I run towards the living room, trying not to slip on the white marble. I freeze in the middle of the room when I see the social worker standing next to Levi in her usual gray suit and stern face.

"Good morning." My voice comes out uncertain. My heart hammers against my chest. I hope she didn't come here to ask me more questions that I can't answer.

"Good morning. I'm looking for Mr. Wright."

It takes me a few seconds to realize she's talking about Michael.

"He's in the studio recording. Can I help you?"

"You are not Levi's legal representative. I need to talk to Mr. Wright."

"I can try to call him to come home. Can you give me a minute to change? I was taking a shower." I don't know why I didn't tell her I was taking a hot bath. Maybe because I get the feeling this woman would have judged me as a lazy slacker just for having immersed myself in a tub.

She gives me a vague nod with her hand that I interpret

as permission, and I walk quickly down the hall, hearing her asking Levi questions. “Does he often leave you in the company of strangers when he’s not at home?” Her voice is full of insinuations that I don’t like.

“Faith isn’t a stranger! We’ve been living together for months. Her and Michael take care of me.”

I quicken my pace and put on the first thing I can find: a pair of linen pants and a shirt too big to be mine. I go to the bathroom, grab the cell phone I’d left on the counter, and dial his number. I let it ring until it goes to the voicemail three times. I don’t leave him any messages, so as not to worry him, but I hope he’ll call back when he sees the missed calls. I rush back to the living room and find the woman sitting in front of a sulky Levi at the dining table.

“Everything okay, Levi?”

“She wants to talk to Michael,” he mumbles without relaxing his arms stiffly crossed over his chest. Levi is a sunny, smiling boy. I wonder what the woman said to make him sulk like that.

“I tried to call him, but he didn’t answer. When he’s in the recording studio, he usually leaves his phone inside a cabinet so he’s not disturbed,” I try to explain so she understands it’s not like Michael to not answer his phone.

“And if there’s an emergency and Levi needs immediate assistance, what does he do? Wait until Michael has finished recording his album before he gets any attention?”

I notice an acidic vein in her words. It’s clear this woman is angry with Michael, and I can’t understand why.

“I take care of him. I’m the adult responsible for Levi’s well-being when Michael is not here.”

"Do you have a car?"

"I don't even have a driver's license, for that matter, but what does that have to do with an emergency? If it's a medical problem, it would be irresponsible to think of getting into Manhattan traffic with a child who needs medical assistance without calling an ambulance. If it's not a medical emergency, there's nothing that can't be solved with a taxi or Uber. Besides, I'm a qualified nurse. I have experience in handling emergencies."

For the first time in my life, I find myself responding angrily to a person and letting the emotions boiling in my veins take over. She wants to make us look like we're incapable of taking care of Levi, and I don't accept that. My father's hostile words echo in my head, but I cast them out decisively, annoyed by the fact that he somehow still influences me, despite having disowned me as a daughter.

Out of the corner of my eye, I see Levi struggling to hold back a smile. A small victory that calms me down a bit. I try to call Michael again, but the phone keeps ringing without an answer as I watch the woman open the red folder she's forever clutching and jot something down that I assume is not favorable. I notice newspaper clippings in the pocket of the folder showing photos of us outside the restaurant where we went for dinner a couple of weeks ago. While I've never worried about gossip magazines, it bothers me that this woman felt the need to buy them.

"Michael isn't answering. Can you make an appointment for another time so you can speak with him? Or you can ask me."

The woman shakes her head and continues to write. She

spends at least half an hour in silence before getting up and leaving our house angrily without a word.

"I hate her," Levi mumbles as he goes to sit on the couch.

I want to tell him that hating is a strong word, that he should be careful of what he says and not hurt people, but I'm not sure I can blame him this time. That woman is hard to take—it's clear she's not giving us a chance. It almost seems like she wants us to fail with Levi, and that's not fair because Michael is giving it all he has.

I sit next to him and try to call Michael again, and the voicemail message welcomes me once again. I try to call Damian, Simon, and Thomas, but the result is the same. I'm not surprised. I know when they're in the studio, they don't let themselves be distracted by anything, and right now they're pretty stressed out by the pressure of writing and recording this new album.

All that day I keep trying to call Michael and, after a while, the phone doesn't even ring anymore, going straight to the voicemail. He must've turned it off, and I'm bewildered. Did he just decide to ignore it despite seeing the countless calls I made? Doesn't he care at least a little bit about us? Or wonder why I tried to call so many times?

The anger begins to simmer in my stomach, along with the agitation of the meeting, and the worry of whether I did or said something wrong, making me pace around the room in a fury. Michael is irresponsible. He's a former inmate. He has to prove that he's fully reformed before thinking of raising a young boy! And here he disappears, turns off his phone, and leaves me alone to face an irate, stubborn social worker.

***

It's ten in the evening when Michael finally comes home and meets my fiery gaze. The built-up tension from the day causes me to jump off the couch and walk briskly towards him.

"Where have you been?" I hiss, anxiety and fear pouring out with my words.

Michael frowns. "In the studio, recording."

"Really? Or were you with a woman? Because I tried calling you all day, and you never once answered."

Michael's face clouds over, a wounded expression veiling his eyes. "Do you really think I'd be with another woman? Is that what you think of me? My phone battery died, that's all. Try calling Damian or the others, ask them," he replies, irritated, walking by me and heading to his bedroom.

"I called Damian and the others. None of you answered. The social worker came by today and wanted to talk to you. She left angry after writing in her damn folder for more than half an hour without uttering a single word. Levi was so upset he cried for hours."

Michael freezes and turns to me with wide eyes.

"I've tried calling you dozens of times today. I needed you to come home and talk to her. She didn't tell me anything. She didn't ask me any questions. She just waited for you, as if it were a matter of life or death, and then she left. I didn't know what to do. I needed you." Tears run down my cheeks, easing the tightness I've held in my chest all day. Michael grabs me by the wrist and pulls me in for a hug.

"I'm here now. Tomorrow I'll call my lawyer and we'll solve this."

I want to believe his words, but I feel his heart pounding wildly in his chest and his hug is so tight it almost hurts. He's

not reassuring me, he's clinging to me to hide his own fear, and I'm not sure I can help him. Michael will smile and pretend for Levi's sake that he's not worried, but I've learned by now that under the smiling facade, he often hides fears and insecurities he'll never confess out loud.

"Will she take me away from you?" Levi's voice draws our attention. After the meeting with the social worker, he'd stayed in his room all day and came out only for meals without saying a word.

"No. tomorrow, I'll call my lawyer and make an appointment with that woman."

"What if she doesn't want to meet with us?" He comes over and wraps his arms around Michael's waist, who turns and embraces him.

"We all have a life. She can't expect us all to drop everything when she comes over. If it was so important, she could have waited until I got home."

Levi looks up at him and smiles, but he doesn't seem comforted.

"Come on, let's see if there are any documentaries on TV you might like," he suggests as he pulls Levi to the couch.

Michael motions for me to follow. I join them, sitting next to Michael and sinking into the pillows as images of Australian kangaroos drift across the screen. No one dares to speak, but when I glance at Michael, I see not only the exhaustion of a day spent in the studio, but also worry over this missed meeting. As much as he tries to reassure us that his lawyer can resolve the problem, I'm sure even he doubts his own words.

CHAPTER 25

Michael

"How the hell is it possible that she can show up at my house on a Saturday morning and demand that we be available?" I pace while my lawyer looks at Evan and Simon, who are with us in the conference room at the record company.

I asked to see him as soon as possible, considering that our phone conversation on Sunday was more or less shouting from me and "Michael, I'll try to investigate what happened" on his part.

"These are surprise visits that social workers make to check up on people who are taking care of the kids they entrust to them," he tries to explain to me for the umpteenth time.

I glance at Faith, who shifts worriedly in the chair behind the counter, throwing us quick looks as she answers the phone.

"And where the hell were these people when they sent Levi to rob those stores? Because there is no logical explanation for this."

Simon tries to intervene with his usual logical reasoning that at the moment makes me even more nervous. "Michael, the issue of social services is complicated. They often have no funds to control the families that host the kids. If there are no obvious signs of mistreatment, they usually trust what the kids say. I can guarantee that when you're in that situation, you lie

to the social workers. You don't want to suffer the revenge of the people taking care of you."

"But they have the funds to send her to our home twice in a month? To a luxury building with a concierge and private security? I must be a really unfit adult to make a kid live in luxury and give him the best teachers in the state to help him catch up and go to college."

Simon turns to my lawyer. "He has a point. It's usually a miracle if they come every five to six months in the beginning. Strangely, they took the trouble to come twice in such a short time, especially since it's clear that Levi is not in danger with Michael."

My lawyer rubs his face, seeming uncertain whether or not to say what's on his mind. This immediately alarms me. He's never hidden anything from me, not even when he had to tell me that my father wanted more money every month to keep his damn mouth shut about my past.

"I was not able to speak directly with her, but with her supervisor. He says she's not a bad woman, just that she's particularly meticulous and doesn't like when someone bends the rules. He believes she bears a grudge against Michael because nothing in this situation is normal. A judge allowed Levi to serve his sentence in your home, then gave you custody without having done all the work to be able to take part in the program. She's one of those people who believe that money shouldn't buy a kid's life."

I doubt that the woman's supervisor used these exact words, but my lawyer is used to sharks, and he knows how to ask the right questions and read between the lines. "So my only fault is that I have the money and the connections to give Levi a good life?"

"Your only fault is that you bent the rules to get Levi. It doesn't matter if you love him or not," Evan says. "Is it possible to do something?" he then asks with his usual practicality and tendency to try and solve all our problems.

"Be present at the next visits, convince her that Levi is in good hands. Make sure she understands this isn't just some whim to make you look good in front of the press."

Wait for her to come back to convince her? What if she decides she wants to see my lawyer next time, but he's not available? Or ask about my family or Faith and deduce that we didn't grow up in a suitable environment? I can't sit here, waiting for someone to come and take Levi away from me. I cannot accept that.

***

"I know she's not in the office, and she can't get to the phone. You said that every one of the twenty times I've called in the last five hours. I only ask you to give me her mobile number, and I swear I will not use it except to ask her for another chance. Hello? Hello?"

Faith looks at me with apprehension. As soon as I got home, I did the one thing everyone advised me not to: call the social worker.

"He hung up," I explain, slumping on the couch where she's sitting.

"Michael, you wore them out. Please calm down and go pack your bag. We have to leave in less than half an hour, and calling again will not solve the situation."

"Don't tell me to calm down. The situation is anything but calm," I snap, and I see her mouth shut, surprised by my ag-

gressive reaction. I'm sorry, I shouldn't blame her, but the reality is that right now, I want to jump out of my own skin at how suffocated I feel.

Faith gets up and, without saying a word, goes to her bedroom, coming out a few minutes later with a suitcase in hand, ready to do her job and join us on the tour.

"Levi, in a few minutes, the car will come to pick us up. Are you ready?" she asks out loud, completely ignoring me as I go to my room to get my stuff.

Knowing I made her angry makes me feel bad, but pride and not knowing how to apologize keep me quiet. The remaining hours that separate us from the hotel in Las Vegas are spent in complete silence on my part, aside from some harsh replies to my bandmates, and at some point they understood and stopped asking me questions.

"Are you going to continue being an asshole to Faith, or will you get your shit together?" Simon's voice behind me in the corridor that leads us to our rooms makes me snort, annoyed. I don't feel like talking to anyone.

"If you don't like how I behave, get lost, because I don't really want to argue today," I mumble.

My friend grabs me by the arm and drags me into one of the elevators closing behind us. He presses the button for the middle floor, which has an exclusive bar for guests, and pushes me towards it when the doors open.

"Now we're going to sit here at this table until you get your shit together. Do you understand?"

"Simon, really, I can't deal with your bullshit today."

"Explain. I've never seen Faith as depressed as she's been these last few hours."

I close my eyes and rub a hand across my face. "I'm concerned about the situation with Levi. I tried to call the social worker, but she's unreachable."

"You did exactly what we all advised against." It's not a question but an observation that smacks of reproach.

"That's right, so what? I'm not going to sit here, waiting for them to take him away from me, okay?"

"I know you can't sit still. You're always jumping into situations and facing them head-on, but this time you can't do anything about it." Simon is always the practical and direct one, but today his sincerity bothers me.

"So I just sit here and wait?"

"That's right. Trust me, social services won't care how many albums you've recorded and prioritize you because you're famous. They'll follow their usual protocol, and you'll have to adapt to their rules, not the other way around."

I inhale deeply and hold my breath until my lungs hurt. Simon doesn't say anything, but he studies me as if expecting to see me explode at any moment.

"I'm going to my room to unpack my suitcase—are you coming?" he asks finally.

"Go ahead. I need to calm down a bit before facing Faith and Levi. I won't stay long, I swear." I smile at him, a gesture much less forced than expected. The tension is gradually leaving my body. Simon is the only one of us who grew up under the protection of social services in foster families, and he's the only one who tells me like it is.

I don't know how much time has passed when Faith joins me, in Simon's place. "Are you going to drink it?" she asks me after a few minutes, pointing to my glass.

Every time I look at her, it stops me in my tracks and I realize how beautiful she is, how that natural, make-up-free face is the closest thing to perfection I've ever seen.

"Do you know that since you and Levi came to live with me, I have not been drunk anymore? I drink alcohol, of course, but not as much as before. When I was going out at night, getting drunk was the only way to have fun in this shallow and superficial business we're in. Since you've been here, I haven't felt the need for it."

"Do you plan to start today?"

"I was thinking that if they take Levi away from me, I don't know if my life will ever be the same as it was. I've finally found a reason to think about the future instead of living only in the present. To be completely honest, I think if they were to take him away from me, my life would become as meaningless as it used to be. Filled with cheap thrills that fill that void the overdose has left in me."

Faith studies me for a few seconds, then leans against the back of the armchair and tilts her head to the side. "Don't give them one more reason to do it. Getting drunk now would mean ending up in the newspapers as the fickle rock star who gave a bad show to his fans. That won't help your resume or help you keep custody of Levi."

Her way of reasoning reminds me a lot of Simon's, and while it warms my heart, it also scares me. If I were to lose Simon, I think I'd lose my mind. Thomas is Damian's best friend and Simon is mine, but in many ways, Faith has become the female counterpart of a best friend. I don't know how I'd react if she abandoned me and the kid.

"If Levi were to leave, would you stay?" I ask her with raw

honesty.

Faith studies me calmly. "Is this what worries you? That I'll leave with him?"

"It's not so far-fetched, is it?"

"Michael, all the decisions I've made so far have taken me in one direction, to you. Call me crazy, romantic, or deluded, but I think what binds us is something deeper than looking after Levi. The three of us became a family the moment you entered that infirmary with him, no social worker can break apart the ties that unite us."

Her words hit me like a brick to the chest. Besides my band-mates, no one's ever stuck with me this long, and I find that I like it. I've always said I'm not made for monogamy, but Faith has never tried to use arguments to convince me otherwise. Maybe it's possible that a woman can stand by me without demanding that I become someone else. Faith hasn't asked me to change who I am and become her Prince Charming, and this realization makes me feel deeply accepted just as I am.

"Do you want to go to our room and relax before the show? There's a huge hot tub!" Faith's wide eyes make me smile.

"This is Las Vegas, everything is big and luxurious. What surprises me, though, is that you're inviting me to try it." I raise my eyebrows and give her my most mischievous smile.

She frowns and watches me, tilting her head, clearly not understanding the implications of a hot tub inside a private bathroom of a hotel room.

"People have sex in those tubs. It's why they put them in these bathrooms," I explain, chuckling and enjoying her scan-dalized expression.

"Really?"

“Yes, they’re expensive to maintain, difficult to clean, and make no sense when every hotel here has at least a swimming pool and a casino big enough to entertain thousands of people. Those tubs offer adults another kind of entertainment when they’re done losing all their money at the tables.”

“Dear Jesus, and here I wanted Levi to try it. Maybe it’s not such a good idea. I mean…forget I asked,” she says red from the neck up.

I burst out laughing. “No, come on. Let’s try it, and we’ll order room service to really live it up. But tonight, I want to use it again in private, with all the bubbles going up in very, very private parts.” I conclude my proposal in a whisper.

“Michael!” she exclaims, scandalized, as I grab her by the hand and drag her to the elevator that takes us to the room.

I can laugh again, and though our problems are far from over, it feels good to have a little breathing room with Faith. Maybe the social worker won’t think we’re perfect, but she doesn’t know that we can always smile again, together.

CHAPTER 26

Faith

I open my eyes before sunrise, looking at the time on the alarm clock above the bedside table: five forty-five. I slept less than four hours. Sleeping in a bed that's not mine, in a room that's not mine, makes for a restless night. I turn to Michael and watch him sleep blissfully, he's used to all these changes, and I hope, one day, I will be too.

I look at his naked chest, his hair lightened by the sun barely glowing on his pillow. It's a little longer than when I met him, and I like it even more. It gives him that scruffy look of a bad boy, beautiful but not unrealistically perfect. I could stay here and watch him for hours, with his sculpted chest and marbled abs, the golden hairless skin covering those perfect and inviting muscles. I've never seen a guy like him, in fact, I've never seen a guy without a shirt. I imagine even some men in my community have great physiques under their loose shirts, especially those who work all day on farms, where physical effort forms a man's body, but I wouldn't know.

I slide a finger over his navel, marking the contours with a light touch. Maybe it stirs him because he turns to me in his sleep, and the sheet slips down, revealing much more than his hips. His semi-erection peeks out, and I find myself staring at it without being able to look away. Usually, when we make

love, I don't stop to look at it, but in the early dawn of this room, I pause to admire the object of my pleasure.

The vibration coming from my bedside table makes me jump, and I turn around and grab the phone before Michael wakes up. It's the number of the apartment in New York, and immediately my heart bounces back into my chest. I quickly put on my bathrobe to cover my bare skin and leave the room before answering in a whisper.

"Hello?"

"Miss Faith? I'm sorry to bother you, but I can't reach Mr. Michael."

I smile at our concierge's way of saying our names. We've asked him to use our first names, but Matthew always feels the need to add Miss or Mr. in front of them. "He's still sleeping."

A moment of pause makes me think that he wasn't expecting this answer.

"The social worker is here and is asking to see Mr. Michael and Mr. Levi."

My heart sinks into my chest. "What do you mean, the social worker is there? It's dawn on a Saturday morning. What is she doing there?"

Another pause that seems endless. My heart pounding in my chest and throat makes it seem even longer.

"It's almost nine o'clock here, Miss Faith." I curse myself when I remember the three hours difference between the two cities. "I didn't want to disturb you, but it seemed like a pretty important issue." He tries to apologize.

"No, Matthew, I'm glad you called. Can you tell her we're not in the city but will take the first plane home? If she can leave you a phone number, we will make an appointment today."

He seems to hesitate, but then gives in. "I'll definitely do that, Miss Faith," he reassures me before hanging up.

Before I return to Michael, I grab my iPad and start looking for flights back for this morning. We had decided to spend the weekend here and return on Sunday evening, even though the Jailbirds played last night and finished up this tour date.

"Michael, you have to get up right away. We have to go back to New York," I tell him as I shake him after waking Levi up and returning to our room.

Michael looks at me with sleepy and confused eyes. "Not even a little good morning sex? And also, why do we have to go back? Has something happened?" His eyes widen in an expression of alarm when he sees that I am getting dressed in a hurry.

"Mathew called. He said the social worker was there asking for us."

"What? The social worker? How the hell is that possible? She was there a week ago." He snaps to his feet, and I stop myself from scolding him for invoking the devil and hell. I don't like it when he does, but this isn't the time to bring it up.

"I don't know. I managed to find a flight for all the three of us in an hour and a half. We have to hurry to make it to the airport. I've already sent a message to Evan to warn him and to have him pick up our luggage. Put something on, quickly. I'm going to check if Levi is ready. A car is waiting for us." I finish tying my shoes and stuff the documents we need in my bag.

Michael has already slipped into his jeans, is looking for his shirt, and when he finds it, he moves towards me and pulls me in for a kiss with his hand on the back of my neck.

"Christ, I adore when you're so organized. I love you." The words suck all the air out of the room. I look at him, stunned, and meet his disoriented expression. "Sorry, that came out of nowhere... I didn't want to tell you *I love you* like this, in a moment of absolute chaos," he stammers in embarrassment.

I try to play it down, but in truth, my stomach is in turmoil. "Of course, it was probably just your subconscious. You've been thinking about it for a while, maybe, but didn't notice. It would have been worse if you'd said you hate me, right?" How I wish what he said was the plain and simple truth. Because as much as I keep repeating that I can do this and accept our situation, I grew up wanting to have a family, a marriage, and children. I gave up on a union arranged by my father, but this doesn't mean that I don't want one at all. I dream of having a marriage and a family with the man I love, that part of me didn't die when I was disowned. It's more alive than ever.

"Well, yes... But can we talk about it again when we're calmer?" He nervously rubs a hand through his hair.

"Will we ever talk about it, Michael? Be honest."

Michael tightens his jaw. "What do you want me to say, Faith? That the only marriage I saw was my parents' and that there was no love? My mother was forced to marry my father to pay off my grandfather's debt to my father's criminal family. Look at Damian and Lilly or Thomas and Iris—they're not married but they're happy. Isn't that enough for you?"

"No, Michael, because if one day one of them wakes up and decides they don't want to stay in that relationship anymore, they can pack their bags and walk out the door without looking back." I feel my cheeks flare up, and anger grip my stomach.

"A married man can do that too."

"But if he wants to marry another woman, he can't do it legally. He has to go back and face his responsibilities. It's not so easy to leave a marriage, and that's why you don't want to commit. You're insecure. You want to have a relationship and a way out at the same time, to keep your options open." I spit it all out in one breath, and Michael's eyes widen, caught off guard by my answer.

"Can we talk about this when we don't have the stress of this whole social worker situation on us?" he asks me sadly.

I nod and inhale deeply. We're both tense, and maybe it's not the best time to bring up my insecurities about our relationship, which I've been thinking about for a while now.

After a moment of complete awkwardness, the door opens wide and Levi enters, ready to leave.

"Should we get going and meet this harpy?"

"Where did you learn the word harpy?" asks Michael curiously.

"After you gave me Percy Jackson's books, I watched some documentaries about Greek mythology. Did you know that there's a bird of prey called a harpy? It lives mainly in Central America," he explains with his usual chronic curiousness.

"Exactly how many documentaries is *some*?" Michael teases him with a smile, but I can hear the anxiousness in his voice. I appreciate that he's trying to keep the topic light so as not to scare Levi, given our complete disadvantage in this moment.

"I don't know…ten, maybe eleven..." he admits blushing as we leave the room and head towards the elevators.

Michael laughs, but without much joy.

***

"Did she leave a phone number to contact her?" asks Mi-

chael without even greeting poor Matthew, who gets panicky as soon as he sees us.

"No, unfortunately not."

"Damn!" he curses, and Levi clasps his arms around me.

"Michael, why don't you and Levi go upstairs to take a nice shower and make us something to eat? I'll join you in a few minutes," I suggest tilting my head towards Levi, who is holding me tightly, afraid and anxious because Michael is agitated.

Michael looks down at the boy and immediately softens. He stretches out his hand and nods his head towards the elevators. "Come on, let's go munch on something and think of a solution. What do you say?"

I like how he never keeps Levi in the dark about this whole situation, but that means he has to try to be even more sensitive to the boy's feelings. It's not easy to live in an environment where they threaten to move you from one house to another like a postal package. And the worst part is never knowing when it will happen; the social worker in charge of your file decides if that family is good for you or not. It can take two, three, ten surprise visits, but there's no rule or magic formula to understanding it.

When the elevator doors close and their figures disappear, I turn to Matthew and smile. "I don't think that woman said nothing at all and left. How did she react when you asked her for her number?"

The guy blushes slightly and stiffens. It must not have been a pleasant experience for him either.

"If I can be honest, she gives me the creeps. She's stiff and cold and seems to have no feelings."

I smile again, waiting for him to go on.

"She said she's not one of your employees that you can call whenever you want. That if you want to complain, there's an office with a supervisor you can deal with."

"Did she say where it is?"

"No, she just left me the landline number. But if you want, I can look up the number and see if the address is public information."

"Would you really do that? Thank you very much."

A few minutes later, I find myself in a taxi with Manhattan traffic flowing past me, heading to Brooklyn.

***

The building is a block of red brick on the street overlooking the East River. Similar to many other buildings around here, only there are no curtains or plants in the windows, just the classic white mini blinds typical of offices. I approach the door and notice there are four bells, and when I ring social services, no one responds. The office hours say they're open to the public Monday through Friday from nine to five and only by appointment. But I'm not going to give up without trying to see if Mrs. Mayer is inside this building. I ring the doorbell of a tailor who makes emergency repairs, and the metallic sound of the door opening gives me hope.

I go up the stairs, stopping in front of each door to read the plates showing the occupants' name or business. A tailor on the first floor, lawyers on the second, social workers on the third. I'm guessing the debt collection agency mentioned on the doorbell is on the fourth floor. The place is illuminated by fluorescent lights that, added to the dark gray tint of the walls, make this place look similar to a prison, and the shiver that runs down my back makes me almost tremble. I don't miss

that gloomy environment at all.

I ring the social services bell but, again, no one answers, so I try to turn the handle in the hope that someone's inside. To my surprise, the door opens to a waiting room filled with gray plastic chairs that contrast with the white walls covered by leaflets and posters about families. In front of me, there is a reception counter divided by glass but no one behind it. Next to it, a low wooden gate opens into the cubicle area that serves as the social workers' offices. At least a dozen stations piled with papers, a couple of gray chairs in front of the desks, and computers even more beaten-up than Levi's.

A single station is occupied at this time, and behind the glass, I see the very woman I'm looking for. I take a deep breath and approach her. When I'm in front of her, she looks up from the document she was writing on, surprised.

"How did you get in here?"

"The tailor on the first floor let me in without even asking me for my name." I smile.

She inhales deeply, closes her eyes, and shakes her head slightly as if she's seen this before and doesn't like it. She motions for me to sit in the gray plastic chair in front of her desk. "If you came to make an appointment, you're wasting your time. The visits are not planned." Her expression is severe, tired, the same one my mother has when she has to scold us.

"I know, but it seems like they almost always happen when we're not at home. I get the impression that we started off on the wrong foot."

The woman smiles, shaking her head. "Miss, we never really started at all. The only visit that was successful was the first, the scheduled one. On the others, Mr. Wright didn't want

to be found. Maybe he's too busy with his career to take care of a child."

I frown and begin to understand why Michael's lawyer thinks she's bearing a grudge against him. There is almost contempt in her voice. "Michael loves that boy more than any biological parent. He literally lives for Levi. He gives him the best of everything." The knot that tightens my stomach almost hurts.

"It's not a matter of loving a person. It's giving him stability. Levi doesn't need love. He needs someone to guide him to become an adult, not go around to concerts and live in an environment that a fourteen-year-old boy shouldn't even know exists." It's almost a reprimand.

"Do you know that in the months Levi's been staying with us, he's almost caught up with the years of school he lost when he was *entrusted* to families who sent him to rob stores? He has the best private teachers around and a guaranteed college fund to allow him to study and have a future."

"But he doesn't go to a real school, with real classmates. He does not have a life with rules, schedules, and routines. Do we even want to bring up the newspapers? His privacy is violated every time he leaves home, the social networks plaster his face around the world, exposing him to all kinds of comments, nastiness, and rumors. Maybe it's fun for you because your Instagram account has a surge in followers, but for a kid who's been in prison, maybe life in the spotlight is not so good. What will Mr. Wright do when they find out Levi was in the same prison as he was? How will they exploit that news? Levi will never be free from his mistakes if those mistakes are made public to the entire world."

I can't say anything. I have nothing to counter her accusations because I don't know even a tenth of how this world works, of social networks, of gossip. I was pushed into the rock star environment through the back door, discovering the backstage before seeing what everyone else sees, and I have no idea how you can defend a kid from all this. I get up and walk to the door, with tears threatening to fall.

"Sometimes, if you love someone, you also have to understand what's best for that person," she says in a calmer voice. "Give up your pride and decide to do the right thing."

I nod and leave without being able to open my mouth. When I close the door behind me, tears I can no longer hold roll freely down my cheeks.

***

"Where have you been?" Michael is worried as he pulls me by the arm to his room.

Levi is perched on the sofa in the living room, carving a piece of wood while watching one of his countless documentaries.

"To see the social worker," I whisper as I close the door behind me.

He looks at me in surprise, then frowns and sits on the bed. I've never seen him defeated, not once since we've lived under the same roof. He's the strong one who either faces situations head-on or lets them go if he knows he can't do a thing about it.

"What did she say?"

I tell him the conversation in broad outlines, squeezing his hand while an endless series of emotions cross his face.

"Damn." He sighs as he rubs his face.

“Michael...” I don’t know what to tell him.

I feel like a liar to pull out the usual cliché “everything will be fine” because I’m not sure it will be. Not everything goes the right way. I experienced that when my father closed the door and prevented me from seeing my family again. God knows how many times I’ve tried to talk to them and how many times the phone was slammed in my face without any chance to explain why I abandoned them.

Michael turns to me, puts his hands in my hair, and kisses me first gently, but slowly more and more with increasing heat. His tongue seems to struggle with mine. His teeth take possession of my lips, biting and pulling them with a fervor he’s never shown before. I reach for his shoulders with my hands, but he stops me. He’s filled with all the anger this situation stirs up and he has no outlet—so he explodes. Michael explodes in an animalistic instinct I’ve never seen before. He doesn’t want to make love. He wants to let everything out physically that he’s been keeping inside emotionally. I abandon myself to him, to whatever he needs to find release, certain that because this is Michael, he will never hurt me.

He pushes me on the bed and then stands up, using his legs to open mine. He puts his hands under my dress to take off my panties, his gaze never leaving mine. He is wild and comforting, new and familiar, impetuous and loving. All the facets of Michael in one moment of intimacy.

He gets on the bed, his legs on the sides of mine. With one hand, he grabs my wrists and lifts them firmly over my head. With the other, he grabs the thin straps of my dress and one after the other tears them with a single decisive move. A yelp of surprise comes out of my lips, and my lower belly flares up

with warmth and desire.

Michael gets up again, grabs the dress by the hem, and pulls it off with ease. Uses both hands to hold my wrists and drag me to the headboard, uses the dress to tie them to the dark wood. I can't run away. I can't move my arms to wrap them around his perfect body. I should be frightened by this complete helplessness but I'm more excited than I've ever been.

He gets out of bed and takes all the time he needs to observe my naked body as he undresses slowly. He kneels on the bed and rests his lips on my breasts, greedily sucking a nipple while his fingers torture the other in a mixture of pain and pleasure that makes me groan. I pull at my restraints. I would like to free my hands and sink my fingers into his hair, but I can't, and the frustration is paired with a mixture of excitement that makes me say his name.

"Michael," I whisper like a prayer.

But pray for what? For him to free me, to fill me with his erection? Right now, I'm in a limbo of ecstasy and frustration that is shattering my ability to think coherently.

While sucking and biting one of my nipples, he slips between my legs and uses two fingers to penetrate my most tender and sensitive spot. He flexes his fingers, massages that part of my body that gives me such intense pleasure my legs tremble. He alternates those movements with more profound and deeper thrusts, making me short of breath.

"Michael..." His name comes out as a moan, making me close my eyes and arch my back with an orgasm that leaves me breathless.

"I want to fuck you without a condom. I want to feel you completely mine," he whispers in my ear and then looks up

at me. A mixture of lust and prayer envelops those blue eyes, pulling me into his world.

"Okay."

It's a huge step for both of us. I've long known that we're both healthy, but doing it without that barrier that physically separates us is like putting your life in the hands of the other person. A gesture of total and complete trust you don't just give to anyone, that makes you vulnerable, that makes us both fragile and at the same time powerful.

Michael slips between my legs, takes my ankles, and puts them on his shoulders. He leans forward and sinks his erection, slow but never stopping. He lowers towards me, forcing my legs to rise towards my shoulders, plunging like never before. I feel everything about him, how he fills me, how his heart hammers against his chest, and when he starts moving his hips without any hesitation, my orgasm mounts again until I sink my teeth in his shoulder to keep from screaming.

I've never experienced such intensity before, and when he reaches his pleasure too, his body trembles on mine, his arms wrapping me in a tight grip that puts all our pieces back together, fuses them in a single and intense act of love.

He slides down next to me. With one hand, he unties my wrists, while with the other, he wraps me in an embrace. He pants as he sinks his face into the hollow of my neck in a moment that will always be ours alone.

"I don't want to lose you, Faith, but I don't know how to be the man you deserve," he confesses in a whisper.

"You already are, Michael. You're so busy defending yourself and the people around you from your demons that you don't realize how wonderful you are."

His lips touch my shoulder in a single sweet kiss, but they don’t reveal any of the feelings I know are stirring in his chest.

CHAPTER 27

Michael

"I decided to go and talk to the social worker," I blurt out at breakfast after Evan convinced me to make a proper appointment to talk heart-to-heart with the woman.

Faith and Levi exchange a glance I can't read. On Saturday night, after Faith and I managed to get out of the room, we explained to Levi that there's a possibility that the social worker would decide not to let him live with us. He cried and hugged us but then understood that we had no control over this. I don't want the news to come like a bolt out of the blue for him. And I don't want him to delude himself that everything's okay when in reality, the chances of him staying with us are becoming increasingly slim.

"I'm coming too," Levi announced.

Faith looks at him, a little worried but says nothing. I know she agrees to let him participate in every decision, but she's concerned some things might be so painful for him that he'll run away again.

"I'm coming too," she says with a smile and a hand resting on Levi's.

"It's becoming a field trip!" I try to play down a moment filled with so much negativity.

"Maybe the harpy will change her mind."

I smile behind my cup of coffee while Faith scolds him for calling people names. When someone asks for it, I'd have to agree with Levi.

We arrive at the woman's office ten minutes early. We show up in the waiting room and sit quietly on the uncomfortable plastic chairs in the reception area. Inside the office, the cubicles are all occupied, the phones ring, and there's no one but us waiting. I watch Ronda Mayer fill out her papers without ever answering the phone, looking at the computer, or in our direction. A stubbornness that lasts for an hour and a half until I get up impatiently and point out to the receptionist that all this waiting is getting ridiculous. She glances over at the social worker's cubicle and then motions with her head for us to go in. I think she was ordered to keep us here until we walked out in frustration.

"That's not how foster care visits work, Mr. Wright."

"I know, but with you, it seems the only possible solution," I blurt out with a little more intensity than necessary.

Faith puts a hand on my leg, and the gesture does not escape the attentive gaze of the woman, so I stretch my hand to cover hers and intertwine our fingers. I don't want there to be any doubt about what kind of relationship this is.

"I have to make sure the boy is entrusted to people who take care of him, not people who pay others to take care of him."

"So the problem is money? Do you know why I don't send him to a normal school but insist on home school with the best teachers? So he can be with me everywhere, and I won't have to leave him at home with a nanny every time I'm out of town. Because I want to have him with me, take care of him, teach him things."

"He should learn them in a stable environment, not gallivanting around the world with a group of adults who live a reckless life. Why don't you change jobs, Mr. Wright? Why are you not the one who's giving up something for Levi?"

Her words cut me to the core. Am I really that selfish that I'm putting myself first?

"Nobody's going to ask what I want?" Levi's voice breaks the silence.

The woman looks at the boy and softens a little.

"I went from living in a house with junkies to one where they beat me if I didn't bring home at least a hundred dollars a day to support myself. With Michael and Faith, I finally found a family. Nobody cares about what I want?"

The woman smiles for the first time since we met her. "Levi, of course, your opinion is important, but sometimes at your age, you're not old enough or experienced enough to judge the environment around you. Right now, it's all beautiful, sparkling, you have a lot of new toys, but you can't rely on those. There are other things in life you're not yet able to fully discern, so someone must do it for you."

"I ended up in prison. What other experience do I need to have? Isn't that bad enough?"

Tears begin to stream down his face, and I reach out to draw him against my chest. "We'll solve this, okay? You're my number one priority," I whisper in his ear to calm him down. I hate this woman more than anything in the world right now.

"Can I come in?" Simon's voice makes my head snap towards the door. What the hell is he doing here?

The woman frowns and looks at him impatiently. "And you are?"

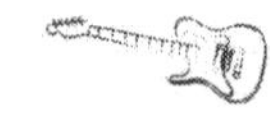

"My name is Simon. I'm Michael's bandmate." He extends his hand to her and smiles, not necessarily the right tactic with this harpy.

"Mr. Simon, this is not one of the clubs you're used to. I don't know what Mr. Wright told you, but not everyone is allowed in these meetings," she reproaches him, angry.

"I know this isn't a club. I spent most of my childhood and adolescence in offices like this because I was also in the foster care system, and was never adopted. I know exactly how Levi feels right now, the fear of losing the only decent place he's ever lived in."

I watch my friend stand in front of her desk, looking confident. I have no idea how he knew we were here, but I appreciate his presence. It gives me the strength to face this desperate situation. This woman will not judge Levi's case fairly; she's clearly biased against rock stars and isn't going to change. She must know about all my parties, the excessive lifestyle, drugs, the near-dead model, and the rehab. For the first time in my life, I'm ashamed of my past, of what I've been, and I curse myself for not having made different decisions, choices that would have led to better ending for this story.

"If Levi stays in that house, he'll not only have Michael and Faith by his side but also me, Thomas, Iris, Damian, Lilly, Evan, and Emily. Those same people can teach him that in life, you can make mistakes but also make amends. We can change lifestyles, work to improve ourselves, and not let our futures be determined by the mistakes we've made. Is there a better example of what we can offer Levi? We went through exactly what he went through and got out of it."

His voice trembles at the end, his hands clenched in fists to keep from trembling. I know how much it cost Simon to come here this morning. He doesn't like to talk about his past. He's never basked in the pity of the bad life he's had. He's always taken responsibility for his actions, and is the only one among us who would make exactly the same choices, including prison. He's the best and most sensitive of all of us, but would do anything for a friend, for someone he loves, including ending up behind bars for him. Levi is part of this incredible family I have, and this woman can never change that.

"Thank you, Mr. Simon. You have pleaded your case, I will certainly take into account your opinions, but you all need to leave this office. You can't stay here." Her voice seems softened, but nothing else indicates that she's changed her mind. She's already decided that Levi can't be with us. Anything we do is absolutely useless.

"Thank you for listening to us," I tell her in a broken voice, then I follow the others out of the office and exit the building holding Levi's hand.

When we get to the sidewalk in front of the offices, I lean against the red brick wall and inhale deeply. The dusty New York City air enters my lungs and calms me down a bit.

"Thank you for coming. How did you know we were here?" I ask my friend, who is watching me with concern.

"I asked Evan why you weren't in the office, and he told me you had an appointment here. So I texted Faith to find out the address, and came to try and help."

I glance at her, who looks down, blushing. I reach out one hand and caress the naked skin of her arm. Levi takes a step towards him and embraces his waist, clutching him tightly. Simon smiles with a disarming sweetness and hugs him back.

Then he lowers himself, looking Levi straight in the eyes. "No matter which family you end up in, we will always be near you, understood? You can count on all of us at every step you take in your life. Never forget it." He puts his hand on the kid's head and ruffles his hair.

Levi nods and wipes away his tears with a sleeve. "Can we go home and watch TV instead of studying?" he asks me as a hiccup shakes him.

"Yes, I think today was enough for everyone." Then I call an Uber to take us to our apartment.

***

I spend at least two hours in the room with Levi after today's meeting with the social worker. I reassure him that, even if the decision is to move him to another family, I'll continue to stay in touch with him, looking for any legal way to reverse the situation. Over time, I've discovered that to fend off his anxiety attacks, you have to do research, formulate plans, spend hours online looking for laws and quibbles that can somehow give him hope that a way out exists. When he finally fell asleep, and I left his room, the weight of those promises push heavily on my chest, almost preventing me from breathing. My hopes are also beginning to fade.

I enter our bedroom and find Faith lying on the bed, wrapped in her knee-length nightgown, her nose stuck in the Kindle I gave her. Little by little, as she's been reading books that were forbidden in her family, her skirts get shorter, leaving room for a little more confidence in having her skin uncovered. But always maintaining a certain modesty, with cotton fabrics and flowers instead of silk and lace. I never thought I'd be excited by the sight of it so much I'd lose my mind.

"What are you reading?" I crawl towards her and cuddle up to her side. Until a few months ago, I never thought I'd use this term in my vocabulary, let alone put it into practice by curling up next to a woman and resting my head on her shoulder.

"The story of an English noblewoman who was forced to marry a lord who risks being imprisoned for debts."

I've learned that historical romance novels are her favorites. Put in some lords, arranged marriages, and spicy sex scenes, and you've conquered her. I love it when she widens her eyes and blushes at certain erotic scenes. I can read it in her eyes when she gets to the part where he lays her out on a bed and teaches her what it's like to be a woman.

"Have you gotten to the part where they consummate the marriage?"

"Michael!" She scolds me but blushes.

I laugh and hold her in a hug, grabbing the Kindle and placing it on the bedside table. She looks at me with disappointment.

"It was a heavy day, and I need to cuddle. Don't make that face."

She raises an eyebrow and crosses her arms. "You just want to have sex."

"That's a cuddle bonus."

Faith rolls her eyes but doesn't move when I stick my hand between her legs and caress her over her cotton panties. On the contrary, she closes her eyes and abandons herself against my chest, letting out a slight groan.

"Are you still convinced you don't want to cuddle?"

"No, you can keep going, but..."

"But?" I insist as I move the edge of her underwear and

gently caress her skin, making her moan a little more. I like to tease her like this and see her struggle to formulate a coherent thought.

"I'd like you to…I mean…what you did Saturday. When you tied me to the bed." She ends the sentence by hiding her face in the hollow of my neck.

I freeze and frown. It takes me a few seconds before I realize what she's saying. "You like it when I tie you to the bed?"

That was a particularly intense moment, where I vented a lot of frustration. I've always had women who don't make me beg in bed and who take control. I must say I'm thrilled by Faith's inexperience.

"I like it when you take control and somehow force yourself on me. Is that too outrageous?" she asks in a whisper.

I smile and hold her to me. "No, it's perfectly normal in the bedroom. But you know you can stop me at any time, right? If you don't want to do something, just tell me, and I stop, okay? Even if you're tied up and all that."

"Yes, I trust you. That's maybe why I like it even more. Because I know you're more experienced than I am and you wouldn't do anything to hurt me. I've noticed you ask me that a lot—have I said something wrong? Or given you the impression that I don't want your attention?"

Her confession leaves me breathless. Her total trust in me weighs on me with a responsibility I didn't think I wanted but am happy to have. "No, it's that my mother didn't have the chance to choose, and neither did my sisters. An act was forced on them that violated not only their body but also their mind, heart, and will, breaking them. I want to make sure you know that you don't have to accept something you don't like just because you think it's your duty."

She smiles at me and shakes her head. "Michael, you made my freedom your crusade. I never thought you forced me into such an intimate act. You're not a monster." She smiles at me and caresses my cheek. "Now, do you want to keep going, or do I go back to reading my book?"

"Don't you dare touch your Kindle. And after I've satisfied you tonight, we'll download the *Fifty Shades of Grey* audiobook and listen to it together. Trust me, you'll like it."

"Is there a lord chasing his little maid through the rooms of the palace?" She teases, smiling and finally looking into my eyes.

"He's not a lord, but he is rich, that's for sure. And you will certainly like one of the rooms in his palace."

She frowns but doesn't press any further as I lift her and throw her on one side of the bed before plunging into her mouth, interrupting a giggle. "Stop there, don't move," I tell her as I slip into the walk-in closet.

When I come out, she's in the same position, with furrowed brows and an intrigued look.

"I had to buy them for costume parties, but I never used them more than once. At least now I know what to do with them." I show her the two scarves I have in my hand.

I approach the bed again, and I take off her nightgown, wasting no time. I like her amused and, at the same time, nervous giggle.

"Raise your arms," I order, and she does it, biting her lip and blushing.

Holy Christ, I could get used to this life! I crawl toward her, grab her wrists, and with one of the two ties, I tie her to the

bed. When I bought the bed, I was undecided between this and another headboard made of a single block of wood and leather. Thank God I chose the one with space to tie her slender wrists. When I approach her with the second scarf, and place it on her eyes and tie it around her head, I don't miss a second of her surprised expression, a little scared but completely excited. I get out of bed to undress, stopping to look at her as she perks up her ears to hear what's happening around her.

She is breathtakingly beautiful, with those long legs, slender body, and two breasts that fit in one hand. She is simplicity personified, and this makes her even sexier and more desirable. I would spend hours kissing, licking, biting that pale skin. Hearing her moans fill this room as if they were music. I approach the bedside table and open the drawer to get a condom.

"Michael?" Her hesitant voice makes me smile.

"Yes..." I whisper as I approach kneeling on the bed.

"Can we do it without a condom? I like that the best." She blushes as if she's asked me to do something scandalous.

My stomach tightens in a pleasant grip, and I smile. "Are you sure? You know how children are conceived, right?" I took it for granted because she is a nurse. But given her past, you never know.

She chuckles. "Yes, Michael, I studied it. But I'm sure I'm not ovulating, or I wouldn't have asked. I'm not dumb enough to think of trapping you with a baby."

I take the blindfold off of her for a moment and rest my eyes on hers. "I never thought you wanted to trap me, and if one day you do get pregnant, I want you to know it wouldn't be a problem. A child is a blessing, I may be reluctant toward

marriage, but I've never thought of a child as something unwanted."

"Are you serious?" I can read a mixture of disbelief and hope in her tone.

"Very serious. I wouldn't joke about these things. I always take responsibility for what I do, and if I've decided to make love to you without a condom, it's because I think you would be a fantastic mother."

Her eyes are shining with an emotion that fills my heart with happiness. "Now, you can continue what you were doing." She laughs and shifts her gaze as if overwhelmed by a wave of feelings she can't process.

I smile and lower the blindfold again. "Your every wish is my command." I kiss her on the neck before going down to her breasts, dedicating myself to her nipples and feeling her quiver under my touch.

I pull off her panties and slip between her legs to devour her sweet taste that I've now come to recognize. I look up and watch her squirm with pleasure with my every touch, arching her back and holding her breath. Blindfolded, without knowing what's happening around her, she lets go more, chasing her orgasm. It's as if she is safe in her own world, aware of the sensations but far from the inhibitions that hold her back when the light is on, and my eyes on her make her insecure. I watch her as I bring her to orgasm and enjoy her hips moving against my mouth.

"Michael," she pants.

"Open your legs," I order when I get out of bed and stop to look at her. Her cheeks are still flushed with pleasure.

Faith hesitates for a moment, but then she opens her legs

wide for me; the traces of her orgasm still visible between her thighs. My erection pulsates almost painfully, but I don't move. I stand there and watch this woman who has given me everything, even the most precious thing for her: her purity. Awareness makes its way into my chest, and something very much like happiness invades me when I realize Faith is mine. She is mine to look after, bring to orgasm, and accompany in her discovery of life. She is mine in so many ways that the mere thought of losing her hurts.

I approach her again and, when I sink between her legs, I push all the way until I become part of her, of her body, of her soul. It's no longer a matter of pursuing my own fleeting pleasure but of making that pleasure complete us both, joining us in a way that transcends anything physical. When the rhythm becomes more pressing, and her hips push against mine in search of pleasure, I feel her reach the limit and overcome it with a groan that enters my chest, making me orgasm with her, pouring a part of me into her body that welcomes me. I'd never before been able to control my orgasm so that I could explode together with the same pleasure.

I collapse over her, struggling to support myself on my weak arms. Her chest fills with air, pressing against mine. We are both short of breath, our hearts pounding in our chests at a frantic pace. I lie next to her and, after untying her wrists, I remove the tie from her eyes to lose myself in her sweet and dreamy look. I always thought I had to be the one to introduce her to the joys of sex, but Faith has taught me what it really means to make love. And it scares me a little.

"Would you really be willing to have a child now but not marry me?" Faith's question comes after a long silence.

I move slightly away from her to look into her eyes and understand what is going through her head. Her forehead is furrowed, waiting. "What can I tell you? A child is always a blessing, even if it's not planned, and marriage is a noose around my neck that I don't want to experience."

"How do you keep the two separate? How do you take on the commitment and responsibility of a child and not of the mother who gave you that child?" Her words are sharp and hurt me.

"Because a piece of paper doesn't make you a good husband like DNA doesn't make you a good father." I get out of bed, raising my voice, while Faith sits up stiffly. "It's all just bullshit that ties you to the church. You can be a good partner even without marriage!"

I head to the bathroom and turn on the water in the shower, ready to wash off the nightmare of this day and this discussion. Faith's light step behind me makes me turn, and I am surprised by the fury in her eyes. I've never seen her so angry, so caught up in her emotions.

"Do you know what I think? You're scared. You've spent your entire life running away from everything that represents your family. You did the impossible by erasing your criminal past, you built an honest career, you fought to teach me to be an independent woman who can stand on her own; for Levi, you became the father you never had. But you don't have the balls to ask me to marry you because that's what your parents did, and you don't want to be like them."

I am dumbfounded by her fury and the volume of her voice that fills this room.

"And don't look at me like that. I said balls, and I'll say

it again. Balls! Balls! Balls!" She emphasizes every word by tapping my chest with her long fingers.

It's such an uncharacteristic response on her part it takes me a while to speak. "That's not true! When I commit to a person, I don't need to put it in writing. I've never been one to abandon someone just because I'm not bound by a contract."

"How many women have you committed yourself to, Michael. Hm?" She crosses her arms over her chest, challenging me and tilting her head to the side.

"Is this what scares you? That I'll leave you? Do you really believe that marriage would keep me tied to you?"

"No, Michael, I'm not worried about you leaving me because I don't even know if we're together."

"What do you think we are, Faith? We live under the same roof, go to sleep in the same bed, and make the most important decisions of our lives together, around the same table while sharing the same meal. What else do you need to make you believe we're a family?"

She looks down and says nothing. I turn around and slip under the hot water, hoping I can wash away the sense of discomfort that's fallen on me. I hear Faith's footsteps move away, and the door closes with a light click. When I go back to the room, I'm surprised to find her sleeping in her half of the bed. I thought she'd go back to her room tonight, but I'm relieved to see she stayed. I slip under the sheets and turn off the light, stretching one foot and touching hers because, in spite of our fight, I need to know she's still with me.

CHAPTER 28
Faith

I practically tiptoe into Thomas and Iris's house. Levi is in the top floor apartment with his teachers, and Michael is in the studio with his bandmates. It was Evan's turn to watch the phones for a while, and when I told him what I wanted to do, he immediately gave me permission to leave and come upstairs.

"Why are you sneaking in like you've come to rob us?" Iris's voice behind me makes me jump.

"I was looking for you but didn't want to disturb you."

"Honey, you're the most polite person I've ever met. You never disturb anyone."

I blush at her compliment, knowing I have a giant favor to ask. She motions for me to follow her into the studio she set up in the room next to the living room. The room clearly shows Iris's artistic flair with its recycled vintage decor. The coffee table next to the restored antique sofa is one of those giant wooden cylinders used for wrapping high voltage cables. Polished and re-polished, it's the perfect mix in this space that's partly gray, partly metal-blue and the perfect backdrop to her black and white photographs of New York City.

I sit on the couch next to Iris's big red cat who starts purring as soon as I sink my fingers into his thick fur.

"How is it possible that this cat loves everyone but me?

Every morning he snuggles up next to Thomas and purrs, but when he comes to me, he stands on my stomach and puts his rear right in my face," she complains, and Emily laughs.

"I think it's because he still remembers the time you took him to the vet, and when he woke up in your apartment, he had no balls. I mean, I would've been pissed off, too, if I'd taken a ride and woke up numb from anesthesia and missing my reproductive system."

I can't help but laugh at the side-eyed glare Iris throws her friend. "I'm not even going to respond to that. Faith, tell me you have something more fun to talk about than my so-called friend here."

"Honestly, I'm here to ask you for a favor," I admit with embarrassment.

The two lean forward with eager smiles as if they were waiting for this.

"As you know, we have no idea how much longer Levi can stay with Michael."

"Michael told us about that bitch. How can she think that child is better off somewhere else? Have you seen how Michael is with him?" Iris seems outraged.

"Have you seen how he teaches him to carve those little wooden animals? They're lovely, and the two of them together are lovely. I can't believe that viper doesn't see it," Emily echoes.

"I know. That's why I need your help. Levi's birthday is in October, then there's Thanksgiving and Christmas, but I don't know if we'll be able to celebrate all of these together. That's why I wanted to organize a party that would include all three this weekend. I know it's only September, and that it sounds like a stupid idea, but I think Levi would like it." Their faces seem to light up as I explain.

"A stupid idea? It's fabulous! Michael will be crazy about it."

"Well, about that... I want it to be a surprise for Michael too. Another stupid idea?"

They look at me, frowning with confusion.

"We argued, and I want him to know that I'm sorry, that everything he's done for me these past few months means the world to me."

"May I ask why you argued?" Iris' eyes soften as she asks me the question.

I inhale deeply, feeling suddenly stupid. "Let's say that if I stay with him, there's no marriage in my future."

The two girls smile and look at me for a long moment. "You know that in Michael's world,
living together is more meaningful than the sacred bond of marriage, right?"

"Yes, I guess it's a big step forward for him compared to his old life, but sometimes I don't understand it."

"Are you worried? Do you think he's re-evaluating your relationship?"

I raise my shoulders and look at my hands, unable to meet their gazes. "I don't know, to be honest. I've never argued with anyone in my life."

"Are you talking to each other?"

I frown and look at them in surprise. "Of course. As soon as he came to bed, he reached out for contact. I pretended to sleep for a while, but then I gave in, and when I turned to him, he pulled me in and held me tight all night. The next morning

we continued our conversations more calmly."

The two girls smile, and their relaxed faces reassure me.

"Trust me, if Michael is angry, you'd know it. Thomas told me Michael got in a huge fight with Simon once, and for a whole week, he didn't talk to him, blatantly ignoring him even when he was in the same room."

"And how did they resolve it?"

"They punched each other, but I doubt he would ever get to this point with you."

"So you don't think my idea is stupid?"

Emily gets up, sits next to me, and looks at me with a smile so broad it almost scares me. "No, you came to the right place for surprise parties. We're experts," she says with a conspiratorial whisper that almost makes me re-evaluate the idea of asking them for help.

"But I was your only friend for years before I met Thomas, and how many surprise parties have we ever organized?" Iris raises an eyebrow challenging Emily and making me smile.

"When I came to your apartment with bottles of wine! Wasn't that a surprise?"

"Emily, that's called sneaking into people's homes for dinner," her friend teases, and I burst out laughing.

"Mere semantics. Did we have fun or what? That's a party!"

Their banter is wonderful. Growing up, I wish I'd had this with my sisters, and the thought makes my heart tighten in a vise. I miss them a little, but the chance of seeing them again is completely impossible, at least for the moment. I don't know if my father will ever reconsider or if they'll ever try and find me. The more I witness the relationships between these people who are not even bound by blood ties, the more I realize that

what I had growing up doesn't even remotely resemble love.

"Faith, count on us. I already have some ideas to decorate your living room. By the way, I'll need the measurements of your ceilings for the Christmas tree." Emily begins to type ideas into her phone like the organizational machine she is.

I frown and cast a worried glance at Iris, whose face mirrors mine. "Christmas tree?"

Emily looks up at me, bewildered. "Do you want to throw a Christmas party without the tree?" she asks like it's the most obvious thing in the world.

I turn to her friend, and she shakes her head as if to say let it go. "For the gifts, I'd like to involve Thomas too. I want him to feel the joy of giving a gift to a kid since he can't see his own nieces or nephews." A veil of sadness covers Iris' eyes for a moment before she recovers her usual cheerful smile.

Of all their stories, Thomas's is the one I feel most sad about because he's the only one who, despite having paid for his mistakes, continues to suffer the consequences. For the most part, the others voluntarily decided to distance themselves from their past lives and their families; Thomas didn't have the luxury of that choice. This shines through the love and attention he pours into Iris's mother and now Levi. It's his way of redeeming himself for what he's done. But unfortunately, he'll never have peace until his sister gives him a second chance.

"No problem, but don't worry too much about gifts. I don't want you to spend a lot of money on something I asked you to do."

"You're kidding, right? That kid will be spoiled by every one of us," Emily admits as a matter of fact.

I smile, suspecting this would happen. "I need help from

the band, though, to get Michael and Levi out of the house on Saturday morning while I set up. Is that asking you too much?"

"Trust me, Thomas and Damian would love to do something with just the guys. They're happy with Lilly and me, but sometimes they need to go back to when it was just the four of them, talking about things we'd never understand."

I think Michael will appreciate that too. Although he's radically changed his life to adapt to Levi's, his friends are still an essential part of it, and he'll enjoy spending a few hours alone with them outside of work.

***

When Emily said they'd help me organize the party, I didn't think she meant turning our entire living room upside down. Five minutes after Michael and Levi left for a spa morning—which surprised me because I thought the "men's stuff" Iris was talking about didn't include mud baths and moisturizers—Matthew showed up at our door with Iris, Emily, and Lilly loaded with bags and boxes and three other delivery men following behind.

In an hour and a half, they have divided the living room into three sections, the birthday-themed area, the Thanksgiving area, and finally the Christmas area. All strictly set up with garland and Happy Birthday balloons, fake turkeys and pumpkins for the November festivity, and Christmas tree and fake reindeer for the December one. The room has become a showcase of all the holidays, the kind you see in a home décor store. The work they've done is nothing short of incredible and, most important, I've never seen people laugh and have so much fun while working at such an intense pace.

"That dress fits you beautifully." Lilly approaches me while

I finish putting some candy on the table, not very healthy-looking but Levi loves it.

I turn to her and see she's changed into a summer dress that covers her arms to her elbows and hits her mid-thigh. I've noticed she feels more comfortable when she doesn't show the stretch marks that run down the inside of her arms. She's a beautiful girl, but I understand her shyness in revealing herself to the world, despite Damian looking at her as if she were the only woman on earth.

"Thank you, yours is gorgeous too. That pink suits you."

She smiles and adjusts the hem of her skirt. "I look like a sugared almond, but I discovered that dresses, especially in the summer, are much more comfortable than jeans and sweatshirts. I didn't think I would ever say that, but I love wearing them."

I smile and look behind her, noticing Iris and Emily walking toward us, all showered and cleaned up. One took my room and one Michael's…which has now become mine too.

"That shower is amazing. So huge it could fit an entire basketball team," Emily gushes, impressed.

"I know. It fits more than one person comfortably."

I look up from the table and find their eyes on me. Their amused smiles make me blush with embarrassment.

"Exactly how many of you were in that shower? Two, three, four people?"

"Emily!" I exclaim, scandalized by her insinuations.

"Okay, she's just discovered the joys of sex. I don't think she suddenly became a porn star," Iris chuckles.

"This is Michael we're talking about. Anything's possible where sex is concerned." Lilly makes matters worse.

"Michael would never share me with anyone else…I don't think."

"No, trust me. From the way he looks at you, I think he would tear the eyes out of anyone who tried to get close to you," Lilly reassures me.

My phone starts ringing, catching our attention. "It's the concierge. They're in the elevator."

A few seconds later, the front door opens into our living room, and Michael's surprised face appears, followed by Levi's.

"Surprise!" we shout in chorus at their confused faces. Behind them, Thomas, Damian, Simon, and Evan are flashing full-mouthed smiles and pushing them forward. I walk over to Levi, who looks at me confused.

"Since we don't know if we'll be together for all of the celebrations coming up, Michael and I thought it would be nice to sort of group a few parties together while we still can," I try to explain, not knowing quite how to explain this unique surprise.

Levi raises his shiny eyes to mine and throws his arms around my waist, holding me in a hug that takes my breath away. I look over at Michael and find him with an incredulous smile and eyes equally shiny with emotion. "Thank you," he mouths before coming closer and joining the embrace.

"So, Levi, are you ready to party?" Damian's thundering voice restores a more cheerful and less tearful tone and, as the boy breaks away from me and joins the others who are already wandering around the table set for the holidays, Michael takes me aside.

"Your friends helped me organize this party. I hope you

don't mind. I wanted it to be a surprise for you too," I tell him, resting my hands on his chest as he pulls me into a hug.

"You're asking me if I mind? This is the most beautiful surprise anyone's ever pulled off, and it's not even for me." He smiles and kisses me. "I love you. And this time, I'm not saying it in the heat of the moment or because I'm freaking out. I've always teased my friends about becoming soft since finding a woman, and here I am, falling in love with you…and I like it. God, I love this feeling of coming home and holding you in my arms."

His words take my breath away, calm the eagles in my stomach and make my legs tremble.

"I love you too, Michael. I've always thought living with a person for the rest of my life was a duty all women have to endure, but you've proven that wrong every single day since I met you. It's never been a burden to be close to you, it's a pleasure and an honor. I finally understand what it means to love someone."

Michael smiles and kisses me again gently on the lips. "Will you promise me something?"

I nod at his serious and intense gaze. "What?"

"That if the harpy decides to take Levi away from us, we'll fight to get him back with all the legal weapons we have."

"I'll be with you every step of the battle." I reach up and kiss him almost desperately.

"Are you two done making out?" Simon's teasing voice brings us back to reality. "We're celebrating without you."

Michael laughs and wraps his arms around my waist, pulling me towards the center of the living room where they're all gathered around Levi, who is ecstatic.

"Simon, how is it that you, the one always looking for a woman to settle down with, are the only one still single?" Michael teases him a little amidst the laughter of his friends.

"You tell me. I do everything right. I open car doors for them, help them with their coats, take them to ritzy places for dinner—nothing. Not one who's stuck around for more than a couple of dates," he complains.

"Have you ever thought about fucking them? That usually brings them back for more."

"Damian! Do you really have to say that out loud?" Lilly scolds him, scandalized.

"Are you saying my prowess in bed didn't convince you to stay?"

"Actually..." she agrees among the general laughter.

I approach the others, munching on some pretzels I grab off the table as I watch Michael go to his bedroom. When he returns after a few minutes, he motions for Levi to join him, and I watch him pull the carving knife his grandfather gave him out of his pocket, the only memory he has kept of his family. He hands it to Levi, who takes it with some hesitation. When it occurs to me what Michael's doing, that he's giving him his most precious possession, tears fill my eyes—just like Levi, who throws himself into a hug with him. In this moment, I'm certain that no matter what happens, we'll always be a family, marriage or not.

When the doorbell rings, I notice Michael's face whitening while the others look around a little confused, wondering who it could be. I move towards him as he reaches the door.

"If she thinks she's taking Levi from us today, she can think again," he hisses between his teeth as he opens the door.

His surprise when he finds Penelope in front of him is almost palpable.

"If that's the face you welcome your guests with, I doubt you have many friends," she says with mock horror as Michael steps aside to let her in. She immediately embraces me.

"Did you know she was coming?" asks Michael, smiling.

I shake my head.

"Faith invited me, but I wasn't sure if I could get back in time from a conference in Houston. Luckily, I managed to free myself in time to catch an early flight, or I would have missed Christmas," she says, looking at the big decorated tree currently occupying a large section of our living room.

Michael wraps Penelope in such a tight hug she has to slap his back to get some air. "I'm glad you came."

"I wouldn't miss it."

Penelope scrutinizes us both with a watchful eye, and when Michael pulls me into a hug from behind, he gives her a wide grin. "I see you've managed to overcome your differences." She's amused.

"Yes, we no longer have problems exchanging body fluids."

"Michael!" My cheeks are on fire as Penelope laughs.

"Have you managed to overcome your doubts about premarital sex?" she asks me quietly, though with her usual frankness.

"I didn't have much choice, as Michael seems to be allergic to marriage." I turn my gaze towards him and he rolls his eyes in response.

"I think I've proven that I'm not going anywhere," he mumbles.

"And is this a problem for you, Faith?" asks Penelope in a

tone somewhere between a worried friend and a psychologist doing her job.

"Not exactly. Like Michael says, he shows me every day that he's not going anywhere, but sometimes the desire for a husband and children still takes over. I'm getting used to our… situation."

Penelope nods and turns her inquisitor gaze on Michael.

"Don't look at me like that. I just told her I'm in love with her!" He squeezes me even tighter, as if preventing my escape. "I'm scared to death they'll take Levi away from me. Can we do one problem at a time?" I put my hand on his and intertwine our fingers to reassure him.

Penelope smiles and looks at him lovingly. "You'll get there, Michael. You need time, but you're on the right track."

"Are you two finished monopolizing Penelope?" Damian's voice makes us turn towards the room full of guests looking at us curiously. He comes closer and holds her in an embrace that lifts her off the ground with his bigger-than-life frame.

"I was just making sure everything was okay around here," she smiles.

"They're a bit messed up, but we keep an eye on them. Michael in love is worse than me." Damian winks at me as he drags Penelope by the hand to greet everyone else.

Michael turns me towards him, an indecipherable expression on his face. "You know I won't run away, right? That I don't want to be without you for a minute." The search for reassurance in his voice almost makes my heart leave my chest.

"I know. I wouldn't be here if I thought this was only temporary."

He puts a hand on my face and pulls me in for a kiss full

of unspoken promises that erase all my doubts that there is no "forever" for him. It just looks a little different than how I thought it would.

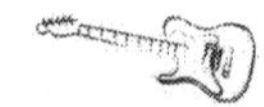

CHAPTER 29

Michael

"We have eleven songs finished or almost finished, and we need a couple more before we can think about releasing the album." Damian throws the setlist of songs on the stool in front of him.

Considering we can't use the ones published by our old record company, and we couldn't bring the ones we'd recently discarded up to our standards, the only solution is to write more songs.

"Eleven isn't a bad number," Evan says. "It's a bit low by your standards, but it's acceptable for an album. The ones you have are really great. And I'm telling you this as a manager, not a friend. Don't get frustrated if you can't come up with something decent. Better two songs less than two tracks that aren't as good."

After almost two hours of discussion about it, Evan seems to be the only one who hasn't changed his mind about the fact that a shorter album can be okay.

I speak my mind on the matter. "I prefer that we take a little more time and put out at least thirteen songs. Our old label released the last one less than a year ago. They promoted it, charged full price. I know we need to bring in money, and that our resources aren't endless, but I don't want our fans to

think we're putting out shorter albums at full price to make money off them. They were loyal to stick with us through this mess, encourage us, and defend us against the press attacking us from all fronts. I don't want to disappoint them."

"I'm with Michael," Thomas adds. "Let's hold off until we have two more songs, and then we'll get it out. This idea of doing concerts as a treasure hunt has given us an advantage with the media, we have interviews planned for at least a couple of months, so let's take advantage of this push, and try to work quickly on the other two."

Damian nods his assent, and Simon also seems to be at peace with this plan.

"Okay, then. Let's get these other two songs written. Does anyone have something, even just a few chords? A vague idea that can turn into the hit song of the century?" asks our manager with a veil of hope in his voice.

"Michael has started writing again," Simon drops the bomb that turns all eyes towards me. In response, he throws me a smile and a wink.

Meanwhile, Thomas, Damian, and Evan look at me with stunned expressions. I'd be surprised if I were them too. Since rehab, I haven't written a single note. But I didn't want Simon throwing me under the bus like this. I'm not sure what I have is good. I'm rusty, and writing songs takes practice and dedication. "I have four or five pieces that are anything but finished. Some are just fragments." I try to minimize the situation.

The silence is overwhelming.

"We've been here for two hours racking our brains about what to put on that damn album, and you're sitting there with five songs and you don't tell us?" says Damian incredulously.

"I said some are just fragments."

"Four or five songs..." presses Damian.

I turn over the iPad with my lyrics and musical ideas, and the grip of nervousness in my stomach almost physically hurts.

"One's called 'Faith'? Are you serious?" Damian snickers with the others who can't hold back their smiles.

"Faith as in complete trust. Faith in God, in humanity, in life. Faith in what you want, but not what you think."

"Of course, whatever you say," he nods, returning to the songs in front of him. Then he turns to Evan. "Give or take, I think we have an album of fifteen or sixteen songs."

"Two hours, Michael. You made me waste *two hours* trying to figure this out, and you had this in your pocket the whole time? You're killing me." Our manager glares at me, nailing me to my stool.

"If I'm not keeping you on your toes a little, you'll get soft," I laugh. "You don't even have to drag us out of wild parties anymore. What do you do in the evening without us?"

"I have a life, Michael, I finally have a life!" He laughs as he grabs the door handle and is startled to find Faith with her hand raised, ready to knock.

"Speak of the devil..." Damian chuckles, but I don't have the heart to answer him when I see her worried face. My stomach turns so violently I almost vomit.

"Matthew called. He said the social worker is waiting for you at home. I've already called Levi and told him to get here. It's better if you go."

The nausea worsens with every word that comes out of her mouth. Three weeks have passed since we visited her office, and there's been nothing since then, no contact. I look at my

friends, who are easily as shaken as I am. The time has come. I have to let Levi go and start the battle to gain back custody. No one speaks; I can't even move.

"Michael." Faith's voice seems far away when I get up from the stool and approach the door.

"Faith, send the calls to my phone and go with him." Evan's voice is sweet, calm as it always is when the situation is terrible but you shouldn't lose your shit.

I thank him with a nod as we all walk out the front door, my heart pounding in my chest and my mouth dry. I haven't felt this way since the day I was sentenced to jail.

***

Though it's only a few blocks away, the trip to the house is a blur of buildings, people, and vehicles that I can't entirely focus on. Inside the car, there is absolute silence; Max has even turned off the music. When we arrive in front of our building, I reach for the door handle and notice my hand is trembling. Matthew comes out from behind his counter and motions me towards the armchairs in the lobby. When the woman stands up to meet us, the first thing I notice is that she doesn't have her folder. Levi is hiding behind me.

"Shall we go up?" I say, since Levi will have to pack a minimum of suitcases before leaving, though I'll have all his stuff delivered to the new address.

The woman, however, shakes her head. "What I have to say, I can say here."

We're all holding our breath. Faith's hands cling to mine, and I don't know if I'm holding her up or the other way around. Maybe we're supporting each other.

"I've come to tell you that Levi's custody is final and there

will be no need to find another home. Congratulations."

My heart pumps so fast I can feel the blood beating in my ears, and everything sounds muffled. My brain struggles to keep up with her words; emotions collide in my chest: happiness, relief, confusion.

"Thank you." My voice breaks with emotion, and I notice a slight smile on the woman's face.

Behind me, Levi is in tears, and Faith sobs quietly next to me. My legs are shaking, and I don't know if I'll be able to stay on my feet for long.

"Can I ask what made you change your mind?" I ask after clearing my voice.

This time the woman's smile widens, and her features soften. "Your friend Simon sent me an email with a video of the party you had for Levi. A family that moves mountains to celebrate Christmas in September deserves a second chance."

Levi frees himself from me and runs towards the woman, embracing her. "You're the best harpy I know! Thank you."

The woman is confused for a long moment, then, for the first time since we met her, she laughs out loud, and Faith and I join her.

"Levi. We need to work on the art of diplomacy. What do you say?" I grab his hand when he finally separates from her.

We're all dazed by the news and, out of the corner of my eye, I notice Matthew witnessing the scene and smiling as well.

"Are you sure you don't want to come up at least for coffee?" I ask the woman who suddenly seems like a decent person.

She shakes her head. "Don't you have a job to go back to,

Mr. Wright?"

"Today, work can wait. I want to be with my family." I grin at her while pulling Faith and Levi closer to me.

I watch her smile as she walks to the front door and goes out into the Manhattan streets, ready to give some other family a hard time.

"Do we really get to stay home today?" asks Levi hopefully.

I nod as I pull them to the elevator.

***

When Simon comes to the door, he's surprised to see me. After giving them the news, I took the rest of the day off to be with Levi and Faith for a while, but I needed to see Simon and thank him in person for what he did.

"Do you want to come in?"

"No, I'm in a hurry. I promised Levi I'd take him to the movies to celebrate."

"So, what the hell are you doing here?" He's smiling.

"I came to thank you. It's only because of you that we have something to celebrate."

Simon shrugs and grins. "They're your family, Michael. You're mine. I'd do anything for you, you know that. No need to get all mushy about it."

I smile at Simon's inability to accept a heartfelt thank you. He's never been able to, even when we were kids. He was the one who saved me when the nightmares kept me up at night, and the only way out I saw was death. But as much as I tried to thank him, I always found him short of words, unable to accept a compliment or gratitude. Simon grew up without ever being wanted and loved by those who took care of him. Always content with those few gestures of love that came to him

from time to time, never expecting anything from anyone. He collected the love he received so sporadically and carried it in his chest like a treasure.

"See you tomorrow in the studio," I wave goodbye with one hand.

"Have fun at the movies tonight." He smiles before closing the door and leaving me to my family.

My family. I never thought those words could taste so sweet and stir up such positive emotions. I grew up with the idea that family was an evil I would never voluntarily submit to, that my friends were enough for me. Levi taught me, though, that while you can't change the family you're born into, you can choose the one you build for the future.

EPILOGUE

Michael

The spectacle in front of us is nothing short of incredible. Although we can't get to the center of the forest because it's forbidden for tourists to disturb the butterflies, even from here, you can see the bright orange color of millions of wings covering the trees in front of us. The walk from the center that welcomes tourists to this amazing place from all over the world was spent in absolute silence. We were too excited, imagining how it would look, to make small talk. Even Levi's random chattering that erupts in the most unexpected moments has remained still. He's wide-eyed and ready to capture every tiny movement like a flutter of a butterfly's wings.

"Wow," he whispers, almost afraid his breath might make them disappear.

We remain quiet, holding our breath, while the warm air of Mexico makes us forget the November frost of New York. When I told Levi and Faith to go get their passports because I was taking them to see the migration of butterflies, they looked at me like I was crazy, incredulous. When I consented to the trip, they thought it would be years down the road, not just a few months later. I asked myself: why not now? The fear of losing Levi has taught me to live every single moment while we have time. What should I have waited for? To get stuck on

another tour? For Levi to graduate and leave for college? Why postpone something we can do now?

Standing in front of this spectacle, I take off my backpack and pause to gather up courage for what I'm about to do. Both of their noses are in the air, admiring the clusters of butterflies descending from the branches of the trees, and I get lost for a few seconds in their astonished faces. I kneel in front of Levi and, when he notices, he looks at me a little confused. I take out a yellow envelope I've been guarding zealously for days and hand it to him. Faith moves in closer and smiles. She knows what's hidden inside this envelope, and I can read the emotion in her eyes.

"Is this some strange marriage proposal? You know I'm only fifteen, right?" he jokes. I really have to stop letting him hang out with my friends. He's always ready with the jokes, he's getting smarter and smarter, and most of all, he's becoming more interested in adult topics, losing a little of that innocence that makes him so full of wonder.

"No, no matter how much I love you, never say that again. It creeps me out. Open it."

I watch Faith hiding a smile. She was the one who helped keep my meetings with the lawyer a secret from Levi.

"What is it?" Levi's voice trembles as he reads the words on the page, almost incredulous.

"If it's okay with you, Faith and I would like to make our family official and adopt you."

Levi's eyes widen as he looks first at me and then Faith. "Really?"

"Really," I say, hugging him. "Unless you feel differently about it. In that case, I would respect your decision."

"No, no! I want to adopt you, I swear."

I smile and hug him again. He's right, in a way. He did adopt me the moment his desperate eyes met mine. At that moment, I had no choice but to fight with all I had for his happiness.

"And now you have to help me with Faith," I whisper in his ear.

Levi nods and kneels next to me with a grin from ear to ear. Faith frowns and looks at us, puzzled. She's not the only one who's been plotting with me to make this moment even more meaningful. Levi came with me to all the jewelers and helped me choose the right ring for the woman who taught me to love.

"Since I'm already on my knees..." I take out the blue velvet box I've been carrying for a month. "The time has come to make you an honest woman. I know that marriage is important to you, and I have no intention of denying you a white dress. We may have more children one day, and I know it's important for you that they are born to a legitimate union. I don't want to deprive you of all that." Though I've never believed in marriage, I believe in the happiness of other people. What I've always considered a piece of paper for Faith is an important ritual that I can't ask her to give up. My only purpose in life is her happiness and Levi's, and if marriage is what makes her happy, I'm not going to be the one to keep it from her.

Faith bursts into tears, and Levi looks at me, worried, as if looking for confirmation that this is a good reaction. In all honesty, the tears are so many I'm not so sure myself. Maybe it's too early? Or perhaps it's not what she wants anymore, since the last time she went through this was a forced marriage.

"Is that a yes?"

Faith nods vigorously between hiccups and my heart leaps in my chest. I take her trembling hand and put the ring on her finger. A very simple diamond set on a platinum band. When she looks at it, a series of sobs shake her chest so hard I worry about her. I expected an emotional reaction, but this is a whole hysterical crisis. I look at Levi, who seems as worried as I am.

"But, Michael..."

Her words stop me instantly; there should not be a *but* after that yes. I look up at her and see her smiling. I don't understand anything anymore. Is it a yes or a no? I already don't understand anything about women, cohabitation, and marriages. What the hell do you do in these situations? I break out in a cold sweat cold, and all the happiness I feel is replaced by anxiety so strong it almost makes me nauseous. Does she want to leave me? She wouldn't say yes if she wanted to end the relationship, right?

She interrupts my chaotic thoughts. "If you want me to have children in this marriage, you should be a little more specific with that whole 'in the future' business, because I'm late."

Words hover in the air for an endless time, and when my brain registers them, they tear the earth from under my feet. I am speechless. I look into her eyes and find a mixture of happiness and insecurity that makes me waver. Is she really saying I'm about to become a father for the second time? I didn't think happiness could hurt so much, but my chest is swelling to the point that I'm short of breath. It took me a lifetime to figure out what a family really was, and damn it, now I can hardly wait for it.

"Late for what? Don't we just have this one trip planned for today?" whispers Levi in my ear, not knowing what to do.

Faith and I burst out laughing as I pull her towards me and kiss her belly.

"I'm afraid a journey much longer than this simple trip has started today. Get ready to share your Playstation with a little brother or sister much sooner than a few years down the road," I say to Levi as I pull him into our hug.

Levi frowns, and then the surprise spreads on his lips. "Really? Does that mean you won't adopt me anymore?" The panic in his voice makes us both turn and kneel in front of him.

"No biological child can ever replace you, Levi. You are already part of our family," she whispers as she squeezes us both.

"You're not getting rid of us," I tell him as I grab his chin between my fingers and have him look me in the eye. "You'll always be my first child, whether DNA binds us or not. Got it?"

Levi nods and hugs us. "But exactly how many hours a day will I have to give them the Playstation?" he asks worriedly.

Faith and I burst out laughing, dazed by the wave of newness in the last few minutes.

"Don't worry, you'll have time to go to college before they're old enough to use it," I reassure him, and he smiles with relief.

Faith and Levi have shown me that a real family is full of love and affection, and I'm determined to make sure that these two things are never lacking in their lives again.

If someone had told me I'd find happiness in a wife and two kids a year ago, I would have laughed until I cried. Because come on, let's face it, who'd want to try family life after growing up in a hell like mine? But apparently, if you put together

three very different hells, you can actually create a corner of paradise.

BOOKS BY ERIKA VANZIN

ROADIES SERIES

Backstage

Paparazzi

Faith

Showtime

THE HUNTING CLUB

The producer: Aaron

About the author

Erika Vanzin is the Italian Amazon bestselling author of the rock star romance Roadies Series.

After traveling around the world with her husband, she settled down in Seattle, enjoying the marvelous Pacific Northwest. She brought from Italy a couple of suitcases, fifteen boxes full of books, and her most successful novels translated into English.

While she is not writing, she enjoys reading books, watching the Kraken hockey games, and working on DIY projects.

Keep in touch with Erika via the web:

Website: https://www.erikavanzin.com/

BookBub: https://www.bookbub.com/authors/erika-vanzin

Goodreads: https://www.goodreads.com/author/show/14437720.Erika_Vanzin

Facebook: https://www.facebook.com/erikavanzinauthor

Instagram: https://www.instagram.com/clumsyeki/

TikTok: https://www.tiktok.com/@erikavanzin

Twitter: https://twitter.com/ErikaVanzin

Newsletter: https://www.erikavanzin.com/newsletter.html

Acknowledgements

This book is dedicated to families. I was lucky. I grew up in a family that loved and supported me unconditionally. I received love from everyone, not only parents and brother but all the uncles, aunties, and cousins who cheered for me, making me grow up strong and reach goals that I would never have imagined. I will never stop being grateful to them for the opportunities they gave me. Thanks to all of you, my successes are also yours.

However, family also means the people you choose to continue your journey with when you grow up. Thanks to Dario, my husband, who jumped on this adventure and makes me laugh, smile, feel loved every day.

Thanks to Stefania, who became part of this crazy life four books ago, she soon became more than an editor. Family means staying up all night, supporting when fatigue takes over, working together to reach the finish line in time. Stefania, you are the perfect companion for this crazy journey.

Annalisa and Chiara, what can I say about you? You are the craziest, funniest, most authentic family that could happen to me. Thank you for always putting up with me, even when I disappear for days, when I'm in a hurry and when life keeps me busy. Thanks for the laughter but also for your support... and thanks also for the photos. You know what I am talking about.

Family means moving to the other side of the world and still wanting to have dinner together. Paola, thanks for the dinners via Zoom, the chats at the most ridiculous hours. But above all, thank you for trusting a writer with your crazy stories. Your adventures and misadventures will fill the pages of the next novels!

And last but not least, I want to thank the Groupies' family. Without you, this adventure would be impossible. Without your enthusiasm, support, and commitment, I could not do this job. Thank you from the bottom of my heart for keeping this dream alive.